HEAT

2

HEAT

2

A NOVEL

MICHAEL MANN

+

MEG GARDINER

MICHAEL

MANN   *wm* WILLIAM MORROW
               An Imprint of HarperCollins*Publishers*
BOOKS

FIRST EDITION

Designed by Bonni Leon-Berman

Library of Congress Cataloging-in-Publication Data has been applied for.

ISBN 978-0-06-265331-4

22 23 24 25 26 LBC 6 5 4 3 2

for my dad

Jack Aaron Mann

who inspired everything

—Michael Mann

For Paul

—Meg Gardiner

HEAT

2

PROLOGUE

At 11:32 a.m. on Thursday, September 7, 1995, the Far East National Bank at 444 South Flower Street in Los Angeles was held up by three men: Neil McCauley, Michael Cerrito, and Chris Shiherlis. A fourth, Donald Breedan, was driving the getaway vehicle. Far East National was a cash distribution hub with large amounts of currency on hand. Bank employees triggered two telco and one cellular alarm, but the signals went nowhere. The night before, Cerrito had cut through the ceiling of the bank's underground garage to access the alarm system's CPU on the floor above and changed out three of its circuit boards. Twenty minutes before the robbery, the alarm system turned itself and its video recorders off. At 11:50 a.m., McCauley, Cerrito, and Shiherlis were walking out—one at a time—carrying duffel bags containing $12.8 million in cash.

Five minutes earlier, at 11:45 a.m., Vincent Hanna of LAPD's Robbery-Homicide Division had received a tip about the armed robbery in progress. Hanna, his detectives, and units of uniformed police raced to the bank as McCauley, Cerrito, and Shiherlis were crossing the sidewalk on their way out. In the next moments, downtown LA erupted into urban warfare.

Hanna had been pursuing this crew since he arrived at the scene of a violent armored van robbery. Pulling in, he found the typical crime scene paradigm: the ordered regularity of street furniture—curbs, lampposts, utility boxes—and then the anomalies appeared: brains, bone shards, irregular pools of blood, the underside of an armored van on its side like a petrified mammoth.

The armed robbers' identities were a mystery. But what Hanna knew at first glance was they were a heavy-duty crew of highline pros.

There were signs, like discarded shards, leavings, that contained messages about what happened. Reversing how they got there told Hanna the sequence of events and about this crew's methods. The spot they picked had good escape routes—on-ramps to two freeways. They ignored loose cash, and the two-minute elapsed time of the robbery meant they knew how long it took LAPD to respond to a 211. The skillful use of shaped charges to cut the precise, rectangular opening in the armor plate told Hanna this crew could go in on the prowl. They could do sophisticated highline burglaries as well. That meant they were capable of taking down a variety of scores any way those scores needed to be taken down. And, if they went in strong, they'd rock and roll at the drop of a hat. They killed two armored guards when one reached for an ankle-holstered handgun. They executed the third off a cold calculation: Since it had become a murder one beef anyway, why leave a living witness? If you happened into this crew's way, that was going to be your problem.

Hanna finished taking it all in before speaking to the detectives, technicians, and uniformed officers from other divisions.

Robbery-Homicide Division was LAPD's elite major crime unit. Its purview was citywide. Hanna had the authority to appropriate any case in any division. He wanted this one. RHD took over.

Working his network of informants, Hanna identified one crew member, Michael Cerrito. Surveillance on him led Hanna to the others, except the elusive McCauley. Hanna knew, as a foregone conclusion, given this crew's proficiency, they were unlikely to leave behind enough physical evidence at a crime scene to tie them to it. So Hanna's strategy became to surveil them, discover what they were taking next, and be there when they walked in the door.

Neil McCauley became aware that somebody was on him. When it happened, his reaction was calm and smooth because smooth was fast. Fast wasn't fast. Shiherlis was inside a precious metal depository, cutting a hole in a metal vault door with a hollow-core drill at three in the morning. Cerrito was up a telephone pole monitoring his alarm system bypasses. Trejo, on lookout, was circling the block.

Outside on the sidewalk the night air was cool on Neil's face as he watched the dark, vacant streets. He heard a sound. It was sheet metal hit by a solid object. It was a sound that should not be there. It came from a row of delivery vans parked across the street in a lot for an industrial bakery. The sound was out of place. They were supposed to be empty. They weren't.

Coolly, Neil reentered the building. Shiherlis, guiding the hollow bit, was moments away from accessing the lock box. After that it would be open sesame. Neil gave the order: walk away. They left behind tools, work clothes, six weeks of preparation. That was their discipline.

Hanna watched it all play out on FLIR images from hidden cameras inside a bakery delivery van. His SWAT teams were staked out and well hidden.

He let them go. He wasn't settling for breaking and entering. He wanted them for real.

Afterward, Neil gathered Shiherlis, Cerrito, and Trejo outside a DWP electrical substation, where the exposed high-voltage conductors created so much RF interference that any transmission from bugs they hadn't found on their cars would be scrambled.

They had to decide there and then—split and go their separate ways right now, or figure out who the hell had cut into them, dump their surveillance, and stay and take the bank anyway.

For Chris Shiherlis it was an automatic. His marriage was on full tilt. He was solid, with a lethal sobriety and pinpoint focus, when he was in the groove on the job. They had been scoring, month in, month out. It was in normal life that Chris was a fuckup. A reformed gambling junkie, he fell off the wagon on a Saturday morning two months earlier at Santa Anita. He lost a load on the third race and started betting wildly on "meta-coincidences" based off numbers and names, including a horse named Dominick, the same name as his son. It lost, too. He blew half of what he and Charlene had stashed after a year and a half of solid scoring.

Charlene had had it after that. She wanted a version of adult life for them and their son. She had pulled herself up out of a downslope life.

To her, Chris was staying "a child, growing older." For Chris, dumping the cops who had cut into them and taking the bank's $11–$12 million was worth the risk.

Sitting in night shadows beneath the soaring ramps of the 105–110 interchange in a Cadillac, Neil was handed a package of counterintel, including Vincent Hanna's personnel file, by his fixer and middle-man, Nate.

Nate was an old-school SoCal bank robber. He and McCauley had done time in McNeil Federal Penitentiary in Puget Sound. Now he was a broker of scores and Neil's fence. Tall, skeletal, and careful, with stringy long hair, Nate worked out of a blue-lit lounge he owned in Encino called the Blue Room. Right now, he was searching to find compelling words to frame his urgent caution.

This Vincent Hanna in RHD wasn't on the job "to serve and pro-tect." He wasn't a careerist working up the admin ladder. He was on to a third marriage because he was out there all night on the prowl. He was one of those dedicated types. And he was all over Neil's crew—all except Neil.

Neil's mantra was split in thirty seconds flat if you spot the heat around the corner. Nate reminded him of that. And Hanna could make mistakes. Hanna could hit or miss. Neil could not miss once.

Neil considered and rejected all of it. He felt no obligation to ex-plain why he'd stay, break his own tenet, evade Hanna, and take the bank anyway.

No one needed to know. He told himself, initially, Eady was a one-night stand and he'd make do with the memory. Her life was a million miles from Neil McCauley's. She was a freelance graphic designer, originally from the Blue Ridge Mountains, working a day job at an architectural bookstore in Santa Monica. With her a door had opened that Neil didn't think was there anymore. It had been closed on a bloody two-lane blacktop outside Mexicali years earlier. He wanted to be with this woman. This score and the life it bought them, somewhere far away, is why he'd stay. He hadn't planned for this, but a future without her had come to count for zero.

At one moment in time, after Vincent Hanna discovered his surveillance on Neil McCauley was blown, he and Neil came face-to-face.

It was because staying covert didn't matter anymore, Hanna realized.

He pulled over McCauley on the 105 Freeway. He wanted whatever he could learn about McCauley, and he could learn more by talking to him face-to-face than from his blown surveillance.

McCauley, too, knew he might have a split second in the not-too-distant future to intuitively decide to zig or zag. So he wanted the sensory intake of who Hanna was.

They sat down at Kate Mantilini on Wilshire Boulevard. They both knew blunt facts about the other, but they were devoid of color. Each man's intake of the other was highly sensitized and raw. They were both predators.

Neil knew about Hanna's burned-out marriages. Hanna confessed it was the price paid for chasing guys like him around the block. Neil confessed he had a woman, but he didn't talk about her or what he had said to her one night: *My life's a needle starting at zero and going the other way, a double blank.* That was until she came into it. He convinced Eady to leave with him.

While revealing nothing that might compromise themselves, they talked with the intimacy sometimes occurring between strangers. They discovered that they took in the real world and the way life rushed at them in similar ways.

Hanna was haunted by dreams, dead bodies at a long table looking at him. They didn't say anything. Their look imposed obligations. McCauley didn't acknowledge obligations. He had dreams he couldn't breathe. He was drowning. Maybe he was running out of time, Hanna offered. They were the same in that both knew life was short, we are footprints on a beach until the tide comes in. And each navigated the future racing at him with eyes wide open. Raw. Polar opposites in some ways, they were the same in taking in how the world worked, devoid of illusions and self-deception.

At the same time, each would blow the other out of his socks with no hesitation. They knew that, too.

But that might never happen. They might never see each other again.

That's how the meeting ended.

In the chaos of the Far East bank robbery, Breedan was killed at the wheel of the Lincoln by Hanna's detectives, Drucker and Casals. Cerrito, shielding himself with a five-year-old, was shot through the head by Hanna. Hanna's partner, Bosko, was gunned down by Shiherlis. Three uniformed LAPD were dead and eleven wounded, three seriously. Shiherlis was hit above his body armor by a 5.56 mm round traveling at 3,100 feet per second. It slammed him to the ground and shattered his clavicle, sending bone shrapnel throughout his upper thorax. Neil half carried him into a supermarket parking lot, where he carjacked a station wagon. They had to get the hell out of LA.

Neil never made it.

Hanna killed him under the approach lights at the foot of an LAX runway. Eady was waiting for him in a Camaro on the driveway next to the Airport Marquee Hotel on Century Boulevard.

Only Chris Shiherlis survived.

PART ONE

Los Angeles, 1995

Realness eats raw meat
and does not waver
He has the staying power of the sun
He walks only in his own shoes

                  —Spoon Jackson

1

Night strobes between slats of blinds, intermittent pink and blue neon from the Korean corner mall outside. Headlights from turning cars cast shadows on the ceiling. Music pounds up through the floor from a music store below. It drums like a pulse through Chris Shiherlis's shoulder and neck.

Get up.

He can't get there.

Get the fuck up. Now.

Shiherlis opens his eyes.

He isn't dead. The dead don't throb from K-pop coming up through the floor. The dead don't bleed.

He isn't home. Home is a ranch house homogenized into the anonymity of the San Fernando Valley. This is a mattress on a frame in a corner. It isn't a jail cell. Upstairs apartment. Koreatown.

His eyes sink shut, riding the oxycodone tide once more. Then he crests awake.

How am I here?

K-pop washes like staccato gunfire. A memory, the swinging weight of the duffel of money slung across his back on its strap. Breedan hit, dead meat at the wheel. Ambushed. More LAPD incoming. Cops. Superior firepower, used to overwhelming civilians. *Civilians? Overwhelm this, motherfucker!* Black-and-white sheet metal turning into sieves, the *sound* drives your pulse into your head, exploding out the top of your skull.

Music thuds, bright and foreign. *Use it.*

"Focus, eyes," he mutters.

Shadows and pink light from the street stripe the grimy walls. Bed, cheap sheets, him in his boxers. His clothes folded on a plastic lawn chair. A darkened TV on a card table. Old cigarette butts stubbed out on a chipped saucer; beer cans crushed in a wastebasket. Voices outside.

The wound track screams. Bone fragments didn't lacerate his subclavian artery. If they did, he'd be dead.

Chris kicks for the surface.

Get the fuck up!

He tries to roll over and sit up. He's slammed back by his shoulder and neck muscles screaming.

How'd he get here? Horns honked at him, startling him out of his stupor at a red light turned green. He remembers slow-driving across lanes northbound over the dark Sepulveda Pass back to Nate's in Encino after he left Venice. He didn't trust himself on the 405.

Venice. Her hand glided through the air in a blackjack dealer gesture. Drawing cards is over. She'd called and left word. Nate argued; he left anyway, drove to Venice. He'd winched himself out of the car, spotted her waiting on the balcony.

Her eyes, a smile—inviting, like when they first met. Then the rising of that look, overtaking her, warning him.

The Koreatown door opens. Nate walks in.

He's tall in a two-button cream sports coat and bolo tie. Stringy blond hair greased back, '70s mustache drooping down his blotchy face. His eyes, quick and small, look Shiherlis up and down, quietly evaluating.

Time is it?

Nate closes the blinds. "What?"

How long I been here?

Words. He hears them in his head. They make sense. Are they coming out?

Nate leans over him. "Hold still."

He drags the lawn chair beside the bed, sits down, and cautiously peels back the medical tape on the gauze dressing that covers the gunshot wound.

The small 5.56 mm round at high velocity had punched into him like a Sidewinder missile, fulfilling its design: large cavitation through body mass, bone turned to shrapnel. Chris remembers being on his back on the asphalt in adrenalized clarity, askew side views of police cars they'd shot to pieces. *Can't move.* Neil hauled him up.

Nate pulls off the dressing. The sutures are black, the skin red and hot.

The overhead light silhouettes. Nate grunts, nods, and presses the tape back against Chris's skin. He leans on his elbows. He searches Chris's eyes.

"You here with me or in Disneyland?" His voice is low and hoarse.

Chris nods.

"Gotta get you outta here. Fast."

Nate moves shit. Merch. Him. Scores. Anything.

"Charlene," Chris rasps.

"You got a couple hours. Then that's it."

His son, his wife. Charlene isn't here . . .

"Neil?" Chris asks.

Nate's eyes go cold, expressionless. A controlled response from a veteran of bad outcomes.

"You stay here? You are dead meat," Nate says simply. "That's all you gotta think about."

"Neil . . ."

"Get your shit together. I'll be right back." Nate hesitates, shakes his head a millimeter, then heads for the door.

Chris sees him, striped pink and blue from the neon across the street. He tries to send his voice across the room to Nate before he goes, over the boom-box beat of K-pop up through the floor. *Don't shake your head, man, and walk away.*

The door shuts.

2

Vincent Hanna paces beside the plate glass, scanning the room. Surf outside beats a drumroll against the sand. The ocean is dark cobalt. The tops of low cumuli catch threaded gold, like braid on a dress uniform. Sunrise. Six a.m. The house is empty. Neil McCauley lived here. He is not coming back.

Hanna's here because he wants this place to tell him things. He wants McCauley to speak to him again. It hasn't been six hours since he fired the three rounds that took McCauley down. He took McCauley's hand through the paroxysms that carried him into death.

They understood each other, as if they were the only two people on the planet. Alone, isolated within who they were, but only they knew how it all really works.

Tactile memory is still in his left palm.

He crosses Neil's living space, looking. The time he has left is evaporating. He wants something—info, data points. The hardwood floors produce only echoes as he crosses. The crash of breakers resounds off the windows. The glass railing on the balcony is stained with seagull shit.

McCauley didn't live here, in this white space. He slept here, ate here, drank the single malt from the one bottle on the counter. McCauley never inhabited the place.

It had been a way station.

No attachments. Walk away in thirty seconds flat from anything and anybody if you spot the heat around the corner. He'd told Hanna that.

So, who was that girl in the Camaro?

Outside, the rising sun opens the sky above the dark ocean. Hanna turns from the windows.

Everything's gone. McCauley's cut of an eight-figure bank score. Cerrito. Trejo. Breedan.

Except the last man, Chris Shiherlis. He is out there. Where?

Sergeant Jamal Drucker sweeps into the living room from the back of the house. He moves like a carbon blade, quiet, sharp, his brown face grave in the dim light. "Nothing back here, Vincent."

"Scraps? Specks? Scintillas?"

His thoughts stream into tangents . . . Someone from Michael Bosko's family will be at the morgue by now. This, he dreads. There or the funeral home. That indifferent look on Shiherlis's face as he fired. No hesitation. The three-round burst killing Bosko. Where's Shiherlis? Hanna's chances of closing in on him are running out in evenly metered units like a tachometer in reverse. With time's usual indifference, it's ripping away his possibilities.

Drucker looks tired, but his deep voice is channeled, focused. "Three identical white shirts in the closet. Books—*Mechanical Metallurgy,* Camus, Marcus Aurelius. Don't ask me why."

Why doesn't that surprise him? "No women's things? Lipstick, mascara, lingerie, Tampax, rubber gloves in pink or turquoise on the drainpipe under the sink? What's in the fridge? Yogurt? Raspberries? Frozen Twinkies? Something besides TV dinners?"

"One bottle of vodka."

But McCauley had a woman. She had a stricken look on her face beneath a tumble of brown hair, standing at the side of the Camaro. She's in the low-res hotel security footage, shoulders crumpling as McCauley turns away from her and runs, Hanna in pursuit. The tags on the Camaro didn't match. No question it was McCauley's ride. Who is she?

Hanna looks at Drucker. "She was taking off with him."

"Who?"

"The girl at the Camaro."

"Maybe she's gone."

"From her looks she's not a player. So where would she go without him? Maybe she knows who was laying on Neil's transpo. Whoever that is is who Shiherlis is using. He's not doing curbside check-in at LAX. Shiherlis no-showed because he clocked we were on Charlene. He knows Charlene's not goin' anywhere. That means he's on the run. Alone. Whoever set up McCauley's transpo is the guy he will go to."

He turns, scanning.

"Anything in this bullshit, sterile, white-with-seagull-shit-on-the-windows place tell us who the fuck that might be?"

He studies the living room, now lit blue in the growing dawn. His pulse feels heavy. He tries to soak up information. But this house holds nothing but reflections.

What can this tell me?

Nothing. Why am I still here?

He's trying to feel Neil's presence, standing where Neil stood, seeing what he saw. A certain melancholy holds him to the hardwood floor. A life gone, irreversible, a man he knew.

They knew how the other thought about personal things in that moment as they sat across from each other at Kate Mantilini . . . at the same time Hanna learned nothing he could put to logistical use about the man.

Drucker moves into the kitchen. Antiseptic, gleaming appliances. A spotless counter. A pen beside yesterday's *LA Times*. He unfolds the newspaper, to look for scribbled notes, phone numbers, names, initials, flight information. Beneath it is a glossy book.

"Vincent," Drucker says. "*Stress Fractures in Titanium*."

Hanna approaches.

Drucker hands him the book. "Great reading list . . . cold, clinical shit."

A price tag is stuck to the back. "Hennessey and Ingalls. You know this place?"

"Santa Monica, yeah. It's an art and architecture bookstore."

Hanna flips through the heavy stock pages. A receipt is stuck inside. "Bought the book last month. Paid cash."

The roll of the surf seeps through the windows. Hanna holds up the receipt. Drucker's already dialing.

"Haul the manager's ass in right now. Neil was in that store three weeks ago buying this. Who was with him? Who waited on him? Who cashed him out?"

Drucker heads out the door. Hanna stands there in front of the ocean.

The night before, airliners roared overhead. He felt Neil McCauley's rushing pulse in his left hand. Now Hanna hears only the surf. His right hand touches the glass.

Neil, maybe Chris, too, stood here, right here, like this. *Where I am, looking through this glass.* He tries to channel Neil's thinking. Alone in the vastness—except for this body, this organism . . . perceiving, until it isn't. That's what Neil would think . . .

Hanna held Neil's hand as paroxysms racked his body, shock from hemorrhagic arteries. If he had to, he'd do exactly the same again, and that changes nothing about this moment. Both are true.

He turns from the sea.

He raps his knuckles against the glass as he walks away. The sound drums in the twilight like a prayer wheel.

3

Nate leans against the hood of the pay phone, receiver to his ear, watching early-morning traffic, watching pedestrians. "*Debe ir hoy. Absolutamente,*" he says in Angeleno white-boy Spanish.

Today, Shiherlis has to go. Waiting longer isn't an option.

He's outside a funky Koreatown drugstore holding a bulging plastic bag full of medical supplies, Gatorade, a disposable razor, and more.

"Half up front—*la mitad antes. Mitad después.* The rest when he gets there." He listens. He watches. People eye him as they pass on the sidewalk, a tall, busted-out rockabilly white guy with a bolo tie from the '50s.

"*El carro*—the car is at my place. In the garage. Blue Room. Yeah. *Azul.*" He nods. "*A qué hora?*" He checks his watch. "He'll be ready."

He hangs up, checks the street, steps back so the cholo approaching from his left can't cross behind him. Prison habits from on the yard die hard. He zigzags across the street and slips through the narrow doorway up the stairs to the studio above the music store and dry cleaner, where he stashed Shiherlis.

Inside, Chris hears the footsteps. He sits up on the edge of the bed, woozy and light-headed.

He has to get up. *The meat machine. That ain't me. I'm me, inside of it. Get up, body. Do it.*

Nate enters. Chris pushes himself to rise.

Something torques within his gut, vagus nerve, nausea, the room spins.

Stand up, motherfucker!

Daylight is a sheet of heated steel outside the window. The oxy is ebbing. Pain is sharpening its teeth. He needs his clarity, even though that means the stabbing with every breath returns.

Nate drops a rustling plastic bag on the bed. "You leave today, brother. You gotta be able to move soon."

Chris is parched, headache throbbing. Dehydration and blood loss. He opens a twenty-eight-ounce bottle of Gatorade and drinks half of it. Nate dumps out packs of fresh gauze, antibiotic ointment, and a bottle of prescription pills.

"Broad-spectrum antibiotic. Don't be allergic." Nate gets a bottle of hydrogen peroxide and cotton balls. "Take your shirt off. I'm changing your dressing."

Chris pulls the shirt off and sits heavily on the edge of the bed. The sound of traffic outside and the light in the room seem to swell and fade, a pulsing, flickering sensation. Chris's tongue feels slow.

"Charlene," he says.

Nate pulls the rusting lawn chair beside the bed, sits, and strips the tape and old dressing from his shoulder. The air on Chris's skin feels weirdly alive. He leans forward.

"Charlene?"

"I heard you the first time."

"Gotta get to her . . ."

"Really . . . ? How'd you know where she was?"

"She called and told me."

Nate eyes him coldly. "What's that tell you?"

No answer.

"That's not happening. That cop you shot?" Nate says. "Dead. One of Vincent Hanna's team. Plus three others. Every eyeball in a uniform is looking for you."

Chris's voice strengthens. "I gotta get them out."

Nate straightens, stops patching the wound. "Then I am cutting loose of you right now, man. You try for that? The only 'out' you got is into a hole in the ground."

Chris lurches up. Great idea. Pain crashes through him like a gong.

Nate waits for him to calm down. "The only way for you to get them out is *you* get out first. Then set it up."

Chris breathes. "How'd they get to Charlene?"

"How do I know?" Nate gives him a flat look, *shut up* in his glare. "I warned Neil. He didn't listen. Now, you fucking listen to me when I talk to you!"

How? How did it go so wrong?

Chris's mind won't focus. All he sees is Charlene's blackjack dealer's wave.

Cops *everywhere*. She risked herself to send up a flare. How'd they find out where she holed up?

"What's with the shoulder?" Nate says.

"I'm gonna take up tennis." Chris crushes his teeth against the pain. Tries to think.

Then it lands, what he didn't want to know but knows.

Nate sees that. "That's right," he says.

Neil's gone. His crew is gone. And Charlene gave him up.

There's no way around it. Whose place was that in Venice? And the cops were waiting . . .

Even with Hanna and the Robbery-Homicide Division, they took down the score anyway. It was all good. Cool. Until it went wrong.

Did they bust her? Did she set him up but change her mind? His stomach abruptly cramps. He hunches.

"What happened?" he says, mostly to himself.

He's speaking more clearly now. Nate is deliberately ignoring him. Cleaning the stitches on his chest with the peroxide. Getting out a pair of medical scissors, cutting lengths of tape, and prepping the new dressing.

Nate doesn't react. "I don't know all of it."

Chris tries to slow his breathing. Nate applies antibiotic gel, places sterile gauze pads over the vet's handiwork, and tapes him up.

Chris doesn't want to look at Nate. Wants to punch him. Wants to kick a hole through the wall, right after he rips his own shoulder off.

"You ain't moving so fast, so you gotta start now. Somebody is comin' for you. Okay? You lag 'cause you got goofy ideas, they will split—and get paid anyway, so they don't give a shit. By and by, I'll try to set a call."

Nate turns. Chris clamps a hand on his arm. "What happened?"

That coldness in Nate's eyes. It's how he deals with loss.

"I warned him. He was clear. On his way to LAX he detoured to whack that fucking Waingro and walked himself into a trap. The cop, Hanna, shot him somewhere at the airport."

"Did he get Waingro?"

"He did."

4

Hennessey and Ingalls is empty. The manager's shaken. It's eight a.m., Wilshire, down from the Third Street Promenade, the area just waking up, the pedestrian walkway hosed down, shining. The store's pale hardwood floor and bookshelves gleam. The manager cues up surveillance video from the sales date. Hanna has McCauley's book and the sales receipt. The manager rolls through the footage, fast-forwarding. Hanna stands behind her, close, arms crossed, chewing gum, rocking side to side, eyes on the screen. She fumbles the switch. She's not used to dealing with police. Drucker paces behind him.

When the clock on the screen approaches the time stamp on the receipt, Hanna stills.

There's McCauley.

Gray suit, white shirt, Mr. Anonymous, moving with precision as he browses the engineering section and selects the book Hanna now holds in his hand. Self-contained, focused, alert. Neil flips pages back and forth. The camera angle shows electronic microphotography of various kinds of steel.

A woman passes along the aisle behind McCauley. She casts a glance at him and the book, slowing as she walks by. Neil doesn't give any attention to her.

"Stop," Hanna says. "Rewind."

The manager backs up the tape and replays it.

Hanna points at the screen. "Who's that?"

She frowns up at him. "That's Eady. She works here. Did."

"Where is she?"

"She quit two days ago."

Hanna feels electric. He says one word. "Bingo."

High cheekbones and wide eyes. Her waves of brown hair could have sprung from a pre-Raphaelite painting. Her stride is athletic, her clothing soft. Something about her manner reminds him of a doe approaching a busy road.

The woman standing beside the Camaro.

Drucker is getting Eady's full name, address, Social Security and driver's license numbers, thanking the manager on the move as he speed-dials RHD to pull her jacket while heading for the door. Hanna's already run outside.

5

The house is nestled on a hillside above Sunset Plaza, a tiny place with an enormous view across the sprawling grid of the basin. Blue skies, bright sun. The place has the clean lines of a blank canvas. A beat-to-shit Honda Civic is parked in the driveway. No other vehicles. Nothing moving on the street, all the shades down. Hanna leads three detectives and four uniformed cops up the drive. He and Drucker aim for the front door with two uniforms. Casals and the others slip around the back. Hanna's fingers tingle. Uncertainty fills him, possibility, urgency. He knocks on the door, but they stand to the sides, Hanna with his Combat Commander .45 and Drucker with a twelve-gauge.

No answer. He knocks again.

"Force it?" The uniform behind him holds a compact battering ram.

Then the lock turns and the door opens. In the shadowed entryway stands the woman Hanna ran past outside the Airport Marquee Hotel.

Hanna grabs her wrist and yanks her outside and stands her up against the wall. A uniformed policewoman does a quick weapons search.

From inside they hear, from Casals, "Clear."

Hanna displays his badge. "We have a warrant to search the premises."

She stares at him, then Drucker. "Am I under arrest?"

"Yes, but what happens next depends on what you do in the next five minutes," Hanna says.

She blinks. Her face is chalky, her eyes red, her hair disheveled. She's wearing old track bottoms and an indie band T-shirt. Hanna takes her by the arm and leads her inside, into the modern kitchen and the living room, where a graphic design studio has been cobbled together. Outside plate glass windows a balcony overlooks the city. Other uniforms stand there staring through the glass, like vultures in black. Drucker unlocks the balcony door and lets them in.

"Clear outside," one reports.

Shiherlis isn't there. No surprise. Hanna hears the tick, tick of seconds running down. He points Eady at a stool by the television.

Drucker responds to his radio, pushes the earpiece deeper into his ear canal. Listens. He signs off, gestures Hanna aside.

Hanna turns so Eady can't hear. Drucker whispers to him, "Totally clean. No priors. She doesn't even get traffic tickets." Hanna turns back to her.

Eady stands with her hands clenched by her sides, as if half of her is somewhere else and she doesn't know where to put her body until Hanna waves her to the stool. He gestures away the policewoman with her open handcuffs.

"Do you know what I want?"

She shakes her head.

"Everything you know about Neil McCauley and his crew. Don't lie, don't hold back. If you want to stay out of a cell facing accessory charges, talk to me."

She flinches. "I didn't know who he was. I don't know about a crew."

Hanna slaps the TV. "This works, right? KNBC comes in crystal clear. You saw the footage from the bank robbery downtown."

"He told me he was a salesman."

"And you believed him? What did he tell you he sold?"

"He said he traveled a lot and sold metal."

That matches what McCauley told him, but Hanna doesn't give it away. He presses closer into her space. "C'mon, c'mon, c'mon! You saw his photo on the news. And you hopped into his car anyway and took a ride to the Airport Marquee Hotel, where mayhem and murder rained down *all* around you, replete with fire trucks, cops, crazy people running around, helicopters, the whole Mardi Gras. And you thought he was selling metal kitchen cabinets or something?"

She seems, for a moment, like someone trapped in a burning building as the walls collapse around her.

"I didn't know *until* last night. And I had to do what he said." She's trying to find words to explain. She can't. "Then, near the end, he told me. And then, yes, I went with him anyway."

This is who McCauley wanted at his side as he made a run to freedom. She had upended her world to go with him.

She'd been standing in the open door of the Camaro, watching McCauley back away and take off. The way she kept staring after him. Frozen. Confused. Hanna now understands. Bereft. Hanna can read her mourning. Her brief glimpse of a different life—a wilder, more urgent passion with this intense man—was over.

He knows she was innocently involved. Technically a DA might try to label her an accomplice. She is not.

"Look, Eady. I can protect you," he says. "But you have to give me everything. Right now. Who else did Neil have contact with?"

She gathers herself. "Michael. He mentioned a friend named Michael. One of the men shot downtown."

"Cerrito," Drucker says.

She nods. "He said . . ." Her voice cracks. "He said, 'When it rains, you get wet. Michael knew the risks.'"

She swallows. To Hanna, it's clear she's thinking, *So did I.*

Around her the detectives loom large, filling the room with an unsettling energy. Punitive, she thinks. Nothing she's ever encountered. They search through things invasively, as if it's their inalienable right to induce disorder. It's like everything they touch becomes . . . not hers anymore. She might return them to where they lay, but it won't be the same. Her personal possessions are no longer possessory. They're being stripped of meaning. Not mementos anymore. Inanimate objects. The careful array of pastels. Rolled Japanese paper, precious in the excellence and care of its manufacture, now merely a thing as the thick fingers of a detective search through the sheets.

Hanna brings her back to right now. "Look at me. Hey, Eady. Stay right here."

Mildly dazed, she looks back to Hanna, really taking him in for the first time.

He sees it. Every news report is leading with the story that McCauley was killed in a gunfight at LAX. By a cop.

She's fighting it, not taking that last step, though Hanna is standing in front of her. Then she shudders, like she's taken an electric shock.

"Who else did McCauley talk about?" Hanna says. "Shiherlis? Chris?"

"No." Her gaze has sharpened. "I saw you. Outside the hotel."

"Trejo? Breedan? Their wives, girlfriends, kids?"

"No. He was always alone." She shakes her head. "You shot him, didn't you?"

"And you went with him, knowing who he was."

He holds poised, right in front of her face. She sways, and her eyes turn dark and shiny. Almost inaudibly, she repeats, "It rains, you get wet."

Hanna doesn't move, but lowers his voice. "Who else did he have contact with?"

She scrapes her fingers through her hair. She shrugs. "He made a stop on the way to the airport. He met a man at the back door of a bar."

The arc of Hanna's attention focuses to a pinpoint. "What bar? What man?"

"North Hollywood, off Burbank Boulevard. I don't know the address. Brick and corrugated sheet metal, ivy on the walls. The Blue something."

Casals gets on his radio.

"Describe this man," Hanna says.

"Fifties, stringy blond hair, mustache. Wearing polyester. All seventies."

Hanna's pulse guns. He nods at his men.

Casals has already identified the bar and assigned two units to stake it out from two blocks away.

Hanna writes something on the back of his card and hands it to Eady. "The policewoman over there is going to handcuff you and take you downtown. We have to book you. Do you have an attorney?"

She doesn't. Her ability to process what's happening is floating off into a black pool. Hanna sees that.

"Call this number. He's a lawyer. He'll get you a bail bondsman. Anybody else tries to interview you, you're entitled to have your attorney present. Understand?"

She nods and looks into his eyes directly. He sees why Neil wanted to take her along to freedom.

"If you remember anything else that helps me, you call. Don't think, don't blink, you call." Before he starts out, he adds, "And, yes, I had to shoot him."

Their eyes connect again and hold for that moment.

Then her look changes. Now it says, *Anything else?* There's nothing else. Everything is over.

6

The sun is beating down when Hanna and SWAT crash into the Blue Room. The bar is a dark neighborhood throwback bar on a faded commercial street.

The search warrant came through at one p.m. Hanna, his team, uniforms, and SWAT approached from the streets behind. They blocked both ends of an alley with black-and-whites. They eliminated a surveillance camera.

If Shiherlis is here, he'll be armed to his fingertips. Who else may be inside?

Hanna, in a ballistic vest with a Benelli semiauto twelve-gauge at port arms, is in the precise scrum, stacked up within the SWAT unit in the tactical ballet, bodies to bodies, precisely aligned feet. He nods to the SWAT team leader, who holds an automatic rifle across his chest, barrel high. The man raises a hand and counts down on his fingers. Silent entry. He reaches zero, aims his hand at the door like a hatchet, and goes.

The door is unlocked. They're in. In an instant they cover and command the space. A long bar runs along the wall on the left, mirror behind it, bottles glowing in the dim light. A few early drinkers stand at the rail or sit at wobbly tables. "Gangsta's Paradise" thumps from the jukebox. The bartender turns.

Hanna shouts with the others, "Freeze. Show me your hands."

A SWAT officer bellows at customers. "Up against the wall, hands behind your heads."

A second team moves tactically up a staircase.

The bartender steps back and raises his hands overhead. A customer dodges for the front door. When he slams it open, Drucker clotheslines him. He and Casals, with a Remington 870, enter.

Hanna arrows toward the tall guy standing at the bar, hands in plain view, one holding a coffee cup. He's who Eady had described. Older SoCal hard case, stringy gray-blond hair, chill eyes watching Hanna in the mirror.

"Hands on the bar," Hanna says.

The guy complies. He smells like Brut and dry-cleaned polyester. He eyes Hanna in the mirror with a subzero gaze. He's frisked. A SWAT team member tosses his keys and wallet on the bar.

Hanna flips open the wallet. The same ice-blue eyes stare from the driver's license.

Hanna reads the name. "Nathan. We're going to talk about a mutual friend."

Nate turns, his face neutral. "I know you?"

"How the fuck do I know if you know me? I know you. And I know one guy you know. Neil McCauley."

Nate's expression is a total blank. "Who?"

"Your pal."

"Does not ring a bell."

"What kinda bell? Like ding-dong, Avon calling? That bell? Security camera out back? Does it put you and McCauley together at the rear entrance? What are the odds?"

Upstairs, one of the SWAT officers calls, "Clear."

The SWAT team leader comes down the hall. "All clear."

Chris Shiherlis isn't here.

"So happens, the odds are zero," Nate says.

Hanna feels the black scorch of anger. Outside, he smiles like a reaper's scythe. "Good. 'Cause rewinding and erasing evinces what we call 'consciousness of guilt.'" He looks around, all-seeing. "Since others have laid eyes on you and your meeting him."

Drucker says, "Why lie? You wanna lie, lie about something maybe we can't prove. Lie about Neil? That lie is a loser. Why lie about that?"

Nate looks around, surveys his LAPD-occupied bar with disdain. "So far, up to now you are eluding me."

"Eluding?" Hanna shrugs. "Shiherlis, Christopher. I figure you're the middleman-slash-fixer. Right now, at a minimum, you're looking at accessory after the fact on the armored van robbery with three associated homicides and a bank robbery, including the murder of an LAPD sergeant during its commission, one of my partners, and three uniformed officers. The killing of Roger Van Zant and, in addition to that aforementioned . . . *car-nage* . . . the killing of an asshole named Waingro"—he leans close—"by Neil, your pal, who told me in person that he was never going back. And he is not."

Nate's cold blue eyes, set within the pink blotching of burst capillaries, drift across Hanna, barely registering him. "Robbery-Homicide Division. RHD. Try your showboat act somewhere else."

Hanna's cool, like still water. "Shiherlis on the run may or may not *elude* me. You will not. For you, I've got a lotta time."

Nate glances away skeptically, then looks back at Hanna squarely. "If you got cause, arrest me. If not, your presence is discouraging my midday business."

"Yeah, yeah . . ." Hanna, suddenly focused elsewhere, glances behind him. Officers are searching the back office. That could take hours. Hanna nods Drucker aside.

"Waste of time," Hanna says sotto voce. "This guy's like talking to last week's roadkill."

"What's the play?" Drucker says.

"Him? Haul him in. Old-school ex-con? Assign someone young to wear him down. They won't get to first base. Chris Shiherlis . . ." He considers it. "Casals hit Shiherlis above the vest. Clavicle. He's too fucked up to risk commercial air travel. Maybe not enough time for Mr. Fix-It over there to lay on a private plane, file flight plans, look legit, all that. Shiherlis is running, but he's on the ground."

"BOLO's out to every agency in California," Drucker says. "Driver's license photo and mug shot."

Hanna thinks about it. "He won't look the same." He eyes the alley through the rear door, tapping his hand against his leg. "He'll get rid of the surfer dude ponytail. Cut his hair short, maybe dye it dark. Get our artist to put together a sketch. New BOLO."

"If he's got no time," Drucker says, "he's heading for Mexico."

"And he ain't backpacking through the desert," Hanna says. "Hit the border crossings. Send the new sketch and BOLO to Customs, Border Patrol, Mexican immigration, and Baja, Sonora, Chihuahua, Coahuila, Nuevo León, and Tamaulipas Judiciales. I want every god-damn border crossing from San Diego to Brownsville wallpapered with his picture."

A SWAT officer comes in the back door from the alley. "Lieutenant?"

Hanna turns.

The man jerks a thumb over his shoulder. "There's a detached garage out here. You want to see this?"

Hanna follows him into the alley and rounds a corner. The door of the garage has been rolled up. Hanna stops, staring in.

A fresh oil stain, not yet soaked into the concrete. Someone left. Recently.

7

The road bleeds by, the freeway, as the car rolls east across the desert. The radio blares. Talk jocks and mariachi out of Tecate slowly fade to static. This afternoon is a blur of white sun and pain. Interstate 8. Chris knows the road. He doesn't know the woman who's driving.

Los Angeles is behind him. All that remains is an oil stain from this car on the floor of Nate's empty garage.

The pain is back. Here, on the road, he's exposed. He can't deaden himself with Percocet. He opens his eyes and bears another second of agony as his neck and back muscles, anchored to the clavicle, pull on the broken but reset bones. His stitches are large and crude. *World-class job, Dr. Bob.* A friend drags you to a vet, you get vet-quality trauma work.

Vacancy washes up through him, a cold, bitter splash. His unthinking take of the world has Neil still in it, until he reminds himself. In Koreatown, when Nate turned that flat gaze in his direction and told him, a hiss had risen in his mind like a road flare.

Nate had sat down and leaned close. *Somebody will come get you. Next person who comes here will be your out. They'll have your paper. Don't worry, it'll stand up.*

Where? Chris said numbly. *Where am I going?*

South. Nate laid out a route.

Chris's head swam. *My cut from the bank score . . .*

Will be safe. I'll set up an account through a Delaware trust. You can access it by phone, fax, computer. But where you're going, don't draw on that money unless it's an emergency. No flash. You can't stick out.

I need to get some of it to Charlene and Dominick.

Charlene. Luring him into a trap. *Why?*

A black heat ran through him. Did they threaten to take Dominick from her? These fucking people.

Nate looked thoughtful. *I'll handle that, but I can't get her anything except cash. Nothing that creates a trail. And not for a while.* He stood. *I'm going.*

Chris struggled to his feet and shook Nate's hand. *Thanks.*

You got it. Nate lifted his chin, a farewell. *Jumpin' Jack Flash, keep your head down.*

The someone who had come for him is behind the wheel. She wears jeans, Reeboks, and four-inch gold hoop earrings and has a tattoo on her forearm of her grandbaby. She can't be forty. She looks like she could bench-press a Chrysler.

He watches her drive. She's been driving for hours.

"What's your name?"

She cuts a glance at him, maybe surprised he's half coherent. "Don't matter."

"You know mine," he says.

"Jeffrey Bergman, Calgary, Alberta, Canada."

Her voice is East LA. At the safe house, she took his Beretta and demanded he hand over his wallet, both of which he did grudgingly. She re-dressed his wound and gave him a preppy shirt and sports coat, dark sunglasses to cover the drug glaze in his blue eyes. She dumped him in the passenger seat of this Chevy and hit the road while he drifted from syrup-sweet stupor into screaming pain.

"What you need to know is my family work with Nate from way back, and I do the job I'm paid for," she says. "You don't trust me, I let you out here and you can fucking hitchhike."

He tries to raise both hands, a mollifying gesture. His left arm shrieks, and his vision goes electric white. He gasps and leans against the window.

"Keep driving," he says.

She nods at the glove compartment. "Envelope's in there, has your Canadian passport, new wallet with a driver's license, credit cards, family photos. American and Canadian dollars and some pesos."

He gets the envelope and slides the passport and wallet into his pockets.

Exhaling, he turns to her. "How do you do? I'm Jeffrey fucking Bergman."

Her lips purse, maybe a smile. "Frida fucking Kahlo."

Now, deep into the bright afternoon, she pulls off at a gas station. "Nate told me to call and check in. No sweat, just hold tight."

She gets out and walks toward a pay phone. Chris heads for the john, feeling his head zoom, trying to walk straight. He washes his face in lukewarm water. In the grimy mirror he looks like a vampire: pale, lips nearly blue, his eyes too hot. *Get your shit together.* When he comes out, Frida is hanging up the phone. Her face is smooth, but her eyes are jumping.

"What?" he says.

"LAPD raided Nate's bar. He didn't give 'em nothing, but they don't need nothing from him. They're not stupid."

"What else? There's something."

"They're adding a new police drawing to their BOLO." She shoots him a glance. "Sketch of you, close to the way you look now. They'll send it to both sides of the border. We gotta roll."

She accelerates through skillet-flat farmland, past trailer parks, cheap minimarts, scrub and sand. The border skates along a few miles to their right. The freeway has been repaved, and more houses, suburban cookie-cutter homes, line the road than there were in '88.

"Mexicali," Chris says.

"Easy crossing," Frida says. "You been?"

"Forget it."

"You think there's a problem?" She eyes him. "Reason you don't want to stay there? Don't worry. We aren't."

"Then why cross there?"

"Airstrip an hour south. Stay cool."

He shuts his eyes and turns his head. But the memory seeps into him. A derelict Chinese-style motel. The score. That rush, man. Then . . . Then . . . He seems to smell mesquite and gunpowder and blood. How things could spin. Could be lost, could be won. In a finger snap.

If Chris ever lost Charlene, he'd annihilate whoever took her from him. He'd vaporize them like an H-bomb.

Sunlight flashes off the hood. It shoots through his skull like lightning.

Neil was home free, Nate had said.

Nate also told him, *Hanna's a motherfucker. And right now Hanna's prowling around the city, mobilizing every asset he can. One thought: you. You killed his partner.*

Now Chris is alone. Far from home. Only one way to change that. Keep going. Last chance. Don't throw it away.

A mile out of El Centro, Frida Kahlo leaves the interstate and pulls over. The afternoon is lengthening, shadows falling across the fields.

She puts the car in park. "Take off your sunglasses. Let me see your eyes."

Chris pulls them off and gives her a stare. "Straight enough?"

"Yeah. You drive us across."

"Why?"

She gets out. "Say I'm your auntie, if they ask. Or the nanny, if that makes you feel better."

He doesn't actually mind the edge in her voice. He gets behind the wheel. Dabbing sweat from his face with his sleeve, he carefully pulls back onto the road. His pulse is jacking. It pounds through the shoulder wound like a hammer.

Five miles south of I-8, in Calexico, they approach the border checkpoint. Four cars are in line ahead of them. Easy crossing, sure. Nobody at the American checkpoint cares if you leave the United States. Not unless you're a drug trafficker or a felon.

Or wanted in LA for taking down a cop.

Chris slows and gets in line. The day is cooling. Sunset will be coming on soon. An agent stands at the head of the line, chewing gum, lackadaisical. But there's a booth, lit, a guard inside, flyers and posters on the wall.

The gum-chewer watches cars pull forward. Cop stance, fingers jammed under his utility belt, reflective shades. Asking everyone to roll down their windows. Waving one car through, talking to the next. Asking for ID.

Chris pats his jacket pocket.

"The license is good," Frida says.

He holds his hand over the wallet.

"Jeffrey?" she says. "Chris?"

He watches the cop.

These people. Their job? Threatening his wife. Threatening his son. Willing to ruin his beautiful shining boy's life to grab him.

Frida puts her hand over his. He turns sharply. She reaches into his pocket and takes out the wallet. He tries to stop her, but she finds it. Among the fake family photos is the snapshot he grabbed at the Koreatown safe house: Dominick in Charlene's arms, Chris at their side, laughing, every bit of it golden.

Frida sticks the snapshot in her jeans pocket and hands the wallet back. She says nothing. Chris wants to kick the door open and boot her out. He grips the wheel instead.

The two cars ahead are waved through. The border cop, Shiny Shades, Mr. I Am God, beckons him forward, one of those *I own you* waves. Chris pulls up. In the booth, the bored guard with a gray buzz cut looks at a computer. And at the flyers posted on the wall, and out the window at him.

Then back at the flyers.

Shiny Shades scans Chris's face as he pulls up.

Chris puts down the window. Tries to look bored. Feels wired.

Frida starts crying.

"Where you headed?" Shades says.

"Mexicali," Chris says.

Frida pulls a wad of Kleenex from her purse and cries into it, actual tears.

Shades leans down. Looks at her, at Chris. "Everything all right?"

"Her grandmother had a stroke. Everybody's worried. We're trying to get there before . . ."

Frida looks at him, eyes wet. "Sorry, Officer. It's been a day."

The older guard, Buzz Cut, comes out of the booth and walks toward them. Chris tenses. *Fuck*, she took the Beretta back at the safe house—why did he let her do that? She's getting them both . . .

Buzz Cut waves at Shades. "Offerman."

Shades gives Chris a long look—at his fatigue, his weakness, his vulnerability. Chris is unarmed. He can barely move. If he smashes open the driver's door, he can hit the gas, flatten Shades, and be across the border before the guy gets back to his feet.

Buzz Cut marches up and with urgency says, "Come on."

Shades looks at Chris, at Frida. "Hope your grandma's all right. Pull forward."

Then he follows Buzz Cut to the car behind them in line. Chris inches away, hands knotted, the sledgehammer pain in his shoulder nearly making him scream. He looks in the rearview mirror.

The guards approach the car behind him from either side, hands on their holstered weapons. Buzz Cut tells the driver to lower his window.

"What's going on?" Chris says.

"Keep driving."

He pulls ahead, barely able to see through his pounding vision. *Don't pass out.*

"It's my brother," Frida says.

"Who?"

"In the car behind us. I called him from the pay phone when we stopped. He looks like you"—she turns—"enough."

He wants to laugh. He checks the mirror again. The driver is out of the car, handing over his license. Tall, fit, he has short dark hair and wears shades the guards are now telling him to remove.

"Elisa . . ."

"What?"

"I mean Frida."

"Nine, ten!" She puts away the tissues.

They skate through the Mexican checkpoint. Then they're in Mexicali. Palm trees, *cambios*, tourist hotels, the welcoming Chinese pagodas painted red, green, and gold beside the big sign that reads BIENVENIDOS A MEXICALI.

Fuck no. It just has to come back around to this place, doesn't it?

I'm going backward. Into the fire. Into nothing.

"I'm not staying here," he says. "There's nothing for me here."

"You're not. Calm down," Frida says.

He keeps driving until she tells him, "Pull over."

Dusty farmland slides toward the horizon. He stops on the dirt shoulder. She gets out and pops the trunk. She returns and hands him a black brick of a satellite phone.

"One minute," she says. "Not a second more."

She ambles toward the fields, hands in her pockets, giving him privacy. He eases himself from the car and leans against the hood. Gripping the phone, he inhales and punches in the number.

He hears static and an electronic ping, and then, finally, her voice. "Hello."

Distant, tinny, insubstantial, but there. She isn't under arrest. She hasn't run. Home.

"Baby," Chris says.

Static. Nothing. Until a sound that might be Charlene exhaling, hard.

"You okay?" she says.

Nowhere close. Maybe never again. But she knows that. And he has forty-five seconds left. Only one thing counts right now.

"How's Dominick?" he says.

"In my lap and asleep. Safe and sound."

His heart eases. "Listen, and believe what I am saying. Someday. Somehow. When I'm set and secure, we will be together."

The static flares. For endless seconds, there's no reply. At the edge of the field, Frida looks at her watch and walks toward him.

"Charlene," Chris says.

"I hear you," she says.

Traffic rolls past: a farm truck, a gasoline tanker. Chris nods and shuts his eyes. He hears Frida approach.

"I don't know what happened," he says. "Don't explain. I don't want to know. What I'll take with me is that you put it all on the line to warn me off."

Frida gestures for the phone.

"Stay strong," he says to Charlene. "I love you."

Charlene's voice is ghostly. "You, too." A sound, maybe a laugh or a sob. "Always."

Frida takes the phone from him, almost gently, and presses End. Chris sinks back into the driver's seat. The sky seems to shimmer. Frida returns the phone to the trunk. Then she gets a lighter from her purse. She takes the snapshot of him with Dominick and Charlene and lights it on fire. She holds the photo for a second, the flame flaring red, eating it. She drops it and grinds it into the dust and gets back in the car.

She slams the door. "Drive."

"Where?" His voice is hollow.

"Past the mountains. It'll be dark. A plane's coming."

"Where am I goin'?"

"Dunno. All I know is get you to the plane, and they said it's a very long flight."

As he pulls onto the highway, he looks back. Sunset rakes the sky violet and orange. He puts down the window. An evening chill is sinking into the air. In the side mirrors he sees the other side of the border, the lights of California, shimmering like a mirage. Nothing is different five feet on this side of the line, except everything. He is leaving the land of death.

Driving into the land of death.

Neil, brother.

Charlene. Dominick.

Somehow, someday, I'll be back.

He stares ahead at the desert plains, at the blue-brown mountains rising hazy on the horizon. This is the land of blood and ghosts. Of unfinished business. *Breathe,* he tells himself. *Just fucking breathe.*

PART TWO

1988

8

Las Vegas

Chris Shiherlis is in town for only eighteen hours, but hours in Vegas are like dog years. He powers up to the entrance at Caesars Palace in a dirty black convertible Corvette. The day is sun-fried. The heat feels eager. Bennies overlay the weed, giving a smooth zoom to the light in the sky and the blood in his veins. He tosses the keys to the parking valet. He has a flight to Chicago in the morning, but today he has a roll of cash ready to lay down. New clothes, a blue silk shirt. Fresh haircut, Wayfarers. He snaps them off when he rolls through the doors. Bulletproof.

Craps, blackjack, and the sports book—it's a feast. He moves through the shouts, the music, the mechanical chug of the slot machines, the ringing of jackpots, quarters sliding into buckets held by dedicated grandmas with cigarettes jammed in the corners of their mouths. Hot women at the roulette wheel. Dark and light and magic. He is here, ready to cast a spell and reap the payoff. *Presto.*

When he walks onto the casino floor, he sees her.

She's standing beside an older guy at the craps table, amber light overhead, neon and glitter behind her. Bright and shadowed. Everything momentarily fades—the incredible buzz, the excitement and possibility. Everything goes soft-focus, except for her. Velvet and sunshine. Storm and sleekness. She looks up, across the table, through the crowd, and her gaze flicks him.

Lightning.

Black hair, glossy, like Cleopatra. A sleeveless black Spandex dress that shows every slow move and every muscle in her powerful body. Smooth bronze skin. A choker with a massive turquoise-and-garnet crucifix lying against her chest. All-American youth, and dark, knowing eyes.

The crowd around the table is riled. The older guy—black suit, silver hair, cutthroat eyes like a New York banker's—lifts the dice and shoots the woman a glance. She runs her hand down his arm, leans in, and blows on the dice. He hooks his gaze on her for a moment too long. Possessively. Uncertainly. Without confidence.

Guy is lookin' to lose, Chris thinks. The divine light in the room has blessed the dice, but the man lacks conviction.

Chris stays back. The banker throws the dice. People around the table moan.

Knew it.

Chris angles around the table, taking his time, aiming in the general direction of the sports book. The roll of cash feels eager in his pocket.

The banker downs the last of his whiskey, a sour scowl on his face. The woman rubs his back, accommodating, commiserating.

Working, Chris thinks. Twenty-three, maybe twenty-four, firm on her feet, doing her appointed tasks. Feeding his ego and looking magnificent—looking ungodly—on his arm and convincing him he's a winner. Even if he's paying her for her time, the banker should know how lucky he is.

Chris veers toward the table. The noise is wild, the dealer clamoring to be heard. Chris leans close to the woman.

"You busy?" he says.

She doesn't look at him. She licks her lips. The banker slams down his empty tumbler, looks at Chris.

"Clearly," she says.

"For how long?"

She looks up from under her lashes. For a moment her gaze seems clinical, assessing him. A good prospect? A loser?

Then the banker spins on his stool. "Excuse me?" A beat. "Piss off."

His shoulders are bunched, like he's ready to butt heads.

Chris's eyes go blank. He stares at him. It's a look from a different world. The banker feels ice between his shoulder blades and it rises up his spine.

He actually blinks.

"You lost 'cause you knew you were gonna lose," Chris says.

The guy stands and grabs the woman's arm. "Let's go." He nudges her. She holds still a moment. "Cinnamon. Come on."

She leaves, but her gaze walks back to Chris.

That's when he smiles. "I'll see you later."

She finds him three hours later. He's up six grand on the Lakers game. She glides in, sits down across from him, and crosses those long legs. She rests her arms on the arms of the chair, languid, like a big cat, nails a vivid scarlet. Her eyes are calm, something rock solid behind them, anchored. A bank of TV screens flashes behind her. Bulls-Pistons. Juventus-Milan. Belmont Park. Her eyes pull him away from all of it.

"You hungry?" Chris says.

"I'm starving."

"The steak house here—"

"*Prizewinning.* I know a better place."

He stands. "My car's outside."

The entire room tracks her as she leads him out. She's so magnetic, he expects coins and keys to levitate out of people's pockets and fly across the casino.

"I'm Chris."

"Charlene."

"Not Cinnamon?"

She rolls her eyes.

He scorches the tires on the drive out.

They eat at a neighborhood place on the east side of town. Dim sum. When they leave the restaurant, she holds out her hand and says, "Keys."

They head for the Strip sharing a blunt. Charlene drives like she's been trained at Top Gun. A screaming eagle. Confident, and smooth, and quick-witted. In control, never out beyond the edge. The engine hums under her.

She'd be a solid wheelman, Chris thinks. *Someone you could count on. Who'd figured all the ifs and buts and alternate routes and never freaks out. Who gets you home every time.*

"What are you smiling at?" she shouts over the wind and the engine.

"Magic," he says.

They come in through the casino floor at the Mirage. The night is lifting, pulsing, energy rolling straight into him.

He turns to her. "I have a room. You want to skip this?"

"Please, yes," she says.

He leads her to the elevator. "You're not a gambler?"

"I gamble every day." She says it lightly, but her voice has an undertow. Then she looks him up and down. "Some days, I bet big."

It's three a.m. when she finally pulls off the black wig, that sleek disguise, and shakes her sandy curls loose. She's on top of him, riding him, engulfing him, electrifying him. The empty bottle of Veuve is tipped upside down in the ice bucket. The smack is carrying him along a warm, sweet river of euphoria. Calm, and centered, and bright with beauty. The view out the plate glass windows reflects the throbbing grid of light outside.

Chris slides his hands along her thighs. She takes his wrists and stretches them over his head.

"Baby," he says.

She drives down on him. He inhales and closes his eyes. He feels the wave sweep over him. He clutches her, moaning, and holds on. Her nails dig into his forearms. She throws her head back and shouts.

Then she lies flat on top of him, breathing hard.

"Where did you come from?" he says at last.

"That's not a question for tonight." She softens and rolls off. "It's not romantic and it's no place you want to hear about."

"Everything about you is romantic."

"Shh. Then don't break the spell."

He props himself up on an elbow. Runs the backs of his fingers down her belly, then leans over and kisses her bare skin. She sighs and smiles with the relaxed assurance of a lioness who's just fed.

He pulls her close, already feeling the sweet lure of sleep. But she inhales, gets up, and begins dressing.

"You don't have to go," Chris says.

"It's work. This isn't."

"You still don't have to." He tries to figure out how to say it. "I'll cover you . . . for the night."

She stops.

"No." He sits up and presses the heels of his hands to his eyes. "I mean, I don't want anybody giving you grief. This is"—he gestures between them—"us." He does not want her to think this is commercial. "You took time for me. Let me make it right for you."

"You mean, with . . ." Then she laughs. ". . . my escort service manager slash pimp?"

"Charlene . . ."

She steps into the dress and wrestles it on. "It's just work, baby. But it *is* work."

He feels a heated coal in his chest. "Yeah, who is he? Let me make it square."

She picks up the wig. "Dude. Don't."

"I want to."

She kneels on the bed and presses her fingertips to his lips. "You're perfect. This is perfect. I have to go."

"How do I find you again? What's your number?"

"A romantic *and* an optimist. Wow." She slides her shoes on and grabs her purse. "Will you still be here tomorrow?"

"No. I'm leaving. Work."

She smiles. It looks melancholy. Shrugs, like she expected nothing less.

Then she's out the door.

He goes out to the balcony overlooking the hotel entrance. The night air runs cool across his skin. The sounds of traffic and street laughter bubble up to him. A minute later he sees her walk out, back straight, armored against the night. She raises her hand and hails a taxi.

Manager. From the way she said it, the way her eyes died, she'd made a bad bargain.

Pimp.

The taxi pulls out, the lights of the Strip sliding over it. Disappearing. *Magical Mystery Tour.*

He stands, letting the night sparkle through him. He'd seen it. Before she got in the cab, she looked back. Looked up toward the room.

He'll come back. He'll find her.

9

The diner juts like the prow of a ship toward the six-cornered intersection. The Near Northwest Side Chicago neighborhood is rolling at 8:25 on a Monday morning. Traffic is building up at the lights on Diversey. Suits—men and women—pass on the sidewalk, heading for the L, shoulders squared, briefcases swinging. The sky is blue, the trees vibrant along the sidewalk. Brick buildings fill the six-way intersection.

Neil McCauley sits solo at the lunch counter. The counter matches the shape of the diner, an isosceles triangle, windows on two sides. An expansive view. Half the stools are occupied, plates and silverware clattering. A radio plays on a shelf behind the grill: "Simply Irresistible," the song everywhere, the video a guy in a slick black suit, women with slick red lips and slinky stilettos. Show that at Folsom and howling men would bring the walls down. Neil drinks his coffee. Nobody in the diner talks. Everybody's heads are in the *Sun-Times* or the *Trib* and their food. The light that slants through the eastern windows is flat. Distancing.

The grill man comes out from the back with a coffeepot in his hand, waiting on customers this morning.

"Top you up?" he says.

"Sure."

The guy pours. He's white, looks forty-seven, forty-eight. Pack of smokes in the pocket of his apron. Forty-two. Neil clocks the muscular forearms and double-sized wrists. He suspects the guy had worked as a pipefitter. Jobs that aren't around anymore. The starched cuffs on his pristinely ironed shirt—that bonnaroo perfection—say he did time. The broken capillaries on the nose say he's a drinker. The guy is a transient, Neil thinks, a short-order cook who picks up work for six, eight weeks and then gets that itch and moves on. From the low melody of his accent, he's Appalachian, living in a furnished room in Uptown around Wilson and Broadway. Neil nods thanks, and the man heads back behind the grill.

Neil raises the coffee cup to his lips. He has a clear view out the opposite windows.

What he's viewing is a 1922 office building across the street, built when seven stories provided a sense of pride. A bright new flag flies on the flagpole projecting from its bow. On the ground floor is Prosperity Savings & Loan.

The S&L is a small-scale outfit. Sole location. The spot was originally a proud 1920s bank that went under during the Depression.

The diner's glass door flashes with sunlight as Chris comes in. He slides onto the stool beside Neil.

"Height of the junction box makes it visible from the L tracks, but it's screened by trees," he says. "Trains are loud as hell when you're on the street under the tracks."

Chris picks up a laminated menu, only to set it back. He tosses his blond hair out of his eyes. He's cool, torqued down, his eyes flat. But Neil knows the energy underneath. Chris is always wired, even when his affect seems flat; he can be explosive with no hesitation. Right now that thrumming is somewhere below. Right now is work. They watch the far windows. They both mark three clerks and the assistant manager entering the S&L's side door at 8:32 for the 9:00 a.m. opening.

"We have to be out by five a.m.," Neil says.

Chris's eyes stay locked on the side door of the building across the street. The grill man comes out wiping his hands on his apron. Chris gives him a blackjack wave off. The man takes Neil's empty plate and leaves.

"Where we meeting Grimes?" Neil says.

"The Belden Deli. Two miles east of here. On Clark Street."

Neil checks his watch. They have four hours. "We'll knock off the supplies. You got cash to cover the hardware?"

"I'm cool."

They split the list. Gloves, goggles, ear protection. Water and food.

Mechanic's toolkits. Electrical gear. All common; all purchased from a large store where no one will remember their trade.

The more specialized Milwaukee Tool circular saw, angle grinder, and heavy-duty tripod-mounted drill—Cerrito already scored all of those.

"I wanna reconnoiter the route," Neil says. "When, on the work cars?"

"Three days."

They'll drive the route in, the route out, the backup escape routes, where they'll dump the work cars, all the tools, and all their clothes, leaving no physical evidence to link the score back to them. They'll double-check the location for cameras. They'll call the city to see where it's planning construction, gas work, and electrical projects over the weekend. The nearest police station is a mile and a half away. Neil knows the CPD's response times to a burglary call and how many units it has patrolling each shift and what time the shift comes on and gets off. He doesn't know how it'll staff up during the Cubs game Saturday afternoon, but there's also a game today. He'll find out.

"They will add cops walking the beat," he says. "Temperature will be in the seventies. They like to walk around when it's like that. First pitch is at two."

From behind the grill, the cook eyes Neil, then scans the other customers. At a corner table, a girl in a DePaul University T-shirt is ignoring her textbook to cast a thirsty gaze at Chris. It's no time to linger.

Neil nods to the cook and tosses extra cash on the counter. Cook looks at Neil for an extra beat and nods back. "Let's go."

10

Belden is a classic Chicago Jewish deli, booths and tables in the middle packed at lunchtime. In the parking lot Neil walks around an innocuous Chevy four-door. It looks like a two-hundred-thousand-mile refugee from Hertz or the Chicago Police Department—what he wants. One point for Aaron Grimes.

Inside, in a booth, Grimes drums his thumbs on the tabletop. Conversations around him racket off the ceiling and windows. A half-eaten pastrami sandwich is in front of him. He's taking a bite when a guy strides up and sits down across from him. Young, ripped, with blond hair and dead, cold eyes. Surfer sociopath in jeans and a flannel shirt. Grimes wipes crumbs and extends his hand.

"You Chris?"

Chris shakes his hand and holds it. And holds it. His grip is cool and relentless, like his gaze. Looking into his vacant blue eyes is like staring into the black ocean at night—you know there are dangerous, cold-blooded things lurking below the surface. Grimes doesn't see the new guy slide into the booth beside him while Chris holds his hand. All at once he's getting frisked by the new guy. Shiherlis's grip is like steel.

The new guy looks strong, if you know where to look. Not pneumatic vanity muscle, but ropy and chiseled, with short black hair, a tight jaw. A starched white shirt under a black baseball jacket. Square aviators, old school. He runs his hands over Grimes with emotionless efficiency, like he does this as habitually as breathing. Grimes looks around. Now he sees the third man, a fireplug with hard eyes that say he'd cut you open and not think twice about it. He's hanging in the deli's small lobby by the pay phone, casually watching the outside.

McCauley finishes the search and half turns. Shiherlis releases his hand and leans back.

"The pastrami's good," Grimes says. "And the turkey club."

"That your beater outside?" McCauley asks.

"It's spoken for. I'll get you one like it if you want," Grimes says.

"Nothing hot," McCauley says. "Gotta be legit and stand a traffic stop."

"Understood." Grimes smooths his T-shirt. "Pop a light, get pulled over, the registration, insurance, no problem. No wants, no warrants, clean rides."

"Plates?"

"If a cop runs the tags, they'll show up as registered in Springfield to a leasing company."

"Driver's licenses."

"They'll be ready."

"Two cars, one panel van, no side windows," McCauley says. "How do you set up delivery?"

"I got a garage on the West Side, behind a commercial vehicle auto repair shop. I will provide you with the key to the garage. Keys for the cars and van will be under the floor mat, ready to rock."

"No fuss, nothing that grabs attention."

"Boring, reliable. Nothing flashy."

"Who owns this auto repair shop?"

"My uncle. I run it."

"He don't ask questions?"

"He's never there." Grimes shakes his head. "You sure you just want the two beaters and the van?"

"Did I say I wanted something else?"

"Asking, that's all. I wondered why you didn't want something faster . . ."

"Why?"

"I was wondering . . ."

"Don't wonder." McCauley takes off his sunglasses. "I hire you to do a thing, you do that thing." He's x-raying Grimes. "Do not fucking ask me what you do not need to know."

Grimes feels the chill. He wants to move away, but there's nowhere in the booth to go. This guy isn't posing. He's from the coast, set up by a guy with connections that are way deep. They're here for something large. Grimes doesn't want to blow it with attitude or overreaching.

"Three rides, ready to go, six grand each, half up front," he says.

"They will have maps in the glove box; they will have McDonald's wrappers on the floor, gum wrappers in the ashtray, and a rosary on the rearview in the van. Scrubbed, but lived in."

"Got it."

McCauley reaches into his jacket and pulls out an envelope.

Grimes eyes the envelope.

McCauley's face is impenetrable. "You tell nobody what cars you are getting, or why or for who . . ." McCauley doesn't finish the sentence.

"I am cool."

McCauley hands him the envelope. It crinkles and has a nice heft. He lifts the flap. The bills inside are fresh and crisp, not even folded. They make for a sleek, thin package. Nine thousand dollars.

Grimes waits a second. Then, feeling the weight of McCauley's stare, he jams the envelope in his jeans pocket.

McCauley stands and heads for the door. Shiherlis falls in behind him. The guy in the lobby follows after they've gone out.

Grimes stares out the front windows. McCauley walks away without looking back.

When Grimes comes out of the Belden, McCauley and his men are gone. Grimes's wary excitement remains. He's doing business with a highline, coast-to-coast crew. One rung up the food chain. He climbs into the Chevy in the parking lot, guns its big block to life, and heads west through sluggish street traffic. The overhead sun bakes the asphalt, the sidewalks, the low yellow brick buildings. By the time he reaches his repair shop and garage, the clock on the dash tells him he's only two minutes late.

At the back in the alley, the man is waiting inside the shadowed cab of his pickup truck, drumming his fingers on the wheel. His number two, Hank, is in the passenger seat.

Grimes pulls up and gets out. The man makes a show of checking his watch. Irritated. His face isn't visible, but the dial flashes in the sun.

Grimes smiles and walks toward the truck with the keys to the Chevy dangling from his finger. "I was tied up with another customer. Sorry."

The man crosses his arms. "Customer? What other customer?"

Grimes shakes his head. "Another customer."

The man holds still for a second, knuckles tight, shoulders heavy. "Can't talk about it?" He turns to Hank, then back to Grimes. His voice goes from hot to amused. "Suddenly you're supplying spooks or something?"

Grimes stays quiet and holds out the keys.

The man grabs the Chevy's keys from Grimes's hand. "The CIA?"

He tosses the keys to Hank, who climbs out of the truck and heads for the car. Grimes backs away.

"The sign, the rest, are in the trunk," Grimes says. "You're cool."

The man fires up the truck. "I'm seeing your brother-in-law later. I'll tell him 'do not disturb,' you're on a secret mission."

He puts the truck in gear. Hank gets behind the wheel of the Chevy. They pull away laughing. Grimes's hand hangs in the air.

11

Alexander Dalecki—Alex, to the woman snorting lines off the living room coffee table—stands naked at the kitchen counter, pouring Johnnie Walker Black into two glasses. The woman, Ginger, is equally naked. Her red hair sticks straight up, wildly disheveled. Stupidly funny for a hairdresser. She wants to go again because he didn't succeed the first time, and she thinks coke will get him over the finish line. But she's about to crawl up the walls to the ceiling. She inhales another line through a rolled-up twenty and flings herself back against the sofa cushions with a whoop. Alex needs to get her back down. Both of them. He pours her a double.

The knock on the door jars him: two loud thumps with the side of a fist.

Ginger pops up, bright, wired like the bride of Frankenstein. "Alex? You expecting company?"

He goes to the peephole. Hank stands outside, rocking the way he does when he gets jacked up, peering up and down the hall.

Alex turns to Ginger. "Get dressed. Now."

She gives him a pout. He pulls her to her feet and pushes her toward the bedroom. Hank pounds again.

"Hang on," Alex says.

His skin is hypersensitive. The lights seem to hiss at him, a nasty sound. He yanks on some sweats and unlocks the front door. Hank slides in. Hank Svoboda always seems to slide, sideways, through cracks, like oil.

"You didn't answer your phone," he says.

"I was otherwise engaged."

"We're on."

Alex feels himself reset. "You said—you said nine p.m."

"It's eight thirty. Get dressed."

Hank's flat Slavic face seems like a skillet, poised to brain him.

"Give me a few," Alex says.

Hank shakes his head. "You shot your mouth off. You want to come along for the ride? I'm parked out back. Sixty seconds. Move."

Alex's pulse feels thready. Yeah, he'd asked. The boss had pointed at him and said, *You're on.*

Maybe the boss didn't think this score was as big as Alex claimed, or that Alex was for real. Going along sure as hell is the way to show all that.

Hank leaves, and Alex hustles Ginger out, looking sulky. Then he dresses in black, shoves the ski mask in his pocket, and runs down the back stairs. Hank is idling in a creaky Chevy sedan.

Alex jumps in, wiping his nose. "Good to go."

Hank pulls out. "Don't take your phone off the hook again."

"I'm here, aren't I?"

You never keep these guys waiting.

Alex says, "What's with the pizza sign on the roof?"

"Figure it out."

They head for Lincoln Park.

The night feels bright. Fizzy, popping. The street is quiet. It's always quiet by the Gold Coast brownstones overlooking Lincoln Park.

Money cushions everything, even sound. Alex sits in the back seat of the Chevy, squashed between Chubby and Angel, his brain an up elevator from the coke, his skin feeling like it's been shaved with sandpaper. Hank is cruising slowly. The boss rides shotgun. The back of his head looks like a cannonball.

The car pulls over fifty yards from the town house. Rich light glows from behind drawn shades. Spring-green trees shiver under the streetlights. A breeze is blowing toward the lake. Leaves scuttle along the street. The sound seems to scrape the inside of Alex's skull.

The engine idles. The boss cracks his knuckles. Alex can hear him breathing. Angel and Chubby are silent.

"Go," the boss says.

Alex rolls out of the car with the other men. The boss slides behind the wheel. Sticking to the shadows, they cross the small lawn to the town house, hurry up the stairs, and flatten against the wall beside the large front door next to Greek urns overflowing with orange bougainvillea.

The Chevy pulls up. Its UMBERTO'S PIZZA sign is illuminated. The boss gets out, wearing a White Sox cap low over his forehead, an Umberto's shirt, and carrying a pizza box. The ski mask is over his face. He walks with contained energy. His eyes look like lit matches.

Alex and the others roll their masks down.

Hank has the house key in his left hand, in case they need it. He has a crowbar in his right. Alex's mask scratches against his hot skin. The leather gloves groan as he flexes his fists. He has to do this. He knows the boss doesn't fully trust him. Alex has to prove he's more than the tipster who scouted the score. Provided intel. He's part of the crew. He has to rise to the occasion, right now.

The boss climbs the steps and rings the doorbell. Then he turns and faces the street. Making sure the pizza box and his shirt are visible, the car visible at the curb, his face hidden.

Alex's knee jitters and his shoulders twitch. Hank grabs him by the back of the neck. His mutter is so low it's no more than a breath.

"Hold. Fucking. Still."

A dead bolt slides back. The door opens.

A man says, "Hang on a minute, I think you have the wrong address." His voice goes muffled as he turns. "Did someone order a pizza?"

The men hidden along the wall spin and charge straight through the door, *bam*. The homeowner yells, and Alex is *in* this house, his heart thundering.

The homeowner, James Matzukas, is backing away from the door, wide-eyed. He's in his late forties, suave, dressed in a cashmere sweater. He wheels around in the marble hallway.

"Andi, run, lock the door," he yells.

Hank swings the crowbar at the man's knee. Matzukas drops like a felled tree. Beyond him, in the doorway of a family room, a woman appears in a robe, towel-drying her hair.

She shouts, "What the *fuck?*"

Mrs. Matzukas. Andi. Chubby bolts after her.

The boss turns and steps inside. He closes the door and takes his .44 from the pizza box.

Andi shrieks as Chubby collars her. Matzukas scrambles like a wounded crab along the gleaming floor. The boss kicks the man's elbow out from under him and steps on his neck. Tossing aside the pizza box, he aims the gun at the man's head.

Then he looks up at the woman. Stands tall. He shouts, "Honey, I'm home."

From behind his mask, Alex can hear every molecule of air entering his lungs. He's panting. He's hot. He's staring at the marble, the swooping staircase, the chandelier. How great is their house. He had imagined it, but it is beyond any glitz he could conjure. It truly sparkles in his eyes. That's the coke, but it *shines*.

Hank grabs his shirt and shoves him toward the front door. "You're lookout. Stay there."

The boss snaps his fingers and points at Angel. "Master bedroom."

Angel charges up the stairs. Chubby drags Andi Matzukas—who's screaming, struggling, swearing—into the hall and binds her wrists with the speed of a team roper, using electrical tape.

The boss turns to Hank. "Get the girl."

Andi thrashes, screaming. With the thick stone walls, nobody outside will hear her.

"Shut up!" the boss orders. She does, eyes wide, panicked.

Hank runs up the stairs. James Matzukas writhes on the floor, his eyes bugging. "Don't hurt my family."

The boss presses his boot into the man's neck. "The cash in the safe. Open it. You do that, we're gone. Done. You give us shit, and . . ."

He gestures. Chubby slaps Andi.

The boss stares down at Matzukas. "I think you know what happens if you give us shit."

Matzukas moans, drooling blood onto the marble. "I'll open it. Don't hurt her. I'm begging you."

The boss hauls him to his feet and shoves the gun in his ribs. "Move."

James Matzukas owns a dozen Chicagoland car dealerships. The boss has been eyeing him since Alex tipped him off and made an impression of his wife's house key. From the moment Alex described Andi Matzukas—the sapphires, the diamond ring, the Porsche, the tight skirt, and the attitude—he's been hot for this score.

Andi is demanding, proud, and thinks nothing's wrong with displaying wealth. Her husband gives her a $10,000 monthly allowance—in cash. Alex has heard her say, *It's hard to spend that much money, but it sure is fun.* Andi goes through life buying everything she wants, including subservience. Alex told the crew that.

The boss force-marches Matzukas toward his study. He glares at Alex and snaps his fingers.

"Eyes out the door."

Alex hunches and turns. He hears Angel upstairs, rifling through drawers. He hears crying. Hank appears, pulling the Matzukases' fourteen-year-old daughter, Jessica, down the stairs. The girl is fighting, flailing at Hank. Her face, always sunny and open when Alex has seen her before, beautiful, cool, seeing but not seeing him as she is swept past, is now a storm of childlike terror.

"Stop it," she yells. "Let go. Don't hurt my mom or dad."

At the wall safe in the study, Matzukas fumbles with the tumbler. "I'll give you whatever. Name it. No one has to get rough." He finally manages the combination and swings the door open. "Take the cash. There on the desk, the keys to my Ferrari. Take it. I won't even report it. Don't hurt my family."

The Ferrari. Alex parked it once. His pulse skitters. He looks through the peephole in the front door. Trees, night, wealth, danger. His blood thuds in his ears, bubbles in his veins. His skin feels like it's covered with ants.

The boss shoves Matzukas away from the safe. "Ferrari? We don't want your fucking Ferrari. We look like hicks from Kenosha who fell into your showroom?"

He sweeps the contents of the safe into a gym bag and grabs the keys after all. Matzukas is breathing like he's about to heave.

"Now," the boss says.

He yanks the man from the study. At the far end of the hall, Chubby and Hank hold Andi and Jessica from behind by the hair, arms pinned. The boss knocks Matzukas to the floor. He pulls out a pack of cigarettes and a lighter and tosses them in front of the man.

"Light up," he says.

"I don't sm—"

He kicks Matzukas in the face with his steel-toed construction boot, fracturing his right cheekbone and orbital socket. Matzukas lies still, eyes rolled back.

Jessica screams. Hank slaps his large hand across her mouth.

"Stop it!" Andi screams. "Don't hurt him. Please, I'll give you whatever you want. I'll do anything."

The boss throws her a wry look. She sees it, parts her robe, exposing herself. His expression says, *Look at that.*

She'll go along, pretend like it's okay, but he'll read her and get whipsawed by her hate and loathing. He's been there.

Sticking the gun in the waistband of his jeans, he picks up the lighter and cigarettes and walks over to her.

"Light up."

He taps a cigarette from the pack and sticks it between her lips. It shakes like a seismograph needle. He flicks the lighter. Andi inhales and the tip of the cigarette lights red. The boss steps back.

"Good girl," he says softly. "Now. Burn yourself or I will. Your choice."

What the fuck? Alex thinks.

He sees Andi's eyes, reflected red with the glowing cigarette, crazed with fear. Hank holds Jessica by the hair, forcing her to watch. Alex sees Andi shake her head. He hears the screams, then the sobs. Jessica yelling, "Stop it. Don't!"

The boss turns and points at Jessica. "Come here."

Jessica freezes. Hank pushes her toward him. The boss grabs her.

"On your knees."

"No," she cries.

"On your knees, bitch, or I'll kill your mother."

She's fourteen, not so sophisticated here at home as she tries to pretend out in the world, Alex thinks. She shakes her head. The boss forces her to the floor and unzips his fly.

Alex is halfway down the hall toward him before he even knows it. "*Stop.*"

The boss turns. Hank turns. Angel and Chubby turn. Staring at him. He keeps coming.

"You're getting loud," he says. "There's a guy on the street walking his dog. Shut the fuck up. We gotta go." It's the best excuse he can think of. He jerks his thumb over his shoulder. "*Now.*"

The boss holds on to Jessica. She's hunched, teeth bared, shivering.

Alex looks the boss in the eye. "I'll gag her, tie her up, lock her in her room. C'mon."

The boss's chest is rising and falling. Behind his mask, his eyes are liquid. He stares at Alex for a moment, then shoves Jessica at him.

She stumbles against Alex's chest. Chubby tosses him the roll of electrical tape.

The boss stalks up and grabs Alex by the back of the neck. He puts his lips to Alex's ear and whispers, harsh and quick, words that make Alex's skin prickle. Then he shoves Alex away.

"Hurry," he says.

Alex puts a hand on Jessica's back and urges her up the stairs.

"Just go. Just do it," he says to her. "Don't resist. It'll be quicker."

Still freaked and crying, the girl staggers up the stairs. She's shuddering. Her eyes are shiny with fear.

"Which room?" Alex says.

She hears the screams from her mother downstairs. She freezes. Alex pushes her forward.

"Don't hurt my mom!"

Downstairs the boss's arm is whipping back and forth as he hits Andi. Then he drags her into the family room.

12

Through the sheers on the balcony window, the headlights down on Lake Shore Drive cast a dreamy light. Vincent Hanna stands up from the king-sized bed. He lifts the tumbler of scotch from the nightstand, where it sits beside his badge, his duty weapon, an extra clip, and a bottle of Bordeaux. Downs the whisky. He pulls on his pants and steps outside into the brisk night. The surrounding skyscrapers sparkle darkly. Lake Michigan is a vast black absence to the east. He stretches and inhales.

Jodie calls to him from the bed. "Show-off."

He turns and smiles. She lies on her back, wineglass in her hand, one leg stretched toward the ceiling, spinning her foot lazily.

"The city wants everything I've got," he says. "They won't get it, but I can give 'em a look."

She rolls over and gets up, pulling on a plush white robe. This is her place, but they've known each other long enough that she feels comfortable having him over.

She steps onto the balcony beside him. "Not bad, huh?"

Better than his first apartment in Chicago. Better than his current apartment in Chicago. He sees pride on her face and a relaxed sense of satisfaction. She's a couple years younger than he is, picky. Discerning about men, he likes to think, knowing that's an ego boost.

"Come here." He pulls her against him and slides his hands beneath her robe.

She smiles slowly, not worrying about the clock. They have the whole evening booked. But when he leans in to kiss her neck, she tilts her head back and says, "Neighbor across the way has a telescope."

"So he'll see what he's missing."

"She."

He runs his hands around her back and laughs.

The beeper is on the dresser inside, with his wallet and keys. He hears it over the sound of traffic and Jodie's cool, clear breathing.

He lets go of her and walks inside. Sees the code.

She comes in, brushing her fingers through her auburn hair. "You going?" She runs one fingernail down his jugular, raises an eyebrow.

He closes his eyes. Opens them. He grabs his shirt. "Yeah." He takes her hand and kisses it as he pulls the shirt on. "I'll call you."

She heads for the shower as he ties his shoes. "Be good."

He leaves her fee on the kitchen island, in cash.

13

Black elms rustle in the night air lit by low streetlamps. Across the street is Lincoln Park. In the middle distance is a granite bridge built in 1893, arching over a bridle path. Empty. Hanna is parked at the curb. Now he gets out and walks down the sidewalk under the lush canopy. He passes on his right a tungsten-yellow bay window in a granite town house. A couple watches the activity down the street. High ceilings, ornate cornices, large table lamp, a *lush vibe of the good life,* he thinks. The rustle of leaves. Dead quiet.

From the house at the end of the street there's a distant blue-white flash of a camera. It's silent, too. Hanna's face changes. A low voltage pulses under his skin, like his heart knows the imminence of the scene racing at him as he takes the granite stairs two at a time. From the side of the house around the corner an ambulance pulls away, lights spinning. White-and-blue units crowd the side street. The ME's body van is half on the sidewalk. From inside among the uniforms comes another flash of the police photographer's camera.

Great. This is going to be a long night, maybe an all-nighter. Hanna pops a couple of uppers. He signs into the scene with the officer stationed inside the door. Detective Robert Easton comes down from upstairs to meet him.

"Vincent."

Easton's shaved head shines under the ceiling light. He's African American, lanky, so tall that he tends to duck his head when approaching doorways.

"What do we got? What do we got?" Hanna says.

"Five men. Ski masks, gloves."

Hanna eyes the door. "No marks on the jamb. Locks are clean. How'd they get in?"

"A ruse. Pizza delivery," Easton says. "Neighbor across the street saw them leave in a car with a sign on top."

Hanna stops inside the vestibule. This is the sixth similar home invasion robbery in the area in the last eight months. Glencoe, Winnetka, Hinsdale—the home invaders have been circling through the suburbs like sharks outside Chicago's perimeter. Now they've spiraled inside the city limits, hitting an upscale Chicago neighborhood. Okay, his turf.

No forced entry. Disguises. Same MO as the suburban scores. Other detectives from Hanna's Criminal Intelligence Division are already scouring the bushes out back. They won't find anything. These guys leave no fingerprints or anything else. The leader of the crew has sexually assaulted four women.

The marble floor in the entry hall is tacky with a pool of drying blood the size of a truck tire. It poured from the head of the dead man with the caved-in skull who lies before him.

"Who?" Hanna says.

"Husband." Easton opens his notepad. "James Matzukas, forty-eight. Owns car dealerships."

"I've seen him on TV. The ambulance?"

"Wife. Andrea Matzukas. Broken ribs and jaw. Cigarette burns on her face, her eye. Raped. Naked, semiconscious on the floor, is how they found her." He shakes his head.

"Who else?"

"The daughter. She's already in the OR. Brain trauma. Sexually assaulted."

Hanna feels a chill. "How old?"

"Fourteen." Easton looks up from his notes, his voice level but sharp around the edges.

An acrid dull heaviness invades Hanna's lungs. He holds his breath. He's immobile. Then he breathes. "What they get?"

Easton walks Hanna into the study, points at the open wall safe. "Cash. Lots of it. Wife's jewelry from here and the bedroom."

"Get an inventory from her as soon as she can talk or from the insurance company. Maybe there's Polaroids. We'll start working local fences, see if it's turning up." Hanna returns to the hall. "Did the same guy attack the wife and daughter?"

"Don't know," Easton says. "Wife was in the family room. Daughter in her bedroom."

Hanna looks at the head wounds. "Number of blows he took—like from a crowbar or tire iron." Seeing the splatter patterns on the walls. "He was already dead before the killer stopped hitting him. Overkill."

He scans the floor. Too many people have been in and out already. The neighbor. The uniforms who responded to the 911 call. The paramedics. The police photographer and the ME's people were careful.

"Get comparison shoe prints for elimination." He looks from the body toward the study. "What I see, though—is what I don't see." He indicates the multiple trails of footprints and points at the study door. "No shoe prints going from the body into the study. No blood in there at all. So they killed him *after* he opened the safe. He opened the safe, and they killed him anyway. Illuminating."

"Illuminates what, boss?"

"He's not there only for the score and free sex. Something else makes this guy go."

He walks toward the stairs to the second floor. "He's angry. Into it. He is not going to stop."

14

Hanna sees Andrea Matzukas in the hospital in the morning. Battered, jaw wired shut, left eye bandaged, hooked to an IV drip. Barely able to talk. Her world crushed beyond repair. And Hanna sees that she fiercely clings to a foundation, some purpose. For the sake of her daughter, he guesses, who is in a room a few floors below in an induced coma to reduce intracranial swelling caused by her skull being fractured when she was beaten unconscious with a table lamp. The woman can't afford herself the luxury of despair, of slipping into the void.

"Five minutes," the nurse tells him sternly, and he knows better than to mess with nurses. He speaks quietly.

"Mrs. Matzukas, I'm a detective. Sergeant Vincent Hanna," he says. "I am sorry this happened to you. It shouldn't happen to anybody. This is difficult, but the sooner you can tell me about what happened, the better chance we have to catch these people. If you cannot, I understand and I can come back when you can."

"Stay," she barely says. Her unbandaged eye is closed tightly, then opens. "White. Masks. Saw skin around their eyes . . ."

Her voice comes as a hissed monotone through her wired jaw. She was a fit, healthy woman from photos in the house; now she's a deflated mass of injuries in the bed. Hanna nods.

"One who gave orders . . ."

"And was he the one who attacked you?"

"Yes. Tall." She swallows. "He entered . . . said, 'Honey, I'm home . . .'"

Hanna slides a hand across his mouth. "The next thing I have to ask you is very hard. Can you tell me what they did? Their specific actions help identify them, if they're similar to or different from the actions in other home invasions."

"Beat Jimmy. Made him open safe." She pauses, staring into the distance past Hanna.

The boss throws Jimmy aside from the open safe. With his ruined knee, he crashes to the floor. The boss turns toward him.

"I'll do anything you want," she says. "Don't hurt my husband! Please, mister . . ." And she lets her robe fall open, revealing herself, turning him from Jimmy.

"Oh, okay. You're gonna be cool, right?" the boss asks.

She nods.

"And you're kinda signifying like . . . maybe being sexed by the malo gangsta bad man in the black mask maybe even gets you off a little? Right?"

She half nods. He moves closer.

"Like a secret part of you is into takin' a walk on the wild side? Getting your kink on? And maybe that'll chill me out, you're thinking? Make it go easier on your family, huh?" His look burns her.

"You think 'cause your pussy's so hot you can con me with that half-assed come-on, you arrogant cunt? I got x-ray vision, baby. You cannot lie to me."

He butts his palm off her forehead, ratcheting her eyes up to his.

"What you're really thinkin' is 'I'm gonna get BONE-a-fide by a maggot. And I gotta do three laps through a pool of Lysol to get his shit off me.'"

"Con me? Baby, from the day I got hatched I got whipsawed by a pro. Uh-uh. We're goin' full apocalypse outta the gate."

"Then he burned me," she continues.

A lit cigarette pushes toward her face. Jessica screams from upstairs. A thud. The flat pools of the boss's eyes. Pain sears savagely. Wild, she rips her head sideways. He forces her head back. The cigarette coming into her eye.

"And he raped me."

Andi's spun around, grabbed by her hair, slammed face-first into the wall. His left hand presses her head there while he rips aside her robe and jerks her ass out toward him.

"Leave her alone!" Jimmy's broken voice.

The boss plunges into her, searing, tearing.

"Killed my husband," she says softly. The deadness in her still looks at a point in space beyond Hanna.

The huge edge of a sheepskin throw rug is large and blurred near her face. Rousing to consciousness, she sees shapes resolve soundlessly. Others are walking away. As the boss is leaving, as if completing a last chore, he lowers over her husband and swings the crowbar down on his head. Jimmy's head bounces up off the marble. He does it again with an irritated urgency. And *again. This time the steel shank smashes through Jimmy's skull and buries there. He yanks it free. The boss glances her way. He leaves.*

She looks at Hanna. Expressionless.

He imagines the home movie that has just played inside her head. Moments pass.

From a file Hanna shows her police photos of the empty safe and ransacked master bedroom. She nods, blinks, raises her left hand. The knuckles are bruised. The robbers ripped her wedding band and engagement ring off her finger. They tore her earlobes ripping away her stud earrings as well.

"Insurance company," she says. "Has inventory."

She gives him the company name. He thanks her.

He heads for the door, but she calls to him through her wired jaw. "Detective?"

Hanna turns.

"Find him."

"Oh, I will," he says. "Believe me, I will."

He heads down to Jessica's floor. The nurse on duty says visitors aren't allowed. He tells her, "If there's any change, anything at all, call me."

Jessica had been conscious the longest during the home invasion. She was the last member of the family attacked. If she comes back— if—she might have more to tell.

The nurse looks at Hanna like she knows him. "I'll make a note."

Levinson's TV & Appliance occupies a cracked-sidewalk stretch of a busy street west of downtown. Hanna and Casals stroll in after lunch. The proprietor sits at a desk in the back, surrounded by televisions and stereos. He's balding, his brown hair slicked back. He turns from watching a cowboy movie on channel 9. His yellow shirt smells of mothballs.

Hanna snaps his fingers. "Larry. Whaddaya hear, whaddaya say?"

Larry leans back. Casals approaches and sits on the side of his desk and starts poking through his papers, intentionally invading his space.

Hanna knows the crew that took the Lincoln Park score stole mounted jewelry. He knows they'll pop the stones out of the settings and lay it all off to one or two fences: one to melt down the gold; maybe another to move the stones. Levinson is the fourth fence they've visited today. He laces his hands across his belly, like he's relaxed, but his eyes skip nervously.

"Hear what, Vincent?"

"About the hole in the ozone layer 'cause of methane from cow farts. Hairspray is destroying the planet." Hanna stands in front of the desk. "Home invasion crew. They took a town house by Lincoln Park last night."

"Don't know nothing about that."

Casals looks over an invoice. "Really? It's riding the airwaves on every fucking news channel. Change the channel on some of these crappy TVs you got stacked in here."

"Middle six figures at wholesale in mounted stones," Hanna says. "Start calling. See if you can get in on the action fencing the stones. Melt down the settings. Make yourself some dough. Give them a good deal and get tight with them."

"I don't deal with home invaders," Levinson protests.

"You do now. And you know who does." Hanna points at the phone. "Dial.

"After you do good by them," Hanna continues, "you're going to shift your ass into flip-o-matic and tell me who the fuck they are. And what they are taking next. You got that?"

No answer.

"Is that clear?" He gets into Levinson's face. "Am I speaking in tongues? Is English your second fucking language?"

"What are you comin' on so strong to me for?" Levinson protests.

"Because you are a part of a criminal subculture. You make your living off of crime. And because I am *angry*, Larry. I want this fucking crew! Am I making my point?"

Levinson hesitates, takes the phone. Dials. Waits. Then . . .

"Hey. Junior. Yeah." Beat. "That score that went down? No, Lincoln

Park. If that's onna street and you're lookin' at it, I'll take a piece."
He listens. His gaze ping-pongs between Hanna and Casals. "Who's
putting out the score?"

Levinson's mouth tightens. "Lemme know if you do. You don't
want none, send it my way. There's a piece innit for you."

Levinson hangs up. Shrugs.

Hanna's already leaving. Over his shoulder: "Keep making calls,
Larry. I will be back."

15

By the time Hanna and Casals pull into CPD's Shakespeare Station,
the afternoon sky is filling with thunderheads. The low brick building is built like a kids' fort in the center of a leafy residential block.
A massive radio antenna rises from the roof. In the bullpen at the
Criminal Intelligence Division, Easton and Detective Rick Rossi are
making calls.

As Hanna enters: "Whadda we know?"

Easton puts his hand over the receiver, indicates the phone. "Re-
interviewing the priors. Looking for commonalities."

The room is crowded, the desks messy. The walls are painted a
shiny, industrial green. A huge whiteboard near the windows is covered with lists. Names. Streets. Businesses. There are hundreds of
items to cross-check.

They need to circle back and speak again to all the families who've
been robbed, sorting for common denominators. Kids and parents,
grandparents, husbands and wives and anyone any of them are
sleeping with on the side. Plumbers, pizza delivery men, teenagers'
girlfriends, boyfriends, alarm system installers, refrigerator repair-
men, cleaners, anyone with access.

This crew never forces its way inside. Sometimes they knock.
Sometimes they open the door with a key. Key? Where do they get
the key? Where did the victims eat before the robberies? Any wed-
dings they'd gone to? Who changes the oil in their cars?

Detecting: 90 percent of it is quantitative accumulation of data from crime scene evidence and interviews and then sorting it. Done right, that earns you the other 10 percent. That's what Hanna lives for.

Hanna drops into his desk chair. He surveys the whiteboard. "Okay. We know the boss commits the sexual assaults. Maybe he's not the only one, but we know he leads it. Torture. And at least two murders we know of. That shit attaches to the rest of the crew. What else?"

Easton answers: "Rest of his crew is sticking with him, according to the matching descriptions of other victims. If they aren't partaking, you'd think one or two of his crew'd get nervous and drop away."

"You'd think."

"Fear?" Casals asks.

"Maybe."

Hanna stares at the puke-green ceiling. Any burglary crew that's any good wouldn't touch a home invasion. At the top of the burglary food chain, highline pros wouldn't even waste their time with mounted jewelry unless it had the Marlborough diamond planted in it. The reason this crew will pop the stones and melt down the settings is because, if you're caught with the jewelry intact, it's identifiable. That ties you to the score. But separating stones from settings all takes time and lower-level fences—any of whom can catch a bust and flip. And the more intermediaries there are between a theft and cash money, the more risk multiplies.

The ideal is unmounted stones out of a wholesale diamond merchant's vault in the 5 South Wabash building—if a crew is good enough to take that down. They're anonymous. Untraceable. So, home invasions are cowboy scores. Add to that this crew's penchant for wanting the homeowners at home . . . What if Dirty Harry or guard dogs are inside . . . and they are at the bottom of the ladder?

"And then here's the anomaly," Hanna says. "Home invaders, as pros, are the low bottoms, or amateurs acting on impulse. But this crew is neither. Their scores are targeted, not opportunistic. They are organized. They're proficient and good at what they do. They know what's in the house before they go in. That indicates research, pre-planning, and prep. And they have access." He points at the whiteboard. "Two of the priors were entered with a key. How? Where's that part of this story? So, their proficiency and what they do don't jibe.

"That means money may be the primary, but it's not the only motivator. There's the other drives, too. They like it."

He crosses to the coffeepot.

"But the bonus round is only for the boss?" Rossi offers.

Hanna pours. "Yeah. And his rapes, the beatings? They are scripted. Intimate. And full of anger. Violence is his bag."

"And if they resisted?" Casals speculates.

Hanna agrees. "He'd *correct* their behavior. He wants them to disobey. Probably there's a history of impulsive, hair-trigger violence in other settings."

Easton adds, "At the corner tavern he'd be known as explosive, 'Don't fuck with Ralph.'"

"How did he talk to the wife? Did he yell at her?" Rossi asks.

"I'll know more when I talk to her again."

"Did this asshole get hard burning her with cigarettes?" Easton asks. "Is the violence erotic?"

"Guessing, but I think the violence is vindictive, not erotic. He hurts the husband. Forces compliance. Then he attacks the woman. That demeans her. So, he replaces the husband in her home and then acts out some kind of living theater for himself on her."

The attack on the teenage daughter, though, sits wrong with Hanna. Not the attack itself. The taking her up to the bedroom. What's that? Every other time this guy likes the show.

"And he said, 'Honey, I'm home.'"

"Home?" Easton asks.

"Exactly." *Home* . . . Hanna thinks. *A fucking comedian.*

Hanna returns to his desk. "Since the sexual assaults are after the husband's opened the safe and he's already got compliance and he's acting out his theater, the scenario is like an antidote to something. That's the high. But the relief would be temporary. He's got to go back and do it again and again."

"Antidote to . . . ?" Easton says.

"How do I know? From what he experienced once upon a time

or is experiencing right now. More specific than that . . . ?" Hanna shrugs.

"Is he taking trophies to fantasize later? Underwear?"

"Cut off a part of her . . . ? Take her liver and have it for breakfast with eggs over easy? He didn't do that. That psychotic? He'd be shitting in the refrigerators, writing on the mirrors. Fingerprints. None of that. The guy is not dysfunctional."

Hanna repeats to himself: "His primary is to score. The score is planned and controlled. But psychosis does not author the event. This sick fuck is *indulging* himself."

"These assholes need to go away," Easton says.

"Really? No shit?"

"Sorry." Easton cares how Hanna regards him. *Shut the fuck up,* he thinks. *Listen.*

"Speculation aside, we are nowhere. Rossi, stay on the phones with prior victims, looking for new common denominators to Matzukas." To Easton: "Bob, segue over to physical evidence on Matzukas. Coroner's best guess on crowbar or tire iron or what. The blood splatter from Matzukas's head—can it indicate direction of the strike? Is the guy right-handed or left-handed? The amount of force to crack open his skull. Like that. Does the angle of the strike tell us about the height of the assailant? Footprints indicating where perps one, two, three, and four stood and traveled. The witness who saw the bullshit pizza delivery sign. All of that . . ."

To all of them: "I want to narratively reconstruct this event. I want to know how every moment physically happened. Beat by beat."

He turns. "Casals, you and I will continue with fences and informants. I'll talk to Andi again and wait for Jessica to wake up . . . if Jessica wakes up."

Captain Charlie Baumann appears in the doorway.

"Hanna," Baumann says.

While Hanna scribbles down a phone number, he holds up a hand to Baumann. *In a minute.* Casals glances at him.

Baumann turns toward his office, gesturing for Hanna to follow.

"Plus, I want a profile on this guy. Casals, call Kessler at Feeb

Behavioral Science at Quantico." Hanna hands Casals the number. "See if he's got any ideas that might help predict behavior. In certain situations this guy is gonna zig or he's gonna zag. Which way he'll fly."

He heads to Baumann's office across the bullpen.

When he enters, Baumann turns to face him. "Who told you you could roust Levinson?"

"Why's it matter?"

"I asked you a question."

"They didn't steal jewelry for dress-up. They're fencing it some-where."

"You think Levinson is fencing this crew's merch?"

"No."

"So leave him alone."

"If somebody lifted a tray of Danish off a bakery truck on Ogden, Levinson knows about it. I want him finding out who is."

"Levinson doesn't work for you." Baumann's meaty forefinger points at Hanna's sternum. "He works for me. Hands off."

Charlie Baumann is the head of the Criminal Intelligence Division. He has snow-white hair, black eyebrows, and piercing eyes. Half German, half Italian, he is as old-school Chicago as it gets. He has a dozen legendary collars and dead bodies to his name. He hangs with Irv Kupcinet and keeps his name prominent in the *Sun-Times*. The armed robbers, serial killers, and sensational murderers he has taken down have created his reputation as Chicago's preeminent tough cop. Below that is a different, more complex matrix of associations—many from his childhood in Chicago's Patch around Grand and Ogden. From that subsurface matrix, Baumann has more chits in his pocket for favors than the First Ward alderman.

In Chicago's parallel political economy, professional thieves, whether they're hitting jewelry salesmen or doing cartage theft of trailers out of the Union Station freight yards, they know they have to down the merch with Outfit fences, like Levinson. Those who think they don't end up as a bad odor in a remote corner of the Randolph Street underground garage until someone reports the vehicle, which comes up stolen, and the medical examiner pops the trunk because he knows ahead of time by the smell what's inside—a professional thief who thought he didn't have to down his merch with Outfit fences. Then he got the news from "Joey the Clown" Lombardo or a crew working for Leo Rugendorf and Milwaukee Phil Alderisio.

On the police side, creating the appearance of equilibrium, is Baumann. His unspoken policy toward Outfit-connected professional crews is live and let live, so long as they don't shit where they eat. That means they operate outside Chicago.

If they violate that condition, Baumann declares open season, and they end up as the dead bodies on the front page of the *Sun-Times,* enhancing Baumann's reputation.

Baumann's not the only one in the room who crosses lines. Both men know Hanna, when he's impelled, when he has the scent and is zeroed in, crosses lines, too, and it's not that Hanna runs red lights. It's that there cease to be lights, red or green. When he's torqued up like that, Hanna thinks, *This is what it must be like to be a junkie.* That metallic craving under the myelin nerve sheaths within his elbows, like an electrical imperative, like jonesin' for a fix that will deliver him into 200 percent of himself. In that state, Hanna commits no errors. Decision-making is smooth and instantaneous. It's music. He's immaculate. That's the high and it is what makes Hanna go.

Baumann is a different organism. He evolved out of a machine of subterranean allegiances to Outfit figures with whom he grew up. Combined with brutality and extrajudicial killings, he's a feature within that system. The system, like Baumann, is lethal.

Hanna isn't part of any system. Hanna is Hanna.

"Use somebody else," Baumann says, repeating the directive.

"I got a fourteen-year-old in a coma. This crew is out there raping and murdering. You're gonna throw a roadblock in front of me?"

"Why you gotta be such a stiff prick? Did the Marine Corps jam a pool cue up your ass?"

"Since when do I need permission to do my job?" No answer. "I am the best shot you got at taking them down and you know it. Go ahead. Pull my ass off of this. Put Novak in. And you can watch it all over the six o'clock news about how this crew is continuing to run wild. *That's a good idea.*"

"You don't need permission. I am *ordering* you. I want every one of these cocksuckers whacked out. Every. One. That's your fucking assignment. But you stay away from Levinson. Go do your goddamn job! Get out."

Hanna doesn't look Baumann in the eye. He looks through Baumann's eyes to the back of his skull. Hanna's momentarily in a different time and place. Then he turns and walks out.

Baumann knows he's going to be trouble.

16

"Come on, kids," Becky Colson calls.

The soccer field is buzzing with red-cheeked nine-year-olds, socks grass-stained and hair windblown after an hour of practice. Two children amble toward Becky, sucking on juice boxes. A girl and a boy. Twins. Becky waves goodbye to the coach and fellow moms and scoops the kids into the back seat of her Volvo 940 wagon. She watches them buckle up, then smooths her hair. She spent an hour at the salon getting a cut and style before picking them up. She wears a loose-fitting tunic over jeans, but when she twists to get behind the wheel, her taut, curvy form reveals itself.

Tease.

She pulls away in a hurry, like she appreciates the turbo engine under the hood.

The boss follows with Hank riding shotgun.

When she pulls into the driveway of her Gold Coast mansion, she hits the garage remote. The door rolls up and she pulls in.

The boss drives on by.

He and Hank are in a nondescript Toyota, eating gyros. The boss is behind dark glasses and under a baseball cap. He's kept back a safe distance. The wife has no clue, in any case. She never expected to be followed, not in that hunk of a Swedish car, while cocooning her arguing kids in its leather seats.

Nice pile of a house. Like a dark redbrick Victorian castle covered with ivy. Like a band would play in the dining room every night while the family eats off the good plates.

Like where I grew up.

Where's that?

Stateway Gardens on South State Street.

That's the projects, man.

That's right.

It's all Black.

Except for my mom. We lived there 'cause she was a social worker.

Really?

Yeah, man. She socially worked the corner on State and Thirty-Fifth.

The husband is a lawyer in the Loop. That word came from *Alex-ander—stupid fucking name, pretentious prick,* the boss thinks. Alex, who is now wrapped up in the crew. But Alex, it looks like, was right.

There is space out front of the house on the street to park. A tall Victorian doorway. Wide. Two could go in abreast.

Becky Colson does philanthropy, charities that call for ball gowns and a hundred grand in ice on her neck, that call for tossing her head back for photos with the conductor of the symphony and the quarterback of the Bears.

You're going to philanthropize me, bitch? You are gonna hate it. I'll straighten out your ass when I see that look. Maybe your husband, too.

A telephone pole in the alley at the back of the property looks like it carries a telco alarm. He can bypass it there.

But if the Colsons are home, having dinner, they won't have the alarm activated.

Sweet.

He drives on.

17

It's a Thursday evening when McCauley arrives at Aaron Grimes's garage with his crew. The sky is piled with thunderclouds, anvil-topped, purple in the west above a red strip of sunset.

Chris hops out of the car and walks ahead up the alley toward the garage. Chicago feels foreign to him, the concrete on the sidewalk rougher than in Southern California, the air humid, the greenery avid. Buildings crowd the pavement. Old brick. Every city block bisected with a long alleyway carrying utility poles and services. He misses the yellow California morning light, the sunsets, the Washingtonia palms, and the varied street layouts of the small towns recently aggregated into LA. It's like nobody told Chicagoans there's a better, newer place to live. It makes him homesick for the 405. Is that possible? Yeah, the 405's not bad with the window open listening to KROQ.

Grimes's garage is a commercial vehicle service and repair facility. Forecourt and entrance on the street, wide accordion doors in the back, opening onto the alley. Inside the repair shop there's a pungent tang of oil and gasoline, the sound of pneumatic tools echoing off the concrete. Four lifts, tools in the pits below them. Other tool chests line the walls. Chris sees Grimes in the glassed-in corner office.

He turns back toward the cross street at the end of the block and nods. Neil comes down the alley, head sweeping the angles. Black baseball jacket, white shirt, Cubs cap.

He fits in. On first look and second. And that's usually all people give a stranger. Chris knows: That is all Neil wants. For people to look past. Utility lights catch the shine in his eyes. Behind him come Cerrito and their driver and lookout, Danny Molina. Cerrito looks calm. Like a grenade looks calm, with the pin in. Molina has a baby face and the chill of a crocodile. He knows the city. He has sharp eyes and a smooth hand with the wheel.

Chris, Cerrito, and Neil enter from the alley. Their three vehicles are lined up at the rear. Keys under the mat. Washed, gassed up, boring. Rosary hanging from the rearview of the van, just like Neil told Grimes.

Molina checks the glove boxes of each vehicle for registration and insurance documents. Neil climbs in the back of the van and checks over their equipment and tools.

"Good?" Cerrito says.

"Good? I don't see the lights, tripod, crowbars. Or the extension cords." Neil hops out. "Check with Grimes."

In the repair shop office, Grimes is talking to a young man who's about his age. Except Grimes is wearing an old work shirt and jeans. The other guy, maybe a relative from how familiar they seem, wears a tight black T-shirt, a suntan, and Tina Turner hair.

Cerrito goes over. "Hey, slick," he calls.

He speaks to Grimes. Grimes shakes his head.

Neil's face darkens. Chris senses a chill in the air around him.

Neil starts toward the inner office. "Where's the rest?"

A pickup truck turns in from the alley and rumbles to a stop just inside the accordion doors. The driver gets out, a husky guy with stony eyes and ponytail, and goes to the cargo bed.

"You're late," Neil says.

"Traffic. I'm here now."

The man takes the floodlights and extension cords from the cargo bed. Chris tells him to set everything out on the floor in the garage. Grimes and Cerrito come over.

The husky guy puts the circular saw and four-foot-long pry bars on the concrete near a workbench. "What you gonna demolish with all this stuff?"

"What?" Neil says.

"I was askin'—"

"What the fuck business is it of yours?" Neil's voice is flat. Cold.

The man pauses.

Neil turns to Grimes. "Where'd you find this fucking guy?"

"He's cool. I know him. He's from Miller Hardware on Division. Known him for years."

Neil looks at the husky guy. "Give me your wallet." And he starts toward him.

The husky guy eyes Grimes, who's giving off a fear vibe.

"Give me your fucking wallet."

The larger man feels the chill. Complies. Neil takes out his license, writes down his home address, tosses the wallet back.

"Who lives there?"

"Why you want to know?"

"Who the fuck lives there?"

"My wife and kids. My family."

Neil stares. "I asked why you wanna know."

The guy exhales, like he's being imposed upon. "I got deliveries to make. I don't need this bullshit—"

Neil slams the guy's shoulder, torquing his body, then spins him the rest of the way, grabs the guy's hair, and smashes his forehead into the side window of the pickup. His .45 is suddenly under the guy's chin.

"You're late, you're sloppy, you're nosy."

"I didn't mean nothing."

The guy's breathing heavy. This is not business as usual.

"Remember, I know where you live. Now get the fuck out of here."

The man staggers, choking, hand to his throat. Neil stands there, frozen. Like he's thinking about saying something. In the background, in the corner office, the other young man withdraws into the shadows, maybe wanting to stay out of Neil's line of sight. The husky guy lurches into the cab of his truck and fumbles with the ignition. Pulls out.

Chris's hand is on his 9 mm SIG under his open shirt in a cross draw. His cold eyes land on Grimes.

"What the fuck's wrong with you?" Neil turns on Grimes. "Why do we gotta cross with people we don't need to meet?"

Grimes raises his hands. He has nothing to say.

Chris and Cerrito load the gear the supplier brought. Neil jumps in one of the work cars and fires up the engine. Chris hops into the passenger seat. He says nothing. They pull out with Cerrito and Molina in the other vehicles behind them. Neil is still breathing hard.

"Motherfucker . . ." he says to himself.

Chris turns to him. "Let it go. He's nobody."

Neil looks over. "Yeah?"

From the way Neil grips the wheel, Chris knows he's not letting it go.

"It was a random thing," Chris says.

"Random? Like the guy who saved pennies I knew once. 'What the fuck are you saving pennies for?' I asked. "Cause a hundred of 'em make a dollar,' he said. Some anonymous asshole sees you and mentions something to somebody who talks to somebody else, which gets overheard, and you wind up being jackpotted, and 'Where the fuck did that come from?' It's invisible but it's operating all around you. Little strings of micro cause and effect. You can't see 'em, but they're there. 'Oh! I had bad luck.' Bullshit. It's for real . . . Fucking moron. I told him we don't meet people. No one but him."

Chris sees Neil wrestling down his anger. They exchange a look. They both know they need to be totally cool now.

"What we can control, we control," Neil says. "No avoidable exposure. No unnecessary risk. Everything that's gonna happen to us, we made happen. Whether we know how or not."

The road is busy, headlights turning on. The skyline is visible to the east. The red dregs of sunset bounce off the tallest buildings.

"You mean we cannot secure our futures playing the lotto?"

"Yeah? You'd like that." Neil's wry grin. They know each other like books. "'Make me a winner,' like life's a roulette wheel. Go ahead, give it a spin. That will fuck you up. It will not save you."

Chris listens to the drone of the tires on the road. They barely glance at Prosperity Savings & Loan as they cruise by to see if anything's different on the night before they score.

Then Neil glances at the Triangle Diner as they pass by. Closed. The ex-con short-order cook is in there alone, wiping down the counter. That's Neil in a different reality.

18

The nurse at the desk looks up when Hanna steps off the elevator. A stethoscope draped around her neck, Latina, wearing scrubs. She's encountered Hanna before. He moves quietly in the subdued light, tie loosened, jacket unbuttoned. Held by the hush.

"How's she doing?" he says.

"Holding steady."

He pushes open the door to Jessica Matzukas's room. The nurse knows better than to try to keep him out.

Beeping from the monitors. Humming from the air vents. The thermal blanket Jessica lies under looks insubstantial. Hanna gently adjusts it. Outside, the night has devolved into fog. The window shows dandelion lights in the parking lot.

He sits down and leans forward on his knees, looks at her chart. "You're steady. That's good."

The staples in the shaved patch on her head are scabbed over. The IV on the back of her hand stands out, her skin so thin. Her breathing is regular. Her eyelids are blue. The rest of her face is purple, fading to yellow.

"Your mom's better," he says. "She's getting back on her feet."

He spoke to Andi Matzukas a couple of days ago. She gave him a list of people they'd entrusted with keys. Housekeeper. Rug installer when they were out of town. Contractor. She was pale and bent, like a reed in a rising river.

Jessica's strong, he said to her.

Yeah, she is. She's a pistol, Andi replied, before shuddering, turning away, and sweeping everything off the nightstand onto the floor.

Jessica's chest rises and falls.

"Your mom told me how you stood up to them. They hurt you and you still fought."

Innocence, he thinks. *That's where your courage comes from. Innocence.* She lies there, breathing. Her lips are cracked. *You know how it's supposed to be, so the wrongness is so violent.*

"Goddamn, Jessica," he says, impressed by her.

Fragile, broken, silent. Jessica should be on a school bus or getting crazy with friends. Blasting music. Some song he hears every time Casals turns on the radio.

Jessica's eyes seem to drift farther closed. She's there, somewhere. He feels certain. She's suspended, wandering somewhere below the threshold of consciousness.

Maybe cocooned on the far side of wakefulness, where none of the horror can crash back in. Maybe desperate to keep away from the blinding light. The sound of her father fighting with them, then being bludgeoned to death on the floor below her room. Leaving his daughter unprotected. The sound of a skull cracking. With only her rage to defend her family while trying to fend off a man twice her size, bent on breaking her apart, who then beat her with a table lamp and raped her.

"The sky fell on you, my girl."

Her chest rises and falls.

"You got a chance. You're going to make it."

He looks at the floor. "I had a Korean girl get shot, once. At random. No reason. Freeway sniper. He could have shot the next car. Through the windshield. She's riding in the back seat. Shot in the head. She was in a coma for a long time. Family came apart. A year later her father's an alcoholic, loses his job, parents divorce. The younger brother starts setting fires. Multiple lives screwed up for forever. That's what can happen."

He reaches for her hand. Jessica breathes. Her fingers are cool and dry.

"My wife was on this floor," he says.

My wife, he'd shouted to the nurse. *Where is she? Sofia Hanna?*

He got the call over the unit radio. He'd screamed into the ER entrance, jumped out. ER doors sliding open, people dodging out of his way to the desk, doctors, paramedics, a young nurse, alarmed, as he bulled toward her, the expression on her face saying, *Oh, man, here we go.*

"I saw Sofia's sister at the end of the hall," he tells Jessica. "Adrienne, she looks like Sofia. Black hair. Intense eyes. She's standing outside a treatment bay. Sees me. She stands there . . ."

Jessica lies still.

". . . like a statue, staring. Behind her eyes it looks like part of her's gone. And then I know. I know."

He knew because that was the look at his father's deathbed, the rip in the world in his mother's eyes.

When he got to Adrienne, he turned and saw Sofia on the gurney, her shirt ripped open, defibrillator gel on her chest where they had shocked her. Breathing tube, tape around her mouth. Her left leg at a wrong angle. Her bloody arm. Part of her face crushed. She was already gone.

The light in the ER had grayed out. Like he was underwater, in rapids, submerged, getting dragged over rocks. Adrienne, off his shoulder, shadowed, facing her sister's empty eyes.

"A doctor came in," he says. "Maybe he said they'd tried."

The doctor put a hand on his shoulder. Hanna shrugged him off so hard he may have knocked him down.

Blood alcohol level sky-high and loaded on Prozac. She drove into the black steel pillars supporting the Illinois Central tracks in a viaduct on West Armitage at 70 mph and caromed off the quarried stone walls.

"Three miscarriages." He blinks. Each time, it knocked her down harder. She was drinking alone on Wells Street.

And where was he?

She was pulling herself back up physically and emotionally.

"She ran a store on North Clark. I'd come home, she's out of it. I tell myself she's withdrawing to punish me for working all night or missing her nephew's baptism or something. Why doesn't she understand?"

She *doesn't understand*?

He stares out the window. She was bright and wild in this crazy great way—she could burn like a flare. And her long dark hair would whip around when she laughed. And she could drop like a flare, too. That dark force that presses you flat. Brain chemistry, loneliness, miscarriages. A cascade of failures, as she defined them. To him she was courageous to keep trying. Maybe to her she was a failure and couldn't imagine her value to Vincent, her family, or anyone else and thought their lives would be better off without her.

"Vincent Hanna, the hotshot detective with x-ray vision . . ."

The machines thrum.

A car alarm goes off outside. It distracts Hanna. Loud. The headlight flashes lighten the ceiling.

The car alarm shuts down.

"I've understood killers, sitting there, bloody. Sons howling like they're the ones who've been stabbed. I don't neutralize myself. Most homicide detectives stay abstract. It makes them more analytical, better at the job. I take it in. I use it. Personalize it to understand the victim, the perpetrator, the anger, the reasons. Keeps me sharp, on the edge. That's what I do," he says.

"With Sofia, who is *gone*, I didn't take anything in." He looks at Jessica, with her eyes closed, as if she's resting, listening to him.

"Isn't that something?"

Back when he was twelve in Granite City, Illinois, floating on his back in a lake, looking up into the night sky and constellations, he all at once understood that we are an accident of happenstance on a speck of dust in a blink of time in the big nothing. It didn't fill him with meaninglessness. It made him feel that consciousness was a rare and recent temporary accident. And that meant life is about what you did with it right now. It infused him with ambition.

There is finality. That's what hit him so hard about Sofia.

It's all over now, baby blue.

The irreversibility.

"You can come back," he says to Jessica, holding her hand.

The Korean girl couldn't.

His voice drops to a rasp. "You are in there. I know it. No matter how dark it is. On this side, there is light. You can come back. We are here. We are waiting for you."

Alex Dalecki finds the boss alone at a table in a bar in Melrose Park, a dark faded place that had once been a Bohemian family's neighborhood pride and now smells of beer and disinfectant. The boss has a bottle of Budweiser in one hand and a rubber-banded roll of twenty-dollar bills in the other. In the dim light, his eyes gleam.

"You saw the Colsons' house?" Alex says. "What do you think?"

The boss makes a *gimme* gesture. "Keys."

Alex hands over the copies he had cut from Becky Colson's key ring.

"What else can you give me on the family?" the boss says.

"Nothing. You got it."

"You talk to anybody about our last score?"

"Course not. No way. To who?"

"Your brother-in-law, for one?"

"Aaron? Hell, no."

"I thought you were close," he says.

"We are, but we don't talk business."

The boss nods, seemingly thoughtfully, and tosses the roll of twenties to him. Alex wants to get out before the boss tells him to come along on this next one. Or bans him from coming along. He doesn't know which he wants more. Since the Matzukas house, he has felt shit-scared and pumped up and powerful. He sticks the roll of twenties in his jacket pocket.

"Sit down, count it," the boss says.

"I trust you."

"That a question?"

Alex is put off-balance. This guy can do that effortlessly, a world expert. Draw you in, then make you worry he's going to spit you out, or worse.

The man leans forward now, and the light finally catches him. His face, with the scar through the eyebrow, goes from hot to amused.

"Sit down."

Alex sits.

The boss drinks. His shoulders are relaxed, but his eyes are keen. "You 'trust me.' I hear a plea there. You want me to say 'I trust you, too, honey'?"

"I don't want anything. I mean, I trust you."

"You want trust? Tell me something." His biceps bulge like footballs under his T-shirt. "This new crew Aaron's in with . . . tied up all of a sudden with their secret mission bullshit."

Apprehension zings under Alex's skin. But also possibility, like deflection. "They're from the coast. Hard-core. Aaron's coming up with shit for 'em."

"Is he?"

"I heard they're ice cold and they take only major scores. If it's less than seven figures it's not worth them getting up in the morning." Maybe the boss needs to feel some competition. Alex's chest relaxes. "Yeah. Aaron's tight with them."

"Tell me more."

"Ask Aaron. Not my business to be talking about his business."

The boss finishes his beer. He stands, walks around the table behind Alex, and puts both of his hands on his shoulders.

"Talking . . . is what the fuck I pay you to do, not just with these rich bitches we're hitting." He grabs Alex's hair and yanks his head back. "Trust, right? Get your ass in gear and find out about Aaron."

The boss smiles and lets him go. Then he picks up the shiny new keys to Becky Colson's house, bound together with a twist tie. He rattles them between his fingers. His eyes are bright.

Neil and his crew roll up to the Prosperity Savings & Loan building at 11:50 p.m. The six-point intersection is quiet. The triangular tip of the building is darkened, only a streetlight shining on the facade.

Through the building's street-level windows, they can see the main floor of the savings and loan. It's loaded with baroque brass and marble from its role as a 1920s showplace.

And it has a large underground safe-deposit vault.

Neil's intel, which Nate conveyed to him directly from Kelso, was that half the safe-deposit boxes belong to politicians, Outfit guys, drug dealers, and miscellaneous others stashing ill-gotten gains.

And Kelso, the wizard in a wheelchair sitting on his hilltop in City Terrace, told Nate, *Have them be on the lookout for what else they might find in those boxes.*

Like what? Neil asked.

According to Kelso, there could be lists of numbered bank accounts in Liechtenstein or the Caymans or Switzerland, or bearer bonds, or anything else liquid.

How does he get this stuff?

How do I know? Nate said. *He sits up there above East LA and pulls it out of the air. He intercepts signal traffic. I dunno. And he's got that stack of computers.*

An added bonus, if they pull this off, is that few of the box owners are likely to admit what really was taken, which makes it harder for the police.

They'll spend the weekend inside.

The store next to the S&L building is vacant. Butcher paper covers the front windows, along with FOR RENT signs. Through that store's basement is how they're going to make their entry.

Tonight is step one.

The wind is blowing in off the lake, lightning spikes in the far distance. Molina drives around the block, then radios: "Clear."

Chris and Cerrito pull the van into the alley behind the vacant store and see no cars, no bums. A dumpster, a stray cat. Beyond a chain-link fence are weeds, trees, and the L tracks.

Cerrito gets out, wearing a hard hat and lineman's yellow vest and leather utility belt. He's eager and wound with energy, like an electric coil. He hates the wait. Wants to go. Always.

He climbs a telephone pole to bypass the vacant store's alarm. With it on the rental market, the building has both power and water. Clenching a penlight flash between his teeth, he opens an ancient metal box. Nearly laughs. The audible alarm is so old, a bird's nest sits on the bell and clapper. He snaps off the rusted clapper arm. That eliminates any possibility an alarm will ring here in the alley.

For the alarm system that goes out over the phone lines, he opens a junction box and examines the bundled wires inside. With his utility knife, he makes a shallow cut through their thick outer insulation. He tears away the papery white layer beneath and carefully pries the multicolored wires apart, gently separating each strand. He needs to find which pair of wires creates the circuit for the dedicated phone line to the alarm company. It's a matter of voltage and pulses. A phone on the hook sends out forty-eight volts of direct current. Off the hook, the same phone sends out only three volts of DC. Ringing, the phone sends out ninety-eight volts of alternating current. Cerrito gets his voltmeter. He's looking for the wires humming at a low ten to twenty-four volts of DC, the sweet spot.

As he touches the prong of the voltmeter to the first wire, a rumble rises. A Ravenswood L train thunders into view, sparks kicking from the elevated track as it squeals by. He holds still. The tree behind him creates cover. When the train passes, the air smells of hot oil and metal.

He tapes off the hot and cold wires making up the dedicated phone circuit and hooks alligator clips to the exposed spots on both wires. He adjusts his black box to mimic the voltage passing through the dedicated alarm line. With the black box simulating a closed circuit, he's ready to render the system moot. If he's got it wrong, this will be the tell. He makes two snips with his wire cutters.

Nothing.

He closes the junction box, climbs down using the logger's strap that has kept him steady atop the pole, and returns to the van. "Done."

McCauley picks up a handheld radio and calls Molina. "Anything on the scanner?"

If Cerrito has triggered a silent alarm to the police, they'll send a unit.

"Nothing." Molina's voice crackles. "All clear."

"We're going in."

"Copy."

McCauley pockets the walkie-talkie. "Let's go."

Wearing coveralls, high-visibility vests, and hard hats, they unload tall, wheeled plastic trash cans from the back of the van. Cerrito pops the lock on the rear door of the empty store, and they slide inside.

It's dusty and dark. Dingy brown light leaks through the butcher paper on the front windows. The stairs to the basement are at the back.

Downstairs, Chris and Cerrito lay one of the garbage cans on its side and pull out the hollow-core drill. They hook up the drill to both power and water. Chris runs his hand over the wall that faces the S&L building.

"Here."

It's poured concrete. They have one job tonight: to get through this wall. The rest will come tomorrow—Friday—after the close of business. Chris attaches the twelve-inch Husqvarna diamond hollow-core bit to the drill. He and Cerrito muscle the drill up against the wall. All three men put on their ear protection. Chris puts on goggles and heavy work gloves. He looks at McCauley.

Neil nods. They wait until they hear the rumble of an approaching L train. Until late in the evening, the trains run every six minutes. That will cover the sound.

Neil watches. Months of prep. All for this.

Chris flips the switch. The drill shrieks to life.

Hanna's in the cocoon of his unmarked car, heading south toward downtown on the Kennedy Expressway. Headlights strobe at him driving out toward O'Hare and the northern suburbs. It's late. The lanes are wide open, the skyline shouldering the view on his left. The Hancock Building, the Standard Oil Building, and, ahead, the Sears Tower. The modernist skyscrapers' energy is alive over the city.

His Motorola MicroTAC lights up. Hanna flips open the cover, extends the antenna. "Yeah?"

It's Easton. "I got the report from Kessler at the Behavioral Science Unit. Want me to fax it to your apartment?"

"No," Hanna says. "Read me the headlines."

"White, twenty-five to forty. No surprise there. 'Minimally educated, minimally employed, probably in casual labor . . . oppositional to authority, but intolerant of dissent from underlings.'"

At the Shakespeare Station, Easton runs his index finger down the page. He's virtually alone in the bullpen. "Our asshole is a 'sociopath who gets a power rush from ownership of the homes he invades. Narcissistic . . .'" Easton turns the page.

"Keep going," Hanna says, listening.

"'Experiences bottomless need and envy. The sexual assaults are sadistically arousing to him. They're also vindictive—anger-retaliation rapes. They are intended to humiliate and degrade his female victims.' Like you said. 'His drive is not to *have* the woman, it's *against* the woman. Raping the woman of the house . . . in a deeply twisted way he's seeking both primacy and solace from the idea of *home*.'"

Hanna listens.

Easton continues reading. "'If his fantasy comes from abandonment or abuse he suffered as a child, he'll have extensive juvenile and adult criminal jackets and a possible foster care history.'"

Hanna thinks about the house keys. The ruses. The urge of the crew to go in when the homeowners are present and vulnerable. The violence, the craving for dominance, payback.

"What else?" Hanna asks.

"Those are the headlines."

"Thanks." Hanna disconnects.

He's heading past downtown toward his apartment in Hyde Park on the South Side near the University of Chicago. Then he changes his mind and swerves right across two lanes to hit the Chicago Avenue off-ramp, and drives east toward the lake past Holy Name Cathedral. All this stolid stone, the city barely 150 years old but making structures to appear as if it had risen along with the continent's bedrock.

He heads for Michigan Avenue. Puts down his window. In the brisk air he hears music, new wave rock, laughter from the sidewalk. The Water Tower is lit up. Its white stone contrasts with the dark glittery vibe. He doesn't want to drink, doesn't want to dance. He thinks of calling Jodie. Instead, he turns right and drives over the Chicago River into the Loop. Some nights, the city gives him its energy, flows into him, like he's part of the large electrical grid extending up Lake Michigan.

He heads down Wabash and parks. The traffic sound under the elevated tracks is sharper. Hanna gets out and lets it infiltrate him as he walks.

The analysis, the data points, the intel he's been taking in, he wants it to synthesize. Intuition. Subconscious pattern recognition.

He wants a light bulb to turn on to illuminate a possible pathway toward finding these people. You keep pushing, never knowing exactly where a lead's going to come from.

He pushes through the door into the Half Step.

The low blue light of the club is a balm. A band is warming up on the dime-sized stage in the corner. Keyboard, drums, stand-up bass, a hungry-looking young guy tuning a Les Paul. Yuki is behind the bar.

She sees him coming and keeps wiping the black wood. The underlit bottles gleam a rich gold behind her on the shelf in front of the mirror, a boozy halo. Her punk-cut dyed blond hair catches the light.

He stops in front of her and leans his elbows on the bar.

She tilts her head. "You catch him?"

"Which him?" Hanna says. Her mood is expected.

"John Dillinger him. Jean Valjean him. Bigfoot him."

"Sorry, baby."

She takes out a shot glass, pulls the Stoli from the shelf, and pours him a shot. She sets the bottle back with a hard *thunk*.

"It's been three months. Your coupon for calling me 'baby' expired," she says. "Though I finished my master's thesis. 'Invisible Beings and Their Irregular Manifestation: A Case Study of Vincent Hanna.'"

He smiles and tosses back the shot. "I like that."

Yuki is wearing a torn black T-shirt over a ripped black tank over acid-washed jeans that must have been slicked on with a paint gun. He likes *that*. She's a grad student in cultural anthropology at U of Illinois's Chicago campus.

"Can you take a break?" he says.

"Hey, Jimmy, I'm taking a ten," she yells at the assistant manager, and takes Hanna's arm, leading him to the rear. "Or maybe it's a four or a five."

He laughs.

The lilt in her voice says she isn't exactly as annoyed as the words suggest.

Behind the bar is an alley. And a doorway where they can't be seen. She says, "Detective Blow, let's go."

She shares a bump with him, the coke instantly burning his

sinuses, sharpening his edge. Her lipstick tastes like cherries. She's smooth and strong, her eyes alight. His heart hammers when he presses into her, her leg wrapped around his as they support themselves against the brick wall.

It's cool, the wind gusting. She claws her fingers into his hair, her head back. He hears people in the distance, someone shouting. Out on the street, cabs honk. Flashing red and blue lights on Madison and a whoop of a siren. That *pull over or move it, asshole* whoop. A police car drives past the alley's entrance. Hanna buries his head against Yuki's neck, buries himself in her, and laughs. She joins him.

They unwind, breathing hard, leaning against each other.

"You can call me 'baby' again," she says.

She kisses the side of his face gently. Ruffles his hair. She likes when it gets wavy in the humidity. She slips from his arms. He follows, taking her hand, as they go back inside. The guitarist is running through a Howlin' Wolf blues riff and checking his tuning.

"I'm coming over to your place later. With some takeout," Hanna says. "Thai."

"I'll pick up Italian on my way home. Just in case."

Hanna looks at her.

"Who knows with you?" She goes on: "A prehistoric monster could be sighted in Lake Michigan."

Yuki smiles and turns for the bar. He takes her hand.

"I gotta make one stop, but I'll be there."

"If you do show up, honey, make it hot. The food and the rest."

"Marry me."

"No fucking way." She laughs, then squeezes his hand and walks down the bar. He puts down a ten for the Stoli and heads back out into the gray noise, his pulse pounding in sync with it.

In his car, he shoots down the ramp onto the southbound Dan Ryan, heading to his apartment to shower and change. It takes Hanna past the Illinois Institute of Technology campus, designed by Mies van der Rohe, a refugee from the Bauhaus who fled to Chicago after the NSDAP in Germany, the Nazi Party, was elected by an overwhelming majority in 1933 and closed it down.

He's about to turn off on Sixty-Third Street for Hyde Park and home. Instead, he guns it past his exit. He activates the Crown Vic's flashers and kicks it up to 90.

He flies through the I-90/I-94 interchange and then due south down I-57. If he keeps going for 350 miles, he'll pass the federal prison in Marion and roll all the way down to Cairo, that last sliver of Illinois pinched between the Mississippi and Ohio Rivers.

That's where the glaciers stopped. They scraped flat four hundred miles of Illinois and then ran out, leaving at the bottom limestone buttes and cliffs over the rivers.

Hanna veers off Interstate 57 before Kankakee. He jogs east to Highway 50, the old two-lane blacktop, and heads south through Peotone to Manteno.

To the right and left of his unmarked Crown Vic is the flat prairie under the black sky and stars in the cold night air. He drives toward Kankakee. He knows this road.

Past the ambient lights of the small town, he flicks off his headlights. The night envelops him. He's driving blind. He feels the roadway through his steering wheel, hears the crunch of gravel when his tires edge onto the shoulder. That's his only navigation. Tension wraps around him. It torques higher. At 65 mph, is he about to fly off the road into the ditch? The amperage climbs up his spine.

Then he brakes, flicks on his headlights. The Crown Vic skids sideways to a stop on the deserted blacktop.

"What the fuck are you doing?"

He guns it through a sliding U-turn, burning rubber, and accelerates back toward Chicago.

At three a.m. he's in Jessica's hospital room again. He tunes in to the regularity of tubes moving fluids in and out of her. She's still in the depths of her coma. She's lit by the side light of the lamp elbowing out of the white tile wall. He sees no movement beneath her eyelids. Is she dreaming?

"What put you here?" he says softly.

He always starts with the immediate remains of an event. Usually those are biological. Dead people. Dead people talk. They tell Hanna where people stood, how close, how far, the angle of an entry wound, what the blood splatter on the wall said about the direction of movement. How fast rigor mortis comes on tells him about the heart rate of the victim. If it was slow, there was no adrenalized urgency pumping blood under pressure throughout the body's muscles. That meant the victim was not anxious about the presence of the killer, which might mean the killer was someone with whom the victim felt at ease, like a family member. Tattooing around the entry wound from unburned gunpowder particles said the weapon was within eighteen inches. The temperature of the liver, taken with a meat thermometer at the crime scene, tells him when the victim was killed because the liver cools to ambient temperature at one degree per half hour. All together it might tell him the victim was shot two hours earlier at close range by a person he was familiar with whose presence didn't alarm him.

He was trying to rebuild a causal chain of what happened. A reconstruction. It didn't matter if it was a body that had been rotting for two weeks under a bed, blown up like a fetid balloon, or Hanna emotionally absorbing the shattered impressions of children who'd witnessed their mother shot and thrown down the stairs.

Entering a crime scene, Hanna took a first step inside and then he stopped. The medical examiners, technicians, photographers, and uniforms suddenly got quiet. They knew his routine. They stopped measuring, photographing, drawing field sketches, and talking about last weekend's BBQ in Michigan City. Hanna would clear his mind and scan the room left to right without stopping. He'd take in the dead woman with the large-caliber head wound, her black eyes, the overturned furniture, the acrid smells from the burned food she'd been cooking. He'd see across the mantel the pictures of her in a confirmation dress, a high school graduation gown; of her holding her baby boy. No wedding pictures. A single mother.

Then he'd step into the room. Work would resume. That first impression, he knew, gave him insights he wouldn't realize until later, when he interviewed her son, a twenty-two-year-old who was indulged and going nowhere, and whose amateur drug dealing went wrong and the people he thought he could screw over came to visit. Not finding him at home, they shot his mother instead.

Right now his eyes take in Jessica's stitches, the bruising, the stubble on her scalp where it had been shaved to trepan a section to relieve the intracranial hematoma.

"You're alone inside your head," he says to her. "But you have a companion. Me. I'm going to discover everything. Then I'm going to hit Rewind. Reverse it. Put Humpty Dumpty back together again and have a causal chain of events from the certain pathways and the ghostly trails that are hard to see right now. And all of that's going to lead me, eventually, through what they wanted and what they did and how they picked you. And then that's going to lead me to who."

But there's a long way to go.

"In the end, I'm going to know more about them than they know about themselves," he tells Jessica.

He was born Vincent Thomas Hanna in 1948 in Granite City, Illinois, the third child of Frank and Gianna Hanna. Granite City was an almost-city in rural western Illinois near the cliffs overlooking the Mississippi. The population were descendants of the original French trappers and the coureurs de bois, who had intermarried with the Osage, Cahokia, and Peoria and given towns names like Cape Girardeau and Prairie du Chien. Freed slaves moved north after Reconstruction was canceled and, later, during Jim Crow to work the coalfields to the south and the early industry around St. Louis. Immigrants from Lombardy came to work the accessible clay deposits into bricks and the stone left standing when the glaciers slid by to the east. Hanna's family of stonemasons was part of that wave of immigrants. His father, Francesco then, was three when they immigrated.

Granite City had seven or eight brick buildings with stores on the bottom and apartments above that looked like they were air-dropped from a commercial street in Chicago. Between them were empty lots, as if room was left for the city about to arrive. It never showed up.

Hanna's father, Frank, returned from France after World War I.

With Prohibition, he decided that's how he'd make a future for his family. He went to work for a bootlegger, delivering whiskey in an armored tanker truck. Hanna has a picture of thirty armed men sitting astride the tanker with rifles, shotguns, and Thompsons outside a rural speakeasy called Dew Drop Inn. One of them is his father.

Frank was drawn into a gunfight outside a cigar store in Granite City. The Ku Klux Klan was resurgent in a nativist reaction against massive European immigration. In the Midwest, it was pro-temperance, anti–trade unionist, anti-Catholic, and anti-Semitic. They had lynched two Sicilians in Johnston City. In the diversely populated areas of Illinois east of St. Louis, the Klansmen found themselves up against United Mine Workers, a Russian Jewish gang leader out of St. Louis, Italian immigrants, and local moonshiners—most of whom were WWI combat veterans.

Outside the cigar store, Asa Barrett, a St. Clair County deputy, who served with Frank Hanna in the battles of Château-Thierry and Saint-Mihiel, shot and killed Klan leader Roger Comers. In the fighting, the back of the Klan was broken, but Hanna's father, who had survived France without a scratch, was hit in the pelvis with a .30-06 round, and a shrapnel-like piece of masonry pierced his throat and damaged his larynx.

It drained the ambition. He got a political job as a St. Clair County deputy and ran a card game out of the lockup. His mother never saw her promised bright future. She raised three children. Hard work and Vincent's sisters consumed her emotional life. His father cared for his family but was lost somewhere in himself and rarely talked. When he did, it was in a rasp.

For young Vincent Hanna, life was a quasi-urban miasma along rural winding roads to cliffs overlooking the Mississippi. He had a desperate yearning for more without knowing what that was.

At eighteen in 1966, he had a choice: enroll in Southern Illinois University in nearby Edwardsville with third-rate frat boys or get drafted. Hanna enlisted in the Marines.

··

On January 31, 1968, he was in the large MACV (Military Assistance Command, Vietnam) base in Phu Bai, in Company H of the Second Battalion, Fifth Marine Regiment. They were prepared to board Stallion twin-rotor helicopters to reinforce Khe Sanh, where General Westmoreland had divined the People's Army of Vietnam (NVA) would launch their offensive, fight for a while, and then, in typical fashion, swiftly vanish. At the last moment, Hanna's company was held back in reserve.

After a year and a half of planning, including the feint at Khe Sanh, the NVA and the Viet Cong launched the Tet Offensive, attacking every population center in South Vietnam simultaneously. The centerpiece was a classic infantry invasion of the ancient imperial capital of Huế on the Perfume River. Previously, it was a war-free zone. They overran it, including the massive walled Imperial City, in twenty-four hours. Then they dug in. They weren't vanishing. They were there to stay.

The commander at Task Force X-Ray, Lieutenant General LaHue, like most of the officer class, believed reports were being exaggerated by green Marines. None of this was happening, because it wasn't supposed to.

Hanna and H Company were ordered up Highway 1 from Phu Bai to sort out what they were told was a couple hundred VC skirmishers attacking a small Marine base in the commercial section south of the river on Trần Cao Vân.

Hanna and H Company crossed the Hung Vuong Bridge, entering Huế from the south, and ran headlong into five thousand dug-in, combat-hardened NVA. They were shot to pieces, with eighteen dead or wounded before they made it one block. They fought their way to refuge and sheltered in the small MACV base.

Hanna was freezing. They had left their packs at Phu Bai, expecting to return in a day. Marines in Vietnam were equipped to fight a jungle war. In Huế they were in hardscape, fighting close-quarter combat, which Marines had not done since the Battle of Seoul.

The twenty-four cold and rainy nights and days of bloodshed and horror produced the largest American casualties of the war. It engraved experiences that stayed with Vincent Hanna forever.

..

Flashers from an incoming ambulance take Hanna's attention. Out the hospital windows, the shadows of trees move against the wall across the parking lot. The siren surrenders. The flashers quit. It's still again under an acid-yellow umbrella of sodium light.

Jessica's respirator kicks in quietly. Hanna looks at her lying in the bed.

"Once there was a flattened lady. We were pinned down by a heavy machine gun emplacement at this wall around a high school, like any high school except the bricks were all dark red."

He says to Jessica, "I remember the street name. Nguyễn Trường Tộ, a block down from Lê Lợi, which ran along the Perfume River. Lê Lợi was like a boulevard in Paris . . .

"In the roadway a Vietnamese woman had been run over by four retreating ARVN M41 Bulldog tanks. She was flattened. Her corpse was two-dimensional, like a cardboard standee outside a movie theater.

"I didn't want to look at her. And I couldn't take my eyes off her. I still see her. Who was she? How'd she get there alone? Somewhere else in the ruins was someone waiting for her to return?"

Anomalies. Those are what stick in memory, he thinks. Packs of civilians running toward them, even though both sides shouted for them to go back, as they raced directly into a crossfire. An affluent villa they bivouacked in once held a family who preferred a dignified suicide. They were all seated around their dining room table. Sometimes the rubble was hallucinogenic, green and blue ceramic fragments in the rain from the palaces and temples.

They fought relentlessly, thanks to top-grade US government dextroamphetamine. Hanna and the others downed it like M&M'S. It turned his world bright and aggressive and electric, and imbued him with the conviction he was invulnerable. Until he crashed. In the down, some men looked around for what they could kill.

After his tour, Hanna enrolled in Boston University in 1969 under

the GI Bill. Antiwar politics swirled around and isolated him. His father died. Hanna buried him and brought his mother to live with his
older sister in St. Louis. Only John Prine's "Sam Stone" made sense,
along with some Tim Hardin. He graduated in three years.

In 1973, he was living in a working-class neighborhood in Chicago
off Armitage, enrolled at DePaul College of Law.

Hanna leans forward and takes Jessica's hand. He looks at it for a
moment, repositions her hand on the bed, and removes his.

"Once in a while . . . I used to drive out at two in the morning
through the black bridges over the Calumet River south of the city,
everything glistening in the rain. Out toward Kankakee on Highway 50.

"Out where there were no more lights, you could imagine the
prairie three, four hundred, eight hundred years ago, when the Sauk,
Fox, and Osage roamed it."

Occasionally he'd turn off his headlights, like he did tonight, dic-
ing with the thrill of a ditch slamming into him at 65 mph. What was
he looking for? What was he running from?

The curriculum of law school was like prison. It transferred visu-
ally and made him loathe the grid pattern of Chicago's streets. He
hated their orderliness, as if they were trying to regulate him, too.
Cravings, like metallic urgings, overtook him, then, and he blasted
out of the city. He did it, too, when the nightmares refused him sleep.

He talks to Jessica as if she's listening to him. "Crazy. What was I
looking for?"

He never found an answer because there was none.

The action of pushing out and pursuing, in and of itself, is what
had become native to him. Pursuing a sequence of unknowns to its
origins in dark and wild places or on the concrete anonymity of city-
scape, that action is what made him go. He quit DePaul two months
later and joined the Chicago Police Department. He made detective
in three years.

Hanna found that the more intense the work, the calmer he became, even as events raced down unexpected tangents from the desperate improvisations of dangerous people. And the heavier the crew

or felon he was hunting, the more dangerous the target, the better he became at it.

After Hanna reconstructs the Matzukas home invasion in the landscape of his mind, works informants, physical evidence, interviews, and psychological profiling, he will have leads. It's never predictable where they may come from. He wants who did this. And he will hunt them down.

The two of them are alone—Jessica on the white bed, under the low lights of the medical equipment, and Vincent Hanna sitting in a chair, watching.

19

Friday night on the Near North Side, the rain clears away to a bright night, and the city is lively. But the six-point corner outside Prosperity Savings & Loan is quiet. The diner across the street is closed. Evening traffic is light. The action is east and south: bars and restaurants on Rush Street, a concert down by the lake. The empty storefront is ignored by the few couples passing on the street.

Prosperity closed at five p.m., when the manager and a guard went to the basement, shut and locked the massive vault door, and set a timer. The ground floor is bolted, alarms set, empty; the S&L keeps no guards on duty over the weekend.

Molina drives the block, front and back, up and down. "Clear."

McCauley parks the panel van in the alley. Between L trains, they unload their gear. In the basement of the empty store, the drilled section of concrete wall is waiting.

Step two: The show.

With the hollow-core drill, Chris has cut a breach in the wall two feet tall and three feet wide. They've dug out the sediment and rubble. Beyond the breach, clean and primed, stands the concrete wall of the S&L basement.

Chris and Cerrito position the drill against it.

They put on ear protection. They wait for the rumble of the next passing train. Chris fires up the drill.

Neil clicks a timer on his watch.

11:57 p.m.

The drill bites into the concrete of the S&L wall smoothly. The wall is reinforced with rebar, but it's the original lugged, diamond-pattern rebar from the 1920s. The core drill goes through it—loudly—with care and muscle. When Chris hits steel on the far side, he stops.

That's the back of the vault.

He and Cerrito reposition the drill to widen the hole. When it finally matches the size of the breach in the store basement wall, McCauley helps Chris pull the drill aside. Chris gets out the Milwaukee cutting tools and uses an angle grinder to file down the rebar protruding from the newly drilled hole, so they won't tear up their gear, their bags, or themselves.

Chris wipes down the edges of the hole and aims a halogen flashlight through the opening. The shine of steel reflects back at him. He looks up at Neil.

Outside, Molina has a police scanner. He has an inconspicuous parking spot up the street, where he can watch the empty store and the S&L building from a work car. But Molina can't monitor every inch of the block front and back. They need more eyes. So, above the back door of the empty store, Cerrito has installed a Panasonic CCTV camera and a Baxall infrared camera, wired into a nine-inch Sony monitor that they've set up in the basement. Neil watches the monitor now for the rising headlight glow of approaching trains.

"We're good."

Chris gets the portable oxyacetylene torch kit, the safety goggles and mask. It's going to be close and hot.

He lies down in front of the breach and army-crawls forward. "If this goes to shit, grab my legs and pull."

He lights the torch.

He puts the torch to the steel panel that forms the exterior wall of the vault. The heat fills the tunnel, instant, overwhelming, the blue flame lightning-bright even through the goggles. But the steel slices like butter. He cuts a section smaller than the dimensions of the hole in the concrete. Then he cuts that into three pieces.

When he shuts off the torch and backs out, he's drenched with sweat. He flips up the mask, wipes his face, and sits for a second. Cerrito squirrels into the opening with a pry bar. With a squeal, one of the three cut sections of steel wall slips free and falls toward him. Cerrito pulls it in and sets it aside.

"Hello," he says.

They're looking at the backs of large safe-deposit boxes. They sit fat and happy in their rack. They're larger than expected, twenty-four by thirty inches.

They pull a few boxes onto the floor of the store basement. McCauley opens one.

It's six inches deep in banded stacks of cash. The color straps read $5,000 and $10,000.

Neil nods, seemingly with satisfaction. Cerrito smiles broadly, like he's looking at a juicy steak. Chris feels his blood pump with adrenaline.

"Fuck yeah," he says. "*Fuck* yeah."

He punches McCauley in the shoulder, then turns back to the breach in the wall.

"Hand me the long-handled flathead screwdriver," he says.

Neil slaps it into Chris's palm like handing a surgeon a scalpel. Then he aims the portable floodlight at the hole while Chris wriggles back into the breach. The light reveals the inside of the door to the safe-deposit box and its double-key door-locking mechanism. Chris carefully unscrews and removes the mechanism. He doesn't yet push the box door open.

Neil hands him a flexible borescope. It has a lighted fiber-optic camera connected to a small video screen. Softly, using the tip of the screwdriver, Chris nudges on the door of the box, just a hair.

They know the vault should have no security cameras. A safe-deposit repository is one of the only places in any financial institution that's free of them. Customer privacy should guarantee nobody is watching. Especially in this old, low-profile neighborhood bank, considered the depository of choice for ill-gotten gains.

The architectural plans for the building show the original installation of the vault. It has no seismic sensors—which would have been a tricky upgrade anyhow, with the L tracks so close. Its locking device uses magnetic plates in the massive vault door and the vault's exterior wall—which they aren't disturbing.

Slowly, Chris maneuvers the borescope to scan the interior of the vault, including the ceiling.

"No cameras. No motion detectors. One smoke detector," he says. "It's clean."

It's 3:30 a.m. They're in.

They slide through the wall breach into the vault, one at a time, pulling portable lights, gym bags, and tools with them. The air is cool. The vault interior is the size of a small swimming pool. Boxes line the walls. Bronze number badges are riveted to each door. Each box requires two keys. Bronze-and-onyx tables occupy the center of the floor with demure table lamps.

McCauley counts.

"Three hundred sixty."

Chris sets up the lights. The external vault door has its stainless, heavy locking mechanisms exposed behind Plexiglas to impress depositors.

"Stay closed, you beauty."

Cerrito glances around. The walls of boxes gleam in the spooky light. "Which one has the Holy Grail?"

Neil opens a gym bag. "Don't matter. You find Jesus Christ, haul him out and hand him a sledgehammer."

He takes out a set of blank lock punches and measures them against the dimensions of the locks on each box. He selects the punch with a matching diameter. Locks it into a long-handled wrench, which he hands to Cerrito. Then he stretches, rolls his neck, and picks up a sledgehammer.

He steps up to the first box. "Let's go."

Cerrito sets the lock punch against the face of the box and stands back, holding the end of the wrench. Neil lines up on it, then draws back and swings like he's hitting a fastball. With a metallic clang, the punch pushes the lock in half an inch. Neil nods at Michael and lines up again. Swings.

Swings again.

They hear the lock push all the way in. Then they hear a hard click behind the box door.

Neil sets down the sledgehammer and aims a flashlight at the hole left by the punched-in lock. He's breathing hard. The click was not the sound of the lock releasing. It was the opposite, a security measure activating inside the box: a relocking mechanism.

The relocker is designed to foil anybody who does what he just did, punch out one of the box's locks.

"Chris," Neil says.

Chris takes out a set of spring-steel hooks. He peers into the hole. Selects a hook that is about eight inches long, like a thief's version of a crochet hook, and carefully inserts it. Working by feel, he maneuvers it around the interior of the locking mechanism. He shuts his eyes.

He feels the hook catch. Gingerly, he pulls. The spring steel yields a fraction of an inch, as it's supposed to, and gently pops the relocker.

The box door swings open.

"Good," Neil says.

Chris pulls out the box and sets it on the floor. They open the lid.

The box is laden with papers: Deeds, stock certificates, a stamp collection. Old photos, look like from World War II. Birth and death certificates. A lock of a baby's hair.

And banded stacks of cash. Neil unloads them and counts.

"Twenty-five large."

Cerrito's smile spreads.

"We take turns with the sledgehammer. Take the cash. Leave mounted jewelry. Forget family heirlooms." He radios Molina. "We're in."

They get to work.

20

The nurse shakes Hanna awake.

Early light is filtering through the hospital window. Saturday morning. He sits straight up.

"I'm going off duty in ten minutes," she says. "Maybe you should, too, Detective."

She's the same nurse he greeted when he came in the other night. Her stethoscope gleams in the sunshine.

He stands, his back stiff. Speaks quietly. "Yeah. Thanks."

She turns to check Jessica Matzukas's vitals. The door hushes open when Hanna leaves. He's standing at the elevator when the doors open and Jessica's mother gets off.

"Mrs. Matzukas."

Andi Matzukas is in a robe and slippers. She's accompanied by an IV pole on wheels and a nurse. She doesn't look surprised to see him. "Detective."

She also carries a fresh bouquet: peonies and daisies, reds and oranges. "Did the nurses tell you? She's steady and doing okay."

"Yes," Hanna says.

He takes her in as she walks toward Jessica's room with small steps. He sees the woman's rigid jaw, still wired, and the renewed straightness in her spine. The heat in her unpatched eye when she speaks of her child. She has climbed far enough out of the pit that she is deliberately girding herself for *her daughter*. She has found a reservoir of strength and wants to deploy that for *her daughter*. It's the two of them alone now.

"Maybe the nurses told you," he says. "I visit her."

She nods. "Is she still in danger? Is there a guard on her door?"

"No. She's safe."

He doesn't tell her about the layers of reasons for why he comes to see her. One is that, perhaps subconsciously, his voice will become familiar, so that if she regains consciousness, she'll trust revealing to him all that happened to her and what she saw. Another is—for reasons he doesn't know—he's impelled to bare his own dark stories, here, with her. A third is simply to root for a young girl fighting to live.

The woman's lips press tight, perhaps guessing part of Hanna's intention. "Head injury. This level, doctor's warned me that she may have no memory of the event." She closes her eye, fighting a wave of tears, and clamps her emotions down again. "But I remember."

She turns her head. "Jessica, upstairs in her room when the doorbell rang. Talking to her friends or listening to INXS, maybe, I don't know. Give me back one minute before Jimmy said, 'I'll get the door.' One moment. I could have said, 'Wait . . . Jimmy, wait.'"

Hanna holds still.

Her chest rises. "He told me to run. It was too late." She presses the back of her hand to her mouth. "And I might have held it together better, but . . ." Her eye sweeps back and forth. "After they grabbed me, the man in the pizza shirt said, 'Get the girl.' That's when I lost it."

Hanna's blood feels electric. "He said 'the girl.'"

She nods.

"Does Jessica's bedroom look over the street?"

"No. The backyard."

"Did any of the men come in from the back of the house?"

"No. All five through the front door."

Hanna stills. When the crew came in they knew ahead of time that the family had a daughter.

Andi looks up sharply with the same realization. "They were watching us? The house?"

Hanna thinks, *Probably. They likely cased the house.* But that wouldn't be all of it.

Andi's breathing quickens. "They were watching *her?*"

"No." He touches her arm. "This is something else." He hears the rising excitement in his voice and tamps it down. "They knew you were affluent. That's what they were after. They knew you had a teenage daughter and they would have to control everyone inside."

"From watching the house . . . ?"

"Or from talking to you or your husband. Or from seeing you with

Jessica somewhere. Where have the two of you been together recently? Tell me about your house keys. How do you keep them?"

"On a key ring with the car key."

"Any place you handed over your keys?"

She inhales, concentrating. "The three of us went out to dinner last week. Jessica and I got our hair cut a few weeks back. We go to the movies on weekends. I don't know."

"That's good."

Restaurant. Hair salon.

Hanna gets to the CID before seven a.m. He walks past the detectives finishing the graveyard shift. Past his desk. He heads for the whiteboard with all its lists.

There it is.

He calls Easton at home.

"Vincent," Easton says flatly.

"Hair salons."

"I checked them. Four families. Different salons."

"The owners. Do they have different or the same owner?"

"Each one's different."

"Okay. What about parking? Valet parking?"

"I don't know," Easton says.

"Check what valet parking services all four use."

Hanna and Easton roll past Ponte Vecchio, where Andi Matzukas gets her hair done, at 10:15 a.m. The salon is on East Oak Street, which means Hermès, Chanel, and other boutiques that hand you a Champagne flute when you walk in. Shoppers stroll the sidewalks, bags rustling, under delicate trees. Even the greenery here looks expensive.

At the curb outside the salon, a parking valet station is up and running.

"Look at that," Hanna says.

At a podium stand two young men in red polo shirts and Dockers.

One is in his late teens, Black with a high fade. The other is white, late twenties, lithe and bronzed, with wide dark eyes and a crucifix earring.

The valets' shirts are embroidered with a logo: PREMIER VALET. All four salons use the service.

Hanna and Easton circle the block and park up the street. Hanna puts binoculars to his eyes. His focus goes to the white valet. The young man has black hair moussed like Billy Squier's in that horrible music video where he's dancing.

Behind the valet podium is a cabinet for car keys. The white valet greets an arriving customer. When he returns to the podium after parking her car, he looks at the keys before popping them on the board. The key ring has house keys attached.

"Five will get you ten they rotate valets across the salons. And it's one or two guys. I doubt it's the company." Hanna adjusts the binoculars.

Easton grabs the radio. Hanna surveys the salon. The receptionist has towering red hair and leggings so tight that if Hanna plucked on them, they would play a high C.

"The half-life on this salon is fifteen minutes once the story gets out a valet's scouting scores and making duplicate house keys for a crew of torture burglars, rapist home invaders," he says.

The CPD dispatcher puts Easton through to Premier Valet. Easton identifies himself and asks for the names of the young men working at Ponte Vecchio.

There's a pause. "Detective?" the man asks. "I don't know if I can divulge that without my attorney's—"

"If you knew what I knew and still want to have a business next week, you will do everything you can to help us in the next thirty seconds," Hanna says.

The owner hears the truth-telling tone in Hanna's voice.

"Are you talking about Alex? Dave is the owner's nephew working a summer job. Alexander Dalecki. If you're popping him for possession, we don't have an obligation to piss test the valets. They're independent contractors, not employees."

Easton and Hanna exchange a glance. Hanna unwraps a piece of gum and sticks it in his mouth. Easton asks for Alexander Dalecki's address, Social Security number, and personal details to run a make on him.

21

Alex Dalecki has a record. Burglary. Shoplifting. Car theft. St. Charles juvie and a stint in Stateville Penitentiary near Joliet.

His address is an apartment on the Near West Side near downtown, but when Hanna and Easton follow him after work, he drives northwest to a tidy neighborhood of single-family homes. He parks in front of a small brick bungalow with faded curtains and potted geraniums on the front step.

Hanna calls in the address. It belongs to Amelia Dalecki, Alexander's mother.

Easton hangs his badge wallet on his pocket and heads up the walk to knock. Hanna circles to the alley behind the house. Waiting by the wooden back fence, he counts down thirty seconds on his watch, knowing Easton is at the front door.

From the far side of the fence he hears a screen door slam and footsteps leaping off the back porch, thudding across the patio and lawn. The fence rocks and hands appear on top, gold chains around a man's wrists. Alex Dalecki flies over.

Hanna grabs him midair and slams him to the ground like he's wrestling a steer.

"*Fuck*, man," Alex yells.

He squirms on the concrete. Hanna holds him down with a knee in his back, a wrist and elbow lock. Easton peers over the fence.

Hanna cuffs him. "Let's go," he says.

"Not in front of the house, man," Alex says from his mother's front lawn. "Come on, this is my mom's place. The whole neighborhood's watching. They talk shit, you know."

"They've been talking about you since you were six and stealing Hula-Hoops from the kid up the street," Hanna says. "The scores you been setting up. C'mon."

"I'm no snitch."

Wrong answer. He implicitly just copped to having knowledge.

Hanna turns as slowly as a winch. "I think you've been setting up your customers at salons to get home invaded, robbed, and raped. Multiple victims remember handing you their keys. They will point at you from the witness stand. You will take the fall. That is not stand-up. That is stupid. They will be out there, laughing, spending money, having a good time in life, while you go away."

A station wagon drives past, the driver's head turning as she goes by. They haul Alex across the street, past a man in shorts who's watering his lawn with a garden hose, and toss him into their unmarked Crown Vic.

"We talked to Premier Valet. Your job is gone. Your game is over."

Hanna speaks evenly. He guesses, looking at Alex, a wannabe Romeo, that he is on the fringe of the crew, hungry, an opportunist.

"And this crew will assume you rolled over, whether you did or not. That means turning out your lights. *Pop.*"

Alex shakes his head. "Fuck you, man."

Hanna lunges halfway over the center console toward the back seat, snaps his fingers. "Look at me!"

Alex looks up warily.

"I get it. All those wealthy women, ignoring you. And they are hot but unattainable. Not for you, right? Perfume that doesn't come from Walgreens. They smell of money. Frustrating. Makes you angry. I get that."

Outside, a neighbor stares at the unmarked car. Alex slinks lower in his seat.

"You believe this clown?" Easton clocks Alex. "He's worried what the neighbors think."

Hanna reaches down to the footwell and picks up the bubble light they use in the unmarked for emergencies. "You see this? We can light it up."

"Christ, come on—"

"We can stick it on the roof. We can tie it to the top of your fucking head and run you around the block like a fire engine."

Easton turns to him. "Do you even have a *clue* what you're lookin' at if you go down for this?"

Alex squeezes his eyes shut and then looks out the window. His crucifix earring flails in the light.

Hanna says, "Okay. Fuck this guy. Let's go to the station."

Easton puts the car in gear.

22

The boss pulls into the alley behind the commercial vehicle repair shop Aaron Grimes runs. Hank and Chubby are with him. The sky is heavy, rain showers blowing through. Traffic on the nearby street splashes past. The repair shop is dark.

The boss checks his watch. "Where is he?"

Hank eyes the alley. "You said five thirty."

"It's five thirty-five." He shakes his head. "He's not on top of this, and I want him here when I check the work cars." He lights a smoke. "Keep him on his toes. So where the hell is he?"

A car turns into the alley, headlights on in the gloom. Grimes pulls up and gets out.

The boss is out of the truck, cigarette in the corner of his mouth. "Time's a-tickin'. Where the fuck you been?"

"Everything's ready."

But, the boss thinks, Grimes looks preoccupied. And not with *him*.

He follows Grimes as he gets out a set of keys and opens the shop's tall accordion doors on their runners.

Grimes has another garage space across the alley. The boss gestures with his head. "What's in there?"

The boss heads for it, but Grimes nods him to the other.

"You're over here." Grimes enters the back of the repair shop. "You're all set."

"What's in the other garage?"

"Nothing."

The boss smirks. "Your CIA client? Your supersecret Batmobile?"

Grimes leads him inside. "Keys are under the mat."

The work car looks suitably nondescript. The van looks impeccable, he has to give Grimes that. Professional lettering on the side, purple and frilly: ENCHANTED FLORIST, MAYWOOD, IL. Washed, waxed, all prim and proper for expensive deliveries to the Gold Coast or the suburbs.

"Registration, insurance?"

"In the glove box. It will all match, come back clean."

"Where'd you get it?"

"Rolled it off the service department at a dealership in Evanston yesterday. It was parked, waiting for a tune-up. Nobody's even going to figure out it's missing yet."

"Cutting it close, aren't you?"

Grimes looks at him with irritation. "You're set, man."

The boss runs his hand along the side of the van. He lets Grimes stew for a moment. Nobody else should get priority over him, Grimes needs to know that.

He nods to Svoboda, who pulls out an envelope and hands it to Grimes. He flicks his cigarette to the ground. Sparks flare.

Time to roll.

In a large, grim interview room in Shakespeare Station, Easton unlocks one of Alex's handcuffs, slips it through a large ring in the concrete floor, and reattaches it to Alex's wrist. Alex is unable to sit up.

"What's this for?" he asks.

Two more large detectives circle him. Hanna stands motionless.

"Round two. That's when asking you questions gets fo' real. This is round one," Easton says.

"C'mon, man, I don't know why I'm here," Alex complains.

"'Cause two victims identified you, you dummy," Hanna says.

No answer. Alex's brio starts to fade.

"'Why am I lucky, Detective Hanna?' is what you should be asking."

Alex looks up at him.

"You wanna know why you're lucky? Okay, I'll tell you. You are lucky because I do *not* have your crew. That is a big deal. Wanna know why? 'Yes, I do, Detective Hanna,'" Hanna mimics Alex.

"Okay, I'll tell you that, too. It's called 'barter.' You got something with which to trade. However. If we get them before you talk, or if one of my guys gets hurt or they hit another family when you could have told us and made that bad thing not happen, that is called 'contingent history.' That means you no longer have what you had. You don't have shit. Nothing to barter. So, we drop your ass in county with a snitch jacket and the race is on to see who turns you into Swiss steak first. Probably your boss, because he *knows* your ass rolled on him. Tick-tock, motherfucker. You are out of time."

"You don't get it," Alex tries.

"Get what? We don't gotta *get* nothin'. Light bulb on yet? Anybody home in that dark, cobwebbed place known as your cerebral cortex?"

"What Kotex?" Alex says.

"Kotex is what ladies put between their legs. Cortex is upstairs."

"You don't know . . ." Alex's head bobs and weaves, trying to navigate, bent over the heavy-duty ring in the floor.

"What don't I know?"

"He's seriously psycho, man. He will kill me!"

Hanna leans down into Alex's face and grabs the crucifix in his right ear and rips it out through the lobe. Alex screams. Blood sprays from the tear.

"Asshole!" Hanna shouts. "What the fuck do you think we're gonna do? You are gonna flip, you dumb prick. You are gonna tell me everything I want to know, you cocksucker!"

He jerks Alex's chin up, stares into his eyes, and shoves forward the cross. "*The power of Christ commands you! I am your motherfucking exorcist. Tell me!*"

"Wardell!" Alex shouts.

"Louder!"

"Otis Wardell!" Alex has said it. He pants like he's been running.

Hanna, abruptly quiet, in a monotone says, "When's the next score?" And Alex says, "Tonight."

23

Hanna comes into the CID like he's riding on rails. The green walls and crowded desks and the smell of cigarettes and men's sweat are just background to his urgency. Easton hustles at his side, pulling along Alex Dalecki, grim-faced, handcuffed, bloodied. He leads him out of the office to the booking desk, to be dumped in a solitary cell.

Alex calls out to Hanna as he's led out.

"Information, man. I just passed along gossip. I didn't know what goes on inside those houses. I never went along for the ride. Okay?"

"Casals, Rossi," Hanna shouts. "It's going down."

The detectives turn.

"We got the crew. We got their next target, which they are planning to hit *right now*," Hanna says.

Casals pushes back from his desk.

"The car valet has been tipping a skel named Otis Wardell and his crew to the scores. He duplicates the house keys," Hanna says, grabbing his vest. "The next one is in the Gold Coast. They've been casing it for days. It is *on*."

Casals is checking his sidearm, grabbing extra magazines. "How they making entry?"

"Through the front door, disguised as florists. They will arrive in a van. Then they will swarm the house."

"Is the family going to be there?" Rossi asks.

"They know the family will be there and what to take. The valet says Wardell likes it that way." Hanna clips to his belt his holstered .45 Colt Combat Commander.

"Pull Wardell's jacket," Hanna says to Rossi, on the move. "Known associates: Hank Svoboda, William 'Chubby' Wozniaki, Carlo Bolzani, aka 'Angel.' They are prepping as we speak. I want us in there ahead of them. When they walk in that door, we will be inside."

Casals holsters his sidearm.

Rossi's on the phone, calling Records, rubbing his knuckles across his forehead.

Easton nods. "Backup?"

Hanna is racing down the hall to the weapons locker. "No time. I don't want SWAT trailing behind us, tipping them off. Keep them distant." They're signing out pump-action shotguns and CAR-15s. "We go in low profile. No lights. No sirens. Hope they aren't already up on the score and spot us." Grabbing boxes of shells, extra magazines. "Let's go."

Eight p.m., Alex told Hanna. That's when Wardell and his crew intend to launch.

The husband's home from his golf game. The kids have cleaned up, done homework. The wife is in the kitchen with a glass of wine. Nice and relaxed. Guard down.

At 7:45 p.m., Easton swings to a stop around the corner from the Colsons' house. The sunset is fading, a calm dusk settling over the neighborhood. The area oozes money. Older large stone-and-brick town houses, cheek by jowl, rise behind sculpted hedges.

Hanna is on the radio, filling in and instructing the CPD dispatcher to keep other units distant. "I want to get this crew as they enter the target home and take them inside. Contain the takedown. Keep this *off* the street. If units see a florist's van, let it roll. Do not slow, do not turn, do not lift your radio transmitter. After it passes, continue out of sight, then call it in. And you call me. You got it?"

Ideally, he would evacuate the residents from the target house and clear out the neighbors on either side before the robbers arrived. He would let the crew pull up in front of the victims' home and make entry. Then he would have units deploy to predetermined choke points, blocking off the streets and alleys.

But this is what he has. He is going to make this work. Like a bazooka.

He jumps out of the unmarked car and rounds the corner to the Colsons' street. The house is a Gold Coast classic, two blocks off Lake

Shore Drive just north of Oak Street. It looks like a college building, ivy climbing the flat stone facade, like you might hear an alma mater wafting over the heavy trees and wrought iron. Hanna hurries through a side gate and runs to the back. The small manicured lawn is peaceful in the evening light. French doors look in on a massive kitchen. Amber light. Two kids watching TV in the adjacent, open-plan family room. A woman in her thirties, casually, expensively dressed, is on the phone, a glass of white wine in her hand. A man in a golf shirt sits at the kitchen table, reading the *Tribune*.

Hanna runs up the steps to the patio. He has a shotgun at port arms and displays his badge. Easton's right behind him. He pounds on the door. The husband's head snaps around. The wife pauses, frozen.

"Police. Emergency," he says.

It takes two stunned seconds for the couple to give each other a sharp glance before the husband unlocks and opens the French doors. Hanna bulls in.

"All right. Listen. I'm Detective Sergeant Vincent Hanna of the Criminal Intelligence Division. You and your family are in danger. Do exactly as I say. You have to do it now."

"What the hell's going on?" the husband interrupts.

Hanna's stepping through, scanning the kitchen, the family room, the wide windows along the back and side of the house, the hallway to the large foyer.

Hanna pivots on him. "You've been targeted for a home invasion. We learned this minutes ago. We want to get you *out*. Right now."

Becky Colson shakes her head, like shaking herself awake. "How do you—"

"Now!" Hanna beckons the children. "Kids. Come on."

"Get us out?" Robert Colson says. "Why don't you keep *them* out?"

"'Cause they're already in the vicinity. They're heavily armed. We don't know where. Let us do our job. The safest move for your family is for you to be elsewhere. *Now*."

Robert's jaw tightens.

Becky is pale. "Are these the people who attacked that family near Lincoln Park?"

"Yes." Hanna nods.

She waves to the kids. "Come on."

The two jump up and hurry into the kitchen.

"Shoes," she says, grabbing her car keys from a basket on the counter, turning toward the front foyer.

Hanna shakes his head. "No. We'll take you out the back, over the fence." He doesn't want Wardell to see the family leaving and call off the score.

Hanna's radio erupts. He pulls it from the clip on his belt.

"Scout car is circling the block," Casals says. "Wozniaki driving."

Hanna's pulse jumps up a notch. "Wait until it's clear, then get in here. Patio door."

He turns back to the Colsons. "Change of plan. Where's the door to the basement?"

"Hold on, hold on." Robert raises a hand.

Becky indicates the basement door.

"What's down there?"

"Rec room and a bathroom and storage," Becky replies.

Becky grabs her children's hands and rushes to the door in the hallway. There's a staircase down. Robert isn't moving.

"You stay right here," Hanna says, "you are putting your family, yourself, and my men at risk."

Easton, flanked by Casals and Rossi, all heavily armed, enters from the patio. The sight convinces Robert Colson.

"Rob!" Becky shouts.

He glares at Hanna and crosses to the stairs.

"Put the kids in the bathroom," Hanna says. "In the tub. Lay a mattress over it or sofa cushions. Lock the doors. Do not unlock them unless you hear instructions from me. Is that clear?"

No answer.

"Is that clear?"

"Yes," Robert says as he runs down. A door slams at the bottom.

Easton says, "Squad cars are way back. SWAT is standing by in an alley off Ashland."

"Close the blinds," Hanna says. "Let's go."

The detectives move into positions behind cover to create lines of fire intersecting the entry at right angles. Hanna walks into the foyer. Stares at the front door.

24

The van pulls up in front of the Colson house with Wardell at the wheel. The street is quiet, the night closing in. Nobody is out on foot. Around here, Wardell guesses, they make their butlers take the dog out back for a shit.

A single car cruises past. The driver pays no mind to the van with ENCHANTED FLORIST painted on the side.

Wardell gets out and lifts a massive flower arrangement from the back. Aaron Grimes, despite his recent lack of attention to him, has come through.

The others in the van roll out the side and hurry to the front porch. Angel, Chubby, and Chubby's cousin Darryl. Svoboda is across town in Franklin Park, readying a safe house where they plan to hole up afterward—with a garage where Wardell intends to stash the Colsons' stolen cars. He climbs the steps to the front door.

The men stack beside it and roll their ski masks down over their faces. Wardell gives himself a moment to inhale. The flower arrangement hides his face. He nods to Angel, who rings the bell.

He can hear a TV playing somewhere in the back of the house. He waits. Angel rings the bell again.

"We go with the key? We're fucking naked out here," Chubby hisses through his teeth.

Wardell ignores him. He listens. Thinks he hears footsteps jogging down a staircase.

Hanna is at the back of the hall, braced in the doorway of a dark closet, his shotgun aimed at the front door, the stock snugged against his shoulder. The lights in the hallway are off. The doorbell rings again.

He eyes Casals, prone on a landing at the top of the stairs, weapon aimed at the door. Rossi, on the left, near the door. Easton, tucked in the kitchen doorway. Hanna raises a hand, fist clenched. *Hold.*

The TV is on, volume up. Kitchen lights on. The Colsons' cars are visible through a window in the garage. The crew knows the house is occupied. Give them long enough, and they'll get tired of waiting.

He hears a key slide into the lock.

Wardell turns the duplicate key. It sticks in the lock.

He sets the flowers on the porch and pulls down his mask. He hears Chubby muttering. He slides the key out and in again. It's a dupe made from a putty mold, an inexact cutting model. He finesses it. He senses Angel tensing. He prefers it when the people in the house open the door. Better to surprise the targets right away, *boom,* and take immediate control. If a man answers, they neutralize a primary physical threat. A woman, good hostage. Instant dominance. But if the Colsons are too fancy to answer their own door, he'll take them by surprise on their designer leather sofa. He massages the key in the lock. Turns it. The dead bolt opens.

Yeah.

He pulls the gun from the waistband of his jeans. Turns the knob. The door is heavy. Standing to the side, he nudges it open, glimpsing the hallway as it swings absolutely silently open. Marble. The foot of a staircase. Pop Art sculpture on a table. Hunter-green wallpaper, paintings. Lights off in the hallway. TV playing in the back of the house, loud, a laugh track. Assholes are unaware. *Come on down, you are the next contestant on* The Price Is Right Between Your Eyes.

Wardell signals the crew. They roll around him and move silently inside. He brings up the rear and shuts the door.

Hanna counts four masked men who come through the door. Under the porch lights, he sees the glint of gun barrels in their hands.

The first three men pause, scanning the darkened hall. The last man holds a massive semiautomatic pistol. The others turn to look at him over their shoulders, waiting for instructions.

That is Otis Wardell.

One of the others, a stout man whose mask stretches over a pumpkin head, mutters, "Where are they?"

As Wardell closes the door, he says, "Back of the house, watching TV. Separate and hog-tie the kids. *Go.*"

They start down the hall.

Hanna emerges from cover and fires the twelve-gauge. "April Fool's, motherfucker!"

Chubby's cousin, crossing in front of Wardell, gets hit and goes down.

The rest of Hanna's team opens up.

All at once . . .

Wardell crouches low behind Chubby.

Casals fires from the stairs landing.

Rossi, from the door to the study with a CAR-15.

Easton, braced in the kitchen doorway.

Chubby firing . . .

Hanna pumps the slide. His Remington roars twice.

Angel's shot hits the floor. Hanna's shotgun blast spins him off his feet. Wardell returns fire rapidly with the large .44.

Chubby, wounded, shouts, off-balance, his gun arm swinging wide. Rossi's fire spins him around. He keeps to his feet, returns fire.

Wardell ducks low and fires from behind him.

Angel, impossibly, rises. Chubby's still on his feet. Fire coming toward his large bulk is a halo Wardell sees around Chubby's bulky frame. Wardell returns fire, while scuttling backward and grabbing the doorknob. Rounds are going into Chubby's chest and legs. Spitting, hitting flesh, bone. One breath, and Chubby's legs are gone out from under him. Wardell fires, one shot after another, dives through the doorway, rolls to his feet, and runs.

..

Hanna slides on the blood as he runs across the hall. A body blocks the front door, a heavyset man. He drags the guy aside.

He opens the door, bracing behind the jamb in case Wardell is outside poised to fire on him. Nothing. Behind him, Easton marches up the hall.

"Clear," Easton calls. "Three down."

Hanna bolts out the door and down the porch steps.

Ahead, Wardell jumps into the fake florist's van. He fires up the engine. Pulse hammering, Hanna raises the Remington. He has a direct shot side-on into the van's cab.

And his background across the street is people at their windows and on the sidewalk. He races across the front lawn to get a clean angle on Wardell.

The van's pulling away, Wardell's at the wheel, ski mask on, dark eyes behind it. Hanna aims, fires.

The windshield frosts white, a hole spiderwebbing the center. Hanna pumps the shotgun. Empty. The van pulls past him. Hanna's running while reloading shotgun shells from his pocket, chasing it.

Squad cars with flashers and sirens are racing in from behind him.

The van jumps the curb, rolls across a lawn. Sheltering civilians dodge out of the way. It comes to a stop in a cluster of bushes. Hanna races up on the passenger side, seeing over the barrel of the Remington. The open passenger sliding door reveals the cab interior. The driver's door is open. Nobody is at the wheel.

"Shit."

Wardell has jumped from the vehicle and is down the street, rounding the corner. Hanna takes off after him.

He hears a shout behind him, Casals calling his name. Hanna follows the clamor ahead, running hard. He pulls his radio from his belt.

"Suspect is on foot. Heading northwest, past Clark toward LaSalle. I am in pursuit."

Heavy trees cover the streetlights, dappling the darkness. He nears a corner and hears a horn and squealing tires. People shout. He bursts onto a busy street. A block south, cars are tangled in an intersection. Drivers are getting out.

Wardell is on his ass on the pavement. He's in front of a Mercedes. The car apparently hit him as he ran into traffic.

"Get back!" Hanna races toward the intersection. "Out of the way!"

The street is bustling. Nobody hears him. The driver of the Mercedes climbs out.

Wardell rolls to his feet, pistol up, aimed at the man. The guy flees. Wardell scrambles into the car. Hanna shoves past pedestrians and around snarled vehicles. Wardell throws the Mercedes into reverse. Eyeing the mirror, he burns rubber away from the tangle of cars in the intersection, veering wildly.

He smashes into a VW behind him.

Hanna runs into the intersection in front of the Mercedes. He raises the shotgun. Wardell stares at him within the ski mask, white disks within the eyeholes, flat black eyes. Expressionless.

The Mercedes revs forward. Hanna fires.

Wardell ducks below the dash. Eight holes blast through the windshield. The car keeps coming. Wardell straightens. Hanna jumps—onto its hood.

Wardell floors it. Hanna slams against the windshield. The shotgun's gone. Wardell keeps his foot on the gas, swerving around cars in the intersection. Hanna tries to anchor himself with one hand, clutching the hood's rear edge, the other bringing his .45 Colt Combat Commander around.

Wardell's first shot goes over Hanna's head. Wardell's second shot, with a sick clang, blows a hole in the hood next to Hanna. Hanna struggles to bring his .45 around into the passenger window. The car lurches across the center line and accelerates against traffic on the wrong side of the road.

Sirens in the distance. Wardell skids through a hard left turn, directly in front of a bus.

As Hanna's grip wrenches away, he snaps off a shot into the Mercedes. He smacks onto the pavement hard, bounces, rolls. Screeching brakes. The headlights of the bus balloon in front of him. It stops near his head. He hears a crash up the street.

Hanna gets to his feet, bruised, knee gimpy, jacket torn, and limps as fast as he can after the Mercedes and Wardell.

He finds the carjacked Mercedes one block west, driver's door open. CPD blue-and-whites are racing in, lights and sirens. An unmarked pulls up, dashboard light spinning red and white. Casals and Rossi jump out.

Hanna, pushing away assistance, circling, stumbling to see up side streets. His eyes on fire with rage to get Wardell. Nothing.

Hanna rides back to the Colsons' house in the unmarked with Casals and Rossi, pressing a handkerchief to a bloody abrasion on his forehead and right ear. The street is a carnival of spinning blue lights. Patrol units block access on either side of the house. Neighbors stand in huddled groups across the street. A CPD helicopter drones overhead, its spotlight bleaching the roofs and road.

"Vincent . . ." Casals says, trying to steer him to a medic at one of the ambulances.

Hanna ignores him and is halfway up the steps when Baumann pulls up beyond the barricade and climbs out. That white hair stands out in the chaotic flood of lights. Police and responders part as he approaches the house wearing a black trench coat, holding a cigar. Following in his wake is his number two, Lieutenant Tom Novak—a solid chunk of a man and a solid cop. Hanna's inside. He didn't wait.

The entry hall is a mess. Lights on, it's blood city. Paintings are knocked off the wall, spattered red. Otis Wardell's crew lies dead on the marble floor.

The men's masks have been pulled up. Easton is directing a photographer to snap photos of the bodies in situ.

Hanna sidesteps the mess. "Easton."

Easton's face is taut. "Full house, jokers over assholes." He looks Hanna up and down.

Hanna shakes his head. "Number one skated." He nods toward the kitchen. "Family?"

"All safe."

Hanna greets them at the kitchen table. "It's over. Everybody good?"

The little boy nods to him. Robert Colson has his arm around his wife.

"We're going to get you out of here," Hanna says.

He hears men's voices at the front door. Hanna limps back into the hall.

He finds Baumann and Novak. Baumann says, "Christ. You got more blood and guts here than at the stockyards."

"And how's your day, Captain?"

"I take it we stopped a robbery in progress," Baumann says. "Family?"

"Safe. The rest? What you see is what you got."

"I see three bodies. A van shot all to hell. News crews lining up."

"They're all yours," Hanna says. "Grab the headlines."

"I will." Baumann points with the cigar. "My advanced skills, in addition to talking, include counting. Three dead? Where's number four and five?"

"At large."

"This Otis Wardell and Hank Svoboda?"

"That's right."

"You couldn't coordinate and cordon off the streets and alleys, block escape routes?"

Hanna sees a shimmer around Baumann's face, an aura. A defocused zone amid the visual noise of the active crime scene. Hanna feels like cool mercury is moving through his veins. His eyes are cold. It's like he momentarily zones into another time and place, out beyond fatigue, fueled up on dexies, in the rubble with everyone else, as they fire, grenade, wound, kill, get wounded, get killed. Zombies in the cold rain.

"Tactical decision," Hanna says.

"And you don't tip off me or Novak? Exclude us from a bust?" Baumann replies.

"Go take the credit. Cameras are right there," Hanna says. "And the crew was already moving in on the family. Tactically, it was the right call. My guys eliminated the most vicious crew you've seen in ten years. I will find Otis Wardell. I am going to take him down."

Baumann goes still. Like a snake. Cold and coiled.

Baumann doesn't care about Wardell. He cares about greasing the machine: Cook County, city hall, the CPD brass, or the Outfit machine. He cares about prestige. Maybe chief of detectives, maybe chief of police. Give him five years. He is embedded in this city like a tick.

Hanna's had rope because Hanna produces.

And Hanna *earned* this job. He thrives on it. He has his team behind him.

"From now on, I want to know every move you're going to make before you make it. No more goin' off like an unguided missile," Baumann says.

From here on, Hanna knows, it's about getting penned in.

That dog won't hunt.

Baumann gazes at him. "You hear what I'm sayin'?"

Hanna, in real time, feels a kind of distortion he can't put words to. It frustrates him. His experiences and what he will do are larger than Baumann and his maneuvering, larger than this place.

"I hear what you're saying. Are you hearing me? Wardell is all mine." Hanna's voice goes to a near whisper. "You hear me now? I want a clear path. Stay the fuck out of my way."

Baumann goes to reach for him. Hanna is ready. Novak holds Baumann back, gesturing to the nearby press.

25

Chris hoists the sledgehammer. His blond hair is dark with sweat. Cerrito positions the lock punch against the safe-deposit box.

Box three hundred.

The vault room stinks of sweat and old cash. They're exhausted. It's Sunday night.

Chris sledgehammers the lock, shoulders aching. Then he works the spring-steel hook into the hole and pops the relocker. The box door swings open.

Neil hauls the box out. Inside are half a dozen US, Canadian, and Mexican passports. Deeds to property. A marriage certificate. And rolls of cash. He stacks the cash in a gym bag. Chris grabs a bottle of water and guzzles it.

Neil sets the safe-deposit box aside and hears something rattle. At the back of it is a set of car keys, a stack of computer disks held together with a thick rubber band, and a Saint Christopher medal.

Chris and Cerrito move on to the next box. The sledgehammer lands with a series of clangs. Chris pops the relocker, pulls out the container, and flips open the lid.

"Yeah." He reaches in.

Gold bars.

Neil lets himself smile.

In here they've found jewelry, Krugerrands, three packets of uncut diamonds, and porn. A lot of porn. Some featuring a US senator.

Cerrito had held up a snapshot. *Neil, this shit could be worth more than anything else we've found.*

Blackmail? No. Rough take so far in cash alone is two million. Neil wiped sweat from his forehead. *And that's an impersonator. The senator isn't actually balling Elvis.*

They've ignored compromising photos, mounted jewelry, accounting ledgers. Set aside are the car keys, the stack of computer disks, and some bearer bonds they may keep or destroy later.

Neil checks his watch. "Thirty minutes left. Last ones."

Cerrito nods and picks up the sledgehammer. He's moving slowly but with tireless drive. They open the next box and Chris yanks the container out.

Cash. Emerald earrings, a pearl brooch. Photos—hippos in a pond in front of a South American hacienda.

Ruby-encrusted nipple clamps. Chris holds them up. "Some people got way too much money."

Cerrito muscles the lock out of the next box, springs the relocker, and hauls it out.

Gold coins. Silver bars. Cash. McCauley loads them up.

It's three a.m. He grabs a plastic garbage bag and begins collecting trash. They plan to leave nothing in the vault they've brought in. Not a scrap of paper. Not an eyelash. He sees a bank book he'd missed, riffles through it. Nothing. He sees the stack of computer disks he had put aside. He pauses. Why were they locked in a safe-deposit box? Kelso, according to Nate, said to be on the lookout for anything unusual. Given Kelso's knowledge of who patronized the bank, maybe they're something. Besides, Nate always says less when he's thinking more. Neil tosses the computer disks in the gym bag.

At 4:55 a.m., they pull the last of their equipment out of the vault. Neil takes a final look around. Empty safe-deposit containers litter the floor. The doors of boxes gape open all around the room. His shoulders throb. Beneath his gloves, his hands are blistered. His eyes are gritty. He slides through the breach in the wall, leaving the plundered vault dark.

Outside, the predawn darkness is cool, a shocking wakeup after fifty-four hours inside. Molina pulls the van up to the back of the empty store. They load everything and roll away in the quiet, before the city begins to rouse.

McCauley shakes hands with Molina when Danny drops him, Chris, and Cerrito at the switch car. Pink dawn light is brushing the street. Molina will dispose of the van and the equipment they used in the vault. Neil drops Cerrito at long-term parking at O'Hare. Michael parked a truck there ahead of the score. He has a two-hour drive to Milwaukee, where he's flying out later today. Michael humps a duffel onto his shoulder.

Neil leans over. "Get home, get ready for a call."

Cerrito gives him a look, bright-eyed. "You got it, sport. How soon?"

"Who knows," McCauley says. "Say hi to Elaine."

He and Chris head southwest on I-55. Their tickets are out of St. Louis, him to LAX, Chris to Vegas. The car is a Ford Taurus, serviceable, beige. Beige reminds him of pasty white men crowded into Folsom cellblocks. Of smothering closeness. He hates beige. But a cherried-out Ford Mustang wouldn't serve, even though he feels like putting the pedal down, feeling an engine roar beneath him, the road race away. Feels alive with success. And freedom.

One step at a time. He keeps to the speed limit. Chris spins the radio dial and finds Van Halen. He turns it up, rolls down the window, and lets the wind and the music scream.

Chris would have rented a Ford Mustang.

Ninety minutes out of Chicago, Neil stops at a gas station and finds a pay phone. The vast sky is a country blue he never sees in LA. Popcorn clouds. Clean. A flat horizon, green and empty. He drops the coins and leans on the hood of the phone booth. Hears a voice on the other end of the line. The day all at once feels even brighter, arcing into him a certainty about what he will make be.

"Hey, baby," Neil says. "I'm on my way to LA. See you soon."

26

Monday morning, ten a.m., Hanna and Casals watch Larry Levinson unlock the door at Levinson's TV & Appliance and flip the sign to OPEN. They come through five seconds later. Levinson hasn't even reached his desk.

His eyes go small. "Vincent."

Hanna shoves him in the chest. "Move."

"What is this?" Off-balance, backpedaling.

"What this is is telethon time. Get on the phone. Find me Otis Wardell."

"What's with you?" Levinson points at him. "You didn't get the message?"

"Message?" Hanna looks to the ceiling. "You mean like the skies parting? A hand came down through clouds. A finger pointed at me. 'Hanna. Hands off Levinson.' That message? I got it. Here's the answer. You're gonna find out where this sick cocksucker is laying off his merch, and you're gonna deliver that to me, because anybody who aids and abets him skipping out by not being forthcoming, forthright, and forthwith, their ass is going down along with this motherfucker."

Levinson doesn't say anything. Hanna spins him around and

pushes him forward to his desk. He stumbles on his vinyl executive chair, his face reddens, but he smooths his bald fringe of hair and pulls the phone toward him.

Hanna knows this will blow back. Baumann will go batshit. Wardell is out there, scrambling, cagey, determined. There's a window and it's closing. The clock's ticking. Hunting down Wardell is in Hanna's bloodstream and his blood is running. Fuck Baumann.

Casals, his voice severe but controlled, says, "You see that movie where the little girl blows up all the TV sets with her mind? That's Vincent two seconds from now."

Levinson gets on the phone. After five minutes of calls, he hangs up. "We wait."

"I'll be back in two hours," Hanna says.

Outside, Casals, tall and calm, seemingly always calm when Hanna gets wound up, says, "Give it time."

As they drive off, Hanna's body aches from the fall he took off the roof of the carjacked Mercedes. The abrasion on his forehead throbs. He is pissed that his suit got ruined. Pissed at the sunlight. Pissed that too many obstacles are in his way.

He knows how it works. He understood the way things run when he took the job. In Chicago, corruption is endemic, fair, and democratic. All citizens have the inalienable right to bribe everybody they can without having to be Standard Oil of New Jersey, the way you do in Southern California. If cash is recovered from a score, half that cash goes into a brown paper bag and disappears into a cop's trunk. Detectives will use it for bribes and informants. Maybe it becomes a new car or a remodeled kitchen. Nobody gets rich. And the cops on the beat and in the detectives' squads accommodate the guys they went to school with back at Holy Martyrs Elementary.

But right now, Hanna's going to make things work his way.

27

The sun is high and sharp when McCauley swings the Seville into his building in Marina del Rey. The salt tang catches him as he gets out, and the undertone of exhaust. Palms shirr in the breeze. He slings the duffel over his shoulder. Upstairs in his condo, the shower is running. He hears laughter from the bathroom behind the closed door. He puts the duffel behind the false panel in the closet.

An open powder-blue Samsonite suitcase is on the floor and a kid's backpack is on the kitchen counter, along with a beach towel drying on a chairback. Someone else is here. McCauley doesn't think twice about it. He takes the phone out onto the balcony.

A wide slice of beach, the spray from the breakers shimmering white in the air. Gulls wheel and shriek. McCauley leans on the railing and dials.

The man who answers speaks over glasses jostling, conversation, music in the background. "Blue Room."

"Put Nate on," McCauley says.

A minute later Nate picks up. "You back?"

"Yeah. You were right."

"How's that?" Nate drawls.

"Something turned up. I want it checked out. Computer disks."

The background Blue Room noise clatters. "I'll set it up."

Back inside the condo, the bathroom door opens. Elisa Vasquez comes out wrapped in Neil's terry robe, drying her eight-year-old daughter Gabriela's hair. She's in a towel, rubbing her eyes, then seeing him.

"Hola, Neil!" Gabriela says brightly, and runs across the kitchen raising her hand. They high-five.

"Hi, kid."

"Get dressed," Elisa says to Gabi as she's embraced in Neil's arms and he kisses her wet hair. She holds herself there while Gabriela runs off into the back bedroom with some clothes from the suitcase.

Neil clears the wet hair off her forehead.

Elisa's dark eyes look up into his face. "So, *mi amado*?" Her voice is low, a deep alto, surprising for a woman as slight and young as she is. "Everything is okay?"

Neil looks sideways, then back at her. That suppressed, under-stated smile. "Better than okay. Zero problems. Everything clicked."

She puts a hand to his cheek, her skin hot from the shower. Then she goes to his fridge, pulls out two beers, opens them, and returns. They clink bottles. She drinks, head tipped back, an arm draped around his neck. Her skin is flawless. Her lips flawless. Her self-possession and slow, hip-swinging walk flawless. Her calmness. The way she looks at him. He buries his face in her neck and kisses her where her pulse throbs.

What throbs within her is relief. It washes across her like a shallow wave on clean sand.

"Stay tonight," Neil says.

"Gabi has school in the a.m. So, I have to drive back. I thought you'd come yesterday."

"Me, too."

"But we have tonight, yes?" Elisa's accent mixes northern Mexico and Rio Grande Tejano. She grew up in Eagle Pass, Texas, and Piedras Negras, Coahuila. Her family has lived along la frontera for four hundred years.

She sinks against him, her lips warm, everything warm, her eyes and her laugh.

And Elisa's pragmatic and her nerves are solid steel. She is more seasoned and steady than anyone he's ever met. She is an open book to him. And he to her. Her cousin Alejandro was in Folsom with Neil. That's how they met. She knows all about him.

"I'm starving," Gabriela says, returning in a Dragon Ball T-shirt and pink Reeboks.

"Okay, hotshot. You up for a steak?"

"How about fish fingers?"

"I want to take your mom someplace special tonight. How about I get you spaghetti at Enrico's?"

"Deal."

To Elisa he says, "I'll drive down to El Centro Wednesday."

She takes his hand.

28

Chris comes screaming back into Vegas in a black Audi Quattro. He checks into the Mirage. He has a plan. He has cash. He has a week before Neil needs him sane and straight and ready to roll. He takes a suite overlooking the Strip, orders a rib eye and a bottle of bourbon, and picks up the phone. Standing at the window with the sun blasting in, he takes out the business card he rifled from Charlene's purse on the night they shared.

The only thing on the card is a 702 phone number. That and the scent of perfume. He doesn't know what. Obsession. Opium. Her.

He's coming off a big win and on a roll. Golden, glowing, and scoring like a champ.

He will find her. He dials.

A woman answers. "Desert Dreams."

Desert Dreams. The service she works for wants to be discreet. He has a plan for that, too, and a connection to make it happen.

"I'm in town on business and I'd like to have a local tour guide show me the sights."

"This is the answering service. I can forward your request, and one of our managers will arrange it and get back to you." He hears typing. "Anyone in particular?"

"Yeah." The sun catches his eyes, an ultraviolet flash. "My buddy said to ask for Cinnamon."

Charlene strides into the bar at the Flamingo before sunset, zipped into a white leather halter dress that contrasts with her tan. The music, the chatter, and the ringing of nearby slots help switch her into work mode. She's early. She's up. Before heading over, she popped two whites to lift herself into the right bright, pliable mood that might impress a new client.

Heads turn as she passes. Men look. Women look. The service said her client tonight is a guy, Bobby Valentine. What's he, a doo-wop singer from the '50s? Her manager, Keith—aka Dead Eye, aka the boyfriend who turned her out three weeks after she met him—has told her it doesn't matter if the client is a man, a woman, or an atomic mutant from the Nevada Testing Site.

Dead Eye thinks he's funny. Sometimes he is. Not lately. She told him she would blow a Minuteman missile if it tipped her well enough. He didn't laugh.

There were times, when she first came to town, when she was hungry, that she let customers take whatever they wanted of her for a few casino chips and a meal. She resists thinking about those days. These days, when she enters a room, heads swivel in desire or envy. But these days aren't, in truth, that much different from the bad times. She's twenty-two. She's tired.

She's getting by. But this life doesn't let you get ahead. Not even in Vegas, this shiny, lying town. She walks, shoulders back, thinking, *I got here.* Got out of North Dakota, that nightmare. Not even sad that her dad has since died of a stroke, the fucker, and that her mom is smoking herself to death. Vegas isn't the end of any road she wants.

At the bar, she slides onto a stool. She puts down a ten and asks the bartender for a seven and seven. The woman, older, in a white dress shirt, black vest, and tie, sets it on the napkin.

"Would you be Charlene?"

She stills. Bobby Valentine had requested Cinnamon. "Who's asking?"

"None of my business, honey." The woman reaches under the bar and pulls out a fat envelope. "This was delivered for you."

Charlene thanks her, and the bartender leaves. She opens it.

"Shit," she whispers.

Inside is a stack of fresh hundred-dollar bills. She doesn't pull them out, but riffles through them. Ten thousand dollars. And a note, on stationery from the Mirage.

Go home, change into jeans and shoes you can walk in. I'll meet you outside Caesars in an hour. The cash is to cover everything you need, anything anybody might ask of you. Tonight, tomorrow, whenever.

Take a chance on me.

Something lights inside her. Anger and laughter. That arrogant, crazy, magical wild boy. She slides off the stool and heads for the exit.

She's standing on the sidewalk outside Caesars when he roars up in a black Audi Quattro, the top-end D11. She's wearing jeans and Chuck Taylors and a white peasant blouse, feeling gruesomely underdressed for the Strip. He leans over and pushes the passenger door open.

"Bobby Valentine?" She smiles.

Chris laughs.

She gets in. Bon Jovi hammers from the stereo. Chris is chewing gum, looking lean, fine, and confident, like a king about to ride into a conquered city. Black polo, black combats, those cloudless blue eyes, that thrumming sense of danger.

Not danger to her, but to anybody who would threaten her.

"Where are we going?" she says.

"Let's find out." He puts the Audi in gear and blasts away from the curb.

They drive into the desert, 90 miles an hour, toward the sunset. Toward the blue shadows that knife from the mountains. It's a cool evening, the music is a drug, and Chris has his hand in hers as he swings off the highway onto a dirt road and rockets across the countryside. He stops atop an arroyo that overlooks the glittering bowl of the city.

He kills the engine. Turns to her. "Admit it. You hoped I'd be back."

She gets out and walks to the lip of the arroyo, hands jammed in her pockets. He comes up behind her and slides his arms around her waist. He's tall and warm, and Jesus God, she hasn't felt anything like his physical *presence* in forever. She's pulsing, every inch of her.

"What are we doing?" she says.

"Told you I wanted to find you again."

"I don't want you as a client, Chris."

"Good, 'cause I want you to quit."

She scoffs. "What, you going to keep me as your own private E-ticket ride?"

"No." He brushes her hair back and kisses her neck. "I want you with me. Period."

She turns and presses herself to him. Jesus *fuck*, he is naive. He is a god. She pushes him toward the car.

"You brought a blanket, I hope."

She pulls his shirt off, kissing him. Unzips his pants. He hoists her up. She wraps her legs around his waist.

She will work it out with him after. After. Holy God.

Later, sitting on the hood of the Audi, she asks Chris about himself, needing to know if he will be truthful.

"Did time," he says.

Admits it. Good, because she's picked up on that from the beginning, starting with his wariness, the way his eyes scan the room, looking for danger and clocking all the exits. And that hair-trigger readiness to take anybody down.

"You like Vegas?" he says.

"Do you like sand in your food?"

"Then why you here?"

"Ever been to Minot, North Dakota?"

"Is that in California?"

"Exactly."

He leans back on his elbows. "You got out of that place." He gazes at the distant shiver of the Vegas lights. "Why not this one?"

It pops into her head: *Next*. She hasn't thought of that since . . . when? It's always *now*. And *numb*.

She came to Vegas to get out from under her fundamentalist parents, the shit parts of growing up as an air force brat. She doesn't tell Chris the bad stuff about men her father knew, who saw a well-developed thirteen-year-old and decided she was theirs to take.

"Life is short," Chris says. "You keep moving, grab what you want, while you can. That's it."

A clear, bell-like sound rings through her.

Think beyond tonight, Charlene. Wake up.

"You're right."

He turns to her. "Then let's do it."

She's sitting with her bare feet propped up on the hood, leaning back, gold-tinged hair swirling around her shoulders in the desert breeze.

"I thought it was chance," Chris says. "Seeing you in the casino. It was magic. And when magic strikes, everything changes." He takes her hand. "I live in LA. Come out there with me and right now."

She turns slowly. Checks him out. To see if he's nuts, or a fool, running way ahead of himself. "What would that look like?"

"You could do anything you want. I work construction. With a small outfit—transportation, logistics, demolition. Good money."

Her expression flattens. "Ten grand in an envelope with my name on it. That good?"

"Seasonal work, the paydays are big. Then I bring it to Vegas and . . ." He snaps his fingers. Grins. "*Boom*."

She looks at him. Serious. Thinking for real.

"I can't just leave," she says.

"Why not?"

Her expression says, *Don't you know? Don't you get it?*

"Think I'm gonna let anybody hurt you?" he says. "Never."

"How's that work, exactly?"

"You want to leave? You leave. Nothing holds you here."

She looks at him skeptically.

"Do you want out of here?" he says.

"Yes." She thinks, *I have to.*

It's time to be smart. *Next.*

"How?" she says.

"You tell him you're done."

"I owe—"

"Nothing. His cut? Your fee? You square it. You're done."

"You know that's not how it works, right?"

He stands up. "Charlene, that's how it's gonna work. For us. And I'll go with you."

He thinks, *It's Vegas. It's magic,* and he's on a winning streak. He is in the witching hour. And he has a plan.

"I know what I'm doing," he says.

The wind rises. The sun falls behind the peaks. The vibrating city lights in the distance look cold and indifferent.

"Yeah," she says. "Okay. But I want to go alone. If I'm going to do this, I want to do it."

He gets it, nods along.

She lives in a cheap apartment with two other girls from the escort service. Been there a year, owns nothing except her bed and the flea-market dresser, doesn't care about any of it. Clothes, her car—when she inventories it, things don't add up to much. Eighteen months here, partying, getting paid to put out, gaining a skill set she can never put on a résumé. Far from Minot, North Dakota, a small stash of cash. Making sure she never has to go back. Burying herself in nothing, in glitter, glazing it with weed, whiskey, smack, whites. Morning, noon, night, none of it matters.

Worn down, worn out.

Until right fucking now.

She packs, throwing her clothes, makeup, and shoes in a suitcase. Doesn't care about the plants or the food in the fridge. She leaves a note for her roommates: *It's yours. Got to go.* She doesn't stick around to hug them goodbye.

She has to wrap it up with Dead Eye.

She finds him at his regular hang, a bar south of the Strip where he has an interest, keeps a booth, takes calls. He is still a handsome charmer, but skinnier than when they first met, his eyes now constantly wired. Success has gone up his nose. He is, she knows, paranoid.

She walks in the dark bar and heads straight for him. He has a tumbler of Jack in front of him.

"Why are you dressed like a hick?" he says. "Your john want to play *Green Acres*?"

She puts down her night's fee, plus an extra three thousand.

"What's this?" Dead Eye says.

"Tonight's take. Plus a little extra."

He squints at her. One eyelid droops, heavy. From a fight, he sometimes says. From getting slashed, sometimes. From a botched forceps delivery, she thinks. He has plenty of lies.

He sucks on his teeth. Suspicious. He's always suspicious now. He organizes her appointments, protects her from the vagaries of the street, simplifies things. He gives her a cut that lets her pay the rent and for groceries and partying. Keeps the machine running. But he has that look now.

"That ain't how it works, sugar," he says.

"Sure it is. We're square."

"What kind of shit is this?"

"This kinda shit ain't shit. It's cash."

"You quitting on me? Jumping to some other outfit?" He tilts his head, his eyes shifting back and forth. "I ain't traded you up and you ain't stupid enough to go renegade. If you think you can choose up with someone else, that won't fly."

She nods at the money. "Count it. It's there, with interest. And I'm out."

She turns and leaves. She makes it halfway across the bar before she hears him knock over a chair as he follows her.

"Don't you fucking walk away from me," Dead Eye calls.

Escalating, like the fool he is. Needing to prove himself to the regulars who are slumped at the bar.

Her heart thumping, she walks out. It's dark, and the walk across the parking lot to her car all at once looks endless.

The bar door slams open behind her. She hurries to her car, jumps in, and hits the locks.

Dead Eye thunders up and pounds on the window. "You're going nowhere, bitch."

She starts the engine. He rattles the door handle. She puts it in gear.

"Fucking whore," he yells.

She pulls away. In the mirror she sees him run to his old Eldorado and jump in.

Charlene accelerates up the wide street, heading toward the Strip.

She wants to get to the Mirage and get out of sight. Meet up with Chris. Drive out in the morning when Dead Eye is too hungover to chase her down.

But in the mirror, she sees Dead Eye's headlights as he pulls out of the parking lot. He swerves and straightens and heads straight for her, a block back, coming hard. He hits the brights.

Her throat tightens. What is she doing? What if he catches her?

No giving up, no going back. She puts the pedal down. The road runs straight. The lights ahead are green. She races through an intersection. Dead Eye's headlights flare in the rearview, closing, painfully bright.

She runs a red. He follows. She hears his engine revving.

Then, behind him, a new set of headlights appears.

The Audi.

Chris closes on Dead Eye. He swings wide, edges his right front wheel alongside the Eldorado, then taps its left rear wheel and steers right. Dead Eye swerves and spins out.

The Eldorado mounts the sidewalk and smashes into a telephone pole.

Charlene pulls a sharp U-turn, mouth wide, and stops. Dead Eye's car is wrecked, flames licking beneath the front wheels and running up the telephone pole. Smoke boils black into the night, swirling under his headlights.

The Eldorado's door opens and Dead Eye stumbles out.

Nearby, Chris has stopped. He climbs from the Audi, strides up to the shambling Dead Eye, grabs him by the shirt, and punches him in the head. Then again. He pours down blows, driving him to the pavement, until Dead Eye lies limp on the asphalt. Chris stands over him, breathing heavily. He kicks him ferociously and walks back to his car.

The night goes firework bright as the Eldorado's gas tank explodes.

Charlene gasps. A roar fills her ears and rattles the steering wheel. Then, blinking her head clear, she spins the wheel and drives away.

In the rearview she can't see Dead Eye anymore. But she sees headlights emerge from the smoke. Chris closes up behind her.

Her heart is racing. She drives.

29

McCauley pulls up the hill in East LA, to City Terrace. A fierce sunset ignites the sky pink and gold. The view unrolls in all directions—downtown, the Hollywood sign, the San Gabriel Mountains, the ocean in the distance. Below, six lanes of red taillights snake eastbound and six lanes of white headlights westbound on the I-10. Up here, the air smells of dust and eucalyptus.

East LA has personality, plenty of it. Murals, Chevy lowriders, bodegas, statues of the Virgin, mariachi, kids in Catholic school uniforms. And young men in white tees under plaid shirts, narco-corridos, and enough gunfire to be mistaken for Beirut despite the million-dollar view. Families who live on this hill keep their windows shut and eyes open against stray bullets. Gang activity doesn't inhibit McCauley. He understands its rules and has contacts with La eMe members in Folsom.

He turns onto Dodds Circle. The place is up a steep driveway bounded by cyclone fencing topped with barbed wire. He stops at a rolling gate and presses a buzzer.

He's bought two jobs from the man who lives here, through Nate, but has never met him. Less exposure. The fewer people who know you, what you look like, your crew, the better. But for this, he's coming in person. He wants to keep the computer disks in his possession.

The gate motors open. At the top of the drive, towering antennas and huge parabolic dishes bristle beside a squat yellow house. Nate's Buick is parked outside. McCauley pulls up on the bare dirt beside it.

At the house, a sliding glass door opens and a long-limbed man comes out in a rugged old wheelchair. Kelso is bald with a Klondike beard, wearing a blue plaid shirt that looks like he wrestled it off a lumberjack, or the grizzly that killed the lumberjack.

McCauley nods at the dishes. "You get Russian sat comms on those, or just HBO?"

Kelso smiles puckishly. "Come in."

His lair is simple: Scandinavian furniture, marijuana plants, and wall-to-wall computers, monitors, TVs, and peripherals, with cables snaking over every surface except the floor where Kelso might run over them. Nate is standing by the windows with a cup of coffee. Long hair slicked back, eyes keen. Neil nods to him.

Kelso says, "Show me what ya got."

Neil hands over the rubber-banded stack of computer disks.

"You looked at them?" Kelso says.

"No."

Kelso heads to a brutish computer with an external drive attached. He inserts the first disk from the stack. Neil stands at his shoulder. The external drive hums and chugs. A dialogue box appears on the computer screen.

Enter password.

"Gonna be a problem?" Neil says.

Kelso's long fingers skitter across the keyboard. "I'll run a pass-word challenge program. We'll see."

Neil looks at Nate, who sips his coffee.

After ninety seconds, Kelso pauses. "Gonna take time. Want to head down to El Tepeyac and pick up dinner?" Keeping his eyes on the screen, he holds up a twenty-dollar bill. "Two Hollenbeck burritos for me."

It takes him two and a half hours. Dinner's finished, paper plates in the kitchen trash, when Kelso hits Return.

"In." He begins opening directories and folders.

"That as complicated as it looked?" McCauley says.

"Triple-factor authentication. Sixteen-character password, but no lockout for failed attempts. That was a security weakness."

Kelso's head juts forward, focused. He opens a folder. Nate saun-ters over.

McCauley peers over Kelso's shoulder. "What do we got?"

"Spreadsheets. It's in Lotus, not some home-brewed program, should be readable—but let's see."

Kelso clicks. A spreadsheet opens, white text against black background. Columns of data. The numbers look random. The headers are illegible. Not a foreign language—gibberish.

Kelso leans back. "The information's coded. Not encrypted, but a cipher." He glances at Neil. "Got any clue to the key?"

Neil stares at the screen.

Kelso takes his reticence as a sign. He ejects the disk. "Come on."

He wheels down a hall to a black steel door. He slides a key card along a vertical lock, then punches a code into a keypad. With a click, the door opens. Overhead lights turn on automatically when he goes in. Nate and Neil follow. Kelso locks the door behind them.

The room is windowless, the walls covered in gray egg-carton acoustic tile. The air conditioner is blasting. Computer fans drone and an electric hum runs in the background. Workbenches line three walls, covered in tools, test equipment, components, and disassembled electronics, along with three desktop computers. Two Sun386i workstations stand side by side along the fourth wall, stacked four feet high atop hard drives.

Neil takes it in. "The hum?"

"This is a Faraday cage. Nobody can overhear or intercept anything."

Neil says, "The disks came from a box rented by a guy connected to the Herreras."

Kelso looks thoughtful. Nate holds still, his small eyes acute.

Neil nods. "Yeah. Those Herreras."

Who have been running major drug distribution from the southern border up into the Midwest through Chicago since the late '40s.

Kelso inserts the disk in a desktop machine. Gets straight in, opens the spreadsheet, and peers meditatively at the screen.

"The code uses the Roman alphabet. Twenty-six letters, no numbers, no symbols—this ain't the Zodiac's spreadsheet," he says. "It may be a simple substitution cipher. I'll start there."

When he finally says, "Yeah," it's been another hour. Neil approaches the screen and sees the headers in plain English.

Warehouse. Waypoint 1. Waypoint 2 . . . 19. Depot. Mileage. Time. Date. Weight. Amount.

"Shipping records," he says.

He scrutinizes them. Kelso uncovers notes typed in the memo field.

They mention the locations of speed traps, list weigh stations, note empty stretches of highway where there are no gas stations or breakdown recovery services. Reports of problems: a flat tire, stopped and ticketed for a busted taillight.

Nate comes closer. Reads. Kelso runs through various columns of figures. After a couple of minutes, he points.

"This is dope going north. Coke and marijuana, I'm guessing. Weights, who's driving." He points at a second column. "This is money going south."

Neil follows the thread. Dates, times, distances. It looks like algebra.

Kelso says, "Delivery records for a stash house. And dollar amounts—by weight."

Neil eyes it all. "The Herreras' Chicago take is collected and rolled up in the city, then transported south." He taps the dates on the screen. "Weekly. This is the transport schedule. Departure from Chicago. Arrival at 'Depot.'"

He, Nate, and Kelso stare at the screen.

"Where's the depot?" Nate says.

"Can't tell," Kelso says. "The log doesn't say."

"Got a map of the US and Mexico?" Neil asks.

"Kitchen junk drawer."

Neil brings it in and unfolds it on the workbench. By cross-referencing it with the shipment logs, they build a geographic model of the routes taken and the shipments being transported.

"It's regular," Neil says. "The cash. Clockwork."

He doesn't care about the drugs coming north. Hijacking a cartel shipment? Aside from the risk, how would he move it? He's not in that business. Nate doesn't care, either, though he is hooked into many markets, domestic and international. But laying off a stolen cartel shipment, they'd eventually find you and get all Aztec on your ass.

But cash money?

Kelso decrypts the rest of the disks. Poring over the shipment logs, they discern the distances. From waypoints they find on expense reports, they discover the route the cash truck drives out of Chicago. As if solving a logic puzzle, working backward from average mileage estimates, based on where the cash truck refilled, they zero in on likely departure points. Neil feels a flash of adrenaline. It's an area of warehouses on Chicago's South Side.

"Give me a number," Neil says. "The cash."

Kelso scrolls through the spreadsheets, grabs a calculator, and smashes some numbers.

He looks up. Serene. "By weight, on the right day, and assuming an equal spread of fives, tens, and twenties from retail sales going south, four-point-five million."

Neil goes silent.

Nate crosses his arms. Kelso looks back and forth between them.

"Forget taking it in Chicago," Neil says. "We took down the vault score in Chicago. Whoever stored the disks in the safe-deposit box will tighten security there."

"They'll also know their routes might be compromised," Nate says.

But the farther the shipment travels from Illinois, the more variable the spreadsheet reports become. After what they guess is St. Louis, the cash truck takes at least four different routes south and southwest. The route it will take on any particular run is impossible to predict. The destination—the "depot"—is never identified. They can't tell the route's endpoint. But they can tell one thing.

Every shipment log ends with a report on a border crossing. Date, time of day, which US border station, wait times, how many guards on duty. Their names. Their attitudes. How greasy their palms are.

Huge shipments of money are funneling into one stash house south of the border.

Neil nods his thanks at Kelso. "Nate said two grand."

Kelso leads them out. "If this turns into something, keep me in mind."

Neil and Nate walk toward their cars. The city below is a shimmering grid of lights.

"The cash truck leaves the Chicago warehouse," Neil says. "Heavy security there. But once it hits the highway, the Herreras won't be looking for trouble. With every mile that nothing happens, they'll let down their guard."

"Don't presume the Herreras' real-world security has holes like their computer security," Nate says. "Guns are more reliable than passwords, and bullets don't need decryption."

Neil stares across the hill at the snaking traffic on the 10. "One hole in their security tells me, look for another one. In procedures, OPSEC, information hygiene, routines. They believe they're ahead of the game. And think about it—whoever's name's on that box ain't doing a news flash that someone got the disks. It's too dangerous for him."

"You think those disks aren't the only copies of the information," Nate says.

"I think they're backups. That was a private box. No other business records. Personal shit. Maybe they're somebody's out—with the cartel, the feds, a rival cartel, if they want to change allegiance." He mulls it. "Whether they're backups or an insurance policy, the disks belong to somebody in Chicago who's not going to warn somebody in the Herrera organization that he lost them."

"Take the cash truck when it leaves the city?" Nate says.

Neil shakes his head. "We could. Easy. But that would be *a* cash truck."

"You think there's more than one?"

"Need to find out."

"That depot." Nate's eyes narrow. "The stash house."

One truck. $4.5 million on a good day.

Nate's expression is cold. "It's a drug cartel. It's probably a fortress."

McCauley falls silent. That kind of score offers up a life-changing payday. Walking away from the possibility seems insane.

But walking into a narco fortress sounds suicidal.

He won't take on a suicidal job. And he won't take his crew on one.

He needs to know more.

"I gotta tail a Herrera cash delivery. Find that depot and see what's up."

Neil drives to Randy's Donuts off the 405, near LAX. The possibilities of this score are astounding. He needs to scope it out.

He orders coffee from the window and walks across the parking lot to a pay phone. The giant doughnut rises above the roof of the shack. Palm trees are backlit by headlights from the freeway. He drops a handful of quarters into the slot and punches in a 312 number.

A gruff voice answers. "Mickey's Auto Repair."

"Grimes in?"

The phone clatters. Soon Aaron Grimes comes on. "Yeah?"

"Call me back at this number from a pay phone."

He hangs up. Drinks his coffee. Watches traffic, LA sludging by, workingmen and -women, doing the day-to-day in the ozone-tinged air.

Possibilities. The more he thinks about it, the more solid it reads to him.

The stash house might be a fortress. Might not. And wherever it is, he and his crew would be operating in a foreign country. McCauley speaks Angeleno Spanish. Shiherlis speaks some. Cerrito none at all. He would need someone fluent. And knowledgeable about Mexico.

The pay phone rings. He picks up. Grimes says, "What do you need?"

"An eighteen-wheeler."

He waits, hoping Grimes won't hesitate.

"What kind?"

"A car transporter."

There's a five-second pause. "How soon?"

30

Otis Wardell has made himself disappear. *Boom*, gone. He can't be found, hasn't been seen, at least not by anybody willing to report it. Not his estranged brother. Not his dead crew's next of kin. Hanna has surveillance on them, has wires on their phones, but nothing. He's spoken to three families who fostered Otis Wardell as a child, after he was removed from his violent, abusive mother. Nobody from the foster families has seen him. No one wants to. One sounds sad. One sounds scared.

The guy has gone underground. Hanna knows Wardell has a network of prison and neighborhood acquaintances, and people under his thumb who might protect him.

But Wardell is *somewhere,* Hanna thinks, maybe still in Chicago, maybe figuring out how to get out.

Because that is what Wardell will do, if he is better than stupid. Get out, try to set up again somewhere new under an alias. Wardell is a wild card. He isn't hooked in. The Outfit wants nothing to do with somebody like him. Maybe Wardell has a woman. Maybe he's holding somebody hostage until he can arrange his out. But he doesn't want to show himself, Hanna feels certain.

At CID, late morning, he's at the whiteboard when Easton fills the doorway, crosses to his desk, puts his sidearm in a drawer, and thumps into his seat.

He examines Hanna's face. "You're starting to look pretty again."

The scabs on Hanna's forehead are healing. The bruises and aches are better. He doesn't care. Basic training at Camp Pendleton felt worse than this.

"When you get covered in assholes, stop, drop, and roll," he says. "For any kind of an out, Wardell needs money. Maybe he's got some from the earlier scores."

"Maybe in a safe-deposit box in Prosperity Savings & Loan?" Easton's expression is sardonic.

"Karma calling?"

"I talked to the uniforms who responded to the bank. They roll up.

Wiseguys are sitting on the curb, heads in their hands. Cops ask, 'Do you have a box in there, sir?' 'No.' 'Lose anything?' 'No.' While they're wiping their eyes."

Hanna grabs the phone and calls Levinson's TV & Appliance. "Larry."

Levinson's sigh seems to have sparks in it. "I was just pickin' up the phone to call you."

"And I was just suiting up for the Bulls to replace Jordan. Whaddaya got?"

"A tip. Look for the brother."

Hanna perks up. "Brother? Whose brother? Otis Wardell? His crew?"

"It's vague, Vincent. His crew are all fringe fuckups. But if you want to find Wardell, sniff out the guys around him and find one of 'em's brother."

"Fringes. Vehicles? Weapons, equipment? Some fuckin' guy who pours him a beer?"

"I got this for you. Do with it what you will." Levinson hangs up.

Hanna raps his knuckles on his desk. To the bullpen, he says, "Everybody you talk to? Ask about the guys on the edge of Wardell's crew. Find out about one of them's brother."

On the desk are snapshots of Wardell and his crew. Maybe one of the home invasion victims will recognize them without their masks. He scoops them up.

"I'll be back."

Andi Matzukas is sitting up in a chair beside her hospital bed. The afternoon sky is bright blue through the window. Hanna pulls her tray table over and lays out a photo lineup. Shots of white men—a mix of mug shots and CPD colleagues, with Wardell's crew mixed in.

He sets five black-and-white pics side by side.

She eyes them carefully. "Can I touch them?"

"Of course."

She has more energy now.

"She's out of the coma," Andi says.

Hanna stops abruptly. "Jessica?"

"She's awake, not all there, in and out. But she's going to live."

His energy stops, jagged and sharp.

"Yeah, Mr. Tough Detective. The nurses told me how you visit and talk to her. Show me the photos."

Now she's staring at them, jaw clenched. She shakes her head.

"I don't . . ." She swears under her breath. "They wore masks."

"Their eyes? Eye color? Lips?" Hanna says.

She pauses. "No."

He lays out another set. She scoffs. Flicks at a photo of Alex Dalecki.

"The parking valet. That little prick. I want to bleach the car to disinfect everywhere he touched."

"You definitely recognize him."

"Oh, yeah. At the hair salon. Running, schmoozing, chatting, flirting."

He nods at the rest of the photos. "Anybody else?"

Her face is tight. Wardell's mug shot is right in front of her. She doesn't clock it.

Hanna says, "No problem. It was a long shot."

She looks disappointed. He says, "Don't be discouraged. Three of these guys are already dead. You do not have to worry about identifying them. We're looking for all known associates of the crew. Fourth and fifth guys are on the run. You are safe, Jessica is safe."

She nods.

He slides the photos into a manila envelope. "Rest up, get out of the hospital. I'll see you soon. I'm going to see if I can see her."

He runs down the stairs two at a time, slapping the envelope against his thigh. He swings down the hall toward Jessica's room. The nurse at the desk sees him and smiles. He pushes through the door.

The TV is on. The machines are beeping. The blinds are half-open, a soft light falling across the foot of the bed. Jessica Matzukas lies on her side, watching a game show.

Hanna stops. He takes her in. Her pale face, the new pose, a girl brought back from limbo. Her hair needs brushing. Her face is the color of flour, dark circles beneath her eyes.

Brown eyes, open.

She slowly turns her head to look at him. He's hoping for recognition.

"Who are you?" she says weakly.

She doesn't know him at all.

He speaks quietly. "Jessica. I am Detective Vincent Hanna."

She blinks. Her focus sharpens, though not by much.

Does she know how long she was unconscious? Does she remember any of it? Does she know her father is dead? He wishes that part could stay blanked out forever.

"I came to say hello, and to tell you that I am very glad that you are back with us," he says. "I was talking to your mom."

Rise, Jessica. Rise.

"Hi." Her voice is cracked, young. She doesn't seem able to say more than that. But she looks at the flowers on the windowsill he brought earlier: daisies and carnations.

"Thought they'd brighten the place up," he says.

All her fragile energy is going into maintaining her newfound consciousness. But she moves her hand, maybe an inch. A thumbs-up.

"I want you to know what's going on," he says, "so you won't worry."

She looks at him.

"You're safe," he says. "The people who hurt you are not coming back."

She doesn't move. Not exactly. But an aura seems to shimmer around her.

She inhales. Her chin trembles. Her eyes glisten.

Hanna steps closer and sets the manila envelope on the bedside tray so he can take her hand, as he's done before. He stops himself. Awake, she doesn't know him.

"You're a survivor. You're strong. I want to make sure you know that," he says.

He isn't going to question her. He only wanted to see for himself that she has turned the corner. But man, he wants to.

"When you're up to it, we'll talk," he says.

The door opens, and a young doctor sweeps in with a nurse.

"Hi, Detective," the doctor says, rushed. "Out. That's enough for today."

The nurse, the one who smiled when Hanna arrived, beckons. He follows her out.

"The doctor's hopped up on caffeine," she says. "Give him a second."

He walks with her toward the desk. A minute later, the doctor leaves Jessica's room. He gives Hanna a cold look and continues down the hall to his next patient.

The nurse reads his mind. "She's going to be here for a while. You can come back."

He raises his hands. "You're the boss."

She gives him a sardonic look. "Right."

A scream erupts from Jessica's room.

Hanna sprints up the hall with the nurse behind him. The screaming continues. He jams through the door. Jessica is sitting up, hunched over, mouth wide. She has a photo in her hand.

The screaming turns to sobs. He takes the photo. It's from the manila envelope, which he'd left on the tray table. It's Alex Dalecki.

She shakes, gasping. The nurse bends over her.

Hanna takes the photo. "You recognize this guy?"

She nods frantically.

"From where?" Hanna says.

"My house."

He feels it like a falling blade. "Your house?"

She bares her teeth and looks like she wants to claw her way through the bedding to the floor and keep on going. Then she explodes with rage. "He took me upstairs. I thought he was going to lock me in my room so they could get away . . ."

Her face crumples.

The nurse tries to get her to lie down.

Jessica won't lie back. "He punched me." She puts a hand to her throat. "Choked me . . ." She's shuddering. "I jammed my thumbs in his eyes."

Hanna nearly shouts, "This guy?"

The nurse points at him. "Detective."

Jessica wants to tell him. And he wants to hear it. Hanna rounds the bed and draws closer to the girl.

Jessica keeps talking. "He pulled back, and his mask came off."

The hair on the back of Hanna's neck stands up. "You saw his face?"

With a shaky finger, she points at Alex's photo. "Him. He punched me again. I was on the floor, and he had my lamp in his hands . . ."

Her breath catches. Hanna takes her hand. "You're okay, you're okay! He's in Cook County Jail. We arrested him. You are totally safe."

She presses her free hand over her eyes. Her other holds his hand tightly.

31

The sun is rising, orange in a steamy Chicago sky, when Aaron Grimes slows and maneuvers the tractor-trailer rig into the alley behind the auto repair shop. He parks, gets out, and rolls up the doors on the commercial garage across the alley.

The legit work cars McCauley asked for are parked inside. Grimes loads them onto the eighteen-wheeler's trailer, the car transporter. The last car is a three-year-old Plymouth. He drives it cautiously onto the top rack and chains it down. He clambers off the trailer. He collects all the keys for the work cars, all the registration documents. He turns and admires the rig.

What a magnificent thing it is.

Gleaming, a blue Peterbilt tractor, older but in prime condition, well cared for. The seven cars and pickup loaded on the trailer are newer-ish, plausible, a mishmash. Nothing flashy. The kind of vehicles that monopolize the highways. American, and an American-made Honda Accord. Bland, common, unremarkable. The rig will be indistinguishable from other eighteen-wheelers on the interstate system heading south.

He circles it. Exceptional.

McCauley appears at the head of the alley, striding toward him without a word. Sunglasses on, baseball jacket zipped. Grimes nods tightly.

McCauley and his crew are like a sheet of black ice, slick and cold. Grimes knows better than to ask McCauley about his business. He's curious. He's certain the bank score on the North Side near Wrigley Field was theirs. And he knows better than to ask about it.

McCauley nears. He eyes the rig. Walks around it silently.

He comes back to Grimes, looks at the rig, back at Grimes. "Good."

"She's ready to roll."

"Documents?"

"In the glove boxes. Rig's all set. There's maps with weigh stations noted. Everything's shipshape. It'll pass inspection."

"Tools?"

Grimes points at the Ford F-150 pickup truck that has a hard cover installed over its cargo bed. "Loaded per your spec."

McCauley hikes up into the cab of the Peterbilt. The keys are in the ignition. He turns it over. The engine rumbles satisfyingly to life.

He takes an envelope from his jacket. "Good work."

He hands it to Grimes and shuts the cab door. Grimes raises a hand to bid him goodbye. McCauley puts the Peterbilt in gear and pulls out, slow and smooth, without looking back. Grimes watches him go, watches the rig make a wide turn onto the street and disappear.

When he turns toward the auto repair shop, Otis Wardell is standing outside the service bay, hands hanging loose at his sides.

"Where's that rig going?"

32

Hanna pulls up in a hurry outside Shakespeare Station. Casals strides out and jumps in. Hanna's tires shriek as he accelerates away.

"Fucking parking valet went on the thrill ride. He was inside the house. He's the one who attacked Jessica."

He hits his flashers, planning to head downtown. Casals shakes his head.

"Don't bother with Cook County. He's out."

Hanna hits the brakes. "He made bond?"

"Last night." Casals points up the road. He knows where Hanna wants to go.

Hanna guns the car onto the cross street and heads for Alex Dalecki's apartment. "How the hell did he post bail?"

"Family," Casals says.

Hanna drives, foot heavy on the gas.

Twenty minutes later, they're coming up the stairs at Alexander Dalecki's six-story yellow brick apartment building. West of downtown in the shadow of skyscrapers, it's nondescript, with struggling trees next to broken sidewalks. Across the street is a strip mall.

The hall is long and dark, the carpet worn. At Alex's door, Hanna puts his ear to the wood. It's dead quiet inside.

"Warrant?" Casals asks.

"I hear screaming," Hanna says. "A desperate cry for help."

"Sounds like a life-or-death struggle," Casals says.

Hanna tries the knob. Locked. He takes a set of picks from his wallet, crouches, and inserts two of them in the keyhole. He's rusty but tenacious. With thirty seconds of nudging, the pins in the tumbler align and the tension wrench turns, the bolt dropping into its slot. A bare nudge of the handle sets the door swinging open.

The apartment is small and messy. A roach clip sits in a butt-filled ashtray. Beer cans overflow a kitchen wastebasket and surround it on the floor, like supplicants trying to reach a shrine.

Alex is in bed, on his back, arms spread like Jesus, snoring. Hanna grabs him by a handful of hair.

"Get up, cocksucker."

He pulls him from the bed, goggle-eyed and gasping, and throws him against the wall.

Alex flails at him, slapping. "The fuck?"

"Motherfucker, you lied to me." Hanna shoves him into the living room.

"I told you everything, man." He's shivering, wearing only jeans, barefoot.

"And you lied to the prosecutor and the judge that all you did was pass along names and addresses of targets to Wardell, and that was it."

"Right," Alex says.

Hanna jabs Alex's bare chest with the heel of his palm. "Where's Wardell?"

Alex is awake now, and terrified. He wants to blend into the paint on the wall. "I don't know."

"You went along into the Matzukas house. You beat, raped, and nearly killed a fourteen-year-old girl."

"No, no, no! Swear to God I didn't do that! I didn't do that!"

Hanna spreads his arms. "God has eyes, asshole."

Alex looks away from him, looks at Casals, at the floor, wipes his nose. "I don't know nothin' about Otis Wardell." He holds his hands up, proclaiming his truth.

Hanna grabs his wrist, snaps it to the breaking point, twists his arm behind him, and projects Alex out the door barefoot toward the stairs.

"Jesus," Alex says. "Where we going? I got no shoes."

Hanna opens the fire door to the roof by shoving Alex through it and up the stairs to the roof. Casals follows.

"What are you doing? I don't know about Wardell!" Alex says. His nose is bleeding.

Alex's fear of Wardell is leaking from his pores like garlic. Hanna wants it replaced with a greater terror. At the top of the stairs he turns to Casals.

"Stay here. Nobody comes out on the roof."

"Shit, man," Alex says.

Hanna pushes him out into the late-afternoon air. Alex looks back through the closing door to Casals, maybe for help, maybe to ask, *Don't let him do this.* Casals's face is blank. The door closes.

"You're a member of this fucking crew. You held out on me."

"No, Hanna. I told you everything," Alex says.

Hanna pushes him across the tar-paper surface. Alex slips. "You afraid of Wardell? Fuck Wardell. You owe me your fear, you prick."

Alex raises his hands placatingly. "You gotta understand."

Hanna throws a right hook that slams Alex to the ground. He rolls and stands up, backing away toward the rear of the building where the tops of tall elms sway in the breeze. The skyscrapers in the distance stand silent. Nobody is around.

Hanna stalks him, yelling, "Where the fuck is Otis Wardell?"

Shaking his head, Alex tries to dodge past Hanna for the door. Hanna is faster. He catches and spins him around, tripping him. Alex stumbles to his feet.

"Is Wardell with your brother?" Hanna says.

"What? I got no brother."

"Is he with your fucking brother?"

"No. I don't got a brother. I got a sister, man—look it up."

"The only chance you have to come out of this alive is for you to tell me where Wardell is." Hanna's advancing toward him again. "I want anybody Wardell would hole up with. Who'll supply him with documents, transpo. How's he getting out of the city? Where'd the work cars come from that he used, the florist's van? You're part of this crew. You know."

Alex trips backward over the cable for a television antenna and catches himself.

In slow motion he shakes his head no. Hanna gets closer and closer to him.

"You ever see *Peter Pan*?" Hanna asks.

"Huh?"

"*Peter Pan*," Hanna asks again.

"The kiddie cartoon?"

"Yeah."

"No."

Hanna takes Alex by the elbow, as if to steer him to safety.

"Tinker Bell asks a fundamental question. You know what it is?"

"No," Alex says.

"Can you fly . . . ?"

"Stop. Stop. Okay." Alex raises his hands to ward off Hanna. "He forced me to come along. Said I had to be all in. All the time. He woulda killed me if I didn't go. I was compelled."

Hanna keeps backing him up. "Where is he?"

Alex shoots his hands out. "Stop, okay? He's holed up at this commercial vehicle place."

"Whose? How do you know he's there?"

"I know he's there. It's my sister's husband's place. He's there."

Hanna pauses. "Your sister's husband? Your brother-in-law?"

"Aaron Grimes."

Not a brother. A brother-in-law. "Part of Wardell's crew?"

Alex's head twists in the sun. "He supplies cars, is all."

"Work cars? To Wardell?" Hanna says.

"That's his business."

"Where's this garage?"

Alex gives him the address on West Roosevelt Road. "C'mon, man!" he shrieks. "I'm giving this to you. My sister will kill me. He's my brother-in-law!" He's shivering.

"Who gives a fuck if he's your brother-in-law? Who's Wardell got with him?"

Alex won't look at Hanna. "Maybe Hank. I don't know."

"Aaron Grimes isn't part of his crew?"

"He's a vendor, dude. That's his gig. He doesn't want Otis there."

"Really?"

"Who would?" Alex says. "C'mon, man! What about me? I'm giving up my own brother-in-law. Okay? We're square, right? Shit, man—I told you everything."

Hanna takes a step toward Alex. "Compelled you? Wardell forced you to come along? Like you were his prisoner and had to do what he said and watch it go down? Right? Wrong. You got it on because you wanted to prove yourself. C'mon, man. Didn't you? He looked at you and he saw fear. Weakness. You wanted to prove yourself to him and read that in his eyes. Am I right?"

Alex looks around. He doesn't know where to go.

"Wardell told me I had to."

Hanna cuts a glance at him.

"Ordered me," Alex says, then imitates Wardell. "'Take her to her room.' And Wardell whispers in my ear, 'She don't get off. She gets it.'" He shrugs.

Hanna blinks.

"I was going to just lock her in, you know?" Alex's lips draw back. "Then she . . . it was like self-defense, man. She was trying to poke my eyes out. So, it was a reflex, I had to defend myself."

Alex's eyes connect with Hanna's, pleading. "I got put in this situation! Out of threat for my life. From Wardell. What am I supposed to do?"

The cheap porn of Alex's illogic roars in Hanna's head. Hanna looks at Alex's face, caught in profile.

"And Wardell's looking at her because, you know. But that wasn't me! What am I supposed to do?" Alex says.

Hanna feels tears push toward his eyes. The sky, the roof—everything has an extra edge of clarity. He visualizes the pattern of Jessica's blood splatter from the lamp on her wall.

Hanna's left foot slides across pebbles. They feel like stones. His weight centers, his head dips, and like a discus thrower, he throws Alex off the roof.

Thirty hours and nineteen hundred miles out of Chicago, McCauley sits high in the cab of the Peterbilt, driving the car transporter toward a desert sunset on I-8. His walkie-talkie scratches to life.

"They're taking the exit to the border," Cerrito says.

"Get ahead, keep them in your mirror," Neil replies. "Time to switch off." He clicks the walkie-talkie again. "Trejo. You're up."

"On it," comes the reply.

Out his window, the Ford F-150 pickup truck pulls even with him in the left lane. The man at the wheel, as hard a con as Neil has ever met, gives him a glance and accelerates. Trejo is cool, and crafty and fit, and nobody who sees him behind the wheel with that black glare would believe how tenderly he can smile at his wife. Trejo pulls ahead to take over surveillance from Cerrito.

All the way from Chicago, they've been rotating the tail cars, following the load the Herreras are running south. Now the cash truck is pulling off the interstate. This is the final route toward the Herreras' depot.

This is where the truck is going to cross the border. Yuma, Arizona.

From the shipping documents on the Herrera computer disks, Neil knows their stash house is nearby on the Mexican side.

He is going to find out where that cash truck deposits the money.

And he is going to take it down.

33

The room behind the office at the auto repair shop is meant to be used as a storeroom but has become Otis Wardell's crash pad. Wardell and Svoboda's. It's been two days now. And the room smells like it, Aaron Grimes thinks.

Now he's bringing them take-out Chinese like a fucking delivery boy. Wardell pays well, but the guy's a nightmare. Why couldn't they have split Chicago?

And Wardell's going to ask about his business with McCauley again, he knows as he enters through the glass-and-steel accordion doors. *Goddamn Alex,* he thinks, *cannot keep his fucking mouth shut.* Aaron likes him, but goddamn.

He wants them *out.*

He heads across the floor of the repair shop to the corner office. He rounds the corner and sees through the glass office wall the empty pizza boxes, beer cans, bottles of Maker's Mark, and stinking socks. He sees Svoboda sitting behind his desk.

Fuck.

Hank has his feet up on it. "How 'bout you get your feet off my desk?" he says.

Wardell's voice comes from behind him. "You've been slow-walking my job."

He turns. Wardell fills the office doorway.

"No, Otis. I'm doing my best, and you are going to get what you need, ASAP."

"That car hauler was the reason why, wasn't it?"

"Not at all."

Wardell had seen McCauley drive out in the tractor-trailer rig and demanded, *Where's that rig going?*

Grimes had kept walking, trying to act blasé. *Down the road, I guess.* He shrugged.

You guess.

Nothing to do with me. Nothing to do with you. I don't know.

Grimes walked past him and into the office. Wardell hadn't shaved in a couple of days. His jeans were dirty. Otis liked to think of himself as having animal magnetism with women, but right now he stank.

A car hauler, Wardell said. *You're just going to leave that hanging?*

Yeah, I am. And that's how it ended.

"You put me second," Wardell says. "I'm your bread and butter. And you put me second for these West Coast assholes? Your secret client?"

He says it sarcastically, but the undertone of menace is tangible.

"Otis." Grimes feels the hair on the back of his neck prickling. "That job was booked before you showed up here. You're always number one."

"No, no, your brother-in-law was bragging about all of a sudden you're working with highline crews planning major scores and shit."

Grimes breathes, trying to stay calm. The smell of garbage is acrid. Wardell is angry. He wants out—and, lacking that, somebody to blame.

Wardell carefully moves closer. "I want to know everything about that eighteen-wheeler. I saw you loading a pickup with work tools. Then you loaded the pickup on the car hauler." He looms. "I asked you before. Where the fuck is that rig going?"

Wardell is right up in his face, the scar in his eyebrow standing out, lightning white against the red rise on his neck.

Svoboda gets to his feet and slides around the desk to stand between Grimes and the door.

"I don't know," Grimes says.

McCauley has called and told him where he and his crew are. Grimes tries to keep his face neutral. That lie is a gamble.

And Aaron sees that he made a mistake. Wardell's eyes are not flat or dark. They're insane and brilliant.

Wardell slams him against the watercooler. It wobbles, and the big bottle tips and falls to the floor with a plastic *thunk,* splashing them.

"Otis, look, man . . ." Grimes says.

The blow comes hard to the side of his head from Wardell's fist. Grimes reels.

"Where's it going? Who was that driving?" Wardell says.

Grimes fights to get his feet under him. He half sees Svoboda shut the office door.

He bunches himself. There's a tire iron on the chair in the corner. He lunges for it.

Wardell launches at him.

34

Neil gets to El Centro late in the afternoon. The desert heat lies like a heavy sear in the air.

The town straddles I-8 near the Mexican border, two-thirds of the way from San Diego to Yuma. An easy drive for him today with clear roads, clear skies.

He pulls up to the modest ranch house with a couple of bags of groceries. Slings his gym bag over his shoulder. The house is freshly painted, bright, in a quiet neighborhood that backs up to a city park. Inside, he unloads the groceries. Out the kitchen window, across the backyard in the park, the sky is filled with kites.

He goes out to the patio. Halfway across the park, he sees Elisa.

The breeze is lifting her mahogany hair like a sail. She turns, slowly, as though he'd spoken to her, though she's eighty yards away.

She walks toward him languorously. Neil returns to the kitchen and cracks open two beers.

Elisa comes through the door, sets her sunglasses on top of her head, and walks straight for him.

"Right on time," she says.

He sweeps her windblown hair off her face. "I stopped by the store."

"The grocery list, I gave that to you last month." She shakes her head. "I've moved on, *vato*."

"Yeah, but I picked up the detergent anyway."

She smiles and play-slaps him on the arm. He shrugs.

He hears light footsteps outside. Gabriela pushes through the door, flip-flops slapping, kite trailing from her hand.

"Hola, Neil." She kisses his cheek.

He puts the back of his hand to her heat-reddened cheek. "Gabi, you're a fireball."

"The sun is the fireball. And it's ninety-two million seven hundred sixty-two thousand miles away. Did you know that?"

"No, I did not." And he says, straight-faced, "Did you measure it?"

"No!" She laughs and looks at Elisa. "*Qué hay para la cena?*"

Elisa answers, "First, you clean up. Then I'll make dinner."

Gabriela jogs down the hall, and McCauley hands Elisa a beer. They clink bottles.

"Check the fridge," he says. "See what else I got at the store."

He raises the bottle and drinks. His smile is evanescent, but he sees that she sees it.

She opens the refrigerator. A bottle of Champagne rests on a shelf. A smile curls at the edge of her mouth. Lopsided, cute, knowing but unpretentious.

Elisa takes him in. The strength in his eyes. That tight smile. She knows him well enough . . .

"You got something new already?" she says.

The excitement is vibrating right below the surface. He's cool and he's going to keep it there, she thinks. But it's big. She can tell.

"South of here," he says.

She raises an eyebrow, nonchalant but interested. "*Otro lado?* Other side of the border?"

"Near Yuma. What do you know about getting back and forth across the line near Yuma?"

Elisa holds Neil's gaze. What does she know?

Her life is all about navigating borders. The way she puts it, the Vasquez family has handled cross-border logistics since the 1850s. They were *tequileros* during Prohibition, and her relatives have run everything from electronics to washing machines, refrigerators, and TVs into Mexico and export the occasional load of grass back into the States. She first ran a key of weed across the border beneath her baby blanket, sitting on her mother's lap.

She's a seventh-generation smuggler. What does she know about getting across the line?

"Near Yuma? Everything," she says.

Gabriela sits at the kitchen table in her Dragon Ball T-shirt and flip-flops, starting arithmetic homework.

He nods. "We'll talk later."

Hanna rolls up to the West Side auto repair shop with Casals. Easton is in the car behind. Two squad cars with four uniformed cops make up the rest of the team. Lights, no sirens. They block the street exit and both ends of the alley behind the shop. Hanna gets out and leads them to the building in a flak vest, armed with his twelve-gauge Remington pump-action shotgun. The roll-up garage doors at the front of the repair shop are closed, the office dark. They surround the building. Hanna has a pounding headache, one now amplified by adrenaline. Rage is a kiln-hot brick deep in his chest.

He and Easton approach on either side of the exterior office door, staying away from the window. Against the wall, Casals stacks up behind Hanna.

Casals didn't say anything when Hanna returned from the roof of Alex Dalecki's apartment building alone.

Slipped and fell, Hanna said.

Casals looked him in the eye and said, *Dangerous roof.*

Now, in the cone of light from a streetlamp, Hanna tries the door. Locked. He radios the uniforms at the back. Everything is locked up there as well, with no visibility inside the garage.

Hanna nods to Easton, who smashes the glass in the office door. He reaches in and unlocks it. They flow inside, clearing the interior.

The office is cluttered, smelling of flat beer and motor oil. An interior door leads to the repair floor. Hanna nods at Casals. He pulls the door open, and Hanna goes through.

The garage floor is dark and empty. No cars. Four service pits, with hydraulic car lifts.

Easton flips on the lights as the uniforms break in the back door from the alley.

Easton lowers his gun, staring. "Christ."

The uniforms' eyes widen. Two of them flinch. One turns away.

Hanna's head pounds, but he's cold and calm at the same time.

An electric chain hoist is mounted on rails beneath the ceiling, centered over one of the service pits. A chain hangs from the hoist. From the chain hangs Aaron Grimes. He's impaled on a steel hook planted under his rib cage.

Hanna lowers his shotgun. Grimes is naked and dead. His flesh is scorched black in parts, his face a pulpy mass. His genitals are burned off. The amount of torture he endured means it took a lot to break him, or his killer kept the torture going for the sake of it.

A cigarette has been put out in his eye.

Hanna breaks the silence.

"Photographer. Crime scene team. ME. Print every inch of this place. Start canvassing for witnesses. Show Wardell's photo around the neighborhood." He tries to think of more. He comes up empty for once. "That's it. Let's go."

He turns to go back outside.

Otis Wardell is gone, trailing a stream of gore. Vanished. And he is never coming back. The sun hasn't broken the horizon, but it sends beams across the sky, streaking jet contrails crimson.

When Baumann pulls in, Hanna's at the edge of the sidewalk near the curb. Baumann eases out of the passenger seat of his unmarked car like a well-fed anaconda. The captain walks toward him, dead cigar jutting from between his fingers, snake eyes vivid. Novak gets out of the driver's seat behind him.

"No collar?" Baumann says. Eyes only for Hanna.

Hanna feels like he is at the wrong end of a telescope on a roof, seeing everything zoomed away, Baumann right in front of him, but small.

Like the system he's part of, he's content and secure.

"Auto mechanic and supplier of work cars to various crews," Hanna says evenly. "Aaron Grimes. Strung up like Action Jackson."

Baumann smiles coldly. Getting the reference. Appreciating that Hanna can tap into Chicago lore.

Same old, same old. Nothing new. A mire.

"Otis Wardell?" Baumann asks.

"He plays the hits, doesn't he?" Hanna says to Casals standing nearby. "He's gone. Far gone and long gone."

There's a sour satisfaction in Baumann's eyes.

Hanna turns to face him, eyeball to eyeball. Baumann, the larger man, is wary, as if expecting Hanna to assault him.

"And so am I." He spreads his empty hands. Then he turns toward the sunrise. He says to Baumann, "I'll write up the report. Then I quit."

He walks away.

"Otis Lloyd Wardell," he says to himself.

PART THREE

Paraguay, 1995–96

35

Heat shimmer off baking tarmac distorts the low pines at the end of the Guaraní International Airport runway in Ciudad del Este, Paraguay. The taxiing Cessna 310 rotates 180 degrees to park before cutting its engines. Climbing out, unsteadily, is Chris Shiherlis, in Ray-Bans and a wrinkled guayabera. By a beaten-up Toyota Land Cruiser, a driver in a T-shirt and jeans waves him forward.

"Señor Bergman."

Carrying only a plastic bag from Mariscal Sucre Quito International Airport, Chris climbs in.

The Land Cruiser speeds off down the side of the runway. Chris clocks the anomalies. On the apron by the service hangars are an ancient DC-3, a DC-2 cargo version, and single-engine Bonanzas. In among them are a Gulfstream G-IV and a Citation X. The combination private fixed-base operations and passenger terminals looks third world. The Toyota exits the parking lot onto the rural highway.

Chris is handed bottled water, drinks, spills some on his shirt. He touches his forehead. He has a fever and it is soaring. He takes off his Ray-Bans. In the subtropical humidity, the light breaks into its spectral components, etching green and blue outlines onto the distant trees and the few high buildings in Ciudad del Este. As the chroma shifts in the heat, Chris feels dizzy. He opens his guayabera and lifts up the stained T-shirt. Beneath it he's still wearing Frida's dressing. He peels back one side and sees red discolored skin streaking away from the wound.

The Land Cruiser hits a crater-sized pothole. Pain explodes in Chris's head. He slumps forward.

Aracaris soar outside a window. The small toucans' harsh cries and bright colors prompt Chris's struggle to consciousness. The walls are high-gloss mustard yellow. He drifts away.

"Señor Bergman," a voice calls.

Chris's eyes snap open. Dr. Ortega, bald with a mustache and wearing green scrubs and a green surgical cap, looks at his chart. A nurse with a starched cap stands beside him.

"Good day, señor. Welcome back," he says in heavily accented English. "I would advise you if you ever require another surgical procedure, you should change surgeons. I had to reopen that wound."

Behind the doctor, against the wall, is a lean man in a black shirt and jeans. He has terra-cotta skin, close-cropped black hair, high cheekbones, and hazel eyes. He's a Brazilian blend of ethnicities: African, European, indigenous. He watches carefully.

"'Cause it looks like I was sewn up by a veterinarian?" Chris asks Dr. Ortega. It *was* done by a veterinarian, Dr. Bob, three days ago in Los Angeles.

Dr. Ortega raises his eyebrows. "Your wound is infected. I installed two drainage tubes. We are infusing you with three thousand units of ciprofloxacin. The anesthesia is wearing off. Expect a headache and some pain . . ."

Chris's eyes close. He floats away.

"My name's Paolo."

Chris blinks awake. The hazel-eyed man stands beside the bed. Time has flipped into dusk heading into night.

"So, you are to come work for me in security." He looks Chris up and down.

Chris doesn't say anything. He scrutinizes Paolo. He's still not clear how he got here, where he's supposed to work or for whom. All he was told is that he would be met.

"My name is Bergman." He remembers stepping off the twin Cessna at the Guaraní Airport and climbing into the beaten-up Toyota Land Cruiser, feeling sick and stoned, and then he woke up in this hospital.

Paolo nods at Chris's wound. "How did that happen?"

"A domestic dispute." Chris's eyes are steady now, holding Paolo's.

Paolo, after a beat, looks down at the passport in his hand. "Jeffrey Bergman. How did you come to get this job in security with me?"

"I applied."

"And?"

"Recommended by a friend. He said I'd like it."

Paolo writes his cell number on a piece of paper and folds it into Chris's passport. His Nokia cell phone rings. Paolo takes the call.

"*Oi, rapaz.*"

Paolo flips the passport with his phone number onto Chris's bed and, as he's leaving the room, points at it and nods, continuing out the door on his cell.

1996

The morning sky is already glazing white when Chris leaves his apartment. The small traffic circle below shines with cars. The fruit stand across the street is busy. Red dirt, low hills, trees he still can't name, aside from the palms. All this green. Mist hovers on the far eastern horizon, rising from the massive Iguazú Falls downriver.

He wears jeans, a green polo shirt, a black sports coat, boots. Glock on his hip. Is it business casual? Urban assault dressy? Whatever, it's business as usual in Ciudad del Este, bolt-hole away from home for Chris Shiherlis, aka Jeffrey Bergman of Calgary, Alberta, Canada. El Americano.

At the bottom of the stairwell, music thuds from a boom box. Señora Hausmann sits on her patio. Both she and her breakfast look thick and German. Chris twirls his keys. She eyes him with suspicion. Their morning ritual. He climbs on the Suzuki, pulls his helmet over his Walkman, and turns the volume up to the max. Tupac. "California Love." The beat descends through his chest. LA, dry heat, a sparkling ocean. He kick-starts the bike and joins traffic.

The vans and buses appear as soon as he turns the corner. An insane scramble. People on foot weave in and out of traffic. Parrots and toucans shriek in the trees. From crowded cafés comes the aroma of hot *chipa,* cheesy bread baked with anise seeds. In most business doorways are security guards carrying twelve-gauges on their shoulders or cradled in their arms like deadly babies, with bayonets that would gut a cow.

This place is the Faraway, as foreign as Mars. The city is a free-trade zone cut out of the rain forest and looming on a cliff over the Paraná River on the triple border between Paraguay, Brazil, and Argentina. The free trade is free of everything: free of conventional law, order, and rules or regs, except for its own rules. Manic, malevolent, rapacious, and totally enticing. A grab bag of people and products to the accompaniment of ringing cash registers and spray from the falls. It's populated by Lebanese, Syrians, Chinese, Koreans, Brazilians, Paraguayans, Argentinians, the descendants of Nazis on the run who fled to the open arms of President Stroessner in the '40s and '50s, Hezbollah from Shia South Lebanon.

The major occupations are smuggling, money laundering, cocaine trafficking, and counterfeiting electronics, computers, software, pharmaceuticals, and luxury goods.

The pull in his collarbone is dull. He lets it smolder. He's off the oxy. Needed it. Partied on it. Can't do that here. Here, he can't afford to surrender to impulse. Here, there are so many unknown variables. Here, it's State of Nature. It has that anything-goes kind of freedom, but a bad roll of the dice is your last.

He passes the cathedral. Capitalism is Ciudad del Este's true, fervent faith, but the church stands there, with its black river stone and wild, abstract stained glass, blazing candles and dimly shining gold. It hisses the history of this place, the dark sacred forest craziness of the Spanish mission fathers and the indigenous people they confronted, saints and martyrs and mysticism.

Sky-daddy shit. Chris gooses the throttle. If you want to talk miracles, shout hosanna for how Dr. Ortega repaired his gunshot wound. A bit better than the LA vet. The hospital specializes in gunshot wounds.

Nothing is back alley in Ciudad del Este.

After his airstrip evac from the desert south of Mexicali, Chris's crazy-ass trip took him through Mexico City to Tegucigalpa, Panama City, Quito, Lima, Cuzco, Asunción. Oceans, deserts, and jungles; skirting the Andes. Seasons flipping; sick, dazed, feverish. Across grasslands and hills and forests. Deep into the continent, to the City

of the East. Home of the nonstop shop and top-flight trauma surgeons.

The scar tissue is tight, but the bone has knit. He's regained muscle. He works out. He runs. Never did before. He knows his body needs
this. He wants to be able to move.

The streets are crammed with shoppers and cigarette smugglers.
Half these shiny cars are stolen from Brazil.

He stops for coffee. A machine-gun battle of multiple languages:
Arabic, Mandarin and Taiwanese dialects, indigenous Guarani and
Spanish. The cashier's till accepts cards in four currencies. In the
alleys, Styrofoam packaging is piling up. It will be six feet high by
five p.m. Then the cardboard and Styrofoam pickers and sweepers
show up. By midnight the streets are completely clean. Someone
makes money from taking the packaging. In the coffeehouse doorway, an armed guard slouches with casual menace.

It's the flip side of law and order: organized crime openly runs
business and industry. The only norms enforced here are clan norms.
The city has the highest murder rate in South America, but the bodies floating down the Paraná River are there for business reasons.
Causality runs it in CdE. No random violence. No street crime.

After almost a year, Chris is deep within its surreal "It's a Small
World After All" ride.

He aches for his family. He'll get them out someday. Not now. Now,
he has command of himself. It's new. Neil, Cerrito, Danny . . . dead
and gone. He's building a reliable, focused strength in this foreign
cauldron.

He's safe but stranded in this strange city. He wants to command
himself and be capable of anything. That's what he wants. Be a new
man on his own. Work out on his body and his mind—that old slogan
from the joint. But true. Men of sufficient egos do exactly that, become jailhouse autodidactic lawyers, writers, better criminals, fiends
of different disciplines.

He has to do that now. He has to *become*.

A shaft of sunlight from behind a cloud strikes a yellow sign. He
can see Charlene's perfect skin lit by the morning sun.

Photos. They came two months ago, in a package with a return address that's a post office box in Delaware. From Nate, the most cautious cat he's ever met. Cutouts. Zigs and zags. Then to him.

No way Vincent Hanna or anyone else hunting him can trace the package to Paraguay.

The Venice Pier. Charlene is smiling into the sun. There's an emptiness in her expression, a downturn in her lips, though. Chris swears he can smell her Chanel No. 5, the scent turned into pure allure by the heat of her skin. He wants to reach into the photo and touch her. The distance, unnavigable. It's a lash across his heart.

Any other contact with Charlene and he'll be traced, tracked, and found.

What's he going to do, he asks himself, beat off to Charlene in memories, make love to his right hand? Fuck that.

Dominick's little fingers curl against hers. His face is lit with unfiltered wonder. If there's innocence in the world, he thinks, it's children.

Meantime, he knows he's fading from Dominick's memory. What does the boy remember? Not much, he worries. Memories have halflives. Soon Chris won't even be a ghost.

Time is running, day by day, increment by increment.

The Xingfu Shopping Center fills a block in the city center, seven stories tall, covered with mirrored plastic tiles, like a disco ball. Telephone and power lines snake to it from poles on the streets, dendrites feeding clustered neurons. It's ringed along the sidewalk by kiosks and stalls selling children's clothing and luggage and frilly polyester bras. Sports gear. Pirated DVDs.

The traffic outside is apocalyptic. Shoppers swarm around gridlocked vehicles like ants, carrying huge plastic shopping bags. Chris parks in the secure garage beneath the building and takes the escalator all the way up, same as every day. Commerce. Hustle.

The Xingfu—meaning "happy"—Shopping Center has a smear of glitz. It boasts an echoing central atrium and Chinese-influenced colors, red and gold. The stores sell electronics. Televisions. Mobile phones. Gaming consoles. Panasonic, Ericsson. Nokia, Motorola. PlayStation, Nintendo. Shop after shop after shop, with Canto-pop and Brazilian soap operas blasting out and wary proprietors sitting at desks in the back or prowling the doorways, sleek and skeevy at the same time. It's a dynamo of moneymaking, owned by a local Taiwanese-Paraguayan family, the Lius.

The merch may be stolen or smuggled to evade tariffs and taxes, and definitely includes counterfeits and knockoffs. The Gucci purses, Nintendo games, Disney plush toys. He assumes that the mall's customers—mostly Brazilians and Argentinians who pour over the border via the Friendship Bridge—know they're snapping up sketchy goods.

He walks along the top floor, looking over the railing at the echoing carnival of retail. He nods at shopkeepers. Mrs. Ling in the phone card shop looks up from her Winston and gives him a squint. He returns it. Mrs. Ling is a tough woman. Sometimes she offers him tea.

Counterfeit Winston, 100 percent.

Paolo is standing in the security office, staring at the wall of televisions that play footage from the two dozen security cameras in the mall. He always stands. Chris doesn't think he has ever seen Paolo sit.

"*Bom dia*," Paolo says offhandedly, not looking at him. Still the chill.

"Mornin'," Chris says.

Paolo is ex–Brazilian air force Para-SAR. Paolo is a lethal man with skills prized by the Liu family: muscle, brains, and deference. Paolo's smile is disarming. He never gives it to Chris.

The shopping center is only one of Paolo's responsibilities in the Liu organization. Chris is still figuring out the byzantine business and family structure. Nate has a connection with the Liu family and set up his free fall into CdE. Chris doesn't know how. He's a security systems specialist, whatever that's supposed to mean. He guesses it means he's a guy who's an expert in security hardware and systems, because he's expert at looking how to beat security hardware and systems. He definitely can identify vulnerabilities. He tells them to dump this system, buy that one. Improve the backup power source. Paolo didn't appreciate being told to put Chris on payroll in the first place. But he followed orders from the family patriarch, David Liu.

You somebody special? Paolo probed.

No. A guy doin' his job, he said.

Paolo has not asked again.

Chris scans the bank of security screens. "What's going on today?"

He speaks English because Paolo has told him to. Paolo wants to improve his grasp of the language.

"Everything look o-kay," Paolo says.

Chris peruses the screens. The property is covered inside and out by CCTV. Armed guards are stationed inside every entrance. The loading dock and service elevators are controlled with multiple physical and electronic locks. Credit card terminals are connected to banks and card companies via phone line, which can, technically, be breached. But Xingfu has dedicated lines for card transactions, plus a red line that, if cut, alerts Liu central security—Paolo and his team— and, if required, the local police.

The outside cameras show the street. Styrofoam packaging fills the sidewalk like a snowbank.

"Except one set of guys." Chris has nighthawk vision for people seeking to exploit security flaws. He says, "Last week, these punks circled the mall on motorbikes. We clocked them, saved their photos. Are they casing the place? Haven't come back until now."

Paolo turns. His expression is disdainful. "What mean 'casing'?"

It's a new word he's trying on.

"Lookin' to find a way to steal. But who'd be so stupid?" Chris says.

Paolo nods. "Argentinians."

"Why Argentinians?" Chris asks.

Paolo snorts. "They'd be that stupid. Because they're comfortable."

This city is teeming with people yearning to spend money. Anywhere else, that would make a shopping center a prime target for pickpockets, shoplifters, and smash-and-grab robbers. Here, nobody tries that. Try that, and you end up dead, floating down the Paraná River. Plain and simple.

Nobody interrupts business in Ciudad del Este. There is virtually no street crime, especially in the multistory shopping malls owned by Lebanese-Syrian, Taiwanese, and Paraguayan families.

But what makes Ciudad del Este the per capita murder capital of South America is when one family tries to take over another family's cigarette-smuggling, arms-trading, money-laundering, cocaine-trafficking, gray-market-pharmaceutical-manufacturing, or counterfeit-software business. That, as well as the nearby Hezbollah summer training camp, contributes to the Paraná body count.

Chris has not met the Lius in person. He has seen David Liu behind thick, tinted glass in his Mitsubishi Montero. He watched the family's son, Felix, shake hands and smile at a schoolkids' event earlier in the winter. Winter meaning August, which is freaky as shit.

"You look like something is brewing," Chris says to Paolo.

"'Brewing'?"

"Coming. Starting."

Paolo eyes him longer than is comfortable. He says nothing. Chris takes that as yet another sign of exclusion.

Chris assumed he got this gig as a favor to Nate. But he's starting to think that David Liu also wanted somebody who was an outsider. Somebody who came with his kind of credentials. Chris doesn't know why yet.

So far there's been no defrost in his contact with Paolo. Paolo prefers to pick his own men. And he repeatedly tests Chris to see if he can step up.

Two months back, Paolo sent Chris out to the firing range with the Xingfu security guards to see what they could do.

Chris nodded crisply.

Paolo has close-quarter combat training, like SWAT, but Paolo is Brazilian, and Brazil doesn't fight wars. Chris fought street wars. Neil McCauley fought both kinds. At eighteen Neil was picked up by the San Bernardino Sheriff's Department after a 7-Eleven robbery. He faced a parole violation, sending him back to Chino, or enlisting.

Five months later he found himself in the strangling jungle greenery of Củ Chi, crawling into Viet Cong caves with a short-barreled, semiauto twelve-gauge in the Twenty-Fifth Infantry Division. During the early weeks of the Tet Offensive, he accompanied a few long-range reconnaissance patrols with Army Rangers engaging units of regular PAVN. The Rangers tried and failed to recruit him. He had other plans. Later, the battles he and Chris fought were with police in the combat zones of urban America.

Chris improved the guards' regimen. He upgraded the firing range with flats to mimic walls and hallways. He invented scenarios requiring firing on the run and from all sorts of cover, graded for accuracy and against the clock. He had the guards cycling five hundred rounds a day, solo, then in teams. He taught them how to assault and clear rooms, engage from moving vehicles, deal with urban environments.

He passed on McCauley's fire team tactics and tactics from his own prison and street experiences, along with Neil's and his attitude: Save your crew. Save what you did it for. If anybody gets in your way, that is their problem.

Paolo knows it when he sees it. He doesn't openly ask Chris where he picked up close-quarter combat tactics. Next, Paolo wants to see if Chris is loyal.

Chris will not disappoint him.

Chris doesn't completely trust that Paolo and his men have his back. He is 95 percent confident that if these men are working close personal protection—bodyguarding—they will protect their principal if attacked. Chris trusts completely only himself on that. Still, he has upgraded the security side to pro status. Pro according to his standards, which include, if you're ambushed, you assault the ambush.

Highline.

But Paolo is twitchy about something. Chris sees nothing on the screens that seems out of place. Just his boss's edgy vibe.

"These guys on the motorbikes," Chris says. "Have you seen them, too?"

"*Talvez.*" Maybe.

"Same guys more than once?" Chris says. "Same bikes?"

Paolo grunts.

"Same route through the street?" he says. "Same time of day? Are they only looking at Xingfu? At other shopping centers?"

Paolo turns. "What are you thinking?"

"Maybe they're laying on a score."

"'Laying on'?"

"Planning to hit the mall. Rob it," Chris explains. "They're scoping it out."

"Would they?"

"They're planning something."

Paolo eyes Chris carefully. "You have done this before."

Once or twice.

"If I'm them," he says, "I know what I'm looking for."

He knows everything a crew watches for and anything that's a soft spot for them to exploit. If they're staking out a score, they're looking for patterns, like who's on a clock, when do the shifts change. Access. Look for one way in, multiple ways out, if they're going in strong. Weird to be on the other side of the fence.

Chris holds Paolo's gaze. "Lemme check it out, see if something is going on."

"*Bom. Bueno.*" Paolo exhales. "Where you start?"

Chris nods at the screens. "Tapes. Find these motorbike guys on the CCTV. Then figure out—are they gathering intel? Probing for weaknesses?"

"Weaknesses. In what?"

"Good question. Identity of personnel. Are they scoping out the guards on the entrances, seeing how alert they are, how quickly they respond to disturbances and threats," Chris says. "Are they search-ing for ways to disable the mall's cameras, alarms, phone and power lines."

"We have the red line. If anybody cuts the phones, we are alerted."

Chris nods. "Could be they're looking to tap into phone lines or cut into computer communications. Maybe to steal credit card numbers"—he thinks—"or penetrate the mall's operating system." He pauses for a second. "Data comm lines run through the phone room in the subbasement, right?" Chris says. "Phone room can be accessed through the garage. Has anybody been prowling down there?"

Paolo looks grim.

"All that, and anything that can be a weakness—searching for an exploit, a way in."

Probing for weaknesses. The shopping center, or something else? Something more? What, he wonders, is *more* in this situation, this city?

He's getting thirsty to know what he's not being told.

He's making a living wage, but he needs to step it up if he's going to get out of here and get his family out of Los Angeles.

"Anything big coming up for the company in the next few months?" he says.

Paolo turns away from the screens. "That is . . ." He searches for the words in English. "Need to know."

"Okay," Chris says calmly. "When do I need to know?"

Paolo gives him a sidelong look. "When you find a suspicious thing."

Who would want information about this mall? Bank and financial information about the shopping center? Could they maybe be digging for clues to the Lius' money trail? Seeking to obtain financial information by getting access to transactions that originate here at Xingfu?

Could they be trying to breach the Lius' internal computer network?

"But all this is retail bullshit," Chris says.

"So?"

"So, if it's more sophisticated, if they're targeting Liu enterprises, I know nothing about that. I can't help protect it if I don't know what they're trying to find." And there's a whole dark continent of Liu business that Chris knows nothing about. "But, maybe, they're going to get zilch."

Paolo finally smirks at that one. "'Zilch'?"

"Zero. Nada. Blank. Double blank." Chris lightens up. "I will find out. I will let you know."

"Good." Paolo takes a last look at the screens and walks out.

What the hell's going on? Chris asks himself.

Near six p.m., Chris walks the exterior of the Xingfu Shopping Center. The kiosks and stalls outside the mall are shuttered. The hundreds of couriers—smugglers, FedEx on foot, men who haul sacks of merch on their shoulders—have hiked back across the Friendship Bridge over the chasm above the Paraná into Brazil. The piles of Styrofoam and plastic packaging left behind on the streets have gotten even larger, mountains of the stuff the pickers will soon remove. What do they do with it?

He has information for Paolo.

The motorcycle boys have surveilled the shopping center twice in the last month. Chris has reviewed the security footage. Two men, early twenties, one Latino, one Asian, no way to tell whether they're Paraguayan, Brazilian, Argentinian. Same bikes, Yamaha sports bikes, with impossible-to-identify plates.

They have absolutely cased the shopping center. First in the morning. They circled the block and drove into the underground garage. They didn't check out parked cars; they're not looking to steal vehicles. But they photographed the locked steel door to the room that contains the phone equipment, the big PBX exchanges, the credit card terminal links, and the door leading to the mall's big circuit breakers and backup generators.

They returned two weeks later, near closing time. Same procedure. Xingfu is a target—for what, Chris doesn't know.

If these guys are foreign amateurs, they don't know this town doesn't allow smash-and-grab robberies, purse snatchings, stranger rape, drunken street fights. Taking scores, robbing retail stores, ain't happening. Period. Not here. Or they're local pros scouting something else.

Chris walks in the direction the bikers drove away. At Café Damascus he orders Arabic coffee and tells the owner, "*Shukran.*" He has come here a dozen times in the last few months. But asking the owner about the bikers would be too forward, too memorable.

He's antsy. Half lonely, half eager to change up into the action or whatever is going down.

Chill. Go for a run. Work out on your body and your mind.

He's been riding the fringes of this for nine months.

He cuts through a street where pop music pours from pizza joints and goes to the private mailbox store. He sticks the key in the lock and opens the P.O. box he has rented under a bland alias.

Empty.

Not even a silent notice from Charlene, he tells himself. He slams the box and walks out into the humid sunset.

It's the not knowing. What are they doing tonight? Who are they with?

He's heading for his bike in the underground garage when Paolo and one of his colleagues exit the elevator lobby.

"Paolo," Chris says.

Paolo keeps walking but nods him along.

"Let's talk," Chris says. "And let me go along on whatever you're doing tonight. Stir-crazy."

Paolo sees something in his eyes, maybe. Chris is good at being vacant, but he thinks that right now, he's not the blank mirror he often tries to be.

Paolo nods at a Range Rover. "Tell me on the way."

Chris gets in.

They're halfway across the city when Chris finishes briefing Paolo. The driver, one of Paolo's silent and watchful inner circle, steers smoothly, eyes hidden behind Oakley tactical sunglasses.

Chris rides shotgun. When he looks over his shoulder, he sees his boss sober and quiet.

"Who?" Paolo says. "Who are they?"

The driver looks at Paolo in the mirror. "*Para quién trabajan?*"

Chris shakes his head. "I can't tell you who they work for unless you give me more information." The SUV rockets onto the highway heading to the airport. "I need to know."

Paolo runs his thumb across his lower lip, brooding. "So do I." To the driver, he says, "*Él vendrá con nosotros.*" He'll come with us.

Chris feels a warm excitement spread down his arms.

Guaraní Airport still seems wildly out of place. The city has a population of three hundred thousand. Guaraní has a runway longer than Asunción's.

On the green plain west of the city, the combo terminal/FBO, surrounded by lacy trees, is a sideshow. The action is in cargo. Across the runway, two MD-11s are unloading freight. An Antonov. Nearby, fifteen gleaming white private jets are parked. Shabby city. All this dough.

This backwater free-trade zone. Families are shoved into cement-block apartment towers with no building code and tin-roof homes with dirt yards.

Money is here. The airport reeks of it.

They park under a psychedelic sunset: orange, magenta, and a velvet blue in the eastern sky above the emerald countryside. They walk through a vaulted hangar and emerge on the apron. Paolo checks his watch. A massive jet banks overhead, the sun painting its wings with a reddish firebird glow.

A 747 touches down, thrust reversers roaring. Paolo hands Chris a set of ear protectors. The ground crew marshals the jumbo to a halt in front of the hangar. The engines spool down, and the nose of the jet swings up. Belly doors open. Cargo handlers swarm and begin unloading pallets.

Stairs are driven to the forward door. The pilots jog down. Paolo calls, "Nǐ hǎo." To Chris, he says, "The cargo. You get it to the warehouse."

"Sure," Chris says.

Two eighteen-wheelers are parked at the hangar. Three guards wait by each, twelve-gauge shotguns slung across their chests. One with an AK.

The pallets are shrink-wrapped in heavy plastic. Whatever they contain, it sure ain't cheap-ass counterfeit merch for shops in the mall.

In Spanish, Chris introduces himself. "Bergman. From Security." He travels in the lead rig, coordinating via radio handset with the second rig and a follow car. They convoy to an industrial park where guards roll open a chain-link gate.

The blue stain of dusk rides the western sky. Bats flit across the background. The rigs back up to a vast warehouse. Under floodlights, forklift drivers swing in with a deft touch. They transfer the cargo inside, ready for inspection.

Chris dares not do that. He was tasked with safely delivering the load, nothing more.

He wants to know what lies beneath the opaque plastic shrink-wrap.

Patience.

Paolo soon arrives and strides in, Beretta shining in the holster on his hip. "All good?"

"Smooth as silk," Chris says.

A minute later, Felix Liu arrives. The Liu family's oldest son is in his late twenties, tall, thin, handsome in a fine-boned way. He is too dressed up for a warehouse. For the job. Pale gray sharkskin suit, tight black dress shirt, no tie. He wears Bruce Lee sunglasses though it's dropping toward night.

Paolo walks up to him. "*Hola, caballero.*"

Felix lifts his chin in greeting. Two minions flank him. Chris can tell: vanity muscle.

They approach the pallets. With a knife, Paolo slices the shrink-wrap. It tears with a thick ripping sound. Felix stands by, hands in his pockets.

Chris isn't sure at first what he's looking at.

It's electronic gear, for certain, wrapped carefully in Styrofoam. So much Styrofoam around here. It should be the Paraguayan flag.

Paolo lifts out a box that looks like a small black stereo receiver: dials, an alphanumeric keypad, circuit boards for innards. Paolo hits a switch, and a display slowly glows green.

Felix eyes the gear. "*Bueno.*"

He speaks in rapid Spanish to Paolo. Chris scans the pallet. The electronic gear doesn't have labels, but manuals are stacked beside it. Some foreign language.

Felix spins and saunters off, entourage trailing. Chris had grabbed only a third of the conversation but caught "casino." A driver opens the door of a Mercedes, and Felix slides in the back, beside someone in a sequined miniskirt.

Paolo stands at parade rest until they drive away, then directs the warehouse crew to secure the pallets.

He turns to Chris: "Good." In English, Chris notes, for his benefit.

"What is this stuff?" Chris sees no point in pretending he knows.

Paolo holds his eye. "Electronic countermeasure system."

Chris keeps his face mild. This is restricted, cutting-edge, extraordinarily expensive equipment. Military grade.

"Not for Mrs. Ling's phone card shop, then," he says.

It's midnight when Chris gets to his apartment. His shoulder aches. But he's buzzed on adrenaline and possibility.

He sees now. The Xingfu Shopping Center is the visible edge of the Liu organization's business. But real estate and retail are not the core of their operations and ambition. Here, deep in South America, the Liu family is selling electronic warfare equipment. The real scope of the world they operate in is dark and dangerous, and must be wildly lucrative.

He shrugs off his jacket and grabs a beer. He turns on the TV for company. He wanders the apartment. He finds himself at his desk, staring at photos of Charlene and Dominick.

Make money to set up an out for his family.

What the hell business are the Lius in?

He wants in. He just needs to convince Paolo he belongs.

He now thinks that robbing the mall is not at all what the sports bike boys have in mind.

36

The diacritical marks on the text in the electronic countermeasures equipment manual are what click things into place. The accents and circles over the vowels, the inverted circumflexes hooked to the tops of letters like ticks. Those trip the lights for Chris.

The 747 came from Taiwan. Chris drove the pilots to the airport for their departure and, through a mix of Mandarin, English, and hand gestures, got the gist of their flight plan. Guaraní–Bogotá–Mexico City–Vancouver–Taipei. Home base. But the cargo isn't Chinese made. When the gear was unwrapped from the pallets, he'd grabbed a look at the manuals. At home, he searched online and identified the language: Czech.

This is surplus—read: pilfered—Czech Republic military gear. Countersurveillance equipment that thwarts detection and disrupts enemy comms. Brand-new, ruggedized. Black-market gold.

Paolo says only that the delivery was a test run. This, Chris intuits, means that the Lius are stepping up and expanding their reach, and they need proof of concept and a quality-control demonstration for their customers.

"In future," Paolo says, "we may not take delivery here. *Talvez*. Too much cost, in freight, fuel, and delivery lag. And we don't—won't need to."

Chris gets it. Once customers buy in, the operation will ship from the point of origin to the delivery address, without hauling everything through Paraguay. Ship gear direct from the factory in the mountains outside Prague or from the military transport train from which it was stolen, to the outbound plane, then through West Africa to the end user. Send the money via Buenos Aires via a different route. They never need to touch hands to accomplish a huge transaction.

Eye-opening. Chris has been occupied in his security job, when, just past his horizon, a world of possibilities exists. He knew he wasn't in Kansas anymore. Now he thinks he'd stayed stuck inside the farmhouse after the twister dropped it and has finally, after months, raised his eyes and looked out the window. Ciudad del Este, Day-Glo fever dream, is a world beyond his expectations.

Family business. David Liu, immigrant entrepreneur, shopping center magnate, is a mainstay in this city. He's always seen in a white dress shirt and black slacks, physically unexceptional but with a calm power in his craggy gaze, his straight-backed posture. Member of the Paraguayan-American Chamber of Commerce. Photo in the local paper of him shaking hands with the bishop.

David Liu is a crime boss.

This isn't the Paraguayan army buying this electronic warfare equipment. Who is? The family's big customers have to include smugglers, arms dealers, pariah banana republics, and Mexican drug cartels. The Lius are running an international enterprise that may be worth hundreds of millions of dollars.

The revelation to Chris's perception is that David Liu clearly doesn't see himself, his family, or his business as criminal. Everything the family does is open. Nobody doubts that the Xingfu Shopping Center sells stolen and counterfeit merch or that one of its many purposes is to launder money. That, in the world of Ciudad del Este, is merely called "standard commerce." You get what you can, and you hold on to what you've got.

Among the Taiwanese diaspora here, the merchant is above and untainted by the commodities he merchandizes. He's a man of trade in the ultimate free market with no rules or regulations. Hobbesian state of nature to the end.

The operational complexity of the world the Lius operate in is another revelation to him. They do deals, control supply chains, transact business through global electronic funds transfers, and they do it quietly, sometimes from a phone in an old Jeep parked overlooking Iguazú Falls. If he's going to be exiled, he's lucky to find himself in criminal Disneyland. He wants to jump on the A train.

37

The rain has let up when Chris arrives at the Lius' nondescript office building south of the city. The roads are slick. Gray clouds puff from the river gorge. Paolo is in the office on the phone. The walls are covered with photos of him in his military days in fatigues in the Rocinha and City of God favelas in Rio. Going up against dangerous gangs and seriously dangerous sixteen-year-olds. Dangerous, but not war. Not LAPD. Not first-rate NVA regulars in caves. *How good is he really?* Chris wonders.

Paolo hangs up. "Assignment for you."

"Okay." Chris doesn't display how charged up he feels. Magic lurks nearby. He's missed this in his life.

Paolo catches it. "You got something?"

On the people casing the mall, he means. Chris hands him a set of photos. "Had one of the Xingfu guards ask around. Off duty. Casual. To find out if anybody recognizes the motorbike boys. Found 'em."

"Sí?" Paolo sifts through the photos. He stops. "They are at the Casino Paraná."

"That's right."

Paolo's face goes unexpectedly stormy. He holds back, then decides. "You need to know."

Paolo stops on a photo of the sports bike boys walking past a fifteen-foot-tall stucco roulette wheel outside the entrance. The casino sits on a cliff overlooking the river, and the gorge is a dark slash in the greenery behind the building.

Paolo's face has the heat of a sizzling skillet. "The Chens own the Casino Paraná."

Chris absorbs that. He should have known that. He mentally zooms out, trying to see the landscape in which this information fits.

Ciudad del Este is a multicultural stew, but separate ethnic groups have a corner on specific markets. The Koreans own the umbrella market. The Lebanese own malls that specialize in high-end counterfeit fashion, the best cafés, and they rule the city's money laundering and cocaine distribution. Everybody sells counterfeit electronics and pirated DVDs, CDs, video games.

But the Chinese are especially into counterfeit software, higher-end arms merchandizing.

The Lius and the other clans—all with deep ties to Taiwan, the

Chinese mainland, and various triads—interact. Their children attend the same schools. They're seen at the same cultural festivals. They donate to the same civic causes.

The Chens own a chain of electronics outlets. The casino surely launders money that is then deposited into the global financial system. Their ambitions might run along the same track as the Liu family's.

They're rivals. And like all organisms in a state of nature, they're fighting for resources and position and longevity.

"So, motorbike, sports bike boys work for the Chens?" he asks Paolo.

"Probably."

"I'll find out," Chris says. "If they do . . ."

"I will take the news to the family."

Discussion over, for now.

"What is the assignment?" Chris says.

"Escort."

"What?"

Paolo frowns. "That is the word?"

"That word means many things," Chris says.

A gust of wind sends a rain shower splashing against the trees and windows. Paolo looks at him askance. Chris smiles. He knows his smile is devastating.

"You mean a guide?" he says.

"A customer arrives. A . . ." Paolo raises a hand. "A maybe customer."

"Potential."

"Potential. To have meetings. Discuss business."

"And you want me to safeguard this customer," Chris says. "And keep an eye on him?"

"Yes," Paolo says. "This man, he comes from abroad. He does not know the city. And we do not know him."

"He's important?"

"Act like he is, whether he is or not." Paolo nods at the parking lot.

"He arrives on the afternoon flight from São Paulo into Foz. Take the Range Rover."

Chris gets the keys on his way out.

Foz do Iguaçu International Airport is rickety but aspirational, surrounded by clapped-together homes with dirt driveways. Beyond the stained concrete passenger terminal is, of course, a long runway.

Waiting at domestic arrivals, Chris thinks about the motorbike boys and the Chens. Paolo's reaction means he needs to get up to speed on the Chens' strengths, weaknesses, and connections and the threat they might present to the Lius. He's standing near the exit when the customer emerges.

He's tall and overtly North American. After months in polyglot CdE, Chris can now discern people's point of origin by how they dress and talk, but especially by how they carry themselves through the world. And this guy carries himself like a big American swinging dick.

He's six feet, mid-thirties. Anglo, tall, brown hair with product. He's wearing cargo pants and a bomber jacket, has a duffel slung over his shoulder. His gaze traverses the arrivals hall.

He looks past Chris and starts toward a Brazilian man in a blue blazer holding a sign with a name written on it.

Chris remains still and silent. American Hair gets halfway to the man with the sign—clearly a driver—then stops. The driver is waiting for someone else. The American peers around, maybe in consternation, before catching Chris's eye. Chris waits.

The guy walks over. "You my ride?"

"You Scott Terry?"

He isn't quite as tall as Chris. He is fit, solid muscle beneath his outfit, which, Chris thinks, is oversold for somebody coming to a wild river region in the heart of South America on business. He holds out the duffel.

Chris pauses a microsecond, then takes it. He leads the man out to the Range Rover.

"Good flight?" he says.

"Tolerable."

Scott Terry glances idly at the scenery, the ramshackle airport, the familiar American car rental companies. He has a Chuck Norris stride, something hard about it. He hasn't shaken hands or asked Chris his name.

They pull out. Chris says, "A/C okay?"

"Sure." Terry stares at people on motorbikes and on foot, carrying huge loads on their backs. "Busy place."

"First time?"

"No reason to come here before now." Terry checks his watch. "I travel a lot and don't get much slack in the schedule."

"Take a minute to get in the vibe. This place is a trip."

Chris lets that be an opening, if Terry wants. The man's eyes are remote. His profile is almost too good: etched jawline, three-day scruff. He's wearing a chronometer, something crammed with small dials, a military aspect to its stainless steel band.

"I'm taking you direct to the hotel, the Arenas Resort," Chris says. "Grab a water bottle."

"Stay hydrated? That's what I get from most drivers."

The guy does sound like an annoyed businessman, Chris thinks. *Jet-lagged, thirsty.*

"Drink the bottled water. It ain't just corporate advertising."

Terry eyes the ramshackle stands spilling into the street. "Place isn't exactly Paris."

"But you can get Dior suits at half the Paris price," Chris says. "Cartier watches. Mirage fighter, maybe."

Terry gives him a side-eyed glance. Chris turns to cross the bridge into Paraguay.

Terry frowns. "Jesus. What's the jam?"

"Ciudad del Este is Black Friday three hundred sixty-five days a year."

Terry's face looks pinched. Chris turns up the A/C. On the pedestrian walkway, men trudge along carrying cardboard boxes on their shoulders the size of dishwashers. The slate-green river looks thick below, its eddies coiling iridescent in the sun. Chris sweeps the view ahead and to the sides, checks the mirrors diligently. He expects no trouble, has not been warned of any potential threat, but he's on the job, and that's the job.

He is thinking about Scott Terry. Thinking that his arrival, so soon after the arrival of the countersurveillance gear, is connected. And Paolo had to assume Chris would associate them.

They cross the bridge and edge down into the insanity of Ciudad del Este traffic.

"Cabs are okay here," Chris says. "But any meetings, you'll be picked up and dropped off."

"I'm not worried about walking around a place like this," Terry says.

"It's safe." He glances at Terry. "Long as you don't crack jokes with the Syrian café owner about Hezbollah summer training camp."

Terry gives him another sidelong look. "I thought that was a rumor."

"Rumors you hear about Ciudad del Este—consider 'em all half true. Whatever you want, whatever you need, people here will find a way to get it for you. If . . ." He rubs his fingers together. "Capitalism *über alles.*"

Terry seems to reevaluate him. "You work full-time for the Lius?"

Chris nods. "That's right."

"What kind of people are they?"

"Not my place to say."

"They speak English?"

"Some do, perfectly. You'll have a translator present."

Terry nods. "Won't be you, will it?"

"Not my area."

"Many Americans around here?"

"Enough that there's an AmCham."

Terry doesn't react.

"Paraguayan-American Chamber of Commerce," Chris says off-handedly. "For all your luncheon banquet needs."

They creep along to the Paraguayan border checkpoint, where an official in jeans and a polo shirt stands outside a kiosk. Chris gestures to Terry.

"Passport."

Terry's is American. Chris already has his in hand. The official waves them through. Chris pulls away and returns the passport to Terry.

"You're Canadian?" the man says. "What brings a guy like you to a place like this? Off the prairie to a jungle city?"

Chris keeps an amiably bland look on his face. "I like the heat."

"What part of Canada?"

"Alberta, but I spent my childhood in the States."

"Whereabouts?"

"Ever been to Minot, North Dakota?"

"Sounds flat."

"You can watch your dog run away for three days."

Terry smiles. He stretches out. "Tell me about the Lius. Things I don't know from phone calls. Coming here, into the lion's den and all."

Chris rolls into the city. "I'm paid well to do my job and mind my own business. And I like doing both."

"Fair enough. I'm curious, I'm about to do business with them," Terry says. "You ex-military?"

Chris shakes his head. "Saluting is not for me." He glances over. "Army Rangers?"

Terry looks out the window, seeming pleased. "It's that obvious?"

"You look too smart to be a Marine."

Terry laughs. "You been to Fort Bragg?"

"I stay away from everyplace that ends in 'nam.'"

Terry doesn't react. Food stalls and drink stands line the roadside, the red dirt.

Chris calibrates what he wants to say. "You work the US market?"

"Thought you didn't want to talk business."

"I don't talk about my business." He offers a half smile. "South America, let people wonder about you."

Terry turns. "You're an interesting guy."

"No, I'm not. A working stiff in an interesting place."

"Yeah, I'm buying for the US market," Terry says.

Electronic countermeasure systems. Who uses those?

"Border and how far north?" Chris says.

"Expanding every month."

"US or not, you use your own security guys?" He shrugs. "I'm a student of the industry."

"In the continental US?" Terry says. "It's based mostly on personal connections."

"Former military?"

"And contractors. People from . . . that unit. Snake eaters with global experience. You lookin' for a job?"

"Maybe. You never know," Chris says. "Military, even for transpo and distribution?"

Terry side-eyes him. "Depends. Distribution's a large subject, as I'm sure you have surmised. We're a heavily compartmentalized organization."

"Who do you go to for your security locally?"

"Aztecas." He says it casually, but there's a note of . . . hardness? Conceit?

Chris watches the road. "You out of San Antonio?"

"How'd you guess?"

The resort is ahead. Chris turns in. The place is cheesy, wouldn't earn a second glance in Vegas, but here it is considered primo. Under the portico, Chris gets out and grabs Terry's duffel.

Terry offers his hand this time. "Thanks."

Chris gives him his business card. "If you need anything."

"You got it, bro. See you again?"

"Likely."

Terry, the important man, saunters into the hotel as Chris pulls out, watching him in the rearview mirror.

He drives to the office, to find Paolo.

38

When Chris swings into the parking lot, Paolo is heading out, striding to his SUV.

"You deliver our customer?" he calls.

Chris hops out and walks alongside him. "Straight to the hotel."

"What is on your mind?"

Chris has been churning on it the whole way here. Double-checking himself. Wondering if he's about to stick his neck out too far.

"You look unhappy," Paolo says.

Fuck it. Say it. "It's your customer. He's a three-dollar bill."

The sun has come out, bright, the sky porcelain blue.

"What is 'three-dollar bill'?" Paolo says.

"He's . . ." Chris searches for the word. "He's *off*, man."

Paolo stops at the driver's door of his gleaming black Suburban. "Explain."

"He's lying about himself."

"To you," Paolo says flatly.

Chris has to make his point. Paolo's in a hurry, and Chris is not among his trusted intelligence sources. "You asked me to pick up a customer. I picked him up. I was cool. I was smooth. I was professional."

"Sounds okay."

"Yeah, and the man has important meetings with the Lius. He is going to meet with David Liu, correct?"

"Need to know."

"He's a phony."

"This word."

"Phony. Impostor." No reaction. "Fake. Pretending to be somebody he is not."

"How do you know this?"

"He claims extensive experience in the US military/contractor world. He hints that he works for a drug cartel, that he's buying equipment to help these narcos bust the US border. But his knowledge is only skin-deep."

"Use words I know."

"He thought I was a chauffeur," Chris says.

"So?"

"Man comes out of the terminal, heads for a driver with a sign. Then he finally notices me, comes over and hands me his duffel."

"Again, so?"

"Implies he's US Special Forces. Got that wrong, by the way. But a former soldier, arriving in a foreign country like this for dicey negotiations, possibly a violent place?" Chris shakes his head. "He would know that I'm security, not just a local driver. And he would never hand over his gear. He would not let it out of his hands. He would also know that his security needs to keep both hands free. I'm not the fucking hotel valet."

Paolo acknowledges that. "But he is not military now. He is getting old, no?"

"Mid-thirties."

"Maybe he was an officer." Paolo's smile is sly. "What is the saying?"

"For noncoms and enlisted? 'Don't call me "sir," I work for a living.'" Chris has to concede that point, but is getting wound up. "He copped to the Rangers, but hinted heavily that he was Green Berets. But they're not the same thing."

"No, they are not."

"And he did not get a reference to Fort Bragg, what soldiers stationed there would call the place. Fayette-nam."

Paolo doesn't respond.

"He also said, on the US border, his outfit uses Aztecas for distribution and security."

"Aztecas?"

"Texas prison gang. But when you get south of San Antonio, it's the Texas Syndicate and HPL—Hermanos de Pistoleros Latinos. Those gangs run distribution for Mexican cartels. They don't work with Anglo assholes who wear distressed bomber jackets and Banana Republic cargo pants."

Paolo exhales. "Look around you. This country. Do you not notice? Nobody is who they say. They exaggerate. They promise things they do not do. Paraguay is a small country surrounded by Brazil, Argentina. Bolivia, even, has started wars and killed the young men of this nation for two hundred years. There is a word, in English?"

"Inferiority complex."

"So everybody lies. And you think this customer would tell you the truth about himself?"

"It's what he lied about."

"Maybe he was testing you."

"Why?"

"You say he is not who he says he is. Are you?"

Ignore that. "Some other plan is going on."

Paolo opens the door of the Suburban. "If you see Mr. Terry again, be polite. Do not ask questions. You do not need to know." He gets in and fires up the engine. "You have another job right now. Pick up Felix Liu and drive him to Xingfu."

He drives away.

Chris has a couple new words he could teach Paolo. *Fuck off.*

Is Paolo being genuinely dismissive, or protecting information being kept from Chris?

Okay. Give Junior a ride. Now he *is* playing a fucking chauffeur?

39

Chris is standing beside the Range Rover, parked outside an office tower, when Felix emerges. The young man is in jeans, a $2,000 blazer, and the '70s sunglasses. He aims straight for the SUV's back door and glides in when Chris opens it.

As Chris pulls out, Felix says, in Spanish, "Turn the A/C up."

Chris spins the knob and maneuvers into traffic.

"You new?" Felix says.

"Yeah." Chris glances at him in the rearview, continues speaking Spanish. "About nine months."

Felix looks out the window. He has already lost interest. His cell phone rings.

"*Sí, sí,* okay. *Suficiente!*" Two miles down the road, he puts the phone away. He stretches, then rolls his eyes in annoyance. "I forgot. We need to pick up my sister."

They head to the big warehouse outside the city. Annoyed, Felix checks his large, expensive Cartier watch.

Great. Now, in addition to this guy, Chris has to chaperone a Taiwanese Paraguayan princess in a party dress.

He swings into the parking lot, splashing through sun-silvered puddles. He's getting out of the Range Rover when the door of the office block opens. A young woman walks out.

"Señorita Liu?" he says.

"*Nadie más.*" Nobody else.

She's in her mid-twenties, wearing jeans and Adidas and a plain plaid flannel shirt. No jewelry. She steps up into the front passenger seat of the SUV, not the back, and slams the door. She and Felix don't greet each other.

Chris gets behind the wheel. "*Vámonos a Xingfu Center.*"

She buckles her seat belt. "English is fine." Hers is perfect. She has an English accent. Not what he expected. He pulls out.

He knows her name is Ana and that she is home on a break from school somewhere. She watches the road, a distant expression on her face. After a mile she turns on the stereo. Oasis. Chris doesn't attempt to start conversation. She looks like she would prefer not to talk. He lets her listen to "Wonderwall" and read *The Economist*. He's struck by the difference between her and her brother.

Hitting the city center, he turns down a back street and crawls toward the mall through the crush of traffic. Power lines run crazily overhead. On a balcony, Arab men sip Turkish coffee and eye the scene. Chris pays close attention, but a part of his mind is chewing over his conversation with Scott Terry. And the brush-off from Paolo.

Small trucks jam the curbs, unloading vegetables and toys and cheap-ass swimsuits. Women and men in soccer T-shirts squeeze around one another on the sidewalk. Ana taps her fingers on her thigh, sanguine about the gridlock, and returns to the article she's reading: "Maritime Boundaries and the Projection of Military and Economic Power."

Ahead, a black Toyota Land Cruiser nudges into an intersection from the cross street. Traffic locks up.

"Asshole," Chris mutters.

Ana looks up lazily from the magazine. In the back, Felix leans against the doorpost, arms crossed, eyes closed.

There's room on the right to slip along the broken curb and turn onto the cross street at the corner.

Chris hears it first: the high-pitched revs screaming toward them.

He eyes the sideview mirror. Seventy meters back, weaving through traffic, is a motorcycle. The driver is wearing a helmet with the visor down. Somebody is riding pillion on the back. Sunglasses. A black-and-white keffiyeh wrapped around the lower half of his face, bandit style.

More buzzing. Ahead at the corner, from the left, a second motorbike appears. Another driver and rider. The two bikes are converging toward the intersection. Are they in concert?

"Hold on."

Chris spins the wheel right and punches it, sliding around stopped traffic, jamming toward the intersection. The Range Rover scrapes against a delivery truck, catches the edge of a vendor's stall, and plows on. Ana sits up straight.

"The bikes?" she says.

"Get down."

Felix jerks upright. *"Qué mierda?"*

Ana's gaze sweeps like air defense radar. "The riders are armed."

He floors the Range Rover, shrieking against vehicles on his left. People on the sidewalk scatter. The gridlocked intersection is thirty meters ahead.

Ana's head swivels between the two bikes. "They're closing."

Chris jumps the curb. Pedestrians run. He reaches the intersection, throws the wheel right. Gets around the corner onto the cross street and confronts a pickup truck heading straight at him. Go straight, he'll slam into the truck's grille. He pulls the parking brake and throws the wheel hard over, heel-toeing the brake and gas. The SUV whips around one-eighty. Now facing back toward the intersection, through spaces between low buildings Chris sees the motorbikes halfway to the corner. He glimpses the pillion rider with the keffiyeh. He has an H&K MP5 on a sling, the muscles on his arm standing out, a tattoo writhing.

The Range Rover accelerates toward the intersection, and then Chris cuts left into an alleyway, paralleling the road, racing in the direction from which the sports bikes are coming. Left hand on the wheel, with his right Chris draws his semiautomatic. They'll cross as opposing traffic, separated by a median of weeds, at double the speed, making shooting from the back of a bike twice as tough. Felix dives to the floor. Ana watches out the windshield.

"I said get down!" Chris barks sharply.

Instead she braces one hand against the dash and eyes the bikes like they're a calculus problem. "Keep going."

Chris throws a look to the right as the sports bikes and the Range Rover pass each other twenty-five meters apart. Ana's face is pale, but her eyes are calm.

The sound of gunfire slaps the street.

"*Down!*" Chris barks.

Ana ducks below the dash, covering her head with her arms.

The noise of rounds being fired is flat, drumroll quick, relentless.

Chris angles right, bouncing the Range Rover across the rough median. Snapping a glance into his mirror, Chris sees people in the intersection diving into doorways. A mother scoops up her toddler and ducks behind a food stall.

The black Toyota Land Cruiser is shot to hell, windows shattered, chassis full of holes. The doors are open. The people inside, who tried to get out, droop from the vehicle, blood smeared, dead.

The motorbikes are racing away into the miasma of traffic.

Chris turns the Range Rover left down a side street and then another left, emerging onto a road overlooking the chasm above the river.

Ana peers up from under her arms. "Clear?"

He presses her head low. "Stay down."

He pushes the car, his vision fine-tuned, his pulse high. Adrenalized. A familiar, too-long-gone feeling.

He checks the road ahead and side streets as they rush past, gun in his hand. He hits speed dial on his console-mounted phone and calls Paolo.

"Clear?" Ana asks.

"Don't know."

Ana sits up anyway. She sweeps the road, the mirrors, and looks at Chris.

The call to Paolo goes to voice mail. Chris leaves an urgent message. He hangs up and again scans the mirrors. "Getting you out of here."

"Where? And what's your name?" Ana says.

He shoots her a look. "Where you're safe. Home."

"You have a lot to learn about my family."

Chris shoots her another look.

From the back seat comes Felix's muffled voice. "Fucking funny."

So, he speaks English, too, Chris thinks. Felix sits up, straightens his sunglasses, smooths his hair. His face has lost color.

Ana exhales, slowly, like a yoga breath. "Never mind. Besides, they were not after us."

"Not at that corner, maybe."

That observation gives *her* pause.

"Where do you think we are, New York City?" Her tone is bone dry.

The road ahead is wide open, arcing toward the green suburbs. Chris's vision is still pulsing on high alert. Paolo calls back.

"What happened?"

Chris takes a beat. What did happen? "Gun attack on a Land Cruiser. Avenida de la Paz. Twenty meters from us. I'm taking Mr. Liu and Miss Liu home."

"I get back to you." Paolo ends the call.

"Ana," the young woman says.

"Excuse me?"

"Since you took me for an evasive-driving thrill ride, you may as well call me Ana. Now, you tell me your name, señor."

He passes the entrance to the local country club, all palms and manicured lawns.

"Chris." He slows his voice. "Bergman."

"Chris Bergman, turn at the next street."

She sounds like she's telling him to pull into a McDonald's drive-through.

He glances at her again. "What did you have for breakfast, antifreeze?"

Her look dwells on him. She gestures at the upcoming turn. Maybe she's covering for unseen nerves. Maybe she's right: they were in no danger, beyond the risk of being caught in the line of fire of small machine guns on full auto, shot from motorbikes.

She points. He turns. They head along a beautifully landscaped road toward a snaking gorge above the river. Birds-of-paradise, hibiscus, security cameras bolted to power poles. When they approach a rolling steel gate, an armed guard in mirrored sunglasses steps from a security hut.

Ana waves. He calls, "*Buenos días*, Señorita Ana," and buzzes the gate open.

Trees arch overhead. Mist swirls. A bridge leads over a narrow chasm to an island. Driving across, Chris gets a glimpse below into the Paraná.

"You have a moat and everything," he says.

"And you have a sense of humor," Ana replies.

They drive into a neighborhood of mansions. On a bend in the road with clear sight lines in all directions, no trees or vegetation obstructing the view from the property, is a massive three-story house. White walls, blue tile roof. And that's all one sees because there are almost no exterior windows. Two golden-hued lion statues flank the wide walk to the front doors.

Chris parks and kills the engine. Before he can get around the SUV to open Ana's door, she's out, striding toward the house. Felix follows.

The quiet, the scent of flowers, the birds flying overhead, the distant rush of the river—sensory overload. An adrenaline flood.

On the shaded porch, she enters a code into a keypad beside the door. Turns. "You going to come in?"

She opens the door.

Chris follows into a three-story-tall great room with a marble floor. A hand-painted mural of a lotus pond covers one wall, beside an indoor waterfall. Leather sofas nestle up to a Ping-Pong table and video game station in one corner of the vast room. Ana drops her backpack and strides toward the interior. Chris trails her.

The windows are two stories up—tiny, thick green glass. Ballistic.

The house is a fortress. Everything is built around a central courtyard, where a pool glitters in the afternoon light. Life faces inward. It's a gilded M1 Abrams tank, where the family lives barricaded.

Ana walks down an echoing corridor to a wing where Chris sees an office suite. "Bà," she calls out. Dad.

Hardwood doors open and her father emerges.

David Liu's weathered face is flinty. He scrutinizes Ana and speaks in Mandarin. Chris catches a couple of words, including what he thinks is "daughter." Ana shrugs, again keeping her cool.

Liu turns to Chris. "Paolo called. I heard." He glances at Ana. "Xiu-Ying says there was no danger. And you are skilled driver." His accent is heavy, his English carefully considered.

"That's my job."

Some job, Chris thinks. Dead end, low level, but he's grateful, even if he doesn't know how he got it, other than Nate's connection.

Liu nods. "Okay."

Felix takes off the shades, runs a look over Chris, and says, in Spanish, "It was no big deal."

Ana barely turns. "You want a reward? An ice-cream cone?"

Chris can't quite get the family dynamic but senses that Felix's louche attitude around his father is both too casual and long indulged. Felix looks like he wants to be anywhere but here. Ana looks like she wants to get back to her *Economist*. Maybe. There's a cold reserve in her eyes that seems both genuine and brittle. Like maybe she got more rattled than she would display to an outsider.

David pauses. In formal Spanish, he says to Chris, "You protect my son and daughter. Thank you."

Chris nods, sharp and quick, deferential. He's two seconds from being dismissed and sent back to town.

Normally he'd expect an adrenaline crash, coming down off his senses jacked to the max, seeing all, even particles of dust in the air.

For nine months he's been staying low profile, looking for the solid ground in this strange reality. Doing basic jobs way below his skill set and standing in the hierarchy of his mind, while he recovered his strength and searched for purchase after arriving from a blown-apart world. Losing Dominick and Charlene. Cerrito gone. Whatever happened to Trejo. And Neil dead—his brother from a different mother.

From the outside, he knows he's being clocked as one of those withdrawn expats who float through the streets here, hiding whatever it is they're on the run from.

Right now, standing here, he feels none of that ebbed adrenaline flatness. He's all 3-D, centered and crystal clear. A professional criminal Clark Kent who hasn't seen the mountain he can't figure out how to climb, the hard time he can't handle. He knows what he knows and knows he can learn anything he doesn't.

"If you have a minute, there is something else," he says.

The Lius face him: father, son, and daughter. David Liu's face is unreadable.

"I work in security for you."

Liu's expression barely moves. "I know."

"You're meeting a man. Scott Terry."

"Who you drove from the airport."

Bring it.

"He is not who he says he is," Chris says. "He's lying. He's phony."

Liu says nothing for what seems an endless pause.

40

David Liu nods, turns away.

He leads Chris into his office suite. High windows shaped like pillbox slits, slatted, allow light through, shafts piercing. His son and daughter follow. Felix drops onto a sofa, coolly disinterested. Ana hangs back, eyeing Chris with what seems like analytical curiosity. She looks small in her grunge plaid shirt and Adidas. But sharp. Escaping from the scene of a downtown gangland hit seems to have turned up her internal wattage somehow.

David Liu walks around his desk and sits down. Chris stands before him. He doesn't expect a seat. Liu catches Ana's attention. He's obviously shooing her out of his office. The daughter, the grad student, doesn't need to be here for men's talk.

He turns his attention back to Chris. "Go ahead."

Felix is sitting with his legs crossed, foot swinging. Ana takes a second. She was beside Chris as he evaded automatic gunfire on a city street. But she's been dismissed. She manages to square her shoulders before heading for the door.

Chris says, "My Spanish is basic. Your daughter might help me translate."

Liu purses his lips, then nods. Ana stays. She gives Chris a bare glance with an emotion he can't read.

Liu waits.

Chris organizes his thoughts. "Here's why this Scott Terry is not who he says he is."

Chris looks at Ana. She translates into Mandarin. Her father listens impassively.

"His passport is phony. He handed it to me. Using an alias means nothing. The problem is the passport was a good forgery. Not a great one. The embossing on the cover was excellent. The lamination on the photo page was imperfect. It's not State Department issue." He lets Ana translate. "Terry implied he works for Mexican narcos. The cartels can forge top-class papers or bribe US consular employees to issue fraudulent passports. The one he handed me was neither."

Ana finishes. Liu digests her translation, says, "What else did you observe?"

Chris explains how Terry didn't seem to know that soldiers call Fort Bragg "Fayette-nam." His elision of the Rangers and Green Berets. And Rangers train at Fort Benning, not Fort Bragg.

"His watch, an over-the-top chronometer." Chris taps his wrist. "No one would wear a shiny band. Nothing that flashes under the moonlight. They'd wear plastic dive watches. Or the original Rolex, which would be twenty, thirty years old."

Liu raises an eyebrow.

"Then there's his bullshit about Texas prison gangs."

Liu looks at Felix, then back at Chris. "Explain."

Chris tells him how Scott Terry didn't know the Aztecas from HPL and the Texas Syndicate. He describes the *wrongness* of Terry's situational awareness. His blindness to OPSEC.

When he finishes, Liu sits stone-faced.

Chris waits. He has leveled suspicions. Are inferences enough? He knows in his gut this guy is wrong.

"With a photo of Terry I can reach out to contacts who might be able to identify him."

Finally, Liu's glance flicks up. "Get a photo. Full face. Bring it to me. Do nothing else."

Liu's head dips, a brief nod.

Done.

Chris's nod in return is equally brief. Clipped. He walks out, his pulse strong and smooth.

And Chris is starting to think maybe assigning him to collect Terry wasn't an accident. Maybe David Liu wanted Chris's sentinel ability. Maybe it's one of the reasons he's here.

41

The next evening a passing downpour is clearing when Chris returns home from a run, drenched, out of breath, pumped by how much energy he has, how the run turned into flight halfway through. He wipes his face with his forearm and puts his hands on his hips to open his rib cage. He's heading for the stairs when a black Suburban pulls up in front of the apartment tower and Paolo honks.

Chris turns, heads over. Paolo puts down the passenger window, sunglasses on top of his head, handsome brown face cold and distant.

Chris leans on the doorframe. "Boss."

"You talk to Mr. Liu, yes?"

"I did. When I drove his daughter and son to the house."

Paolo looks displeased. "You talked about the man you met at the airport."

Chris pauses. *Play it straight.* "Yeah. I told him I thought the guy was a phony. One thing led to another."

"Another" being the photos he snapped last night, from concealment, of Scott Terry at the concierge desk at the Arenas Resort, collecting Chris's welcome-to-Paraguay gift of Canadian Club whisky.

Did he violate some macho chain of command? Probably. He scrapes his hair out of his eyes. Paolo waves for him to get in.

"Come. Mr. Liu wants to see you."

"How about a shower first?"

Paolo checks his watch. "Three minutes."

Chris pulls off his shirt. Paolo checks out his scars.

When they cross the security gate and the bridge to the island, the white walls of the Lius' house are washed pink with the setting sun. The high windows gleam silver. Ana opens the door in a Tottenham Hotspurs hoodie and jeans with worn cuffs, a bowl of ramen in her hand. In the dining room, people sit around the table: a woman Chris presumes to be Ana's mother or aunt at one end, several other middle-aged adults, a couple of little kids squirming and laughing. David Liu gets up from the head of the table and makes his way out. Felix jogs down the grand staircase in front of the waterfall. He raises an eyebrow at Chris.

"*El mago,*" he says. "*Lector de la mente.*"

Reader of the . . .

Ana sidles up. "You are a magician. A mind reader."

David approaches. "Paolo. Chris. *Mi oficina.*"

This time, Liu points Chris to a chair in front of his desk, along with Paolo. Felix paces behind them, eyeing his watch. Ana pads to her father's side.

David sits. He looks at Chris. He speaks Mandarin, and Ana translates.

"We have uncovered Scott Terry's identity. Your suspicions were right."

Chris's pulse kicks up a gear. He looks from Ana to her father. Paolo sits with arms crossed, calm and cold.

"And your insights into American 'businessmen' are"—Liu stares at Chris—"very good."

Chris says, "I'm glad my observations could be of service."

Felix paces. Ana looks bright-eyed. David Liu looks calculating, assessing him.

"This man Terry did not conclude any business with us," Liu says. "He did not come here to conduct business. That was a story."

Chris notes the past tense. What happened to Scott Terry?

Liu does not tell him. Paolo does not tell him. Felix seems uninterested in telling him. Felix seems late for a rave. Ana is quiet.

Chris notes nobody is asking him to give Terry a ride back to the airport.

The door of opportunity is open. It can slam shut in a snap. Chris checks his gut. What he feels is not uncertainty, not loss and desperation; he feels confident. If David Liu hired him because he knew Chris's background and thought his perspective might be valuable, this is his moment.

"You gave me a job, Mr. Liu. You understood from the people who sent me to you I can handle security."

Ana translates. Her eyebrow rises, just for a second. Liu listens.

"And I have some skills handling explosives, metallurgy, and basic electronics. I can't tell you anything about Paraguayans. But I am a genius at reading Americans like an x-ray machine. That includes Mexicans, the border, and the drug trade." He takes a beat. "I assume the photo went to contacts who can access a foreign country's intel database."

Ana translates.

Liu has a wry look. Glances at Paolo, then back at Chris. "That is right." Liu offers nothing more.

"So here's what I'm asking. Step me up. What do you need done?"

"With Mr. Terry? Nothing. We *are* done." Liu glances at Ana, perhaps shading his words, using euphemisms for her benefit. "Tell him what issues remain," he says to Paolo.

Paolo, in English, says, "We did not learn who the man was working for."

Chris thinks. "Maybe it was a cutout and he didn't know."

Liu's hands are immobile. To Paolo: "His other meeting."

Paolo expands to Chris. "We got from him information about another meeting in the city."

Chris lets his mind go. "An impostor arrives here. He has a meeting set up with you. He had credentials? He claimed to represent certain interests?"

Liu nods.

"He was going to learn more about your product and make a purchase?" Chris says.

Felix bites his thumbnail as he paces. "Spot on, Sherlock."

"And you want to know who, for real, this guy was acting for. And whoever they are, what are they after." Chris holds Liu's gaze.

Ana translates. Liu nods.

"His second meeting here," Liu says. "That may be with people who hired him. Maybe yes, maybe no. I want to know who he planned to talk to and why."

Paolo says, "Very compartmentalized. He didn't know the people he is supposed to meet. I am certain he did not lie. He did not know them. They do not know him."

Chris takes a breath. "Why don't I go instead and find out what I can find out?"

Liu watches him carefully.

Chris has stepped out onto the end of the high dive. Maybe above the gorge of the Paraná.

"You can do this?" Liu says in English.

Chris takes a second.

Liu sits forward. His Mandarin is brusque. Ana's translation dilutes the strength of his tone, but Chris gets the challenge in the question.

"This is good information for us if you can get it."

Great. A life-threatening audition.

Chris feels everyone's attention on him. Ana's eyes. Even Felix stops pacing. Chris keeps his gaze on David Liu.

"Sure."

42

Chris follows Paolo to the center patio in the Liu family's fortified mansion. Inflatable plastic swans float in the pool. The sky overhead is a searing blue, streaked with pink and gold strati.

Felix heads out the front door, swinging a key ring around his index finger. Paolo sees Chris eye the young man as he goes.

"Pay attention," Paolo says in a low voice. "That one, he wants to party, not work. He is not, what do you call it . . ."

"A player?" Chris says.

"A player."

A *poser*, Chris thinks. "But he's the number one son, right?"

"He is. The boss to come."

Inside, Ana jogs up the stairs, light on her bare feet in her old jeans and hoodie. Chris can tell she's the brains of the next generation. But she doesn't rate.

Paolo grows sober. "Now, you need to know."

Chris can't tell if Paolo is pissed at him for stepping out of line, for taking his suspicions about the Lius' American customer to the head of the family. Paolo's ex-military; these guys can have a rigid sense of hierarchy.

"I saw it, I called it," Chris says. He looks squarely at Paolo.

Paolo has no reaction. Is that because of Chris's diminished prospects, given what's next? Chris wonders. Undercover? What the hell? Walking into a bank in a suit with an assault rifle slung under his jacket, smiling at a teller—that doesn't count. Purchasing tools of the trade with a fabricated identity—brief. This is complex role-play with a long duration. Do this wrong and he'll end up floating naked in the Paraná, bobbing for his own junk.

"Who did Scott Terry say he was?" he asks.

"A middleman who was buying an extensive electronic warfare

system for Amado Carrillo Fuentes's Juárez Cartel. The electronic countermeasures. And, possibly, a signal intercept system, a highly sophisticated communications package. That's who this guy claimed to be."

Okay. He notes, again, Paolo's use of the past tense.

Chris lowers his voice. "So, assuming Mr. Liu has access to a globally respected government security service, providing background checks via facial recognition software . . ."

Paolo's smile flashes again. "Yes?"

"Which service?"

"None of your business."

"FSB?" Chris guesses.

Paolo half laughs. "You're so smart about Scott Terry with his fake passport, bad knowledge of the US Army."

And prison gangs, Chris thinks.

"So, now you are the point of contact. Yes? Congratulations."

"And I will play the part and *smart* my ass off for you. Tell me what to do, and not to do, and how to act. Will they ask for the passport?"

"We will arrange for you to have a passport in the name Scott Terry."

"When's this meeting?" Chris says.

"Tonight."

"What am I standing around a swimming pool for?"

Paolo eyes him. "We are not able to learn much of this man. We know he is from Missouri, was for a short time in US Customs, maybe did some undercover street buys in El Paso or McAllen. Then worked for Lykos Consultants, a small security outfit in Alexandria. No connection to the Juárez Cartel. Do not talk much about Mr. Terry. Stay to the business."

"And what will I say?"

"That the Lius want to go ahead. You're nearly certain you will obtain their electronic countermeasure product."

They're on their way to the door when Ana calls to Chris from the stairs. She comes down and walks with them.

"Couple more things," she says. "This meeting. Assume Terry's contacts set it up to debrief him, that his contacts expect information, not just about the ECM purchase but the equipment's components, the software upgrade, and the Eastern European connections that enable Liu enterprises to source the raw system in the first place. Additionally, they'll want information on who you talked to at my father's company, what you can tell them about its operations and who runs it below him."

"Got it."

As they head toward the Suburban, Ana slows and elaborates to Chris, "Tell them you'll go back to us. You are still negotiating, but you now have access to the people who make the decisions—and developed the software. That you will be able to get anything they want, but that takes more time, more meetings with the Lius."

"Get myself out, is what you're saying."

"Preferably in one piece." She looks him straight in the eye. "After you draw them in."

"You worried about me?"

"It won't be much of a report if you're not here to make it."

"I can take care of myself," he says.

"I would expect so. Isn't that why we hired you?" She looks at him with innocent curiosity. "How did you get this job anyway?"

Chris wonders what she sees when she looks at him. What's she searching for? She's slight, physically unexceptional under loose clothes and with raised eyebrow.

He looks right at her. "Friend of a friend." Zero expression.

"That's it?"

"That's it."

Her look is taut. After a moment, she relaxes. "You worked with a man named Nate. He was in McNeil Federal Penitentiary with my uncle Marvin. He was my late mother's brother. They made a deal. Nate looked after him. My uncle didn't get extorted, knifed, or turned out. They became friends. You being here is payback to Nate."

She's testing his discretion. She knows more than he does. And she's revealed she is dead smart and not to be underestimated.

"Go get us what we need, Mr. Bergman," Ana says.

She turns and walks back to the house. Paolo starts the SUV. They drive back to town under a sunset that burns nuclear red.

..

Paolo delivers Chris the passport ninety minutes later, along with a rented black Chevy Tahoe. He is not about to go to this meeting without his own transpo.

Chris wears his Glock under his untucked shirt, cowboy boots, tight jeans. American macho. Paolo hands him a note written on Arenas Resort stationery. It's directions. *Hwy 600. Presa de Itaipu.*

Chris looks up. "They're meeting at the dam?"

"Tourism." Paolo says it deadpan.

"Maybe they'll give me a parrot to put on my shoulder for the souvenir photo."

"They want to impress him. Theater."

And they can throw him off the dam if things go bad. "There more than one exit from the hydroelectric plant?"

Paolo's face turns knowing. "A tunnel and maintenance road from a small island beneath the spillway. To the electrical substation on the Paraguayan side."

Chris nods. He doesn't know what kind of meeting this is supposed to be. Client? Report from a private intelligence firm? Hired gun?

Paolo holds out a cell phone. "Terry's."

Chris takes it. Its call and text history are empty. "Burner."

The man whose phone this was gave up the password and no longer needs it.

"The resort?" Chris asks. "If somebody turns up with a photo of Terry . . ."

"The staff at the Arenas are paid well to speak for the Liu organization. They are loyal. If anyone asks about that man, they will get faces of wood."

Face of wood. A blank look.

Chris pockets the phone. "I'll call you and leave the line open."

Paolo gives Chris a last look, gauging him. "I will be listening. And waiting."

Represa de Itaipú—the Itaipu Dam—spans the Paraguay-Brazil border on the Paraná. It's 650 feet tall, five miles wide. When the water is high and the spillway is open, the power of the runoff could blow a skyscraper off its foundations. Fifty floodgates protrude in massive pipes from the bottom of the dam, big enough to drive a bus through.

The night is starkly clear, moonlit, stars cast about like careless diamonds. Chris drives across the bridge. A silver sheen coats the water roiling through the gorge below.

Electronic warfare systems. Chris feels himself moving further from comfort, from certainty, from purchase, into the world of chance. Of possibility.

Gambling.

The rush, the feeling of a win, of portent, sweeps over him. He sets himself.

Two miles out from the dam, he calls Paolo. "Approaching."

"Copy."

Chris slides the phone into his pocket.

The road rolls through manicured countryside. In the distance the dam spreads across the horizon, a concrete cathedral. The single security checkpoint, a kiosk in the center of the road, is unoccupied.

Half a mile on, Chris spots three vehicles in a parking lot overlooking the river.

Saddle up.

He pulls in, letting his headlights sweep the vehicles: a heavy-duty pickup, an old Jeep Cherokee, and, in the center, a hulking black Suburban. He swings around, tires crunching on crushed stone, and parks facing the exit.

As soon as he opens his door, men get out of the pickup and the Jeep, their doors opening in unison, like choreography. Chris walks toward them, as casually confident as possible.

Four men station themselves in front of the vehicles. The driver of the Suburban gets out and waits for Chris to approach.

A bell tone rings through him. Recognition. His reconstructed clavicle feels a deep ache, some kind of warning.

The driver of the Suburban, the one standing with his hands loose at his sides as Chris walks up, is one of the motorbike riders. The tattoo on his right arm is clear now. The one Chris thought he saw in the security footage. The one he now realizes he glimpsed on Avenida de la Paz as the bikes converged on the Toyota Land Cruiser. It's a two-headed snake.

The man is in his late twenties, hard around the eyes. Chris doesn't break stride. He looks past him at the Suburban, like the man is merely a hood ornament.

The man steps into his path. He says nothing, doesn't raise a hand, but makes his point clear. Chris stops. He hears boots scuffling on the crushed stone around him. The men from the other vehicles are coming closer.

"*Tú*," the man says. "*Yo conozco.*"

You. I recognize you.

43

The night is cool, the air still. The river undulates, eel black, lit by slippery light from the moon and the floodlights atop the dam. The driver of the Suburban, with his slaty eyes and twitchy fingers, stands in front of Chris. The men from the other vehicles slowly draw toward him.

Chris faces him, the man he has seen surveilling the Lius' marquee shopping center. The man with an H&K MP5 on the back of a motorcycle in the city center, who opened fire on the Land Cruiser.

Chris takes a pack of gum from his front pocket and unwraps a piece and sticks it in his mouth. It's the most dismissive, American thing he can think to do.

"*Buenos noches*," he says, in an intentionally sloppy accent. "*Qué tal?*" In English, he adds, "You're not the one I'm supposed to meet."

Motorbike Man looks at him and at the others, the men gathering behind Chris's back. Chris gives a half look in either direction, letting them know he's aware.

Motorbike Man looks like he's deciding whether to admit he speaks English. In Spanish he says, "I saw you. Yesterday, in town. You were with Ana Liu."

Scuffling feet on the crushed rock. The water from the dam spillway rushes and roars.

Chris chews gum.

"Ana Liu," Motorbike Man repeats.

Chris looks at him. "And?"

"You were driving." He raises his chin toward the SUV Chris arrived in. "Not that car."

Chris can feel the other men circling him. He can sense people in the Suburban, sitting there in the dark, watching and listening. The people he's supposed to meet. The river plays tricks on his eyes, sinuous, deafening, deep.

He stares at Motorbike Man. "Yeah. So?" He leans around him, looking at the black Suburban pointedly.

"Why were you with the Liu girl?" the guy says.

"Seriously?" Chris says in English. He stops speaking in Spanish at all. He raises his voice, directing his words at the people in the Suburban. "I was with her because I flew halfway around the fucking planet to meet with her father's people. And they assigned her to me as a tour guide and minder." He spreads his hands. "I am the customer. Her daddy's company is the vendor."

He isn't sure Motorbike Man has understood all that. He leans in. "Where'd you see me? In the city, where some street theater broke out? I was twenty yards from a black Toyota with no intention of sticking around to get hit with stray gunfire."

He shakes his head. "And I thought that vehicle might be recognized." He throws a thumb over his shoulder. "New wheels, Jesus."

Motorbike Man stares at him for a few seconds, stares past him at the men who have set up a ring around him. Waits. The dam rises like a blade, blocking out half the sky. The river rushes below them.

The back doors of the Suburban open. Three men get out.

One of them waves to Chris. "Mr. Terry."

If the three men were game pieces, Chris couldn't tell you what board they came from. One is short, Anglo, in chinos and a zip-up Ralph Lauren sweater, like he got called to this meeting from his weekend home in Connecticut. The other two are ethnic Chinese. The older is wearing a Brooks Brothers suit without a tie. Horn-rims.

Hands in his pockets. The solemn stolidity of an accountant. The third man is not quite Chris's age, with the build of a distance runner or maybe a dancer. Tall, confident bearing. He's wearing a green military-style jacket with gold braid and epaulets and rhinestone medals on it, along with skinny jeans and loafers with white socks.

He's dressed like Michael Jackson. He stands in the middle, waiting. The boss, then.

Motorbike Man and the chorus of security thugs retreat and stand out of earshot by their vehicles.

Chris walks to them casually, as if it's a social event. "Good evening."

Michael Jackson paints him up and down with his gaze, like Chris is a lollipop. He says something in Mandarin. Chris waits.

The accountant adjusts his horn-rims. "Mr. Chen would like to know what you have discovered."

The accountant's accent is a mélange, like that of many people Chris has met here. Perfect English with slight British overtones, strong Chinese inflections beneath.

"You have met with the Lius, yes?" the accountant says.

Chen.

They're the Taiwanese family that owns the clifftop Casino Paraná. Major money launderers. Chris keeps his eyes on the younger man. The guy's vibe is weird. Like beneath the King of Pop jacket, he's made of electrified barbed wire.

Chris realizes he's meeting a rival Taiwanese organized crime family. And their gunman recognizes Chris's face. The gunman who had carried out an assassination in the heart of the city.

What does Chris know about the Chen family? Not enough. They own the casino. They are well established here. This guy, the Paraguayan Smooth Criminal—Chris tries not to think *clown*—is not the head of the family. Number one son, Chris thinks.

"I had my first meeting with the Liu organization," Chris says.

The accountant translates. Chen doesn't react, just continues staring at Chris.

"What, exactly, do you want to know?" Chris says.

The Connecticut Anglo speaks in Spanish-accented English. "The equipment. You saw it? The Lius have it?"

Equipment.

"They have it."

He waits for their reaction as the accountant translates. Chen nods. Connecticut licks his lips. Chris feels like he's tiptoeing through a minefield.

Chen speaks briefly. "Electronic countermeasures packages?"

He nods. "Mostly Czech, but not all. They have a pipeline. Supply is not an issue."

The accountant translates, looking at the ground, fingers on the edges of his glasses. Chris feels his heart pounding. Chen listens and turns to the river. Connecticut huddles with him, speaking sotto voce in Spanish. Chris can't catch much of it. He feels a chill at his back, a revulsion against turning away from the armed men who wait in the parking lot, clearly hair-trigger thugs.

Chen turns and approaches. He speaks in English this time. "Documentation, performance stats, schematics. Sources for over-the-counter components. Yes?"

Chris slow-walks his reply. "How to hook up with the engineering side of the house? That will be a series of meetings. They pop me the *clavo*? Easy. They already vetted me, but—"

Chen interrupts. "How'd they vet you?"

"How do I know? Ran me to someone they bought who can access a national database to do a background check. Maybe through US Customs or EPIC in El Paso. And they'll verify the source of funds. 'Show you mine, you show me yours.' But for this, I gotta get a lot deeper."

"The engineering." Chen's shoulder twitches. "The Lius talk to you about system upgrades?"

Upgrades. What kind? "They alluded to them. It's possible. For a price."

"Their software. You need to get it."

Software. "I can. And what I'm telling you is that's more time and more work."

"If you don't, you will not leave here."

"I just said I would. And I do what I say." Chris pauses. He's supposed to be a player in this transnational shit? Okay. Roll the fucking dice. "But it's gonna cost you."

Chen reacts like an entitled princeling asking the help for a second coffee. Chris wonders if he's pushed too much. But it's done.

"I'll get this for you. And you won't touch me. You'll pay me. You'll pay me enough to fly to Monaco on a private jet. Because it'll be worth it."

The younger man inches closer than is comfortable. "You will meet with us again. Tomorrow."

"I gotta social engineer this. I'm not going into their offices on the prowl, thinking I can steal this shit." He spreads his hands. "But you'll get it."

"Tomorrow."

Chen walks away, waving his fingers. His two minions follow. The accountant looks over his shoulder. "We will call you at the hotel and set the meeting."

They drive away, racing up the road in a convoy. Chris stands by the edge of the grass, listening to the roar of the water through the dam, the river seething in the moonlight.

He climbs in his Tahoe. Drives away. Says nothing. Miles down the road, he pulls off, takes a scanner from the glove compartment, and checks the vehicle for bugs. He had his back turned.

He finds a tracker beneath the rear wheel well. Is that the one he's supposed to find? He checks under the car, finds a second above the drive shaft. Somebody crawled under the car. He leaves it in place. Finds no audio bugs.

He U-turns to take the back route back into Paraguay, through the tunnel beneath the dam's spillway. He takes Terry's phone from his pocket. The call to Paolo is still connected.

"I'll talk to you when I get back."

"I'll be waiting," Paolo says.

Chris ends the call and steps on the accelerator. He watches the mirror until he hits the far side of the tunnel and drives into the Paraguayan countryside.

44

The guard at the steel gate lets Chris through. The mist from the river gorge rises like smoke as he crosses onto the island. At the Lius' house, Paolo lets him in. A TV is on in the far corner of the empty, echoing great room. A grade-school-age girl is in the kitchen, playing with a puppy. The pool in the courtyard is lit from below, patterns warbling on the surface of the turquoise water.

Paolo is his usual wood-faced totem, but his eyes are intensely curious. "I heard only a few words. And?"

"The Chens," Chris says.

"*Nem fodendo.*" No fucking way.

"Young Mr. Chen was there, dressed for the 'Billie Jean' video."

Chris watches Paolo's face. Anger. Confirmation. Calculation.

"They put two trackers on my rental. I drove back to the hotel and removed them both. They'll think I'm still there."

"Come," Paolo says.

When he knocks on the door of an upstairs study, an executive from the Liu organization opens the door. Inside, David Liu is watching a Taiwanese action movie. He's sitting on a pink combination sofa bed–airplane cockpit of some kind, with individual plush leather seat backs, consoles on either side, and padded equipment that raises up like uneven parallel bars at the foot of the thing. What the hell kind of gymnastic sex acts is it designed for? Liu wears the same outfit as always: black slacks, white shirt. He raises a remote to silence the TV.

Paolo leads Chris in. "*Es los Chens.*"

Liu eyes Chris as if making sure he's alive and intact. He gets up and walks to a desk. He lights a cigarette. He looks at Chris, speaks Spanish. "What did they want?"

"The electronic countermeasure systems."

"Of course."

"But more. The accompanying documentation. Schematics. And your software upgrades."

Liu looks at the executive, gray and impassive, who's standing in the corner.

Chris takes a risk. "I presume you have developed proprietary programming that improves the performance of the system. That, I think, is what they really want."

Liu eyes him. "Why you think that?"

Chris has to speak English to speak carefully. "Because they could get the same equipment elsewhere. All they have to do is try hard enough. Make the contacts. Or steal your contacts. But they can't obtain your programming, your code. How? Crack your encryption? They can't. For that, they need Terry, me, to give it to them or provide an insider."

Liu takes a drag and blows smoke from his nostrils. He presses an intercom button on the desk. A moment later, a female voice comes through. "Bà?"

Liu speaks in Mandarin and releases the button. A minute later, Ana arrives. Chris notes that Felix is nowhere to be seen. Ana is wearing chunky black glasses, her hair in a sloppy ponytail. She nods curtly to Chris.

"My father would like me to translate. There are some . . . subtleties in what he wishes to understand and to convey."

Chris nods back with equal brusqueness.

David Liu taps ash from his cigarette and talks for a minute. Ana waits till he finishes.

"My father says our competition, the Chen family, you said, want to steal our code." She makes sure Chris understands. "Software design, improvements on blocking and jamming systems, like that . . ."

Chris nods.

"They are aggressive, the Chens. It's commerce. Extremely competitive. We have taken a position in this field ahead of them. Now, it seems, they want to steal our programming."

There's conversation in the hallway, and Felix comes in. He looks like he's just arrived back from clubbing.

"*Qué pasa?*" he says.

Ana's glance at him is as cold as freezer ice. David Liu waves a hand, and Paolo explains in quick Spanish.

Felix drops onto the massive sofa-starship. "It's all gamesmanship."

David Liu looks at him, his face flat. "No."

Felix spreads his hands. "They're going for it. But it's meant to distract. I mean, bringing in a phony customer? They're trying to mess with our heads, get us to sell something to people who don't exist. Look like fools."

Chris bites back a reply. David Liu says nothing, not immediately. Then he mutters something in Mandarin. Ana eyes him and her brother, and then Chris.

She says, "Intelligence, not games. Code, not gossip."

Chris thinks he knows what she's talking about. "They flew an operator halfway around the world, set him up with a cover identity to obtain equipment and computer code. They got him through an intel outfit. Private consultancy. The guy wasn't up to snuff, but that's what they wanted and they still want."

Ana translates for her father.

Chris continues. "This Chen . . ."

"Claudio Chen. The son. I know him," Ana says. "We all know him."

"Claudio Chen was specific about wanting a software upgrade. I told him I would get it."

She opens her mouth but doesn't immediately translate.

"And I can," Chris says.

Ana's eyes tell him she understands what he's about to suggest. She speaks to her father. He takes another drag. Stands and circles the desk. Talks looking at Chris. Ana translates.

"My daughter says perhaps we should provide the Chens with what they're after. They will be very happy, and the program will contain malware, deeply buried inside its code, that will eventually cause the product to malfunction, catastrophically."

Chris holds Liu's gaze. He tries to name a feeling that's coursing deep within him.

It's not his high around a craps table when suddenly he's into a streak and impresses himself with himself, feeling like a winner. Successful scores give him that, too. Both last only for a while.

This is different. This is working outside of any system. Your fate is dependent on you and you alone. He's heard about others who feel this same rush. When they're working out in the wild dark zones, making it happen, scoring, with no safety net, no backup—with people and in places where there are no boundaries.

What it is, he realizes, is raw ambition.

Chris speaks with a coolness that covers his intensity. "How soon can we get it ready? They want to meet again tomorrow."

45

Chris stays overnight at the Arenas Resort, in the suite reserved for Scott Terry. The carpet is thin. The next morning Paolo turns up with Felix, who says he's there for show.

"If the Chens have eyes on you," Felix says.

Chris pours yerba maté for Felix. "If the Chens have eyes on me, they will think this is a regular meeting with the family's oldest son. That's not it. I want them to think I'm having meetings with someone who will sell you out in a heartbeat and slip me the software."

Felix thinks. Nods. "Okay." He looks at Paolo. "Who?"

Chris can't decide if Felix is irked, frightened, or over his head. In any case, he looks like he'd rather be on a golf course. Chris says, "I'll go to the warehouse and the office and let the tracker on the SUV follow me. It doesn't matter."

Felix says, "What about Ana?"

Paolo shakes his head. "No."

Chris says, "No. Why would you even suggest that?"

Felix shrugs. "Because she's not me."

Chris thinks, *Your father keeps Ana from power in the family business, and she hates that.* But he has seen nothing to suggest that Ana would ever sell out the family or that the Chens would consider her anything but the dutiful daughter. Grad student who can't wait to get back to London and her study of EU monetary policy and exchange rate algorithms.

Paolo says, "Ana won't be involved." His voice is even, but Chris gets the deeper sense of what he's thinking: *Asshole.*

Chris feels like he's at a big door to a bigger world just beyond. First he has to pull off this second part of the op.

Felix stands up to leave. "Keep me in the loop."

He can't wait to get out of there.

The phone rings three hours later.

A male voice speaks in Spanish: "Nine p.m. The casino."

"I'll be there," Chris says.

The casino, when he pulls up, is blasting. The tourist buzz in Ciudad del Este happens during daylight hours. The gunmen-in-doorways vibe puts off Brazilian and Argentinian tourists, who scurry across the bridge to staid package resorts across the triple border. The people rocking the place at night are locals.

The massive plaster roulette wheel is lit up, neon. He sees the dark Suburban at the back of the parking lot. A cigarette glows red from the driver's seat.

Motorbike Man, Chris thinks.

He has Terry's phone connected on a call to Paolo. He parks and walks into the casino.

The place is like a Chuck E. Cheese version of Vegas: cheaper, louder, darker. People slide by, chips in their hands, sequined tops on the women, shirts unbuttoned to the waist on the men. Mostly young, mostly thirsty, eyeing the crowd, maybe for better partners, maybe for the coke dealers. It's a plastic kiddie ball-pit version of high life, but in the community that counts, that makes the money, after a while Ciudad del Este is world-class.

Chris walks across the casino floor. Noise floods in from a stage somewhere. People shout. He has no itch at all to walk up to the craps table, not even a taste. That's weird.

He's here for a bigger win. Much bigger.

Ana has provided him with the software program. And, with her father's permission, she has explained what it does and why the Chens want it so badly.

The Czech ECM units have off-the-shelf capability for electronic blocking and jamming of radio systems, including satellite, she said. *What we have engineered—what is revolutionary—is GPS spoofing.*

Spoofing provides inaccurate geographic coordinates. It fools opponents—drones, planes, missiles, the DEA, a Marine platoon—into thinking they're somewhere where they're not. It makes a target impossible to locate and might cause an airborne vehicle to crash into terrain.

And, unlike blocking and jamming, a spoof does not advertise that it's active. Normally, opponents know when they're being jammed. They hear noise. Jamming disrupts their signals. But with spoofing, they don't realize they're using fake GPS data until their missiles go off course and crash into a mountain or they get lost. The spoofer doesn't disrupt the signal—it *takes over* the signal and inserts false data.

It's cutting edge. More valuable than diamonds.

A disco ball spins above the casino floor. Chris doesn't have to turn around to see Motorbike Man following him. The guy appears in the mirrored tiles that cover the walls.

In the bar, the bland executive in chinos who met him at the dam, Mr. Connecticut, stands up from a table.

"Señor Terry."

Chris takes a second to surveil the room. Claudio Chen is waiting, a tumbler of whiskey in front of him. Tonight he's wearing a vivid silk shirt with an animal print and heavy eyeliner. Motorbike Man lurks along the wall.

Claudio gestures at the seat across from him. Chris sits. He hates leaving his back exposed, but the mirrored wall tiles give him a 360-degree view. A waitress instantly appears.

"Have a drink. On me," Chen says.

Chris says, "Budweiser."

"You have enjoyed your day?" Chen smiles. He looks at Chris like he's examining a monkey, like Chris—Terry—is a pawn who doesn't know it. "You have meetings today, correct?"

"Yeah, somewhat successful," Chris says.

The waitress brings his Bud. He wants to wipe the rim of the bottle but knows that even a supposedly stupid, culturally blundering American wouldn't do that in front of the owner of the establishment he's sitting in. Not when the beer is comped. He takes a swig.

"Tell me," Chen says.

"I'll show you," Chris says. "But first I want to discuss my compensation. For extra meetings."

Be blunt. Be in their faces. Be all about the money. That's how he wants to present. Don't bother finishing your beer. Don't spend an hour getting to know them. Let them think you're a greedy motherfucker.

Chen leans back. The look on his face mixes *I knew* it with disdain and curiosity. He is young and handsome and has something hungry in his gaze. *Womanizer,* Paolo told him and Felix echoed. But the look he's giving Chris is too appreciative. It's lustful. Chen's eyes are dark behind the smoky kohl eyeliner.

Chris feels a moment of discomfort, something primal. Gets past it. Looks straight at Chen, letting him know he's playing along with this game, letting him admire.

"We can work it out," Chris says. "Bonus into my account, separate from the original fee."

Chen nods. "Bonus. Yes, if you give us what we need, you are bonus." He smiles. It's lascivious. "Ricardo will work it out with you." He eyes Connecticut.

Chris takes a CD from his pocket. He sets it on the table and puts his hand over it. "I've verified it on my laptop. But if you want to check . . ."

Chen slides his hand across the table and lifts Chris's palm. His fingers are cool and dry. He takes the CD. "We will confirm this. Tonight. If it contains what you say, you will be paid." He holds Chris's gaze. "And the decryption code?"

The Liu spoofing program is encrypted. Claudio needs the decryption key, an authentication code that must be entered before the program can be loaded and activated in the ECM equipment.

Chris takes Claudio's hand and turns it palm up. With a ballpoint pen, he writes a sixteen-character alphanumeric code along Claudio's lifeline.

"Don't wrap that around anything wet," he says.

Then Chris drinks down his Bud in one long swallow, tilting the bottle back. Stands up. Leaves. He walks to the Tahoe, the hair on the back of his neck standing up.

It's a win.

He drives away, back toward the resort. Makes sure he isn't followed. After a few miles, he switches off the headlights and zigzags into a warren of streets in an unlit workers' neighborhood. He takes the SUV back to the rental car outfit and picks up his bike.

Back at his apartment building, he climbs the stairs and stops.

Ana Liu is waiting outside his door.

"Tell me everything," she says.

46

Chris's apartment is cool and dark. Ana kicks off her shoes in the front hall.

"Habit," she says. "Even in Paraguay, Chinese manners linger."

He hits the lights in the kitchen. "Drink?"

"Who was at the meeting?" she says. "Where was it?"

"I'm going to tell Paolo, and he'll report it all to your father."

"And I can get the gist through the children's puppet show they put on for the local school?"

He stops.

She jams her hands in the back pockets of her jeans, lifts her chin. "You succeeded, I see that from the shine in your eyes. I want to know everything. The nuances. What I won't hear thirdhand from your report to Paolo, who will abridge it further for my father, who has time for the bullet points. I want your insights."

"Insights," Chris says.

"Your acuity. Sagacity. Deep, intuitive understanding of it. Shall I buy you a dictionary?"

"Sure."

"Who was there?"

"Claudio Chen. And the blond Nazi who looks like he belongs in a Disney movie. Motorbike Man, the one who took out the Land Cruiser."

She stills.

He hands her a bottle of sparkling water. "You were very chill, by the way. Focused. That's not easy," he says.

She twists the top off and drinks. "I give good facade."

"What?"

"I can maintain a facade like a pro." She pauses, looking him over, curiosity and questions in her eyes, like she's wondering about him. "I threw up after you left. Twice."

"Like a pro, I'm guessing."

She half smiles. "Claudio."

"He is—"

"A decadent freak who goes to Rio to indulge with high school girls and ladyboys or imports them to Foz do Iguaçu. He is everything you imagine and more."

She walks to the plate glass door by the balcony. The view is moonlit, trees forming a graceful canopy across the neighborhood.

"He will soon run the Chen organization," she says. "Don't let his costume jewelry fool you. He is every inch the ruthless, strategic incipient overlord my father wishes Felix would be."

Okay, Chris thinks. *Let's get into the family dynamics.*

"Felix is sanguine, casual, about Claudio," she says. "They know each other. He thinks our families are business competitors, nothing more. He's in denial. Felix wants people to get along. He parties sometimes with Claudio in Foz. He is . . . *entranced* by Claudio's ability to get whatever he wants in the club scene, and sexually."

She goes on. Felix is near to becoming Claudio's hanger-on, an aspirant to a degenerate entourage. He sees the drugs, the cocktails, the clubs, the women, the men if he ever wants one. Claudio is thriving, Felix thinks—why shouldn't he? Why does his dad not see that? Not to mention his overly diligent sister. Claudio is a hedonist, absolutely.

His first appetite, though, is the dominance and ruthless success of the Chen operation. That's what Felix doesn't get.

She starts pacing. "A year back, Felix suggested to our father that I should be married to Claudio. 'Stop all this competition. Do the dynastic thing. Marry the two families, align our business interests. A merger.' I nearly vomited. I wanted to feed Felix to the piranhas."

"That's pretty medieval."

"The piranhas or the merger?" She stops and waves the thought away. "You are American, correct?"

He has a Canadian passport, but she sees through that. "What's your point?"

"Family. Business. The diaspora. Connections and traditions. I don't think you understand about family."

Chris roots to the floor.

Ana stops and gives him a look. It lingers a second. "America is a new country," she says. "You are Anglo, your roots are fragile, the ties to wherever your people came from are nonexistent or reed-thin."

His voice is low and harsh. "I thought you wanted to talk about my meeting with Claudio Chen."

"I am talking about that," she says. "We are old families, but we don't go by old ways."

"Looks Old World to me," Chris says. "You pushed aside, while Felix is trained up."

She is chill, but beneath it, Chris senses cracks in the ice. A sharp look passes behind her eyes. Not sour, but painful. An old ache. It seems deep on such a young face.

She paces. "The Chens arrived in Paraguay after the Liu family, maybe forty years ago. We were already established here. We were blown across the ocean. I speak Taiwanese dialect, Mandarin, Spanish, English, and some Portuguese. I look like maybe half the people in this city. But we can never count on anything. We escaped the Communist takeover, the Great Leap Forward, the Cultural Revolution. Commerce and wealth are hedges against catastrophe. And we can never rest. We are willing to reinvent ourselves."

"Clearly."

"You are doing that, too."

"You don't know the first thing about me."

She sends him a slashing glance, like she wants to know what lies behind his opaque gaze. "Tell me about the meeting."

"Claudio wanted the CD. I gave it to him."

"What was he wearing?"

"Tiger print and Max Factor."

"Did he try to pull you?"

"What?"

She waves her hands. "To flirt. I don't think he would really try to seduce you. Pull. British expression."

He pauses, water bottle halfway lifted to his lips. "I must be irresistible."

She cuts a glance at him. "I bet. But what I am thinking—are the Chens trying to cut into our deal? Or are they looking at a new business model?"

"Not my area."

"It should be," she says.

That surprises him.

"Don't limit your ambition. I don't. Even in my family's business."

"What do you have in mind?"

"Long term?" She smiles. It's bright, cold, and evanescent. "Vast potential."

Chris feels like a meteor has just streaked past the corner of his eye. He wants to see more, but Ana's smile has already vanished.

She turns. "Short term?"

Graduation, he thinks.

She sets the water bottle on the counter. She looks at him searchingly, like she's trying to find a subterranean fault line she knows must be there, something deep and dangerous that she can't yet understand. She pulls the hair clip from her ponytail. Crosses the room. Stands in front of him, hands on her hips, a foot away.

He doesn't move. She doesn't blink.

She puts her right hand to his chest. Feels his heartbeat. It has suddenly ticked up.

She presses her left hand to his cheek. Her skin is soft and warm.

He sees her eyes, dark in the low light of the apartment, backlit by the moonstruck trees outside. She seems full of unfathomable and sudden power. A slim girl, surprising him. A pang runs through him. Loneliness. The immense, seemingly infinite rift in his world. The sense of being lost, of being torn away from everything that enriched him.

She holds his gaze.

He wraps his arms around her and lifts her off her feet as he kisses her.

She doesn't want the moonlight alone. In the bedroom she says, "Turn on a light. Low."

She undresses him. She doesn't pause when she sees the scars, but she does run her hand over them, as if learning their contours will educate her about him. Her hair waterfalls across her face. She scores her fingers down his chest and around his back, and then she is on him.

She's eager, she's lithe, skin beautiful in the subdued light, like she's water flowing around him.

She shoves him onto the bed and is on top of him. When she nears climax, she throws her head back, but grabs his hand and puts it over her mouth, so she can yell without the neighbors hearing.

Then she bites him. Playfully. She kneels back, panting. When she eyes him admiringly, she looks ready for seconds. He gets up to get a drink and she pulls him back.

"On top of me. You, now."

He looks at her, smiles. She's outrageous.

She laughs.

It's like she's a fighter pilot who has landed an F-18 on a carrier deck. With the engines at max power, she's ready to accelerate and take to the sky again.

"I . . ."

He's back in bed and slinks himself atop her. She tightens her legs around him, ankles crossed, and scrapes her fingers into his hair.

"There's only so much time," she says. "We have a finite number of seconds. Every single one counts."

He has a number of minutes before he'll be ready to make love again, but she's biting his ear, blowing lightly on his sweaty skin, and scrolling an index finger down his spine, and oh, Christ. He puts his lips to hers, then to her neck, shoulders, breasts, belly.

"You're beautiful," she says.

He puts his lips to her thighs. She shivers.

"Oh my God," she says, and grabs his head, and starts panting.

She climaxes again with what seems like ease and surprise and unrestrained delight. Lies briefly spread-eagled, gloriously naked, unexpectedly delicious and powerfully beautiful.

Chris tries not to think, just to feel, feel and float, but she's set him firing on too many cylinders. She lies beside him. He pulls her to him protectively, like he would a lover of many years.

Habitual, he thinks.

Then she slides on top of him.

"You now," she says. "Tell me what you want."

We only have so many seconds.

It reminds him of Neil. *Whatever time you get is luck.*

It reminds him of whose lives he's missing out on. Every second ticking away.

"Make time nonexistent," he says. "Knock me out."

She laughs. It's as refreshingly, unexpectedly uninhibited and new as everything else she's done in the last hour.

"Be careful what you wish for," she says.

This time he laughs and tilts his head back as she straddles him.

"No," she says. "Don't close your eyes. Not yet."

It's past midnight when Ana finally lies facedown across the foot of the bed, her feet kicking lazily in the air, the tight, lovely curve in her ass catching the golden light. Chris is crosswise to her, spent, winding down.

She takes the time to draw a long breath and blows it out with a near whistle. "Okay. Time to recharge."

She gets up, spring-loaded, and finds her clothes.

Chris feels languid, sated, and, for the first time in months, refreshed.

"You don't have to go," he says.

She has already pulled on her jeans and tank top. "I know," she says. "I will, though."

She slides into the oversized plaid shirt, flips her hair off her shoulders and twists it into a loose bun at the back of her neck.

"Another sparkling water?" she says.

"Help yourself."

She strides purposefully from the bedroom. He watches her backside as she heads for the kitchen. He doesn't want to move. He doesn't want her to leave.

He gets up and pulls on his jeans.

In the kitchen, Ana gets two sparkling waters from the fridge and hands one to him.

"The thing," she says, "the way to go where we can truly have impact and score, is in selling systems. Not things."

Chris frowns. "Say again?"

The light from the fridge etches her profile. The plain girl he took her to be is nowhere in existence anymore. She's not plain. What she is is stripped down to the essence, and it's raw, beautiful, unadorned— the radical center of something he's never experienced before. And she just switched channels into a completely different mode.

"Retail, real estate—the Xingfu Shopping Center, other places in Paraguay and Brazil—those are because we're diversified. They're legacy businesses. Nostalgia," she says. "The big moneymaker is selling whole systems . . . whole systems and hardware. It's global, and the more digital the better."

He stands there, listening to her talk. The Lius' enterprises, moving contraband and breaking embargoes, fly above and outwit any one nation-state's legal system. This is the future. This is the *new* new.

Behind her pedestrian appearance, this young woman is bold, driven, and dead serious about the family business. And she's showing it to him. She has a ruthlessness that's certain and cold. Ana knows she's the brains of the next generation—and that it would take an earthquake for her father to accept it. That, he can see, drives much of her ambition. Forget the flannel shirts and good-student vibe. She is self-possessed and fascinatingly accomplished. Clearly, she sees her family as the ultimate free-market mercantilists. Entrepreneurs. Transactional. And something from her Chinese diaspora culture makes this family consider themselves above the commodity they sell. Whether it's tapioca or RPGs, it doesn't affect who they think they are. They don't self-identify as part of a criminal subculture.

Chris has never met anyone like her.

"Ana?" he says.

"How long am I here, you were going to ask?"

He laughs. She'd read his mind.

"I have two more terms at LSE. I get my MBA in nine months. While I'm back in London, Fù Qīn will continue to encourage Felix to take more responsibility in the business. It won't work. My beloved brother is not engineered for that role."

"Ana."

"What?"

She downs the water, like she is replenishing the fluid levels on a finely calibrated sports car.

"The possibilities are massive," she continues. "LSE has been a plane ride into the new world—Davos, globalization. Transnational connections in Europe and Asia. Risky, as it always is on the cutting edge. But we're solidly positioned to aggressively reorient our business."

She buttons the plaid shirt.

"I'll see you again."

"Yes, you will."

"How do you know?" She smiles.

"Because I want this to happen."

"Good." She heads for the door. "So do I."

He is as off-balance as he's ever been in his life.

PART FOUR

US-Mexican Border, 1988

47

They see the truck coming across a desert floor that shimmers like mercury in the morning light. Sand blows along the asphalt. Yuma is a smear of heat to the east. Neil is in a McDonald's parking lot, at the wheel of the F-150 pickup, facing the state highway.

Cerrito's voice comes over the handheld radio. "They just exited I-8. Half a mile from you."

Engine noise growls beneath Michael's voice. He's in the Pontiac with Chris, tailing the Herrera cash truck southwest toward the border. And the cash truck is right on time.

Last week they followed it to the border crossing. This week they're going to tail it across *la línea* and find out where the money goes when it reaches Mexico.

"Coming up on you now. Quarter mile," Cerrito says.

Neil raises his radio. "Back off. Put traffic between it and you."

"He's through the lights. I can see the McDonald's sign."

"Going."

Neil slips into weekday traffic on the four-lane highway, holding a Styrofoam McDonald's coffee cup, sunglasses on, Arizona Wildcats hat pulled low on his forehead. Driving like a laid-back local.

The cash truck pulls even and then passes him, going the speed limit.

A box truck, it has a rental company logo on the side. A man with a heavy, focused face beneath a Phoenix Suns cap is at the wheel. Another man with slitty eyes is in the shotgun seat. Neil knows there's a third man in the back of the truck, in the dark with no windows, guarding the haul. He saw how the truck's crew worked when he tailed the last load. He lets the truck draw ahead.

They cross the Colorado River into California. Turn south. Two miles on, the truck pulls up at the border checkpoint on the US side.

The guard, wearing a tight brown uniform and mirrored shades, waves the truck through. Keeps waving. Neil rolls past, his pulse even, barely elevated. Two hundred yards on, the Mexican guard gives the

F-150 an equally cursory look and motions him past the entry check-point.

Three minutes later, Chris radios. "Through."

The cash truck is four hundred yards ahead. Eagerness beats in Neil's chest.

"Welcome to Mexico," he radios.

Highway 8 runs parallel to the border through farm- and ranch-land. Neil feels it, that itch. They have to be careful now. They're laying on the score. He considers this a dangerous recon. Foreign turf. The road is narrow, straight, no cover.

They've painted the F-150 and the Pontiac since last week. New colors, to reduce the chance the cash truck crew might recognize the vehicles. New plates. Neil watches his mirrors, checking that no backup car is shadowing the cash or him. They roll west under the beating sun.

Into Mexicali.

The city manifests. Stockyards, railroad sidings, warehouses. Palm trees, eucalyptus windbreaks along the highway. Schools, parks. A flowery sign: BIENVENIDOS A MEXICALI, CAPITAL DE BAJA CALIFORNIA. This is a tourist destination for American Marines and frat boys look-ing for a weekend blowout. Bars, concerts, the bull ring.

Reaching a dispirited stretch of highway, the cash truck slows. At a faded corner, it signals and turns into an abandoned property.

The Herrera stash house is a derelict Chinese-themed motel, sun-bleached red and gold. Pagoda design on the empty office, swoop-ing, wilted. An empty swimming pool sits out front, surrounded by withered palms. The place is L-shaped: two wings, two stories. Most windows on the ground floor are boarded up. The place looks ex-hausted. The electric sign at the edge of the road, half smashed, says MOTEL LA CHINESCA.

What a perfect disguise. Neil drives past, watching the cash truck. He radios Cerrito and Chris. "Truck's going around the back of the motel. Take the side street. Scope it out."

Fifteen minutes later, Cerrito and Chris meet up with Neil at a supermarket parking lot.

"The truck pulled into a loading dock along the back side of the motel," Cerrito says. "Couldn't see more without loitering in the open." He half laughs. "Chinese architecture in Mexico."

"Lots of Chinese Mexicans. Some built the railroads and stayed. Others landed here when the gringos ran them out of California." Neil is chill. "We need eyes on the back of the place, that loading dock."

He watches traffic and the people coming and going from the market: women with kids in shopping carts, men in jean jackets coming out with six-packs of soda and cigarettes. A guy dressed in a similar jacket had been sitting by the pool at La Chinesca.

"They have a guard out front at the motel. The Herreras don't hide that they occupy the place." Neil looks at the white afternoon sun. "See if we can find another abandoned building."

They drive into the neighborhood behind the motel. Entire streets around the place feel deserted. A block from La Chinesca, they find the vantage they're after: an empty beer-bottling plant.

Cerrito stays in the Pontiac as lookout. Neil and Chris climb through a busted-out window and ascend the stairs to the second story. The smell of hops lingers on the empty factory floor. At the window, Neil raises a pair of binoculars.

The rear of the motel looms in his view.

The two wings of La Chinesca are separated by a breezeway. That's where the stairway is. The breezeway provides a cut-through from the rooms at the back to the front side of the motel, the pool, and the office. A parking lot wraps around behind the motel, bordered by a cinder block wall.

The ground-floor rooms on the back side of the motel are not boarded up. Curtains are mostly drawn, doors closed. The building simply looks decrepit.

At the loading dock, midway along the east-west wing, the cash truck has backed in.

Neil feels a twinge of excitement. The truck's three-man crew is unloading shrink-wrapped plastic bales onto dollies and carts, then rolling them into the interior of the motel. He lifts a Nikon that hangs from a strap around his neck and snaps photos.

Chris, watching out the window on the far side of the floor, says, "What you got?"

Through the camera, Neil scans the loading dock. "Two armed guards flanking the truck. Shotguns."

He pans. At the tip of each wing, in the shade outside the rear rooms, a guard is stationed, revolver shoved in the waistband of his jeans. The guy guarding the north-south wing is sitting in a plastic lawn chair. He has a transistor radio on the concrete beside him.

Neil's radio crackles. Cerrito. "Cop coming."

Neil crosses to the windows overlooking Cerrito's parked car. A police car is cruising this way. Michael pulls away from the curb, nice and easy, and motors up the street. The cops keep driving.

They pull in at the motel. At the loading dock they stop and put down their window. One of the Herreras' armed guards saunters over to speak to them. Men continue unloading the cash truck. After a minute the cops continue a slow tour of the rear parking lot. The guard with the transistor radio acknowledges them with a salute. They drive off.

Neil radios Cerrito. "Cops are gone. Find cover or keep moving. We watch to see if they patrol on a schedule."

Cerrito's voice is raspy. "Every building within two blocks is empty. Think that's deliberate."

Neil thinks so, too. This is a busy city. The cartel has cleared this neighborhood so it can spot anybody who gets too close.

The F-150 is parked in the dusty driveway outside the bottling plant. Neil whistles to Chris and tosses him the keys. "Move the pickup. Away from these streets."

Chris heads for the stairs. A minute later, the pickup pulls out and disappears.

The sun rakes the motel. The men finish unloading the cash truck. Neil can just hear the vehicle's metal rear door clatter down. The driver lights a smoke. He and the other men go inside.

Neil writes on a notepad the length of time it took to unload, the time of day the cops drove by on their check-in. He watches.

Where's the count room?

Directly above the loading dock, a service elevator opens. The truck's crew roll their dollies and carts out. They push them along the exterior walkway, past the breezeway with the stairs, and turn the corner to the north-south wing. Halfway along the walkway on that wing, they stop at a door and knock. A man opens the door. They push their carts inside.

Connecting rooms, Neil thinks. The cartel will have set up ante-chambers, defenses, rooms that must be crossed to reach the count room. He waits.

He's counting. Three men from the cash truck. Three guards on the motel exterior, minimum. Unknown number of people in the count room.

One of the guards, the one who talked to the cop, gets in a red Crown Victoria and heads out to patrol the neighborhood. Maybe because the cops told him they saw Cerrito's parked car. This outfit is wired in—eyes on the street, solid coverage. Getting in will take tight teamwork and exact timing. Risky.

Taking the cash truck on I-40 in Arizona suddenly looks like a better choice.

Neil watches the second-floor rooms where the money carts disappeared. From the bulk of the packaging, the currency was probably fives, tens, and twenties—cash the Herreras' Chicago dealers collected from buyers on the street.

Neil's not here to risk himself and his crew for bills with Abe Lincoln's face on them.

In the motel parking lot, sunlight flashes from a windshield. Another box truck turns in. It backs up to the loading dock. Men get out and start unloading.

A third truck soon arrives, and a fourth.

Forget I-40. Mexicali is risky. Fucking risky. But this is the place.

He watches dozens of bulging packages of cash get ferried to the upstairs room at the back of the motel. The Herreras won't be spending that cash at the corner *mercado,* he thinks. Not sweaty crumpled bills. They're going to tally it, then send it on. How?

Ten cars pull into the rear of the motel. Ten people, men and women, get out and head up the stairs. The guards let them into the room. The door closes.

Five minutes later, they come out carrying new gym bags. Heavy. Bulging.

Neil radios Cerrito and Chris. "Cars are about to leave the motel. Follow them."

"On it," Michael says.

Chris says, "Got it."

Neil watches the cars pull out of the motel parking lot. He settles against the wall of the empty bottling plant. Cerrito radios half an hour later.

"*Cambio*," he says.

Neil nods to himself. "Keep on them." Then, "Chris?"

Outside the bottling plant, a Camaro pulls into the driveway. The driver, young, tough looking, gets out.

Somebody saw the F-150 parked there earlier, Neil thinks.

On his radio, Chris replies: "*Cambio*."

Neil turns the walkie-talkie off. The Camaro driver approaches the building. He examines the tire treads in the dusty asphalt on the driveway, looks up at the building and back at the ground. He crouches.

He's reading footprints.

Neil moves swiftly to the building's interior stairs. He runs silently up to the next floor, checking that he has left no footprints. He hopes. He finds a fire escape, climbs out, and waits. When he hears the young tough enter the building below, he ascends. He rolls over the lip of the roof and flattens himself. The wind catches him.

He draws the Colt 1911 semiauto .45 he has tucked in his belt, rolls onto his back, and holds the gun aimed at the top of the ladder.

Five minutes later, he hears the man start his car and pull away slowly.

He lowers the gun. The Herreras are good. They're cautious. They have heavy coverage in the neighborhood. He lies back.

He wants this score.

It's going to be tough. Incredibly tough.

The Camaro's engine dies away. Neil cautiously raises his head, behind a heating unit, to get a view. The car has turned a corner and is cruising away from the motel, maybe on a planned perimeter sweep.

He turns the radio back on. "Head toward the border and hold. I'll call."

He belly-crawls to the lip of the roof facing the motel. From this height, he can see the sign out front, the office, and the empty pool; the rear parking lot and the loading dock. He stares at La Chinesca as if observing a game board.

His pulse quickens. He holds, assessing, making sure he's not imagining it.

Then a car pulls in. One of the women who'd collected a gym bag earlier comes back, the same gym bag now looking square, neat. She climbs the stairs, knocks on the count room door, goes in.

Neil slips downstairs to the second-floor window. Two more cars return to the motel.

They're back for the recount.

After another ninety minutes, all the couriers have returned. Again, they emerge from the count room hauling the gym bags. It's a regular dance party. When the door opens, Neil gets a quick glimpse. A guard with a gun stands inside.

The guard nods goodbye as the couriers leave, gives one woman a smile and blows a kiss.

Down on the street, the cops make another loop.

By the window, Neil checks himself, his thinking, his calculations. His pulse is gunning.

He slips out of the bottling plant through the broken ground-floor window. Distantly, at the motel, he can hear the transistor radio playing pop music.

He walks, searching for surveillance cameras, analyzing.

The weekly Chicago cash load leaves the warehouse on the South Side. The Herreras' men drive it down and across the border at Yuma. Other drivers deliver cash loads from more collection points. They bring the haul to their stash house, a derelict motel that sits right out on the street, seemingly open and available for any bum or drug addict to break into, but in fact is spotlessly clean of trash and broken glass in the parking lot, front and back. It's manicured to look abandoned.

But the blood, the graffiti, and the markings on the walls of buildings on Neil's walk out tell a different tale. The regular patrol by the *judiciales* tells it. The man with a gun sniffing around the abandoned bottling plant tells it.

Get close, get spotted, get killed.

He walks a mile north, beneath strangling electrical and phone wires, past bodegas and tire shops and 7-Elevens and dusty neighborhoods. He radios his men once he gets into greener blocks—the university campus, a hospital—with trees, landscaping, new cars parked at the curb. Chris and Cerrito are waiting in patchy shade at a city park.

Neil approaches. "Tell me about the *cambios.*"

Cambios. Foreign exchange bureaus. Ubiquitous in a border city, a tourist town, a place where lots of people cross the US border to work. The local version of souped-up ATMs, Mexican-style American Express. Turn your *dolares* into pesos.

Or, in a town slowly becoming awash with narco money, turn it into cleaner dollars.

Michael is so excited he's nearly vibrating. "The couriers take the gym bags to *cambios* around town. All those fives and tens and twenties, you're right. That much cash, it must stink." His eyes slide around, at Neil, Chris, the park. A jagged light glints in them. "They take the stanky cash inside. Cashiers count it. They have machines, but it takes a while because there's so much freakin' money. What the couriers get back in exchange are stacks of crisp, clean hundreds. They have the colored bands around them. They're stacked two feet high by the cashier's window. The courier loads them in the duffel and heads out."

"So the Herreras roll their US street take through foreign exchange houses here," Neil says. "The small bills come south. The local *cambios* turn that into hundreds. Couriers bring it back to the stash house, count it again. Then the couriers head out with it one last time."

Michael and Chris are listening. Neil makes sure they're attentive, because he needs to lay it out.

"We could cut into the delivery on the road between Chicago and Mexicali, hijack the cash truck outside Winslow one night at four a.m. I do not doubt we could take down the truck in under two minutes and get away clean. These aren't Brinks trucks. Hit it, *boom,* done."

They look chill and focused.

"But," he says, "do that, and they know we identified their routes out of Chicago. Maybe figure out we ripped off their computer disks. They look for us. And cartels do not stop looking until they find you."

He lets that hang in the air.

"We get one shot at this. We do it on this side of the border. Two reasons. One, because that way it can't be traced back to the spreadsheets and our score." He looks at them. "Two, because we tailed a single truck, but four trucks delivered money to the stash house today." He pauses. "We hit the motel. That's the honeypot."

Michael nods. "Fuckin' A."

"How many *cambios?*" Neil says.

"The woman I tailed hit six."

Chris nods. "Man I followed went to seven. Same at all."

Neil does the math. "It's eight figures. Maybe ten million plus. They bring it back to the motel, fucking check it down to the last bill. And once they do that, they send it out again."

"Where to?"

"Don't matter. Probably getting rolled up for deposit at international banks around Mexico." He looks at them. "The point is, we will have a short window to take the hundreds."

Michael's face lights up. "We're doing it."

"I know where the count room is. It will be tough, and tight," Neil says. "But there's a weakness in the motel security. The way the guards are stationed, they have a blind spot." His heart is pounding. "We exploit that. It's our way in."

He heads for the F-150.

"Michael, go back to Yuma, different route. Chris, you drop me off."

Chris walks to the truck. "Where?"

Neil nods toward the border. "El Centro."

Elisa's house is fifteen miles due north of here.

48

Neil walks behind Elisa in the quiet night. She's climbing, her hips swaying, hair glossy in the moonlight. The dunes have dissipated the day's heat. Traffic drones on I-8, distant. Mountains and canyons slice the view. The sand slides beneath Neil's feet.

Elisa stops at the crest of the dune, hands on her hips. Her shoulders are thrown back, her chin high. She's barely out of breath. Neil catches up.

"See what I mean?" she says.

He stops at her side. Her eyes absorb the night. The Algodones Dunes flow from horizon to horizon, a sea beneath the stars. The Mexican border is two miles south. He can't see it.

Elisa can.

She points. "Dark scar along the west. There. It's rock, *arroyo seco.* Dry creek. Cuts through to *la línea.*"

"Who patrols?" Neil says. "How frequently?"

"INS, Border Patrol. Federales?" She shrugs. "Once a year."

"We plan to drive," he says.

"Of course." She turns. "But you want me to show you these routes."

"I do." He slides his arms around her.

"That arroyo," she says. "A dirt road leads down a canyon. Too steep for most drivers. Cops ignore it. *Contrabandistas* hike in. Small loads. Dope. People."

A breeze scuttles around their feet. The sand shirrs, a scrim, scintillating in the moonlight.

"That would be plan Z," Neil says. "Backup to all the backups."

Elisa turns. "But now you know it's there. And why it's plan Zeta." She gestures, arm sweeping, at a barely visible dark track. It skirts the dunes and disappears into a ravine. "There."

Neil puts the binoculars to his eyes. Under the moon, he can see the snaking road, rising through the rocks.

"That's where *contrabandistas* get ambushed," Elisa says. "When they're . . ." She snaps her fingers, searching for the word. Her English is flawless, but she wants the right emotional inflection. She switches to Spanish. "Slipshod. Careless. They think they are in the clear because they're across the border. But *pow*."

Neil wonders if this is romantic tale-telling of smuggler tradecraft or a warning.

"We'll be coming in the daytime, unlike most other smugglers out here."

"And you're careful. You have eyes in the back of your head."

"On a swivel."

She looks at the horizon, then at him. She trusts him, he knows. Trusts his skill, his focus, his purpose. Like he trusts her knowledge of this country.

She tucks her hands in her jeans pockets. "The three official crossings, you should use them all. The two in Mexicali, straight into Calexico. And the Winterhaven crossing, for Yuma."

Elisa knows a hundred secretive smuggler's paths into Mexico and—by different routes—back across the border. She knows every guard who takes bribes at checkpoints. She isn't in the crew, but she is an integral part of the team that will get the crew safely back across after the score.

"What?" she says.

"Admiring you." He turns back to the dunes. He scuffs the sand, erasing one of his footprints.

She switches back to English. "You will not cross the dunes."

"No." He exhales. "Just reminding myself how quickly things get erased. It all comes, it goes."

"You philosophize?"

"We're all footprints on a beach. The tide comes through and you were never there."

"A guy named Albert Camus wrote that." She tilts her head. "What kind of name is that?"

"French," Neil says.

Elisa looks at him, her eyes shining in the dark. "I'm here now."

"Exactly. That's the point. We're here now. No big reason we exist. No purpose. No heaven or hell waiting on how we pray. The only real question is, why keep on living? Is life worth it? Why not just kill yourself? The only judgment is how we use the now."

"I don't want to put an end to it. If this is what we have, better live it."

"Yeah. All we have is this moment. We live it, conscious of what it means. Nothing. But completely live it. That's what it is."

"Where you read this?" she asks.

"Folsom. What's my life? Why do the time? What am I doing? What's any of this mean? Hit the library and said, 'Where's the philosophy about why we're here, about time? What my life means?' Dude with the book cart turned me on to Camus."

"That's heavy," she says. "That's why I love you, crazy man."

He holds her a moment, nerve ends awake from the night, the recon, and especially from her. That scent, gardenias. The confidence and joy in her eyes.

"You should cross a few times beforehand," she says. "Let the border guards know you. Maybe as a US businessman, going to the *maquiladoras*." She runs a finger down his black button-down shirt, tugs the zipper on his baseball jacket. "But you have to dress better. A suit. Pretend you're a capitalist."

"I am a capitalist."

She laughs. "Catch me, running dog. I want to show you something."

She spins and plunges back down the dune. Neil catches up and passes her. They race to the car. He wins and leans against the hood, arms crossed. She waves him off, sweeping her hair back.

"You're like Gabriela. So competitive."

"Where to?"

They drive east on a state highway, then a county road, and turn off at a dirt driveway with a gate and barbed-wire fencing. Elisa hops out and opens it. The sign over the gate, once proud, now nearly rusted through, says FLYING A RANCH. The driveway leads them over a cattle grate and past empty corrals and water troughs to a darkened house.

Neil stops, headlights shining on it. "Safe house."

"Like it?"

He kills the ignition and gets out. The rambling ranch house is an adobe barracks.

Elisa gets out. "Room here to park your car hauler."

He nods as he ascends the step to the covered porch. His car hauler is currently stashed at the back of a shopping mall parking lot in Yuma, but he wants to get it off the road, out of public view.

"This is good," he says.

He goes in the adobe. Elisa follows and flips a switch. The main room lights up.

The place is spacious, spartan, clean. Furnished. Elisa crosses to the open kitchen. There's a coffeepot and fruit on the counter. She opens the fridge. It's pre-stocked with soft drinks and iced tea.

"I'll load in groceries when you're ready," she says.

Neil heads along the hall. The place is an old bunkhouse for ranch hands. It has five big bedrooms. The beds are made. Three rooms for the crew, doubling up. A big room at the end of the hall for him and Elisa. A smaller room for Gabriela.

"Who took care of this?" Neil says.

"Tío Tomás. From Nogales. My old uncle."

"He's on top of it."

"He has experience." She lingers at the door to the small bedroom. "He'll watch Gabriela."

Tonight, Gabriela's at home in El Centro with a babysitter, a neighbor girl. But after the score, they're going to take off for a while, drive to Colorado. School will be out for Gabriela. Elisa does not want her daughter at home when she will be in Calexico on the day. She wants her with Tío.

"Tío and her can play board games."

"Chess. She'll cream him," Neil says.

"Come on." Elisa nods at the front door. "I'll show you the other one."

She has secured a second house, even more derelict, out in the desert, where Neil and his crew will meet after the score to switch out their cars.

Neil takes her arm in his hand as they leave. "Thank you."

"What for?"

"Perfection."

He spins her around and embraces her, her body against his, her pelvic bone saddled against his hips. They fit. They always have. They were perfectly in tune the day they met. Instant confidence about being together. The singularity of focus of mind and body.

When she kisses him and pulls him back inside to the bedroom, he feels like the *now* has always been.

49

The day is clear, the morning cool with a gold sun rising. The adobe barracks is busy. Neil and his crew are bunked down. There's coffee in the kitchen, plus bacon, eggs, toast. Chris eats like a linebacker. Cerrito puts three sugars in his coffee. Neil stands at the front windows.

The car hauler is parked outside, the blue Peterbilt rig gleaming in the sunrise. The cars have been unloaded: the boring suburban clunkers, the F-150, the fast car, the old Eldorado, the big Mercury with the false panels in the doors and below the floor mats.

On a big wooden table in the living room, their gear is laid out. Six CAR-15 rifles. Ammunition. Flash-bangs—noise- and light-generating grenades—to distract and disable any opposition. Flex-cuffs. Duct tape. Electrical tape. Maps of the United States and Mexico. Range-finder binoculars.

The next cash load is due in three days. Today they're making another recon across the border. They have to assess cartel communications capabilities. They need to prompt the traffickers' reactions to emergencies, so they can clock the response times of the *judiciales*. They know the cops are on the Herreras' payroll. They have to lock in escape routes and gather rock-solid intel on the cartel's drivers, money handlers, and security forces at the derelict motel.

And Neil wants Chris and Michael to verify what he saw the last time: the hole in the cartel's security.

That blind spot. It still thrills him.

A dented Chevy pickup rumbles up, dust blowing behind it, and Tío Tomás gets out. Neil walks outside to help him bring in supplies.

"Hola, Neil. *Qué tal?*" he says.

"Going good."

Tomás Vasquez is sixty-six, dressed like a vaquero: snap-button shirt, jeans, square-toed cowboy boots, and a straw cowboy hat tilted back on his head. His face is sun-creased, his eyes quick like a falcon's. He hands Neil a toolbox, then gets the latest load of groceries.

Inside, Chris looks up from his plate. "Hey, man."

Chris's face is bright, his skin shiny. Neil knows it's because of the upcoming score. Chris is on fire. Okay, good, it means he'll have energy to spare if and when they need it. That's when Chris cleans up his act—no booze, no blow. He's astute, all vivid energy, seeing everything. Nothing sluggish, as if chemicals allowed his acuity to rest, and now, no longer asleep, he is bright and wakeful. Innovative, freethinking, fast. And there's more now. Chris told him there's a woman.

Michael comes out of the bedroom with a loose plaid shirt over a white tee, sunglasses, keys in his hand. Sanguine, slow moving, it seems. Big mistake if you think so. He'd kill you as soon as look at you. Affable sociopath. Neil knows he's got at least two pieces and two knives on him.

They finish breakfast and get ready. Tomás will stay and guard the house while they're gone.

Chris grabs a final piece of bacon as he runs out the door. He waves. "See ya, Tío." Jogs outside.

Two cars again. Easy crossing from Calexico to Mexicali, from California to the slightly more disheveled, far livelier side of the line. Buses of kids in school uniforms head for some kind of fiesta. End of the school year here, too. They drive through the bustling section of the city that crowds up against the border. The cathedral, Nuestra Señora de Guadalupe, is a flat orange church on a street lined with shops that sell First Communion dresses. The sun is fierce. They're only 250 miles from Los Angeles, hardly farther south, but the inland desert, the dry air, turns everything sharper and contrasts with Calexico, with its dust bowl origins and '50s neon signs—a different, more optimistic time.

They vector toward the motel at an angle. The dead zone around La Chinesca will have borders, some clear, some fuzzy. They don't know how far out the cartel's surveillance extends, what forms it takes, and how to circumvent it. Not yet.

The Monte Carlo Cerrito is driving has been painted again, this time brown, a dusty color to blend with the neighborhood around La Chinesca. Nothing on it shines. He peels off to circle the dead zone.

In the F-150, Neil and Chris join morning traffic on the road that runs in front of the motel. They'll make two passes: going, coming. Anything more might trip an alert security team that they're being cased.

A block away, Neil says, "Here we go."

Chris raises the Nikon. As they drive past, he clicks the shutter, on auto. The camera whirs. Neil cuts a look at the property.

No cars are parked out front. Everyone who works at the motel has parked in the back.

Neil cruises on. Four-lane road, no median. Highway entrance a quarter mile east of the motel.

"This is our primary route," he tells Chris.

He turns onto the highway, a wide, divided boulevard, checking the turn, the paving, the traffic. One of the border crossings they'll use is nearby. Scrub, sand, and palms line the road.

"Presume we'll cross midafternoon. Shouldn't be busy," Neil says. "People who work in the US cross first thing in the morning." He turns the truck around. "If there's a line, there's a line. We'll be in the switch car."

Neil drives past the motel again, heading west this time. Chris shoots more photos across the cab, as Neil checks out La Chinesca with his peripheral vision. His pulse ticks up.

Chris scans the road carefully and radios Cerrito. "Inbound."

The walkie-talkie crackles. "Meet you at the supermarket."

In the *supermercado* parking lot, Cerrito approaches the truck and Neil puts the window down.

"Nobody guarding the motel moves around," Michael says. "They all stay at their posts."

Neil nods. "Here's the thing. No cars out front. To protect the guards' sight lines, maybe." He frowns, thinking, verifying the angles in his memory. "There's one guy. Sits on a lawn chair behind the empty pool. Like he's defending a dry moat."

Cerrito nods. "And?"

"I'm seeing something he's not." Neil doesn't want to jump the gun. He needs verification. "Chris, how many cameras did you clock on the front of the motel?"

"One," Chris says. "Single camera over the door to the office, under the parking portico. And it's aimed down, like in a convenience store."

Neil looks at him. "The cartel hasn't changed it since they took over the place."

Cerrito says, "More cameras on the rear of the property, I'm sure."

"We check that next." Neil starts the truck. "After dark."

At sunset, when the arching sky screams red and violet, Neil parks in the bar district off one of Mexicali's central plazas. He and Chris walk two miles along busy streets, then cut through residential neighborhoods and shuttered commercial and industrial blocks. Traffic dims. The stars rise through sandy haze and smog into a cobalt sky. Dogs bark behind chain-link fences.

But when they get to the dead zone, there's nothing. No sounds. They split up when they approach the abandoned beer-bottling plant. Neil waits across the street, in a stand of trees, watching Chris slip inside. Michael appears and goes in as well. No cars. No barking. No streetlights come on as night thickens. He waits half an hour. Nobody comes past on patrol. That tells him that there aren't surveillance cameras turned this way, covering the street here.

Blind spot number one.

He slips through the broken window into the bottling plant. Chris and Michael wait on the third floor, kneeling at a window facing the motel. The dirty glass lets in sketchy amber light. Neil takes the binoculars from Chris.

The motel is no more busy than last time. But there are more cars parked out back now. Behind several windows on the second floor, light leaks around drawn curtains.

He points and speaks quietly. "North-south wing. Lights on. Count 'em. Six rooms."

Chris tilts his head. Michael shakes his.

"Two in the middle . . . I don't see no lights," he says.

"Those are the sally port and the count room," Neil says. "They have the windows boarded up, maybe bricked. Can't tell from here."

Chris nods. "There's a guard outside the door on the left."

Neil lowers the binoculars. "Another weak point."

Chris pauses a minute, working it out. "We don't go through the door from the walkway straight into the count room?"

Neil looks at him, pleased, and feels a warm excitement in his chest. "Exactly. It will be boarded up from the inside. We go in through the connecting room."

"And because all their security is focused on the count room door . . ." Chris stops. Holds out his hand for the binoculars. When Neil hands them over, his excitement increases. Chris has seen it too. "There's a blind spot," Chris says. "Fuckin' A."

Cerrito grabs the binoculars. Stares. Looks frustrated—what are they seeing that he isn't? Then he smiles. "If the count room is that one, they have rooms blocked off on both sides of it. But motel rooms only have connecting doors on one side."

Neil steps closer to the window. "Right. So the room to the right, where the light is leaking through—they've cut a hole in the wall to create access. They've turned the motel into a rat run. A maze. And they don't think anybody knows it."

Chris stands taller, his energy coiling.

"The other thing," Neil says. "The guards are still stationary."

Cerrito nods. "Shit, yeah."

Chris leans close to the glass. "And . . ."

Neil waits a second. "And there's a hole in their coverage."

They all stare at the motel. L-shaped. Two wings. The office and loading dock are on the east-west wing. The count room is on the rear side of the north-south wing. Stairs in the breezeway where the two wings meet. The empty pool out front, where one guard sits. The second guard, the one with the transistor radio, sits outside a room on the back corner of the north-south wing. The third sits outside the back corner of the east-west wing. Loading dock guards come and go with the arriving cash trucks. The rest of the time, when individual couriers arrive and depart, they float along the upstairs walkway on the back of the motel.

Chris says it. "The guard out front by the pool. Nobody else can see him."

"Right," Neil says.

One guy out front, facing the street. Everybody else on the back, because that's where the action is.

"They don't walk sentry," Chris says.

"They think it's enough to control the surrounding streets," Neil says. "They think the dead zone protects them. The Herreras made examples of people who violated it. Now the guards think nobody else would dare."

Chris shifts, like a cobra tensing. "The guards have gotten comfortable. They think the Herreras' reputation scares off any threats. That can't be enough, can it?"

Neil watches the guards. It's dark. They sit.

"No, it's not enough," Neil says. "They have backups. They have runners, tipsters, people on the payroll who patrol the dead zone. And not regular, which makes it more dangerous."

"Plus the cops," Chris says.

"Time to test the *judiciales'* response time."

Cerrito nods. "Let's do it."

He and Neil hike to the pickup. Michael has the flattened spare tire. He lowers the tailgate and sits on the back. It's after midnight.

Traffic is spotty. Neil approaches La Chinesca at a normal clip, with cardboard over the right headlight to disguise the truck.

Chris is waiting in an auto wrecking yard across the street.

As they approach, Michael rolls the spare tire off toward the motel driveway. The tire sails across the forecourt and crashes into the empty pool with a loud clatter.

They keep driving, taillights out.

Chris ducks and watches the motel. The stopwatch on his Timex is running.

Lights come on at La Chinesca, floods in the withered palm trees. Three guards stand over the pool, pointing, talking, waving their arms. One is on the radio. Another jogs to the office and makes a phone call.

When the *judiciales* arrive, two units, they don't come with lights and sirens. They pull in, and they confer with the guards. They slowly circle the motel, side spotlights swiveling. They drive into the dead zone. They come up the street toward the auto wrecking yard. Chris flattens himself on the ground. As they drive by, windows down, he hears them talking with each other and over the radio.

"*Nada*," one of the cops says. "*Nadie.*"

They drive on.

Within fifteen minutes, they're gone, and the guards return to their posts.

Chris runs for the meeting point. He jumps in the pickup. Neil pulls out.

"Four minutes thirty-four seconds," Chris says.

Neil considers it, driving toward the border crossing Elisa has told him to take at this time of night.

"And?" Cerrito says.

"We're going to take it," Neil says.

"How?"

Neil knows Michael will saddle up. He's never seen Michael anything but eager to grab his guns and say, *Let's go.*

Neil looks back at the motel. The sagging pagoda, gray in the shadowed night. The shaggy palm trees. The darkened windows.

"We take the guard by the pool, then the two who sit in the chairs at the back. Then we go up the stairs and take the count room while the couriers are inside waiting. We assault anybody else who's there."

50

It's two a.m. The sound of tires on the freeway is a distant whine.

The Pontiac Trans Am cruises the surface streets, up and down, back and forth. Otis Wardell rides shotgun, Svoboda at the wheel.

Wardell's tired. The radio plays some Yuma station, Iron Maiden.

Svoboda reaches a corner. "Which way?"

The engine idles. Wardell looks up and down the cross street. Points right. Svoboda turns.

"How much longer you want to give it tonight?" Svoboda says.

Wardell watches the street crawl by. A McDonald's. A car dealership. Parking lots.

"All night, all day, until . . ." he says.

He has a walkie-talkie. The rest of his new crew is on the east side of town, doing the same thing he and Svoboda are.

"I have black sky night vision. And that car transporter is too big to hide. Drive."

Hey, McCauley, wherever the fuck you are. I'm here.

Svoboda drives.

51

It's twilight when Neil steps out on the porch at the adobe barracks. A wash of stars is breaking out overhead. He takes a breath, lets the dry heat of the fading day clarify his thoughts. Inside, the crew is prepped. Their gear is laid out. The map of the Mexicali neighborhood is spread on the big living room table.

The Herrera cash truck is on its way down from Chicago, somewhere outside Amarillo now, on I-40. It will arrive at the Winterhaven border crossing in thirteen hours, then drive through the northern Baja farmland to La Chinesca.

Neil and his crew will be waiting. They'll leave here at 3:30 a.m.

He has just gone over it with them one more time.

Standing over the big table, he had tapped the map. *We infiltrate the dead zone, four to four thirty a.m. Concealment in these three abandoned buildings. Guards change shift at eight. Judiciales patrol at seven and eleven.*

The crew watched coolly, clearly, ramping up.

When the couriers all return from the cambios, we go, Neil said. *Take guards one, two, and three—the ones who sit on the plastic chairs outside the motel. Then up the stairs to the back side of the wing with the count room. In through the antechamber. I take point. Chris and Michael with me. Trejo and Molina outside on the walkway, flanking the door, with covering fire sectors. Marcos on overwatch.*

Nobody spoke. They watched Neil.

The crew has prepped for CQC, close-quarters combat. Neil, Chris, and Cerrito will form a three-man assault squad. Neil has run them through it, using the long porch out front here at the adobe as a training ground. They're not military, but his assault plan will use them as a cross between the Viet Cong and US Army. They'll have Trejo and Molina as lookouts and backup on the exterior, with their intersecting quadrants of fire.

We neutralize the guards in the antechamber. Flex-cuff the couriers and people overseeing the count. Load up the banded hundreds on the rolling carts. He turned to Trejo and Molina. *I will alert you to bring the car to the loading dock. We roll the money carts to the service elevator above it. Come down, load up. Split. Get the switch cars. Cross. Hook up at the meeting house.* He took a beat. *Out by three p.m. Gone.*

He eyed the crew.

Questions?

None.

Now he listens to the desert.

The night before the score is all about anticipation. Always. That's good. That means focus. That means energy. Purpose. That means Neil zeroes himself and plays out every single possibility, every tangent, every random twist that could derail the job. It means he thinks of everything he hasn't thought of and brings it to the surface, examines it, and plans how to incorporate it into the takedown.

It's how he lives and survives. How they all will.

In the desert, the night falls hard. It seems like just a few minutes before the black sheet of the sky is overcome, pierced, with more stars than he's seen in his entire life, streaming like a river of light. Cold, relentless, immense.

He hears the door open behind him. Elisa comes out. Voices pour through behind her. Cerrito talking in the kitchen with Tío Tomás. The television, *Monday Night Football* crowd noise and play-by-play. Chris and Trejo shout about something on the field, a penalty call.

Elisa sidles up beside him. She leans against one of the posts that hold up the porch roof. "Stargazing?" she says.

Her eyes are dark, her voice a deep pool. She's wearing jeans and a T-shirt, but manages to look slinky. Her feet are bare.

He surveys the cars parked on the dirt. "Something like that."

"We're set here," she says. "And at the meeting place. What else? Batteries in the radios."

He glances at her. "Thanks."

"I put new ones in all of them and checked they work."

He smiles. "Of course you did."

He pulls her to his side. Her hair smells fresh. She's calm, like always. In a groove. Ready. He thinks she was born ready. She's not part of the crew, but she is an anchor, a lighthouse for him. Maybe for them all.

She puts her hand to his cheek thoughtfully, as if checking his temperature, seeing if he's running a fever. "You sleep tonight?" she says.

"I always get rack."

"*Estás mintiendo.*"

"I never lie to you."

"I know. Now I do. At first I couldn't tell," she says, "because . . ."

"What?"

"When I met you, I thought you were cold."

"I was," he says. "Three weeks out of Folsom. I was colder than ice."

Wandering untethered in the open world, away from the order and the institution. Returned to a state of nature, freed, unmoored, strange. Wary. Violent. Ready to strike out at an instant's provocation. Then . . .

"I was a closed door," he says. "Alarms, locks, guarding myself. Used to it. Too many years. And then"—he strokes her cheek—"I see you."

"Homely widow with shifty eyes. A smuggler who barely knows how to cook."

"Glory of my life. Complete surprise." He tries to find the words. "Sunrise. Warmth. Elisa, you brought me back to life."

"Funny. So did you, for me. Weirdos attract."

The way she says it, the word sounds enticing. *Weirdos.*

She smiles. "Come. Tuck Gabriela in."

They go in. Chris is charged up and eager. It's halftime and he's on the old wall phone in the kitchen. He paces back and forth, receiver to his ear. "No, great. Busy day. Hot, but good." Chris's eyes gleam, something dreamy in them. "How was your day?"

Charlene, Neil knows. That's the name of the woman who has lit Chris on fire. Neil hasn't met her yet, but he knows that Chris came in from Las Vegas with her. She's now in LA. Something serious going on there.

"Cool, baby," Chris says as Neil walks past.

In the small bedroom, Gabriela is sitting on the bed with a book, reading by an amber desk lamp. Elisa goes in first.

"Time for sleep, *mariposa*," she says.

The little girl has soft brown hair. The strawberry birthmark on her neck is shaped like a butterfly. She is self-conscious about it, but Neil has told her that it's what's called a "distinguishing mark." He thinks she's distinct, she's a champ. Elisa worries that Gabriela will get comments or be teased, so she reminds her that it's like a special kiss, a beauty mark. *Mariposa.* My butterfly.

Elisa claps her hands softly and Gabriela dives under the covers. She's quiet and bookish, thoughtful. And, Neil thinks, observant. Self-sufficient. Not watchful, not nervous. Self-confident.

That's not just inborn personality, he thinks. That's Elisa. That's a mother pouring out total assuredness, day and night.

That wasn't in his life.

Elisa pulls the covers up around Gabriela and smooths her daughter's hair. "Sleep tight, baby. I have to get up early with Neil for work. Tío will get breakfast for you."

"*Huevos con queso?*"

"Sure, and you help do the dishes," Elisa says. "I'll see you in town."

Gabriela squirms. Her eyes light up. "And then we're going to Colorado."

"*Sí.*"

Gabriela draws a big breath. The excitement is making her wiggly. "Read me a story?" she says.

"No, sleep."

"*Por favor,* Mama. Come on. Please." Her voice is soft, clear.

Neil comes over. "How about you read me one?"

Elisa kisses her on the forehead and smiles at Neil. In the low light, her T-shirt is the emerald green of a jewel. That green is in his memory. She leaves, quietly pulling the door closed on her way out. Neil sits on the edge of the bed. Gabriela props up the pillow, snuggles against him, and opens the book.

She looks up. "What are you thinking about?"

"The smell of new paper. It reminds me of a neighbor I had when I was a kid your age," he says. "Mrs. Borejszo. She used to give me a sandwich sometimes when I walked past her house on my way home from school when I was seven or eight. She had pictures of men she used to know in Europe. One was in a fancy uniform. Another was of herself dressed as a dancer. In beautiful frames. She had a piano. There was sheet music with Russian and Polish names."

He heard her arguing with his father one time to take better care of him and his brother. His father got angry. She got angrier.

"And she helped me learn how to read. She was a very nice lady."

She gave him his first knowledge of maternal caring. She reached out to him for no reason other than she saw him and wanted to.

All he has of his mother is an impression of her green dress with sequins and her perfume as she kissed him on the forehead one night before leaving with a man who was not his father. Maybe Neil was three.

And he remembers her heavier, exposed, watching a game show on TV and screaming at his father, who took off the belt he always wore and beat her with it.

The civil war ended when she left. Neil was four. His brother was two.

There was the day Mrs. Borejszo went to the hospital. She came home emaciated with cancer. Then she was gone. It was soon after that his father placed them in foster care because he found it too difficult dealing with them. He checked in once or twice and then disappeared from their lives.

As an eleven-year-old foster child, Neil went to school in mismatched, handed-down clothes from Goodwill. He was ostracized, resentful and angry. He got remanded to a juvenile facility because there was no one to deal with him. His brother was sent to a different foster home. They lost track of each other.

Gabriela looks up at his silence with innocent eyes. Neil nods at the book on her lap.

"What's it about?"

She opens it. "The ocean."

She brushes her fingers along the thick pages. Glossy. Pictures of bright schools of fish, flicking silver. Light playing on depthless seas.

"The ocean is seventy percent of Earth's surface," she says.

She tells him how the Pacific Ocean stretches halfway around the globe, from Alaska to Antarctica. She speaks with soft wonder.

She turns a page and says conspiratorially, "This is my favorite part."

On the page are pictures of azure-and-turquoise waters. Nighttime. Glowing.

"What the hell is that?" Neil says.

"Fiji." She looks up. "It's in the South Pacific." Her fingers trace the shimmering surf. "It's iridescent algae."

He almost frowns at her. "Iridescent."

She leans toward him. "It glows in the dark. The whole ocean. When you touch it, when you swim in it, the ocean lights up. Like magic."

"Wow."

"Can you imagine that?" she says. "You swim through it and it's like a falling star follows you."

"I can fully imagine being there and swimming in that."

"Can I come with you?"

"Sure. Absolutely. You and your mom."

Gabriela smiles. "An ocean of lights. Isn't that something?"

"You bet it is."

52

The road is narrow, empty, no lights this far out of town. It's been days now, and Otis Wardell is pissed. Svoboda can tell. He's going through the motions now. One more road. One more turn. One more hour. *That car transporter has to be here,* Otis thinks. Svoboda thinks it's becoming Otis's white whale.

They came down here from Chicago full of fire, Otis full of rage, after leaving Aaron Grimes hanging from a hook in his auto repair garage, like a gutted fish. Cleared out, after that botched home invasion on the Gold Coast.

Svoboda doubts he can ever go back.

Otis has decided, through Otis logic, that his problem *and* his solution is Neil McCauley and his highline crew and a fat score they're planning. They've been driving up and down every street and parking lot and scorpion trail in Bumfuck, Arizona. They have three more guys in two other cars, patrolling I-8 from Tucson to the California border. Otis knows the car hauler has to be here.

Sure.

Sure as he thinks this magical score is going down. Svoboda has his doubts.

Hank Svoboda wants to drive north and spend the rest of his life in Canada. But here they are, fucking around on the southern border.

Sand and heat and, so far, nothing more. If they don't find the car hauler, they're going to run out of money soon. That means a liquor store holdup or a bank score.

Wardell is edgy, itchy. This guy McCauley is nowhere in sight. Otis's eyes are cold in the late-night dashboard lights. He's running his palms up and down his thighs, like wiping off sweat.

The road curves. The headlights sweep the vista—nothing but sand and cactus.

"How much farther you want to go?" Svoboda says.

"To China," Wardell says, griping now. "No. Fuck it. Turn around."

Svoboda slows to make the U-turn. The headlights catch a driveway: dirt, cattle grate, barbed wire fence. Up a dirt track, barely visible, an old adobe bunkhouse for ranch hands.

A glint of metal.

He stops. Hits the brights.

There's a blue Peterbilt out front.

Svoboda turns slowly, as the headlights crawl over the sight.

It's the car transporter.

53

The night is quiet when Neil wakes up. Elisa is asleep beside him, warm and soft, arm across his chest, but when he climbs out of bed, she stretches and silently joins him, getting dressed.

In the kitchen, Tío has brewed coffee. Taciturn, competent, he hands Neil a cup.

"*Gracias*," Neil says.

The men come in. Quiet, purposeful, they spark with energy. The curtains are down. Beyond the house, it's still full night. They eat wordlessly. Cerrito. Shiherlis. Trejo. Molina. Marcos, Elisa's cousin from Piedras Negras, who will serve as lookout. He's twenty, a bantamweight boxer, calm, explicitly trustworthy. Meaning Elisa trusts him. *Nerves of iron*, she told Neil, which Neil believes, because Elisa knows nerves of iron. She has them.

Elisa creeps down the hall to check on Gabriela.

"Sound asleep," she says when she returns. She drinks another cup of coffee, then gets her car keys and waits for Neil to hand her a radio. She will monitor the border crossings today.

Elisa presses the Transmit button. "Check," she says.

On the table, from multiple handsets, her voice comes through clearly.

Neil checks his Colt 1911. Ejects the clip, reinserts it. Seats it home with a hard smack from his palm. Pulls back the action to chamber a round. Holsters it under his baseball jacket.

They're all wearing black: black tees, black jeans or combats, black shoes, black jackets. Black ski masks rolled up and ready to pull on. Over that, for the border crossing, they pull on plaid work shirts, sweatshirts, or pale T-shirts.

"We have the codes?" Neil says.

Everyone nods. They won't use names over the air. They have verification key words to let one another know when things are clear or when there's trouble.

The men take rifles and full boxes of cartridges and shotgun shells from the big table. They put spare clips in their pockets. Grab flash-bangs. Flex-cuffs.

They will stage while it's still dark. They'll wait, concealed, for the cash trucks to pull in and for the count to be carried out, for the couriers to take the small bills to the *cambios* and then return to La Chinesca.

And when the couriers haul the week's takings into the count room in the form of clean, crisp hundred-dollar bills—maybe $10 million worth of them—Neil will give the signal.

He looks at the crew. "Let's go."

54

At 4:35 a.m., Mexicali feels empty. The road in front of La Chinesca is bare of traffic. Neil waits in the dead zone with Chris and Cerrito.

They're concealed a hundred yards from the stash house, in a slanting abandoned garage. They have an unobstructed view of the motel and surrounding streets.

Trejo and Molina have positioned their switch cars near the border crossings they'll use after the score. They're now patrolling the perimeter of the dead zone in an old Eldorado.

Elisa's cousin Marcos is on the far side of La Chinesca from Neil, on the third floor of the abandoned bottling plant, on overwatch, with an unobstructed view of the motel, the parking lot, the surrounding streets, and the dead zone.

Elisa is on the US side of the border with a radio and binoculars, surveilling the border crossings. Safe and distant. Eyes and ears. Neil has an urge to call her, to hear her voice, that low, ringing laugh.

Tonight. They'll be on the road, heading north to the Rockies. He puts that thought in his pocket as he stares out a broken window at the motel. It looks lifeless.

He tells Chris and Michael, "Get some sleep."

Michael settles against a wall and closes his eyes. Chris keeps staring out the window, wound up, reflexes keen.

"You need to be this sharp in ten hours," Neil says. "Get some shut-eye."

He acquiesces grudgingly. Neil hears his breathing settle. In two minutes he's gone.

They swap at six. Neil flicks his synapses to idle. It's seven when his eyes open again. In the pale dawn light, Chris stands staring at the motel, a totem pole with vacant blue eyes, watching.

"The guard by the pool fell asleep for fifteen minutes," he says. "It took a cement truck driving by to wake him up."

From the shadows, Neil peers at the motel. The guard now slouches on his white plastic lawn chair, gun across his lap, drinking from a thermos cup. Casual. Again, Neil thinks, *The cartel is convinced they've cleared this neighborhood, convinced they've scared everyone away. They will not expect a raid to be launched from within the dead zone.* His energy spins up.

..

The dusty, boxy cash truck from Chicago arrives at 8:06 a.m. Exactly on time.

The rising sun flashes orange off its windshield as it reverses and backs into the loading dock at the rear of the motel.

Marcos radios. "Three men in the truck—driver and two gunmen. Two guards from the motel. Two other men helping unload."

Exactly like last time. Good.

The other trucks arrive between 8:17 and 8:42 a.m.

Neil, Chris, and Michael watch. Fifteen minutes later, the elevator above the loading dock opens. Two guards walk out, then two men pushing a tall, cage-like cart stacked seven feet high with dark sacks. They wheel it along the walkway, past the breezeway, and around the corner to the north-south wing.

They repeat the process seven times.

Chris shoots Neil a look. "Big week."

Real big. Huge. Way more than they've ever seen delivered.

The radio squawks. Trejo. "Cops incoming on their regular patrol."

They slink back into the shadows.

On the California side of the border, in the farm country east of Calexico, Elisa parks and walks through the windy morning sunshine to a Jack in the Box on State Highway 7. She orders two tacos and a Coke. A pimply teenager hands her a sack that's soaked orange with grease. She sits by a window, with a view down the block to the border crossing.

Traffic is thin. She sips her Coke. Manages two bites of the wilted taco before wiping her hands with half a dozen paper napkins. The radio in her shoulder bag is silent. It's been silent since Neil and his crew left the safe house before dawn.

After kissing a sleeping Gabriela on the forehead, Elisa loaded all their things in her Corolla for their trip north tonight. She left Gabriela with Tío and a couple of books. She drove to all three border crossings the crew will use later today—Andrade–Los Algodones, Calexico town center, and this one—seeing nothing unusual. Normal day traffic.

She's not nervous.

She's nervous.

She has crossed the border countless times. Literally countless. It's what she does. What her family has always done. They've traveled this land since before borders existed here. Borders have made their business possible. Borders are a transaction cost in a capitalist economy. Borders create the business model and market opening that *contrabandistas* exploit. Smugglers take the risk, outsmart the bureaucrats who suppress free trade, who pretend they can outlaw home-brewed mezcal or homegrown weed. They bring the cheap electronics and appliances that everybody in California and Arizona and Texas gets, tax free, to people who live five miles across an arbitrary line in the sand. She knows how to slink through every crack in the system and provide people on both sides of the border with what they need, want, and enjoy.

Sometimes it's a game. Sometimes you pay, forfeit your load. Sometimes you end up getting ripped off, or handcuffed and have to spend a night in a cell and pay a fine. Unless you're running drugs—not a couple of keys of weed, but smack or cocaine—it's not so dangerous. You don't fear the people who pay you to take the job. You don't risk your life. Not usually. Not even her late husband. Antonio had been hauling dope, yes, buried under potted palms being brought across at Nogales. But being hit by a jackknifed gasoline tanker on a rainslick highway wasn't a risk inherent in smuggling. That was chance. Life. Death. Inevitable. She sends a thought to his spirit, somewhere, forever twenty-six years old. She thinks, *Your baby girl is growing into a rose. Bright, sweet, strong.*

She stops herself.

Don't think about death.

Because Neil is not driving a few refrigerators from a California warehouse into Mexicali. He's not sweet-talking a Mexican border guard out of looking in the trunk of his car, where he might find stone carvings from the National Council for Culture and Arts. He's not even running dope for a well-oiled cell of border rat smugglers. He's taking down a high-stakes score against armed opposition who own the local cops, and they ain't playing, they don't forgive and don't forget. She knows he feels responsible for his crew—Chris, Michael, Trejo, Molina, and her young cousin Marcos—though Neil would say they know the risk, know what they sign up for. He watches over them nevertheless. He knows the Herreras will unleash violence on anyone who tries to touch their money.

So much money. Neil hasn't told her how much is at the stash house, but it's so much, he thinks it will change his life. For a long time. It's so much, he wants her and Gabriela to go away for a while with him. Far away, on roads the Herreras never travel.

Elisa doesn't pray. She wears the medallion of la Virgen de Guadalupe, which her grandmother gave her as a child. Lita's medallion—that's as close to organized religion as Elisa gets. Her real faith is stored in the locket she wears on the necklace with the medal. It contains two photos: one of her daughter and one of Neil. Gabriela gave it to her. She touches it, wraps her palm around it until the metal grows warm.

Vuelve a mí, amado.

Come back to me, Neil.

It's up to her to make sure the three crossings he and his crew will use are clear and safe. And to watch out for her cousin Marcos, who has been shaving for only five years and hasn't experienced the worst the world offers, who still has pop star posters on his wall. Susanna Hoffs, the Bangles. A vision of his large eyes and his reckless, admirable determination—to stand up and be a man, no matter what—fills her with worry.

She tosses the soggy tacos in the trash and takes her Coke outside. The sun is burning down. In her car, she focuses binoculars on the crossing. It's a calm day. She turns the ignition and heads east to make sure the post-score meeting place is ready.

..

The couriers arrive at La Chinesca at 11:00 a.m. They leave with awkwardly bulging gym bags at 11:30. They begin returning from the *cambios* around the city at 1:30 p.m. The last car arrives at 2:24 p.m. A slender woman takes two huge duffels from the trunk. She lugs them, shoulders straining, up the stairs.

The sun is high. No shadows for cover. Plain scorching daylight.

The current guards have been on duty since eight a.m. This is the last ninety minutes of their shift—they're tired, hot; they've eaten lunch. To their minds, Neil thinks, the risky part of the day has passed. The cash haul has been transferred and is safe in the motel, surrounded by guns, in a zone they think nobody in the city would dare invade. They're not at their peak.

Moves the probability needle into his favor, but don't count on it. Or anything . . .

Marcos radios. "The courier just knocked on the motel door and someone let her in. The guards on the corners of both wings are stationary. In their seats. Armed but relaxed."

Decision time.

"Let's take it," Neil says.

55

They drive out of the abandoned garage in a bronze 1978 Maverick with Baja California plates, Neil at the wheel, Chris shotgun, and Cerrito in the back seat. They backtrack through the dead zone, then turn onto the main boulevard, join traffic, and aim toward La Chinesca.

"Inbound," Neil radios Trejo, Molina, and Marcos. "Four hundred meters."

Chris is chill, H&K in his hand, cut-down Mossberg and CAR-15 on the floor. Michael resembles an ingot pulled from a forge: immobile, burning to go.

Trejo radios. "Got you in sight."

Two hundred meters.

Marcos, from overwatch. "Everyone at the motel is stationary."

La Chinesca is ahead at the next corner. One hundred meters. Traffic is desultory.

Neil puts in a radio earpiece. "Here we go."

He slows, like he's checking the street signs. He signals and turns right, onto the cross street at the corner with the motel. He can hear his heart pounding, his pulse in his veins.

He slows alongside the motel's front entrance. The guard sitting by the pool looks up.

Neil turns into the motel like he's lost and is using the parking lot to turn around so he can return to the main road.

The guard stands up and raises a hand, telling them to halt. The Maverick keeps rolling. Neil pulls down his ski mask. The sun is shining directly down on the windshield, obscuring the view into the car.

The guard jogs toward them. "Alto!" Stop.

Chris and Michael have their masks pulled down. The guard is ten feet away. The traffic on the boulevard is mindless. Chris lowers his window. He has a suppressor on his H&K.

The guard gets two more steps in.

Chris aims at him. "Drop your—"

The man swings up his shotgun.

Chris fires three rounds.

The man drops. Cerrito is out the back door of the car. Chris is right behind. Neil pops the trunk. Michael and Chris lug the guard into it and slam it shut.

Neil's pulse thunders. He pulls the Maverick under the portico outside the motel office. Jumping out, he leads the others past the pool toward the north-south wing, which contains the count room. The curtains in every room are drawn. Scraggly oleander bushes provide cover between the motel and the street.

Concealment instead of visibility for the security team—that's an error on the Herreras' part.

The count room is on the back side of the wing. They approach the corner, single file. Neil stops and raises his hand.

Around the corner, ten feet away, he hears a transistor radio playing Mexican pop music. He edges forward.

Marcos comes through his earpiece. "The guard is sitting in his chair facing me. His back will be to you."

Neil pulls a plastic bag from his pocket. He swings around the corner. Takes three steps and flips the plastic bag over the guard's head. Throws him to the ground. The man thrashes. Muffled screams. Chris presses the H&K to his temple. Michael pulls out a roll of electrical tape and whips it around the man's jaw, gagging him. He yanks the guy's hands behind him and binds them with flex-cuffs, then cuffs his feet. Chris takes his weapons.

Neil leans close to his face. Beneath the bag, the man's eyes are bugging.

"Shut the fuck up and I'll let you breathe."

The man frantically nods. Neil unsheathes a Ka-Bar knife and pokes a pinprick hole in the bag, at the nose. They might need him later. He drags the guy around the corner from his chair and zip-ties him to a drainpipe, where nobody upstairs on the building's exterior walkway can spot him.

With the knife, Neil slices the man's Achilles tendon. His screams sound strangled. Michael knocks him unconscious with the butt of his CAR-15. The radio plays on.

Marcos radios. "The third guard is picking his nails with a pocket-knife."

They slip past the pool to the east-west wing, the wing with the loading dock on the rear side, and they take him down, same as the guy with the radio. Drag him into the motel office. They zip-tie him to the metal handles of a built-in cabinet out of sight behind the front desk.

Over his earpiece, Neil asks, "Street?"

Trejo replies, "Clear."

"Now."

"Coming. Fifteen seconds."

From the office, they head to the breezeway between the two wings of the motel. They run silently up the stairs. The count room is on the back side of the north-south wing. They pause before turning the corner.

Marcos: "One guard outside the door, six doors down from the corner. Stationary."

Neil takes an empty beer bottle from his jacket pocket. Ducking, he leans around the corner, rolls it toward the guard, and pulls back. It clinks along the walkway.

Footsteps approach, coming this way to investigate.

Chris goes around Neil, H&K raised. The guard gives him a shocked look, eyes popping. The rifle on a strap over his chest swings up. Chris is ten feet away when he shoots him.

Four guards down.

Three more inside that they know of. Plus ten couriers who may be armed, may not. Neil suspects the Herreras limit who's allowed to carry in their stash house, and it won't include locals who might be tempted to turn a gun on the people protecting towers of cash.

Trejo and Molina come around the corner from the breezeway, dead serious, weapons out. Neil, Chris, and Michael stack against the wall on one side of the door, Trejo and Molina against the other. Neil knocks—the signal knock, which he has observed through the binoculars over and over during the past surveillance. *Tap-tap. Tap-tap. Tap.*

With a rattle, the chain slides off the latch. Voices inside. The door opens a couple of inches.

Neil slams his shoulder against the door, rifle up. He booms in.

The man who opened the door is short, wide, like a wrestler. Strong. His rifle is leaning against the wall inside. His eyes widen and he cocks a fist, then decides to grab for the gun. No time. Neil jams the barrel of his CAR-15 into the guy's throat. It isn't a bayonet, but it still smashes the man's larynx. The man grabs his throat as he lurches back.

Chris and Michael sweep in behind him, each focused on a sector in the room. Trejo and Molina take up positions outside the room on the walkway. Chris kicks the door closed.

In the room, the motel bed has been removed. There's a desk, like this is a secretary's office outside an executive's suite. A man sits behind it—fifties, chunky, in a sweater over a button-down shirt and khakis.

Neil aims at him. He grabs the man by the collar and hauls him straight over the desk, away from the phone. Michael clears the bathroom and closet. They gag and bind the choking guard and Sweater Man.

"*Quieren morir?*" Neil aims the rifle at them. "*Los mataremos a todos ahora. Sí o no?*"

Die, yes or no? Sweater Man looks terrified. Yeah, Neil thinks. Maybe the guy will decide it's better to let Neil kill him right now than face the Herreras afterward. The man shakes his head. Cowers.

The door to the right, to the connecting room, is closed. Chris lines up against the wall, holding a flash-bang. Neil and Michael stack up behind him.

Michael pulls open the door, kicks the second door into the connecting room, and ducks back. Chris throws the flash-bang. The three of them turn away, eyes shut, hands over their ears.

The noise is sharp, the flash white even behind closed eyes.

They hear screams. They go in through pale smoke, holding their breath.

Twelve people, disoriented, crying. The window in the count room is bricked over. The door is nailed shut.

Stacked on a desk and on shelves against the wall are banded stacks of hundred-dollar bills.

The smoke swirls, flour white. The people inside are blinded, stumbling. Chris and Cerrito take them all down: bind, gag, zip-tie.

The gym bags are half packed. The rolling carts are in the corner.

"Load it," Neil says.

As the smoke clears, men cough and moan. Women cry behind their gags. Neil and his crew go to work. Fast, efficient, locked down.

Neil gets a look at the wall on the far side of the room. Like he suspected: a hole has been bashed through it with a sledgehammer. He climbs through into the room beyond. It's dark and empty. He opens the connecting doors to the subsequent room, clears that one, then the next, again climbing through a sledgehammered hole. He makes it all the way to the end of the building. Rat's nest.

He returns to the count room. Michael is zipping duffels and tossing them on the rolling cart.

Neil keys his radio. "Get ready."

Trejo clicks three times in reply. *Ready. Clear.*

Neil slings the rifle over his back by the strap and joins the others
in loading the cash.

Marcos stands at the third-floor window in the bottling plant, watching the motel. He scans one wing, then the next. Outside the anteroom door, Trejo and Molina stand perimeter defense, rifles ready,
each guarding a pie-shaped sector of fire. He sees nobody else.

Then a dented Chevy pickup truck pulls into the parking lot out
front of the motel.

Neil is shoveling banded stacks of cash in a black duffel when his
radio scratches to life.

"Truck just pulled up out front," Marcos says.

Neil stops. "What's happening?"

Chris and Michael look up. Neil gestures at them to continue loading the cash. On the floor, several of the couriers eye him and one
another.

Marcos holds the radio close to his face, watching the Chevy pickup
that has parked at the motel.

"Two guys are getting out."

Enrique and Emiliano Garcia are cousins. They work for the Herrera
cartel. They consider themselves soldiers. They're due to take over
the afternoon shift at La Chinesca at four p.m. They're early.

They have been out all night at clubs downtown. And with the women they left with. Strippers, pros, Enrique thinks. Emiliano agrees.

They didn't want to go home dirty to their wives to get cleaned up before coming to work today. But you work at a motel, you can turn up early to shower, catch a nap, so you're fresh for your shift.

When Emiliano pulls into La Chinesca, he's planning an easy hour to get himself ready for guard duty. His Smith & Wesson revolver is in the glove compartment.

Enrique sees it the same time he does.

"Whose car is that?"

A sun-faded brown Maverick is pulled up under the portico outside the motel office. Emiliano swings toward it. Nobody's inside.

"Where's Guzman?" Enrique says.

The plastic lawn chair behind the pool has nobody sitting in it.

Emiliano kills the engine. "Let's see if he's in the office with whoever came in that car."

They get out.

Marcos keys the radio. "Two men. Looking at the Maverick. Heading for the motel office. Pointing at the empty guard's chair."

Neil hears through his earpiece. To Chris and Michael, he says, "Pick it up."

They zip the duffels and load them on the rolling carts.

Enrique goes into the office. Emiliano circles the brown Maverick. He touches the hood. It's parked in the shade, but the metal is warm. Not hot, but it feels like it's been driven here recently.

He ducks to look through the passenger window, sees nothing suspicious. He saunters toward the back end of the car.

In the office, Enrique pauses and turns his head.

••

Neil slams money into a duffel. Keys his radio. "Report."

Marcos stares at the men who have arrived at the motel. The one in the office walks toward the desk. The one outside circles to the back of the Maverick.

Standing behind the Maverick, Emiliano peers around the parking lot. Still no sign of Guzman. In the office, Enrique ambles over to the abandoned front desk.

Emiliano hears something. A dripping sound. A soft splatter.

He looks up at the portico roof, but it's bone dry—it's a hot, sunny day, and there's no piping up there. The soft drip continues.

He turns to the car. He crouches. The drip is coming from the bottom of the trunk. Thick, dirty, reddish brown. It smells like iron.

From the office, Enrique shouts. He's looking over the desk.

"Fuckers!"

Neil's radio crackles. Marcos says, "You're blown."

56

Neil's vision turns electric. He snaps his fingers.

"We go."

He tosses the duffel he's loaded on the cart. Michael zips a bag and does the same. Chris slings another bag over his shoulder and brings his rifle up across his chest.

Marcos radios. "The guy who found the Maverick just ran into the office. He's on the phone."

"Copy," Neil says.

He clicks a button on his watch to start the stopwatch. "Time," he radios.

Four and a half minutes.

••

In the motel office, Emiliano slams down the phone. "They're coming."

Behind the front desk, Enrique kneels beside an injured guard who lies gagged and bound, his jeans soaked with blood, his Achilles tendon cut. Enrique uses his switchblade to slice off the zip ties. The man is half conscious. Enrique slaps him awake.

"Where's your gun?" he says.

"Don't know. Gone."

Enrique draws his own. "Whoever did this, they're in the count room."

Emiliano runs out to the pickup and grabs his Smith & Wesson and a shotgun from the toolbox in the cargo bed. In the office, Enrique drags the wounded guard to his feet.

"Get out there. We got backup coming. And the cops. But we take these assholes down before reinforcements get here, understand?"

The man's face is striped with pain, but he nods. If the attackers escape from the count room with the week's cash haul, the Herreras will kill him. He hops outside, using the wall as a crutch. Emiliano hands him the shotgun.

"They gotta come downstairs," Enrique says. "They have to exit the count room and get to the staircase or service elevator."

Emiliano nods. There's only the one set of stairs, in the breezeway between the two wings. Halfway there, they spot the third guard who was on duty, bound to a drainpipe. Enrique frees his hands and feet. He's too weak to stand, but Enrique hands him a .38 he has strapped to his ankle.

"Anybody comes out, you kill them."

The man nods.

An Impala packed with men screeches into the parking lot. Enrique runs for the stairs, waving at them to follow.

"Impala, out front. Five men. Long guns," Marcos radios. "The two men from the Chevy pickup coming up the stairs. One more outside the office, limping, just fell down."

Chris and Michael hear the same news in their radio earpieces.

Eight men—minimum. Heavily armed. Neil looks at the money cart. No way they can push it to the elevator now.

But the cash. Those clean, crisp hundreds are stacked and banded with currency straps, neat packs that total either $5,000 or $10,000. They have stuffed nine duffel bags with it. He picks up a second one from the cart and slings it over his back. Cerrito and Chris do the same.

It's $12 million at least. Worth nothing unless they get out alive.

He nods at Cerrito. "Let Trejo and Molina into the anteroom, then block that door with the cart." He radios them. "Get in here."

Michael rolls the cart from the count room through the connecting door. When Trejo and Molina come in, he jams the cart under the door handle. Neil tells them, "Grab duffels."

Footsteps pound on the concrete walkway outside.

Neil points at the bashed-out hole in the plaster wall between the count room and the one beyond it.

"Go."

The crew ducks through. Neil backs after them. He swings his rifle up. He has flash-bangs in his pocket. He hears keys rattle in the entry room door and screeching as the cart jammed against it blocks the attackers from entering. Hears yelling.

He turns. The room they're in is empty and dark. He's seen how the cartel hollowed out the rooms on this side of the motel. He knows he didn't follow the maze all the way through. And mazes can be entered from either end. He doesn't know what lies ahead, just that he and his crew cannot retreat.

"Move."

They forge across two more rooms, scrambling through the holes in the walls, before they reach rooms where the windows are no longer bricked up.

Behind them, they hear the door to the anteroom finally burst open.

Cerrito runs across the room they're in and opens a connecting door. The door on the opposite side is shut. He kicks it wide. Enters, clearing left, Chris immediately behind, clearing right. Neil follows after Trejo and Molina. He shuts and locks the connecting door behind him.

Back in the count room, noise erupts. Shouts.

"Ahí. Esa dirección." That way. The people tied up in the count room are telling the gunmen which way Neil's crew is going.

Michael looks at him sharply. "Where?"

Two options.

One: They can go out the motel room door onto the exterior walkway.

Into the radio, he says, "Status."

Marcos comes back, his voice stressed. "Two men are running along the walkway. Shotguns."

Two: In the back wall of this room, by the bathroom door, there's a hole bashed in the plaster. It leads to the room on the opposite side of the motel.

Gunfire. Deep. A rifle. Behind them, rounds hit the connecting door from the far side. Somebody kicks it. Chris spins and fires a three-shot burst. They hear a body fall. More shots come through the wood, splintering it.

Marcos: "Three men just entered a room on the west side of the building, across from where you are."

Those men are going to hunt backward through the maze, this rat's warren the motel has been turned into. The cartel is coming from all directions.

Neil checks his watch: 3:13 left before the judiciales turn up.

He points at the doors and window in this room. Chris fires a succession of three-shot bursts at each.

Neil leads them through the hole in the back wall. Chris lays down more suppressive fire, then climbs through the hole after them. The light in the room on this side filters through the closed curtains.

The door is nailed shut. Neil pulls the curtains aside. The window is crosshatched with duct tape and glued along the sill.

He spins. As he hoped, this room has a hole in the far wall, leading to an adjacent room—in the direction of the stairs. They clamber through it. Cross the ensuing room. Again, the window and main door are inaccessible. But there are connecting doors to the next room.

Neil hears voices from the far side. The cartel gunmen Marcos spotted are heading toward them.

With hand gestures, he signals Trejo and Molina to guard their rear. They return to the previous room. He, Chris, and Cerrito flatten themselves along the wall beside the connecting door. It opens and three cartel gunmen come through. One is the guard they tied up in the office.

Cerrito takes them down.

They rush into the connecting room. Hear noise ahead and behind. It's on.

They clear that room, each taking his sector of fire. Neutralize two more gunmen.

They cross through three more rooms, then press their backs against the wall when they hear two more talking in low voices, coordinating. The cartel gunmen are moving slowly, now aware.

Neil pulls the pin on another flash-bang and tosses it through the hole in the wall. There's a yell, then the explosion. Chris spins and fires into the smoke-filled room.

Michael rounds him, goes in, fires two shots. Neil leapfrogs, clearing the far sector and bathroom.

All down.

Ninety seconds left.

"Close up," Neil radios.

Trejo and Molina join them. They sweep out the door onto the walkway along the front of the building above the empty pool and run toward the stairs. The Eldorado is waiting at the bottom of the stairway.

They're at the top of the stairs when they see him: the guard they'd neutralized when they first arrived, the one who was sitting in the chair listening to his radio. He's bloody, on his knees, unable to walk, but he has crawled halfway up the stairs. He holds a .38 revolver in his shaking hands. Chris is moving too fast to get out of his way. Neil swings the barrel of his rifle down and sees the muzzle staring back at him, right in the eye.

The shot comes loud, echoing, and blasts a hole in the guard's chest.

He topples.

Neil spins. In the parking lot below, chest heaving, stands Elisa's young cousin Marcos, rifle still aimed at the spot where the guard had been.

Neil dashes down the stairs. He's too grateful to be angry that Marcos left overwatch to join the fight.

Brave fucking kid. They race to the Eldorado. Michael brings up the rear, rifle aimed up the stairs. Trejo jumps in the driver's seat. He's as cold as a shank of sharpened steel. Everyone else piles in, Neil and Chris in the front, Marcos nearly heaving in the back, sandwiched between Michael and Molina. Michael's looking out the back window.

Neil checks his watch. Forty-five seconds. Getting out of the parking lot won't be enough. They have to get away from the dead zone, out of the neighborhood.

Trejo pulls out and swings onto the main road. They're a block away, turning onto a cross street, when Neil sees the green-and-black police cars rocketing toward the motel.

He watches the mirrors. The road. Eyes Trejo. Turns and sees everyone in the back seat lit up with adrenaline.

"Fuck yeah," Cerrito says.

Marcos looks like a bottle rocket about to kick off. The words, an echo, nearly burst forth from his chest. "Yeah. Fuck."

Chris is grinning like he just won the lotto.

They have it. At least twelve mil.

Neil watches the bright sunlight, the explosive day, counting every second until they reach the switch cars.

57

Parked far enough away, Elisa waits outside the Calexico West Port of Entry, the sun reflecting off the hood of her clean Corolla, the radio in her hand silent. Her heel bounces up and down. She watches the crossing and sips her Jack in the Box Coke like she's waiting for somebody, maybe somebody who's going to cross on foot.

She's aching. Usually, she's cool at a crossing. She's aloof. Or charming and chatty. Or annoyed, pretending to be in a snit with whoever's at the wheel of the car, or at the kids in the back seat who are crying and slapping at each other, having the tantrum she told them to have. Though Gabriela is not good at those. Gabriela is good at rolling her eyes like she's sixteen, a total teen, even though she's just eight.

The radio stays silent.

She chews on the plastic straw in the Coke cup.

Her aunt Esperanza will never forgive her if anything happens to Marcos.

Neil, come on. Andalé.

People walk past. An eighteen-wheeler lumbers by, the driver up-shifting.

The radio pops to life.

"Outbound."

Her nerve endings fire, every pore going hot and cold at once with relief and a sense of dreadful expectation that she didn't know she'd been harboring. It's Neil.

Outbound. That means the crew has departed the motel, has split up, and is about to cross.

She puts the radio to her face. She has to clear her throat first and blink her vision clear. "It's sunny."

That's their prearranged code. The crossings are clear.

She puts her hand on the car keys and pauses a moment. To center herself. To see clearly. To be calm. You gotta be calm, centered, clear-headed, every second you're in this life.

A feeling of gratitude shoots out of her heart, like something from a saint's medallion. She laughs. Our Lady of Smugglers. She turns the key.

The meeting point is north of the Fort Yuma Indian Reservation, off a dirt road in such dusty backcountry that not even hardscrabble farmers ever bothered with it for long. The abandoned cabin, however, has an attached barn where they'll dump their work cars and divide up the score. One hand on the wheel, Elisa rolls through Calexico, nice and easy, and swings onto I-8. She checks her watch: 3:45 p.m. She'll arrive at the meetup spot well before Neil and the others.

Marcos is okay. Our Lady is watching. She half laughs. She wants to call Neil and hear everything. Every single breath, every moment, to watch his eyes, see him relive it. He is incredibly intense. Driven. Conscious. She loves that about him. And he's terse. A man of so few words. Every one of them, when she can draw them out, is worth the price of pearls.

The range of her radio is somewhere around twenty miles. She waits until she's in range to make the next call. Checks her mirrors. No traffic, not out here with the sand and tumbleweeds, nobody close enough to care or notice.

She clicks Transmit. "Vaquero."

Code. Calling Tío Tomás.

She trusts that her uncle wasted no time sterilizing the safe house. Not a single scrap of paper or fingerprint will be left at the adobe barracks. The car hauler can be abandoned there—far out of town, off road, nothing illegal about it, nothing suspicious—until Neil's Chicago contact picks it up. That's arranged. That's nothing she or Tío will concern themselves with.

Everyone has a role.

She releases the Transmit button. Hears static on the radio. She's winding between hills, an iffy place for reception. She waits to try again until she reaches clear territory, the sky pale blue overhead, the concrete almost white, the sand the color of a Band-Aid.

"Vaquero," she repeats.

Finally, after a scratch, her uncle replies. "Prima."

Her code name.

"I'm done for the day," she says.

Again there's a scratchy pause. "See you back here soon, huh?"

She passes a slow-moving farm truck with wooden slats on the sides. Men sit in the bed, holding their hats against the wind.

Back here.

A cold drip seems to trace its way down her neck.

"You still . . ." *Back here.*

"Yeah, just waiting for you all to get back. Been a long day here by myself. I'll start a pot of coffee."

He's still at the safe house. The barracks.

That's wrong.

"And I will open that bottle of tequila," he says.

He's been speaking Spanish, but now, in a strangely strained voice, he's speaking English. When it's just the two of them, they don't do that.

"Good," she says.

"So hot today. You hurry back, cool off."

The coded phrase freezes her blood.

Trouble.

58

In the safe house living room, Tomás sits on a hard chair. The radio is near his lips. He's facing the windows, looking out at the wide, covered porch. The car hauler gleams in the sun. The heat is heavy. The house smells of wood and sweat. The blood from the beating he has taken runs down his face. It soaks his embroidered western shirt. He can't wipe it from his eyes. His hands are bound behind his back.

The men loom over him. Five Anglos, thugs. They aren't from around here. Not the main two, anyhow. Those seem midwestern. They smell of beef and greed.

The one who's in charge, the one with the scar through his eyebrow, who struts and grabs his belt, wanting to grab his crotch, leans over him. This man strolled in behind the others, like a movie star making his entrance. He wears a too-small T-shirt and jeans that strain over his heavy thighs. He has Tic Tac breath. His second in command calls him Wardell. Wardell beat him with the butt of a pistol.

Now he holds the radio to Tomás's face. Tomás speaks to Elisa as calmly as he can: "So hot today."

The code phrase for *trouble*. Code doesn't help with the rest of it, but his words, the supposed small talk, should.

Here by myself. It's a message to Elisa, and someone else.

In the back of the house, Gabriela is hiding.

The little bedroom is hot, so hot. Gabriela huddles in the closet, in dim half-light. She can barely hear the men out in the main room.

She has been hiding here, shaking, since she heard the shouting, the blows, the furniture being knocked over.

She'd been reading while Tío Tomás packed up the house, the book about Fiji keeping her enthralled. *Enthralled*—that was a vocabulary word this year. It was in the spelling bee. Then she heard the cars pull in. She peeped around the blinds, and when she saw five strange men get out, her stomach turned into a lump of wet cement. She opened the bedroom door and stepped into the hall to call Tío's name, but he was already in the main room, staring out the windows with a trash bag in one hand and a bowie knife in the other, and he didn't even look at her. He spoke softly, oh so softly, oh so clearly.

Hide, little one.

Now she hears Tío on the radio—and, barely, her mom's voice in reply.

She crawls from the closet, *quiet quiet,* and peeps through a crack in the bedroom door. She can just see the main room. She puts her hands over her mouth. *Quiet quiet quiet.*

Tío is slumped on a chair. His hands are tied behind him. His face is swollen with bumps like broken baseballs. Blood everywhere. The strange men prowl around him like wolves.

One, with tough-guy muscles and a scar through his eyebrow, leans over and holds the walkie-talkie to Tío's face.

Tío talks to Mama. ". . . here by myself."

The men don't know she's hiding in this room. They haven't looked. They think Tío Tomás is alone in the house.

He speaks into the radio.

..

Elisa bombs through the neon afternoon, sun blazing, sand shimmering, metallic colors shrieking from road signs and trucks on the
interstate. The radio crackles in her hand.

"It's cool," Tío Tomás says in English. "*Pequeña segura aquí.*"

She passes traffic like it's stopped. She glances at the speedometer:
95 mph. She lifts her foot. Slowing down feels like tying a noose around
her neck.

She has to get to Gabriela.

"Yes, like I say," Tío adds, "everything is fine here."

That's not what he said. The message in Spanish, oblique, meant,
The little one is safe here.

She forces a calm tone into her voice. "Good. See you soon."

She sets the radio on her lap. Both hands on the wheel. Tears rise
in her eyes. She blinks fiercely and shakes her head. Tío is compromised. Captive. And whoever has him now has his radio.

That means they can intercept Neil's comms.

Gabriela holds still behind the crack in the door. Tío Tomás leans
to one side in the chair. She can hear him breathing. It sounds like
something is stuck in his throat. She wants to cry. He's hurt so bad.
Tío, who is strong, who tries to sound gruff sometimes, and is gruff
sometimes, but who gives her hot chocolate and cinnamon toast.

Pequeña segura aquí.

It was a weird thing for Tío to say. And the man with the scar in his
eyebrow made him say it again in English, but when he did, he said
something different.

The man with the scar, the one the others call Wardell, lowers the
radio from Tío's face. He backs up a step. Then he takes out a pack of
cigarettes and lights one up. He blows smoke in Tío's swollen eyes.

"How long?" he says.

Tío says nothing.

"How long until they return, old man?"

Tío tilts his head up. "Soon. You should run."

Wardell pauses, like Tío has slapped him. Then he smiles. He picks up one of the other dining room chairs.

And he smashes Tío with it.

Gabriela can't move.

The man hits him and hits him. Tío's chair falls over. The man hits him more, grunting. Blood flies.

Tío is on the floor. His head is down.

He's looking this way. Down the hall. At the crack in the door. At her.

Gabriela holds frozen. Tío's eyes connect with hers.

The chair comes down again. Wardell throws it aside and starts kicking Tío.

Tío holds on to Gabriela's gaze, like all his energy is coming to her. Everything, the last bit of it. *Hide. Live.*

Then there's nothing more. The man keeps kicking. But Tío is gone.

Gabriela can barely see. But she feels the last moments of his life hovering over her.

She hears the men. They say Neil's name. They think Neil is returning here with the haul.

Elisa doesn't know how she's going to do it yet, but she knows what's going to happen.

My baby. Gabriela.

I'm coming.

59

The adobe barracks is northwest of Yuma, six miles off I-8. Six empty miles of rugged hills and played-out mines and forgotten patches of land where failed ranchers tried to scratch a living. Elisa drives hard toward it.

Don't storm in. You're not armed.

Not heavily enough. The .22 in the glove box won't defeat an army of men.

Think.

She pulls over, kills the engine. The stunning silence falls in on her.

I must save my daughter.

She puts her fists over her eyes and leans on the steering wheel.

She punches the dash and screams. Long, and loud, and incoherently.

She straightens.

She can fall apart afterward. But now, right now, she is Mama. Mother of one, mother of all, the world held in the palm of her hand and the decisions she makes in the next few minutes.

Fear can come later.

Tears can come later.

Gabriela is all.

The engine ticks. She thinks.

She isn't alone in this. She has Tío, protecting and sheltering Gabriela.

She has Neil and his crew. She has Marcos. Six men who will go to war with her to rescue her daughter. They're coming. But they're not across the border yet.

Anything she says over the radio will be intercepted.

That's a problem.

That's an opportunity.

Borders and trails and holes-in-the-wall. Seeing and being seen. Present yourself as something you're not. That's the smuggler's way.

She has to smuggle her most precious possession out from under the noses of men who would do her harm.

She doesn't know who these people at the safe house are. The Herreras? Impossible. Neil said *Outbound.* They're clear of the Herreras. Out clean. These have to be others.

What do they want? Money?

Neil?

How did they find the safe house? Did they follow the crew, or her? Or the Peterbilt?

Doesn't matter right now. What she does in the next few minutes does.

••

Half a mile west of the safe house, a crumbling road leads to an old mining camp that has been left to the sand and wind. Elisa races up, parks the Corolla out of sight, and runs across the scrub to a rocky promontory. Dropping to her belly, she crawls to the lip of the rise and gazes downslope at the ranch house. The rocks are pumice black. The earth is the color of baking dough. The afternoon air is silent, the animals of the desert asleep, hiding from the heat.

The Peterbilt gleams in the sun. The car hauler is nearly empty, just the backup Honda Accord that Neil had been using on the way down here from Chicago. Two strange cars are parked in front of the adobe barracks: a black Pontiac Trans Am and a heavy-duty red Chevy Blazer SUV. There's no movement outside the house, nobody in sight.

She scrabbles behind a boulder, out of the wind, and keys the transmitter on the radio. "Keyhole, come in."

Keyhole is the code word for Neil's whole operation. The stash house takedown. And the way Elisa has just said it, the word *sounds* like a code. That's what she wants.

She must clue him in that their op has been compromised, that their comms are being intercepted. Neil and his crew will know she is using the word the wrong way.

She releases the transmitter. Waits. If Neil or his men are at a border crossing, they've turned off and hidden their radios.

Neil's voice crackles through the handset. "Keyhole, copy."

Elisa's heart pounds. She takes a breath. "You got everything?"

"Everything."

"I'll meet you at the Taco Bell on Highway 95. The parking lot. Be quicker that way. Make the transfer."

"You got it. Keep people from prying," Neil says.

"Yeah. Then we head to the adobe. Don't want to get stuck in a tight place, people seeing too much."

"On my way. Out."

She clicks the radio off. The sun beats down. She turns and crawls back to the promontory, the overlook.

What she wants, what she has one chance to accomplish, is to get the strange men out of the safe house. The charade she just went through with Neil might do it. *Please.*

Thirty seconds later, men come out the door of the safe house. Both the Trans Am and the Chevy Blazer pull out. They bump down the dirt driveway and race south, to intercept a fictitious meeting.

She watches the house. There's no more movement. After five minutes, she can't stand it. She runs down the hill toward the ranch.

Neil is at the wheel of the tan Mercury, slow-rolling through downtown Calexico. He had no problem at the border, not with the Mexicans, not with the US border guards.

Ski mask, gone. Clothes, changed. A plaid work shirt over a white tee, workman's heavy khakis, Timberland boots. An American who's a foreman with one of the industrial companies that operate *maquiladoras* in Mexicali, coming back from a work trip across the line. Tidy, blue-collar as hell. Face washed. Sweat washed off. Cool slicked back on.

Money in the false compartments of the car doors and beneath the floor. $3 million plus.

Chris and Michael are crossing to the east, the smaller Calexico crossing. Trejo and Molina near Yuma. Marcos—brave, reckless, lifesaving Marcos—is driving to Nogales. The plan is to meet at the abandoned cabin near the Fort Yuma Indian Reservation. Split the take, officially. Scatter fast, after dark, becoming invisible, melting away.

Not now.

Elisa. Something's gone wrong.

They're not supposed to go back to the adobe barracks. Never.

Somebody has cut into their action, into their comms. And Elisa is terrified.

He can think of only one thing that could terrify her. Gabriela's in danger.

••

Elisa runs toward the adobe barracks, feeling exposed. Fifty yards out, she slows and creeps to the edge of the house, where she can see the courtyard and the long covered porch.

It's been thirteen minutes since the cars left. It will take them twenty-five to reach the Taco Bell parking lot she spoke of on the radio. She checks the road. No sign of them coming back.

Heart twisting, she rounds the corner. The windows reflect the afternoon sun. The lights are off inside. She can't see in. Carefully she opens the door and steps into the main room.

She gasps and edges back.

On the floor, tied to a broken chair, Tío Tomás lies dead.

No question, no doubt. And he suffered. *Oh, Tío.*

Her heart hammers. She steps deeper into the room, looks down the hall. The door of the little bedroom is closed. She opens her lips to call Gabriela's name. Something stops her.

The front door slowly closes behind her. The square of light she's standing in vanishes. She spins.

A man stands there. Tall, in a tight black T-shirt and jeans. Dark hair, dark eyes, a thick white scar running through his eyebrow. A shotgun in his hands, aimed at her chest.

His eyes shine. "Honey, you're home."

60

Think, Elisa, think, she tells herself, as her vision pulses, her heart hammers. *Pronto!* Quick. This man is sneaky and smart. She holds still. Says nothing.

He takes a swaggering step toward her and nods at Tío's body. "Think I didn't know that jagoff was sending secret messages to the woman on the radio? Jumping into Spanish." He smirks. "But I am tuned to an ultrahigh frequency. I hear everything."

Quiet my mind, Elisa thinks. *Disappear into the role I need to play, the person I need to be, the words, the vibe, I need him to believe.*

She doesn't need to know who this man is, not right now. Because she knows the one big thing.

This guy has no clue Gabriela is still hiding in the back of the house.

If he knew that, he'd have the gun against her daughter's head. But he doesn't. He's taking another step forward here in the main room, holding that shotgun low near his waist, aimed upward at her heart.

She has to get him out of the house.

She could keep him here, talking, engaging, if it would allow Gabriela to escape. But she has to assume her daughter is in the small bedroom where she's been sleeping. The bedroom door opens onto the hallway. The window opens onto the covered porch. Both are directly in their line of sight. As long as this man is on the property, Gabriela is trapped.

"Hands up," he says.

Elisa raises them. He frisks her roughly, grabbing her breasts and crotch, and finds the .22 in her waistband. He puts it in his back pocket.

She has to get him out of here. Away, down the road. And she has to signal to her daughter, somehow, that once she and this man leave, Gabriela must run, must get out of sight of the house and hide.

The man tilts his head. "Think you're a genius, did you, *muchacha*?"

"I was only hired to be a lookout," she says.

"Where's the crew? When are they coming back?"

"They are not coming back."

"Bullshit." He lifts the shotgun an inch, aiming at her chest. "You came back."

She sweeps a shaky hand toward Tío's body. Her voice cracks. "To check on my uncle."

"Boo-hoo," the man says. "Should have known better than to hire on as cleaners to a highline crew."

The shotgun comes up another inch. Elisa can look down the barrel, a black maw. The man's eyes never leave her.

"When is the crew coming back?" he says.

"They are not."

With his left hand, the man takes a pack of cigarettes and a lighter from his T-shirt pocket. He tosses the pack to her.

"Light up," he says.

From the closet, Gabriela hears voices. She hups a breath. The man called Wardell, who hurt (*killed, killed, he killed*) Tío Tomás, is talking, low and rough. To Mama. Gabriela skitters to the crack in the bedroom door.

Her mom stands in the main room, near where Tío lies. His blood has spread into a red pool and along the seams of the floorboards. Her mom doesn't look at Tío. She's talking to the man with the shotgun. She has a pack of cigarettes in her hand. But her mom doesn't smoke.

Wardell says, "Light up."

Her mom hesitates, then taps a cigarette out and places it between her lips. The man flicks a lighter. She inhales, barely, choking down a cough.

"When is the crew coming back?" Wardell says.

"Never."

"Two choices," Wardell says. "You tell me the truth, or you burn yourself with that cigarette."

Gabriela presses her hand over her mouth to keep from crying out.

"They are not coming back," her mom says.

Wardell takes a breath. It makes him look bigger. "I lied. You tell me, you burn yourself, or you get your brains splattered across the back wall."

He inches the shotgun toward her mom. Gabriela feels a full body wave of fear. She clenches everything to keep from screaming, from crying, from peeing herself.

"The plan," Mama says, "is run. Anything goes wrong, clear out. On your own. Wait until nobody can see you and go. Out of sight. *Comprendes, mariposa?*"

The man makes a face. "Stop with that shit. I *comprendes*, bitch."

Comprendes, mariposa?

Mama is talking to her. It's a message. A definite message. Mama knows she is here. Mama is trying to help her.

Telling Gabriela she must help herself.

Wait until nobody can see you and go. Out of sight.

Gabriela trembles. She must be brave. Mama is brave. She must do what Mama says.

She knows she has to wait. She has known since the strange men came that she couldn't leave this room. They would see her. She had looked at the ceiling, thinking that maybe she could get into the attic and crawl along the rafters, but the ceiling isn't made of big acoustic tiles that can be pushed up, like her bedroom at home; it's solid wood. She has to wait.

That's Mama's secret message.

Wait, then run. She'll know when.

She hears noise in the main room. She puts her eye to the crack in the door.

The man is hitting her mom. He's grabbing her. All over. Gabriela chokes down a cry.

Her mom is fighting back.

She pushes the man away. He rips her T-shirt and grabs the cigarette. He pushes her against the big table, tries to throw her on top of it, pressing the cigarette to her skin, above her bra. Her mom spits at him. He slaps her.

"They are not coming back," Mama says. "Not."

The man pulls her up and slaps her again. With her shirt torn, he sees the necklace Mama wears. It had slipped beneath her collar.

He grabs the chain and twists it, tightening it around Mama's throat.

"Then where are they?"

Elisa faces the man, close, his breath on her face, the cigarette burns stinging, the slap stinging. The chain from her necklace is not thin enough to break. It's twisted tight around her throat.

She looks him in the eye. "I sent your men on a wild-goose chase."

"Stupid bitch."

He tightens the chain, trying to strangle her. She claws at it. He shoves her back against the table. She can feel him. He's hard. Her skin runs cold with panic and adrenaline.

"The men I'm working for," she says, "they are not going to the Taco Bell. I said that to confuse you. So you and your crew would leave. And I could come help my uncle."

"Lying whore." He twists the chain harder.

"He paid me," she says. "The crew boss. Paid me to make sure I help them get away. That I don't tell where they are."

"You ain't getting paid. Not that way. You're *gonna* pay, right now, if—"

"They are meeting at the black rocks!" she blurts out, tears in her eyes. "Don't hurt me."

She gasps for air, not faking her fear, holding the man's gaze. He's searching her face for signs of deception.

"What black rocks?" he says.

She has to get him to go—and take her with him. It's the only way Gabriela can escape and she herself might survive.

"A cut across the border, in the desert, where they're meeting to divide the score, then scatter. Back road, out of sight. Everything else—it's a cover."

He twists the necklace. "Take me."

She holds off, just a second. When she sees his lips draw back, she nods and whispers, "Okay."

"First you call McCauley, make sure he stays there. No leaving without you."

He puts the radio to her lips and presses Transmit.

After a second's thought, she says, "Keyhole, I got delays. Traffic. Plus eyes on a cop behind me. But I'll be there."

The reply scratches. "Copy."

Wardell pulls her out the door by the chain and hauls her to the work car Neil left here, a Honda Accord. The keys are in the ignition. He forces her to crawl through the passenger door and get behind the wheel. He settles in the passenger seat.

"Drive."

Elisa bumps down the rutted dirt driveway and turns onto the road. With his right hand, the man holds the shotgun aimed at her head. With his left, he grasps her necklace like a leash.

She holds her head high, refusing, against every instinct, to flinch from the barrel of the gun. She stares straight ahead. But she checks the mirrors.

Back at the safe house, at the window of the little bedroom, the blinds pull back, just a few inches. A small hand presses against the glass.

She swallows her relief and joy and fear. She stares at the white line in the middle of the road and heads south. The man is breathing hard. The medallion of Our Lady of Guadalupe and the locket that is a gift from Gabriela are clutched in his fist.

"The black rocks." He squints. "That's not what you called it on the radio call with Neil McCauley."

She keeps her face flat. She has much practice at that, at staying calm when people try to throw her off-balance. But this is confirmation and a probe. The man is after Neil. He has come after Neil from somewhere.

"What's your name?" she says.

He scrapes his gaze up and down her body. "What do you care?"

"Curiosity."

He leans across the car and whispers in her ear, a wet, hissing sound. "Wardell. But you can call me Daddy."

She stares at the road.

"The black rocks. Explain," Wardell says.

"A smuggler's place. Old time. From a hundred years back."

"What's there?"

"Nothing. It's hidden, that's why it's a place. To unload or meet up. Then get away."

"Sounds remote."

"Of course." *Don't look at him.*

Or maybe look at him. She turns her head. He has set the gun against the door, braced, still pointing at her midsection. He has Tío's radio.

"How many?" he says.

"Coming?"

She wants to say four hundred. All armed, all crazed, all ready to rip you to slivers.

"Four," she says.

"Where is this place? Give me directions." He tightens the chain of the necklace. "Exact directions. No fucking around."

She tells him. Exact directions. He gets on a cell phone. He calls his men and relays the information.

"We're coming south on the highway now," Wardell says.

Elisa drives. She's heading for the dunes, the canyons. The place where, on a starlit night a few weeks back, she gazed over the crystalline desert landscape and told Neil McCauley tales of the switchbacks and overlooks where unwary smugglers have been ambushed.

That's where she's taking Wardell. She hopes Neil will be there, waiting.

The black rocks. The funnel of death.

Neil races east on the interstate, mind revving.

Nightmare.

Traffic. Eyes on. The worst possible coded message. Someone has Elisa.

What happened at the safe house? They were clean. Everything was clean.

But not. Somewhere there's been a breach in security. Somehow, someone found out he was taking this score and decided to hijack it. Hijack him. Rip off his score.

Who? Somebody who knows that Neil can't call the cops. But somebody who didn't know enough, who didn't know the post-score plan, their out.

It's nobody in the crew, loose lips. He trusts his men 100 percent.

He doesn't think it's Elisa's people, Tomás and Marcos. He doesn't know much about family. But he knows that for Elisa, it's everything. She trusts these people absolutely. And he trusts Elisa with everything. With his life.

She's hostage, on her way to the black rocks. The place she warned that unwary *contrabandistas* can get waylaid.

That's where she wants him to ambush these fuckers.

He sets the Mercury on cruise control so he doesn't inadvertently bust the speed limit. He takes the US Geological Survey topographical map from the glove compartment.

"Keyhole," he radios, repeating the word that tipped him—that would have tipped everyone in the crew—that they have trouble. That somebody has cut into comms.

Chris comes back. "Copy."

"Inbound. Clear on that bridge over the Colorado. See you in two."

"On my way."

Neil rounds a curve between two knobby hills. The sky is a glazed blue. Heat shimmers off the roadway. He shakes the folds from the map and sets it on the steering wheel.

He waits. Has Chris picked up the clue, and can he access the map too?

"I did the addition," Neil says.

Chris replies, "Yeah, man. Tell me. How'd we do?"

Chris is looped in. They'd never indulge in talk like this off a score.

Neil reads off a set of coordinates, coded as two sums of money. "Got that?"

"Cool."

Chris clicks off. The entire crew should have received the message. They should know he wasn't reading out their cut of the take, but the latitude and longitude where he wants them to meet, armed and ready to attack.

To save Elisa.

61

The dunes spread to the sky in the distance, empty, relentless, bleak. Elisa swings off the highway onto a crumbling back road.

Wardell scans the horizon, and then his gaze slides over her face, her torn shirt, her legs. The sun is sinking toward the peaks of the hills to the west, shadows and light shifting as the road winds upward. Behind her, in the mirror, she sees the borderlands spreading to the far horizon, the world, the dunes shifting, the cracks in the rocks hiding trails and pathways.

The black rocks—volcanic basalt—are ten miles ahead. They rise above the saguaro-speckled landscape, jagged and imposing. She's aiming for a stretch of road just before the summit.

Wardell sees her eyeing the rearview mirror. "What are you looking at?"

She returns her gaze to the road. "Your men."

Wardell's crew has joined up with them in convoy: the black Pontiac Trans Am and the red Chevy Blazer. Front and back. Protecting Wardell. Boxing her in.

Ahead, driving the Trans Am, is Wardell's second-in-command, Svoboda. Slippery, with piercing eyes. He and Wardell speak familiarly. Old acquaintances. A thug rides shotgun, a skinhead with white supremacist prison tats and iron pile muscles and a cloverleaf tattoo. Some neo-Nazi piece of shit.

Behind, riding her bumper, is the hulking red Blazer, jacked up on big tires. Two men in there, sunglasses, guns. The one in the passenger seat lowers the window and spits chewing tobacco. Local.

Elisa has accomplished her main goal. She has pulled Wardell and his crew away from the safe house. She sees again Gabriela's hand pressed to the bedroom window as she drove away. Gabriela is out. What happens next for her, she doesn't know. She'll probably hide somewhere outside the house, but nearby.

She has to stay alive and get back to her baby. Wardell holds the shotgun, the barrel centered on her head. She drives. And thinks about jumping from the car.

It will have to be lightning quick. The right moment. She will only have one chance.

She scans the rising road. Once it enters the canyon, it steepens and switchbacks. If she waits for a sharp bend, she can throw herself out the door into the ravine. Wardell would have to scramble to get control of the car before it runs into a wall or off a cliff. There would be confusion. She would fall, roll, through crumbling rock and appalling drops, but it might work.

Wardell grabs her necklace again. "What are you looking at like that?"

Her head jerks. The chain breaks.

She straightens and glances at him. "The road. It gets twisty."

He's glaring, checking her out. Her breathing. Her torn shirt. The bruises on her face. He seems to like what he sees. And to be angered by her.

"Don't get cocky," he says. "I got this T-boned. Solid."

She drives. The gold chain of the necklace drapes from his hand. The religious medallion and the heart-shaped locket swing back and forth. Wardell reads the inscription on the back.

"*Te amo—Gabriela.*"

Elisa's stomach cramps with fear.

He looks at her sharply. "Who's Gabriela?"

With his thumb, he flicks the locket open. He sees the photos inside. On the left, Gabriela. Elisa's brilliant, beautiful butterfly. On the right, Neil.

He pushes the shotgun against her temple. "You just *work* for McCauley? You and your uncle, you clean his house?"

The barrel is cold. She can barely see, barely breathe.

She points up the canyon. "That's the meeting point."

The pinnacles, toothy black rocks, jut above the canyon like punji sticks. Neil races toward them. The dirt road is narrow. On the USGS map it's only a thin line.

He holds the map open on the wheel. Dust boils behind him. The sun glares a sick gold. The Mercury's suspension bucks. He doesn't know how long it will take his crew to get here. They heard Elisa. They won't add radio chatter. They'll come. But he's closest. For now, it's just him.

He crests a summit and stops. Below, the dirt track intersects a paved road.

Downhill, sunlight glints, miles away. Cars are coming up the canyon.

He parks the Mercury across the paved road, blocking it. Grabbing his CAR-15, he jumps out and runs up a rise to a line of boulders.

The heat pounds him. Sunlight flashes off the cars down the canyon. Scrambling atop a boulder, he raises his range-finder binoculars. Expensive gear. He'd almost decided against buying it. Worth every penny now.

He scans downslope. The switchbacks on the road, the faded, chipped asphalt. The opening of the canyon, 5.7 miles below.

He has his Colt 1911 with three extra clips, his CAR-15 with four more. He expended ammo at the motel in Mexicali. He has 147 remaining rounds he can fire.

The sun is behind him. His binocs won't reflect. The people coming up the road have the afternoon glare in their eyes. He's pulled on a dun-colored canvas jacket, and that and his khakis should camouflage him against the terrain. He settles into a crevice at the lip of the boulder and lies flat.

The wind is blowing from the west. He can't tell how it's swirling around the canyon walls downslope. He can account for bullet drop and the downhill angle of fire. The Colt rifle's effective range is four hundred meters, but he plans to hold fire until the vehicles draw much closer. He will fire at a greater distance only if he sees an opportunity. Or a stark threat.

Elisa.

She's hostage, terrified, maybe hurt—he can't bear to think about it.

So he doesn't. He folds his fears neatly, like a sheet of origami paper, and slides them into a slot at the back of his mind. He focuses.

His heart is beating harder than it should.

Sunlight flickers again. He raises the binoculars. Three vehicles, now 5.1 miles away. A black Pontiac Trans Am. A red Chevy Blazer. And in the middle of the convoy, a Honda Accord—the work car he left at the safe house. Is Elisa in that car?

He watches the convoy, watches the numbers on the range finder scroll down. Something scratches at him. That car in front. The black Trans Am. He refocuses the binoculars.

The car's three or four years old. Unexceptional. Dirty. The sun is glaring off the windshield. He glimpses a bulky man at the wheel and a bulkier man in the passenger seat.

It's the fading paint, the scratches, and the lack of upkeep that sends the hairs on the back of his neck up.

That's a work car. One he has seen before. In the garage in Chicago behind the auto repair shop where Aaron Grimes works. *Motherfuck.*

Where's Elisa? He turns the binoculars on the middle car in the convoy.

Elisa rounds a turn behind the Trans Am. Wardell's face has taken on an eager, dark cast. Hungry. Like he's heading for a banquet, expecting to devour everything he finds there. Including her.

"How much farther?" he says.

"Maybe six miles. The cabin is past that summit. A dirt track, hidden by brush."

Wardell puts his arm out the window and signals to the Trans Am in front, a hatchet gesture. *Keep going.*

Elisa has crossed the border via this road at least twenty-five times in the last fifteen years. She has the curves and dips memorized. The convoy heads into a rising bend. Past it, a sharp curve at a sharp drop is coming. She sets herself.

One chance. She'll have to dive below the lip of the drop-off and let herself crash down the ravine to have any chance of evading gunfire from Wardell and his men.

Ahead, the Trans Am smoothly navigates a bend. Behind, the Chevy Blazer remains ass-close, crowding her, aggressive just for the hell of it, she thinks.

The rocks rise high on the right, pinnacles. The road curves and flattens. A hundred yards ahead, she sees the drop-off. Crumbling roadway, immediate plunge. She slowly sets her left hand on the door handle. Readying.

Ahead, the Trans Am swerves.

It veers across the center line, then overcorrects and swings back sharply.

Gunfire roars from the canyon walls around her.

Flat on his belly atop the boulder, Neil absorbs the recoil of the CAR-15.

Ninety meters downslope, the Trans Am swerves toward the drop-off, its windshield pocked white with a bullet hole. It overcorrects, straightens, and accelerates.

Neil fires again. Hits the roof. Fires again, a three-shot burst. Shatters the windshield and sees blood explode against it.

The passenger is hit, maybe dead. The car pours on the power. Behind it, a second later, so do the other two vehicles.

The red Blazer rams the Accord's bumper, forcing it to accelerate. *Yes,* Elisa's in that car.

Neil cannot let any of the vehicles get past his position. He fires again at the Trans Am, multishot bursts. He takes out the left-side tires. The car skids headfirst into the canyon wall.

The Blazer brakes, burning rubber. Neil swings the rifle and unloads three bursts into the windshield. He takes out the driver.

The Accord slams on its brakes as it screeches toward the wrecked Trans Am. Neil can see Elisa in the driver's seat, a man in the passenger seat. He fires at him. Too high. He adjusts his aim and puts rounds into the Accord's engine block. Steam erupts from under the hood.

The driver of the Trans Am scrambles out, a burly guy with a flat face. He dodges for the far side of the car. Neil swings the barrel, hits him before he can reach cover.

He goes down, wounded.

Neil's clip empties. The Trans Am driver crawls around the car out of sight. Neil ejects the clip, grabs another, inserts it, slams it home, and turns fire on the red Blazer again. With the driver dead, it's rolling to a stop. The passenger jumps out on the far side of the vehicle. Neil fires straight through the Blazer's windows. A dozen shots. Glass flies. The noise echoes in the canyon.

Blood sprays. The man goes down. Stays down.

The echo of gunfire fades. Neil hears the driver of the Trans Am shouting to the man in the Accord. They're trying to triangulate Neil's firing position. The Trans Am driver is crouching behind the car, but, maybe because he's injured, he hasn't ducked low enough.

Neil rises on one elbow and fires a tight three-shot burst. The first shot misses left, striking the rocks on the hillside, sending pebbles ricocheting back at the car.

The second shot hits the man in the shoulder. It spins him away from the Trans Am.

The third shot catches him in the open, smashes him in the chest. He's already falling backward. The gun clatters from his hand and he drops from sight behind the car.

Four down. Who's left?

Neil turns the rifle on the center car. The Accord. He unloads on the tires and the front end, pouring rounds into the engine block. The hood and chassis and grille bubble with bullet holes. The radiator blows steam.

A second later, the passenger door kicks open. A man drags Elisa out, shotgun to her head. A human shield.

In the adobe barracks, the silence and heat are overwhelming. Gabriela gathers herself.

Mama told her what to do. *The plan is—run. Anything goes wrong, clear out. On your own. Wait until nobody can see you and go. Out of sight. Comprendes, mariposa?*

Gabriela understands. But her heart has been pierced by the sight of her mom being taken to the car by the bad man, with the locket twisted in his fist.

She doesn't know where Mama is. Where Neil is. Neil would help her if he was here. When Neil is nearby, Gabriela feels safe. But Neil isn't here.

Shaking, she creeps to the bedroom door. Hears nothing. But she knows what's out there.

She slips into the shadowed hall. On the floor in the main room, Tío Tomás lies still. His chest doesn't rise. He stares but doesn't see anything.

She feels freaked out. She thought when people died, their eyes closed. She backs away. Then stops. Tío didn't tell the bad men she was here. He took the pain. He died.

He died.

She can't stand to leave him like this. It's scary—so scary—but she walks, trembling, into the main room. She takes a Navajo blanket off the back of the couch. She approaches Tío with dread. She drapes the blanket over him.

She hesitates. Decides the silence is not good enough.

"I'm sorry, Tío," she says. "I hope it doesn't hurt anymore."

Taking a breath, she crouches and closes his eyes. She whispers, "Thank you."

She slips out the back door.

The man holding Elisa has eyes like an incendiary bomb. Enraged, Neil thinks. Cornered.

The guy frantically scans the canyon, but he can't spot Neil in the crevice on top of the boulder. He holds Elisa in front of him, up on her toes, covering him as he keeps low. Neil sights but has no clear shot.

"Throw down your weapons and come out," the man shouts.

Neil can see Elisa's eyes. He can read everything in them. Cold fear. Determination. Hope.

His chest hurts.

The heat glimmers off the pavement. The man spots the Mercury across the road. He edges toward it. He jams the barrel of the shotgun beneath Elisa's chin.

"Throw down your weapons and come out. Or I kill her."

Neil needs a new firing position to get the drop on this guy. He slides off the boulder.

"Did you not hear me?" the man shouts. "Come out unarmed or I kill her, McCauley."

The man's voice turns muffled. "Tell him."

Elisa shouts in pain. "He is serious."

"I'm counting to ten," the man says. "That's all the time she has."

There's a gap at the base of two boulders. Neil flattens himself and peers through the breach.

"Ten," the man shouts.

The man has Elisa by the hair, shotgun forcing her chin up as he inches toward the Mercury. Neil still has no shot.

"Nine." The man's head swivels, trying to spot him. "Eight."

He has to entice this guy into his sights. "Let her go and I'll give you the keys to my car."

"Seven." The man continues creeping toward the Mercury. "I said *seven*."

He draws back his fist and punches Elisa in the face.

"Six."

He punches her again. She reels. Neil still cannot get a clear shot.

"Five."

Neil steps out from behind the rocks, rifle low on his hip, keys held high. "Let her go."

The man keeps inching, holding Elisa close, trying to read Neil's face. "Toss 'em."

Neil pitches them up the road at the Mercury. "Release her."

The keys hit the pavement near the edge of the road. The man nods. Keeping Elisa between them, he backs away from Neil toward them. There's an inch between himself and Elisa's back. Then six inches. Then a foot.

"One," he says.

He swings his twelve-gauge and shotguns Elisa in the shoulder.

Neil screams, "No!"

She spins. Rag doll. As she falls, the man kicks her over the crumbling lip of the road onto the canyon slope.

He swings the shotgun toward Neil. Neil covers behind rocks. The shotgun roars. He hears gravel tumbling as Elisa slides helplessly down the slope out of sight.

Neil lunges from behind the rocks, leaps over the lip of the road, and plunges downhill to stop her from tumbling helplessly toward the bottom of the ravine.

She's sliding, limp. He digs his heels into the loose scree, grabs her, stops her slide. He throws himself on top of her, covering her with his body, and raises the rifle toward the road.

He hears footsteps running. A car door slams. The Mercury's engine fires up.

Heart thundering, Neil wraps an arm around Elisa and pulls her uphill toward the road. He pauses at the edge of the pavement. The Mercury is in reverse, backing crazily up the road. The man spins the wheel and throws the car into a skidding U-turn.

The man jams the Mercury into drive. He looks Neil in the eye and raises his right hand. It holds Elisa's necklace. The saint's medal and the locket swing back and forth. As Neil gets to one knee and fires the rifle, he floors the car and roars away over a rise to the west.

Breathing hard, Neil pulls Elisa onto the roadway and drops to his knees at her side.

Her shoulder is pulped. Her arm hangs by tendons. He's seen this in battle. Her white shirt is a sopping mass of blood. Point-blank, twelve-gauge. His head feels full of splinters.

She blinks, panting.

"My men are coming," he says. "We'll get you out of here."

He rips open her shirt. The wound is chugging blood, a mass of bone and muscle and shredded skin. That beautiful, smooth, strong line of her body has been turned to mulch.

"I have to stop the bleeding," he says.

He pulls off his jacket, rolls it up, puts it to the wound as a pressure dressing, and leans down on it to stanch the flow of blood. She gasps and her eyes roll back.

His heart clenches.

He did this to her.

Caring distorts your decision-making. Attaching, getting involved. Emotion lures you into tangential event streams instead of down the critical path of least risk, most reward. It gets people you care about hurt.

His fault.

"Gabriela," she says weakly.

"Where is she?"

"Safe house. I told her to run and hide. Send Marcos or Trejo. Find her."

Neil grabs the radio. He pauses, wondering if it's still worth worrying about the man who has his comms. And his car. His cut of the score.

"What's his name?" he asks Elisa.

"Wardell," she says.

He doesn't know it, but he will find out everything there is to know about this man.

"He knows I have a daughter. We have to get her."

Neil presses Transmit. Tells the crew to hurry, to get Marcos to the safe house. Hears static in reply. A distant voice, briefly, before it cuts out. The canyon walls are blocking reception.

"Tío is dead," Elisa says. "He fought them. Kept them from finding Gabriela."

Neil looks around, desperate now. The sun has arced beyond the peaks of the pinnacles. Rays shine through the crags, like God through torn claws. Shadows stripe the empty road. All he can do is keep pressure on the wound and wait for his crew to get here.

"You came," she says.

"Of course."

Her breathing sounds agonized. Her eyes have a dark cast. She knows things are bad.

He looks at her, really looks. Beyond the blood, beyond the bravery, he sees bruises on her face. He sees cigarette burns on her chest. A cold heat suffuses him. Rage.

"*Amado*," Elisa says.

Her voice is dry. He has no water for her. He says, "I'm here."

"All I wanted was to get away from the ranch barracks. All I wanted. Get Wardell far from my baby. Give her a chance to run."

"She got it. You did that."

"The rest. The code. The canyon. I threw that out, words, like scattering seeds. I was desperate. I was trying anything." Her eyes shine. "I did not dare hope you would come."

His chest constricts. "For you. Beautiful girl. For you. Everything."

Everything. Everything gone wrong.

His doing.

"Talk to me, Neil," Elisa says.

"Chris is coming. Cerrito is coming. Trejo is coming."

"You're not Catholic."

He frowns. "What?"

"You say their names like the litany of saints."

"They're coming. They're going to get you to a doctor."

She looks like she wants to believe that, but her eyes chide him. She knows.

I'm lying. Lying to her. Fucking hell, it'll take two hours to get her medical help.

"They're coming."

"Saint Christopher, pray for us," she says.

He inhales. She gives him a wry look.

"Saint Michael, swear for us," she says.

He laughs. It feels out of control. He squeezes her hand. "Holy Trejo, fight for us."

"Neil McCauley, stay with me."

"I'm here." There's a crack in his voice.

"Footprints in the sand," she says.

"What?"

"The dunes."

His gaze rolls down the canyon, to the desert floor and the sculpted rise of the Algodones Dunes on the horizon. Then he takes in Elisa's face. It's pale. Her eyes are growing hot, against the pain, against the draining of her blood. He continues pressing on the gunshot wound, hoping, working, to tether her to the now, to life.

He does not want to think of her washing away with the tides of time and death. He wants her with him forever, warm, breathing, laughing, loving him. This woman. This miracle.

He raises the radio. "Come in."

He hears static. No reception. Presses Transmit again and stops.

He sees it, blinding bright. He can't wait for Chris, for Michael, for Trejo. Can't load Elisa in a work car and find a doctor who will treat her in an office or motel room, off the books.

She needs a hospital, needs trauma surgeons. She needs blood, an IV, fluid resuscitation to stabilize her, to keep her from going into hypovolemic shock. If she loses too much volume, there won't be enough blood for her heart to pump through her body. Blood pressure will crash. Organs will fail, *boom*, one after the next. He's seen it. In Củ Chi. Squad mates grievously wounded while crawling along a three-foot-wide tunnel and gone before they could drag them out to reach a medic.

Elisa needs paramedics. Now.

"I have to get to elevation and call an ambulance."

"Neil."

The canyon slope is crumbling rock and desert sage, but climbable. It's three hundred feet to the summit. He puts her right hand over the pulsing exit wound in her shoulder.

"Press. I have to get up the hill where I can get a signal. Call my crew. They'll call 911. I'll be back. Sixty seconds."

"Neil."

Something in her eyes. Like she knows something he doesn't, sees something about him that he's not seeing for himself. For a surreal instant, his vision zooms out. He sees her as if from a great height: Elisa lies in the roadway, small, her blood surrounding her. A dark vision of a saint, la Virgen de Guadalupe painted on the asphalt, deep red. Beyond her, downslope, are Wardell's three wrecked cars. Four scattered bodies, dead spirits in a Goya painting, splayed, lost.

He holds the radio in his hand. Looks at the pinnacle above him, so promising, so necessary. Three hundred feet above. Too far. Elisa will bleed out.

He drops down beside her, presses on the wound. "Kid," he says, breathless. "Hold tight."

"I tried to tell you."

My men are coming. They're coming.

She turns her head to look at him. "I was empty."

"What?" He adjusts the rolled-up jacket. It's sopping.

"Empty," she says. "The world. After my husband died."

"What are you talking about?"

"It was gray. Nothing. No hope for me."

"Elisa."

"I kept it together for Gabriela." Her voice is dry. "I got up. Worked. Put food on the table for her. Held her. Loved her. But the world was gray."

"The world can be gray. But you are brilliant color."

"*Amado mío,* shut your mouth and listen."

"Let me talk. You rest."

"No. Let *me* talk." A look comes over her face. Not desperation, but clarity. "You. A surprise."

He brushes a strand of hair from her face. "Cold and hard, huh?"

He is trying to slam shut a cage around his heart. To lock it, to seal it up, to weld it shut against the words she's saying, because she's saying the words right now because she thinks there will be no later.

Footprints on a beach. The tide comes through and you were never there.

"True to yourself," she says. "Aware. Waiting. Seeking."

"That's what you saw in me?"

"Handsome guy who didn't know it. Too closed off, too wary to let down his guard. But somehow I slipped past."

"You broke me open," he says, and knows the lock on his heart will not hold. "You were irresistible."

He fights it for another moment, clutching tight to the world he's in, to the world he wants, the one that's about to disappear. Because of his actions. Because of the things he has brought upon this broken glory who lies here on the road.

"I love you," she says. "That is the only truth that matters."

"I love *you*." He hears the rip in his voice. "You brought me to full color."

"You brought me back to life," she says.

He looks down the mountain. Listens. Hopes to hear car engines. Sees nothing but two vultures, far away, riding thermals in the late-afternoon sky.

"*Querida*," he says. Beloved. "I'm sorry."

"Shh."

Heat, a black scrim, falls through him. "I should never have let you get close to this."

"Don't."

"You're not part of my crew. You didn't sign up for this."

"I did."

"If I'd never gotten involved with you, this wouldn't have happened."

She raises a weak hand to his lips. "*Silencio.*"

He breathes.

"Neil." She whispers it. Her lips have a blue cast. A shadow rides behind her eyes. "We have this time. Let me tell you. I am happy. You make me happy. You give joy to my days. My mornings. My nights. My mind. My heart. My body. Every second has been worth it."

He lets it all go. The cage splits open. He hasn't been hiding anything from her, only from himself. And there's no time left for that now.

"I am a lucky man," he says.

She's beginning to shiver. They both know: He has lost everything he came here for today. There's no way to stop it now.

"Stay with me," he says.

"I wish."

"Stay."

"More than anything. To stay. With you. To see . . ." She closes her eyes. Tears leak out. "To see Gabriela again."

"She will be safe. I promise you."

Her lips tremble. She opens her eyes. The tears pool in them. Neil wants to wipe them away, but he is holding pressure on her shoulder wound. The blood has covered his hands, his shirt, his pants.

"Go ahead," she says.

"What?"

"Let go."

"I can't."

Her voice is barely audible above the whir of the breeze rolling down the canyon. She blinks and the tears slide away. Her eyes are hot and dark and clear.

"Hold me, Neil," she says. "Let me kiss you."

He is holding her, but that's not what she wants, not what she's telling him.

She's telling him how she wants to say goodbye.

"Elisa," he says.

"Please."

The sun sinks away, shadows etching the slope and sliding across them.

Chris guns the rugged Dodge up the slope into the canyon, pushing it. It's been twenty minutes since he last heard from Neil. In the shotgun seat, Cerrito looks wired, edgy, antsy, his eyes so wild with unease that he's nearly gone blank. The radio sits silent in his hand.

"Try again," Chris says.

Michael presses Transmit. "Come in."

Silence. Chris jams the pedal down.

"What do you think?" Michael says.

"Check your mags."

"Yeah." He takes his SIG Sauer from his waistband, ejects the magazine, reseats it, and pulls the slide back just enough to reveal the cartridge in the chamber. He shoves the gun behind his back.

Chris peers up the canyon, the view coming and going through rocky promontories, disappearing as the road switchbacks yet again.

He rounds a curve. "Shit."

He slams on the brakes. Cerrito lurches forward, stopping himself against the dash. The car screeches to a halt.

On the road ahead, three cars are shot to all hell: a red Chevy Blazer, the Honda work car, and a black Trans Am. Shattered glass, bullet holes, flattened tires.

Chris and Michael get out carefully, weapons raised.

Four men lie dead among the vehicles. Blood runs off the asphalt into the sand at the side of the road.

Chris and Michael look at each other. Snugging the CAR-15 against his shoulder, Chris takes the left flank around the wrecked cars. Michael takes the right, sweeping his weapon in a tight arc, left, right, down at the ground.

Chris rounds the red Blazer. He freezes. His heart seems to explode. He swings the barrel of the CAR-15 up. Michael appears, inhales, and stops.

In the middle of the road, Neil sits on the asphalt, covered in blood. Held tight in his arms, pale as marble, limp, drained of life, is Elisa.

He stares through the day, through the rocks, through Chris and Michael. He cradles Elisa's body tenderly, desperately. Broken.

Chris drops to one knee on the road and lowers his head. The dusk falls like a shroud.

62

The sand under the mesquite bushes is cooling down. The sun has fallen below the horizon. Concealed in a thicket up a hill from the adobe barracks, Gabriela waits and begins to shiver.

When she hears a car coming, she creeps forward. The bushes block her view. Tires roll along the driveway. Dust blows in the air.

A car door slams.

She hears boots on the wooden porch. A hard sound, like cowboy boots.

Her mom wasn't wearing boots. Neil wasn't. Chris wasn't.

Who is that?

Her mind fires white with fear.

··

At the adobe barracks, Marcos stands in the doorway. The battered body of Tomás Vasquez lies on the floor in front of him.

"Mother of God."

Tomás has been covered, gently, with a Navajo blanket. Holy Lord. The blanket was placed over him by a child. With care, trying to ease a pain Tomás no longer felt. To comfort him.

"Gabriela." Enraged, aching, Marcos runs through the house. She's not there. He dashes outside and calls her name. The sound flattens in the rising wind.

Scrambling to her feet, Gabriela turns to run. The desert opens before her, shadowed, unforgiving. Then she hears it.

Gabriela.

Her mama's voice, something *real*, something *close*. Loud in her head. Like coming from giant speakers, but beyond the world.

Now, Gabriela. Now, and always.

She stops and turns back toward the house.

"Gabriela!"

She bursts into tears and runs toward Marcos.

The night has fully fallen when Neil finally gets back to the safe house. His mind is a steady dial tone—loud, high, insistent. Blank.

He steps through the door. Marcos is there, exhausted, shoulders slumping. The day has dissolved from triumph to disaster. He meets Neil's eyes.

Neil says nothing. He looks at the spot on the wood floor of the main room where blood has soaked into the dry wood.

"Tomás?" he asks.

"I wrapped his body in blankets. It's in the cargo bed of my pickup. Hard shell. Nobody will stop me. I will see to his burial."

Neil nods.

Marcos turns to look down the hall. Neil follows his gaze. Standing there, half hidden in the shadows, is Gabriela.

"Mama," she says. "Where's my mom?"

Neil drives the highway alone as the night turns to morning twilight.

Marcos has taken Gabriela. Neil knows that Wardell has Elisa's ID and her locket. Wardell knows that Elisa has a little girl.

Neil has told Marcos to take her far away, across the border. Keep her safe. Nobody must know where she is.

The locket. Links. Attachment.

It gets people you love—people you should never have been involved with—killed.

It turns the world to ashes.

Neil will take Elisa's body to a funeral home, to a mortuary Marcos knows—people who have worked with their family for generations, who will give her dignified and tender care.

He feels the tires leave the asphalt and scrape over gravel, heading for a ditch. He corrects. He tries to breathe against what feels like strangling wire around his chest.

He's still driving when the sun comes up. He heads for the meeting point, the derelict house north of Yuma that Elisa arranged. The place she never made it to.

He stares at the desert sunrise. At his hands. They're empty, except for Elisa's blood.

PART FIVE

Paraguay, 1996

63

Three weeks.

When Chris walks into the Lius' corporate offices at the utilitarian business park outside the city, it's been three weeks since he has seen Ana Liu. Three weeks since the meet with Claudio at the Casino Paraná. Since he handed over the CD carrying the code and malware and felt Claudio's pulse as he wrote on his palm.

Three long weeks.

He's a little out of his head.

It's been radio silence on the results of the meeting. There's no way for him to know what the Chens have done with the sabotaging GPS spoof program, or what the program has done to their clients, if anything.

That's the second thing on his mind. The woman—the urge to see her again, to hear her voice, for any contact—is the first.

Rain showers have scoured the day, blustery and gray. When Chris arrives, Paolo is pacing in the lobby, talking on his cell phone. He hangs up and approaches, looking quick and alert.

Chris tilts his head, lets a question rise in his eyes.

"The Chens. They are a little angry," Paolo says.

Chris stills. "You mean it worked."

"Yes."

Chris's pulse pops. *Winning.* Then he sees a shadow of concern behind Paolo's gaze.

"And so? What's the risk? Payback? They gonna take a shot at the Lius?" he says. "Have I got a bull's-eye on my back?"

Paolo thinks for a minute.

"Motorbike Man?" Chris says. "Let's cut the crap. Why don't I put this cowboy out of business?"

Paolo holds Chris's gaze. Shakes his head. "No."

The blank look in Chris's eyes says this is going to happen, if not now, later.

"And you are right about the surveillance of the Xingfu Center," Paolo says. "Put together with Mr. Terry, the Chens wanted to hack into the Lius' computer system, to spy and steal their code. They were looking for weaknesses. Could they hack into the Lius' intranet through the phone and fiber-optic lines? The motorbikes were looking for access, the PBX room in the garage. We are hardening the systems."

"The hit on the Land Cruiser?" Chris says.

"An insider who skimmed money from them. That was personal. What you did is business."

Chris digests it. Ciudad del Este business.

Then he hears her voice. Ana comes around the corner on her cell phone. She ends the call and looks back and forth between the two men.

"Whose dog died? Such grim faces."

She's in Adidas and green plaid flannel, chunky glasses propped on top of her head. She looks to Chris like a bright-burning flame.

Chris says, "The Chens are upset."

She gives him a look. "They installed the GPS spoofing software you gave them."

Her face is briefly unreadable. Then: cold satisfaction.

"We have no inside source," she says, "but we hear rumors. When the ECM was activated, the spoofing program did its magic and then shut down after fifty-seven minutes. In every unit. As designed."

Chris fights a smile.

"To pinpoint the defect, the Chens and their clients disassembled the units, examined the hardware. Then they loaded the CD in a networked computer to search for buggy code. The malware is spreading like mold through their systems."

"Bad luck."

"A meteor strike is bad luck." She turns to go, then looks back over her shoulder. "That was good work."

She walks away.

He can't believe the draw to her he feels. His heart, his entire frame, simply wants to move toward her, take her somewhere around a corner out of sight.

He makes sure his eyes are blank and turns to Paolo.

Business?

In Los Angeles, a money launderer, Roger Van Zant, also did "business." Neil, Chris, and the crew took down an armored van and stole bearer bonds. Some were Van Zant's. Since Van Zant was insured, they made a deal to sell the bonds back to him at a price and everybody would make out. But Van Zant felt impelled to retaliate. That didn't work out so well for him.

"Motorbike Man can slide," Chris says. "But the vibe of these players tells me someday . . ."

He gazes down the hall, in the direction Ana has gone. It's involuntary.

Paolo sees, draws into himself. His hazel eyes flash in his copper-brown face, but they're impossible to read. Instead, "There is a thing here called 'equilibrium.'"

"What's that?"

"They made a move on us. We made a move back."

"Okay," Chris says.

"What are you thinking?"

He's thinking about Claudio Chen, about his machismo, his pansexuality, his profit motive, his Machiavellian proclivities.

El mago. Lector de la mente. Time to be a goddamn mind reader. With some heavy backup.

"Let's go get ourselves some equilibrium."

The Suburban rolls through narrow streets. Paolo is at the wheel. Beside him, Chris chambers a round in his H&K USP. He reholsters the weapon. Power lines flay the view overhead. Stalls are up and running. Sunshine glares through the windshield. It's seven a.m.

The café is outside the Mega Bright Mall. Gunmen stand in doorways, looking sleepy, though they are not. On a balcony above, Lebanese men sit at a card table smoking and discussing the morning papers. On the street, stall hawkers rehash last night's *fútbol* match.

The Suburban pulls to the curb, followed by a Jeep with four of Paolo's men.

The café has one narrow door. Chris pauses for a taut moment. He and Paolo lock eyes.

They get out.

The café has tiny tables with plastic chairs crammed around them. Speckled linoleum. Arabic music on the radio. The driving beat sounds mesmerizing and discordant to Chris's ears, alluring and alien. And in this minute, it's a reminder that he is on foreign goddamn turf. The Chens own this mall.

Claudio Chen sits at a table in the back. He's having breakfast with the Connecticut Anglo. He looks up from his espresso when Chris's shadow fills the doorway.

Chris walks straight at him.

No appointment. No phone call. No warning. No alert.

64

In the café, Claudio looks up through the golden morning light. He's wearing an aqua suit and aviator sunglasses. Chris walks in with Paolo behind him. Paolo's men have taken up positions in the doorway and on the sidewalk.

Chris bluntly walks toward his table, hands in plain sight, eyes dead center on Claudio's forehead.

Claudio is chill, but sparks seem to flash from beneath his skin.

At other tables, chairs scrape as Motorbike Man and two more thugs rise and reach under their shirts. They pull out handguns.

The counterman spins and disappears behind the swinging door into the kitchen. A waiter ducks down the back hall. Chris hears the rear door open and a shout. One of Paolo's men is stationed outside the back door in the alley.

In a corner by the window, a tourist couple looks up from their breakfast, cheesy bread halfway to their mouths.

Across the street a guy with an AK steps into the sunlight. Paolo's man on the sidewalk stands rock still, facing him. Gun holstered. Carefully doing nothing.

Motorbike Man is breathing heavily, his skinny chest rising and falling beneath a Diego Maradona jersey.

Chris has a neon-clear microflash in his mind's eye. Charlene's eyes. Dominick's wide-open smile, full of curiosity. Will they do okay without him?

Another flash. Ana on a Ciudad del Este street, wide open to a drive-by.

He walks straight up and pulls out the chair opposite Claudio.

Claudio doesn't twitch. A religious medallion hangs around his neck. When Chris sits down, he sees it's Ayrton Senna.

Chris sets his hands on the edge of the table, loose, visible. "Yeah. It's me."

Connecticut stiffens like a taxidermy fox. His eyes cut back and forth between Chris, Claudio, Paolo, and Motorbike Man.

Claudio removes his shades. He is cooler than a rattler.

But the Chris he is seeing is not the Terry facade. Chris doesn't look at Claudio. His blank stare cuts through Claudio's eyes to the back of his skull, where he would like the .45 round from the H&K USP holstered in his back to go.

Claudio takes a pack of Marlboros from his jacket. He lights up and takes a long, languorous drag. "Go ahead, Mr. Not Scott Terry."

"I'm with the Lius."

His eyes bore in on Chris. He slides the Marlboros across the table. Chris refuses the pack.

"You tried to steal the Lius' software."

Claudio takes another drag.

"You tried to fuck us," Chris says. "I'm here to tell you, face-to-face. It's me. I fucked you."

The tip of Claudio's cigarette glows red.

"In case you put a bull's-eye on my back, I am also here for me. I could split. You'd never see me again." Chris pauses. "But I don't want to."

Claudio exhales.

"Two choices. We can get down, and I will whack you and half your fucking family." Chris holds Claudio's gaze. "Or we consider the status quo is status quo. Equilibrium. We go our separate ways and continue drawing breath and making money."

Claudio blows a smoke ring at the ceiling. The Arabic music skates across the room, hypnotic and unsettling.

"You work for the Lius or you work for you? You like to play it both ways?"

"I work for the Lius. I played it exactly as it came."

Claudio gives him a pensive look. He taps ash onto his saucer and looks at the cigarette as if consuming it gives him sexual gratification. Claudio takes a final drag, stubs out the cigarette on the saucer, and picks a flake of tobacco from his lip.

"As long as there is no more fucking, Mr. Not Terry."

He flicks the tobacco away and leans back, as if dismissing Chris from a dressing-down.

Chris stands and walks into the sunshine.

Chris drives David and Felix Liu to a Chamber of Commerce meeting. It's a mundane yet privileged task. David takes calls in Mandarin. Felix asks Chris about America, East Coast versus West Coast rap.

"This feud, it's real?" Felix says.

"Real and fatal."

Humor him. It's trivial. Chris regards being spoken to by Felix as a breakthrough. He does not tell Felix and David about the meeting at the café. He and Paolo say nothing else about Claudio. Right now, there's nothing else to say. But he is still wound tightly.

And it's that night, eight p.m., when he's come back from a run, that Ana knocks on his door.

It's darkening outside, the night washing blue, headlights and music rising up across the neighborhood. Again, she kicks off her shoes. She has a take-out bag of Chinese food that she unloads on the kitchen counter. "Shower up."

He stands with his hands on his hips, watching her.

She pauses. "All right, then."

She snaps her fingers and points him at the shower. And follows, smiling.

The shower is steamy when she strips and joins him, looking like a wrestler about to enter a cage match and dismantle him. He laughs.

Afterward, she finds a terry-cloth robe and wraps her hair in a towel turban and goes back to the kitchen. He pulls on jeans and joins her. She has served them both healthy plates and is scavenging through his kitchen drawers.

"You have no chopsticks," she says. "Barbarian."

"Yes. That's why you like me."

It's a tossed-off quip, but she flips a wary glance at him, like she suspects his past might contain dark and violent currents. He doesn't react. She goes to the living room, opens her computer bag, and retrieves two sets.

"I will train you in everything?" she says.

"No. You like me wild."

She laughs as she sits down and pulls her plate close. "Wild, but open to suggestion."

They eat heartily, and she gets dressed.

"Thank you," she says. "I will see you again."

"Ana," he says, almost like a strangely lost mantra.

She strolls to the living room for her computer bag and turns to him. "You have more in you than you know." She hesitates a moment. "Yes. You are bold. And you have many more skills than you've shown any of us, I think. But I am talking about what's in you that you do not know. Do you want to exploit those qualities?"

"Yes."

"If what I want to happen happens, you'll have possibilities. Life-changing ones. But I need allies, advisers, and . . ."

"A sentinel?"

"With quick insights and more . . ."

She's standing in front of his desk. She stills and goes silent.

The photo of Charlene and Dominick sits prominently on the desktop. He lets her take her time looking at it.

After what feels like an age, she looks over her shoulder at him.

He walks toward her. "I want to be up front with you."

She turns back to the photo. "I didn't ask. When I came here tonight . . ."

He can't see her face. He rounds to her side. Doesn't touch her.

"I have a wife and a son . . ." His voice feels like it's going to skid. "They're not here. They're never coming here. They can't. I can't go there. But I am going to reunite with them someday. I don't know when. I don't know how. But there is that."

"Yeah." She continues looking at the photo. She doesn't touch it or him. Finally she nods. "No future, you mean. For me and you."

"And no lies."

"I understand."

He can't read the look on her face. He may have blown it. "It" being whatever the hell this is.

"No future," she says. "Then nothing to worry about."

What is she talking about?

Her voice quiets. "Your boy is beautiful."

He feels a stabbing sensation, like his heart has just been shoved all the way out of his body. He merely nods. Ana looks up at him.

Her smile is brief and, maybe, wry. "Jacked, a married American with false papers. What a prize you are." She smiles and goes on. "This is not a match that I would ever be encouraged to make. It is not anything we should talk about to anybody in my family."

"You mean I'm not sleeping my way to the top?"

She laughs. "Are you Taiwanese?"

"No. I am insightful."

"I'll see you soon," she says.

He has never felt more enflamed. It's not only Ana. It's her world that is opening to him. The *new* new. In full color.

She walks out. He goes to the plate glass window and watches her leave. Her car is parked at the curb. She gets in and drives off without looking back.

He leans against the cool glass.

The warehouse is cold when Chris walks in at the beginning of the week. Paolo is supervising an eighteen-wheeler crew. Across the warehouse floor, Ana stands at a particleboard table, typing on her laptop. She doesn't look up.

Paolo finishes up with the truck and approaches.

"That thing," Chris says.

"*Tudo bem.*"

"That's definite? No chatter, no sign things are going to . . ."

"Escalate? That is the word?"

"Yes."

Paolo shakes his head. "Status quo. We make money."

They exchange a look. Chris will never completely let down his guard. He sees now that Paolo won't, either. Good.

Ana closes her laptop and saunters over. "You are not still talking about the Chens, are you?"

"Our job, *señorita,*" Paolo says.

"And we appreciate how well you do it."

He nods in thanks and excuses himself to talk to a driver. Ana turns to Chris.

"The Chens were angry, but the Chens are small change," she says. "Claudio is a guy who would pull the wings off Tinker Bell for fun, but he and his family are stuck thinking within the boundaries of Ciudad del Este."

"You're thinking bigger?" he says.

"As both a hedge and a frontier. I like every deal I make that takes me further into the world than here. I like the high wire," she says. "I am not going to be my father's successor. I am starting my own business unit to run things new ways without limits."

"And you will do it."

A smile skates across her face. "In the meantime . . ."

She crooks a finger and leads him deeper into the warehouse. They round a corner and Chris stops. A wing of the building is full of high-tech gear, floor to ceiling.

"What's all that?" he asks.

She shakes her head. "A month's inventory. We cycle through this much every three weeks."

Chris tries to keep his eyes from widening.

"It's the start," she says.

He almost laughs.

The Lius do deals; access supplies, finished goods, hardware and components, available supply chains; make bank transactions through global electronic funds transfers. They have access to government databases in Russia and Israel for intel on customers and any law enforcement that may impede them. They mostly avoid jurisdictions like the United States and thereby fly above legal strictures. They don't break laws; they soar beyond them and above national judicial systems, operating from this open city, this free-trade zone. They operate outside the hostile police forces, judges, grand juries, parasitic lawyers, and dealmakers within which Chris's criminal career had been submerged.

However, there is no safe harbor. It's a state of nature, a lethal jungle. You make your fate. It is in your own hands. Hunter and hunted roam unconstrained. Your intelligence, discipline, and willingness to engage in all forms of violence are the functions that determine whether you survive.

Chris has never felt so *free*.

He's walking through a small door into CinemaScope; exile has transformed into revelation.

Ana looks at him.

"I'm your man," he says.

On the way home, Chris stops by the post office box, feeling strong enough to throw the dice today and take whatever comes. He opens his box. His heart drops a heavy beat.

There's a letter from Charlene. It's been sitting there for a week.

He walks down the narrow, cacophonous street to Café Damascus. When he sits, the waiter brings him coffee and *chipa*.

He knows what will happen when he opens the letter.

Inside are photos of his beautiful son, of Charlene holding Dominick and kneeling beside him on the beach.

Charlene's letter says, *I love you, baby. We miss you. We need you.*

He's not a ghost. Not to her. Not to his son. He's real.

The streets outside rumble with the fray of commerce today. Tomorrow? The horizon promises domains he can create. His history abruptly feels dated.

What the hell was it? Neil McCauley, Michael Cerrito, Chris Shiherlis, Trejo. With all their expertise, what were they? They were maybe the best. But at what, being nineteenth-century bandidos robbing banks?

He feels alive and vital in this present, the electric now.

And all at once, his life feels spectral. Tenuous. He holds tight to the photo.

PART SIX

Los Angeles, 2000

65

The crime scene lies off the 210 Freeway in scrub-covered hills north of the Valley. A night wind hisses through gullies and ravines. The city below is an ocean of small lights. Vincent Hanna swings around a curve on the crumbling back road. Ahead, LAPD black-and-whites and the van from the Field Investigation Unit are lined up on the shoulder.

The wind sends Hanna's suit jacket sailing behind him as he walks across the uneven ground. It's a familiar tableau. Strobing lights, red and blue. A uniform guarding access to the site. A police photographer's camera flashing. Los Angeles plays the hits.

Drucker is inside the tape, backlit by portable spotlights. Gloves on, talking to a uniform. Beyond him, jets on approach to the Burbank airport line the horizon like a string of blinking jewels. The smell hits Hanna when he's still fifty yards away.

Drucker excuses himself from the uniform and hikes over. "Vincent. Kid off-roading on a dirt bike found it, around sunset."

Hanna ducks under the tape and accompanies Drucker across the field. The lights, the stench, and the buzzing flies show the way.

"Rough estimate?" Hanna says.

"Animals have had at the body, so real rough—she's been dead two days, three."

Hanna dabs his forehead with a handkerchief. He feels thirsty, itchy. Drucker glances at him, those wise eyes quiet and sharp.

Hanna doesn't have to be here. Two other Robbery-Homicide detectives are on scene, Sansara and Rausch, from the Rape Special Unit. But when the call came over the radio, something pulled at him. He told Drucker to respond. Drucker isn't asking why yet.

The woman lies facedown in the eighteen-inch-deep grave. Her body is already partially skeletonized—vultures, insects, mice.

"Hundred yards from the road," Hanna says. "Concealed, but sloppy. A quick job."

Drucker gestures at paw prints in the disturbed earth. "Coyote dug her up."

The body is carelessly sprawled, as though she was dragged into the grave by one arm. She's slender and small, and her long black hair is browned with dust. Teens, twenty max. Wildlife has reduced half her face to bone. What remains shows East Asian features. She's naked except for a single red spike-heeled sandal.

Hanna crouches. There's a craterlike shotgun wound in her back.

"Point-blank." He doesn't turn her, doesn't touch her.

"Violence is off the charts." Drucker nods at the Rape Special Unit detectives. "They think she's off the Fig or Van Nuys track. What pinged your radar?"

Hanna can't tell if Drucker is saying that with concern or hope. He wishes he had a bottled water.

"All right." He rises, surveying the scene. "Her age, the abuse, she's naked, shaved, wearing a cheap stiletto like she was on the stroll? Yeah, she's trafficked. Likelier off the Van Nuys track than Figueroa," he says.

The sex crimes detectives have headed to their car, calling something in. Drucker's looking at him. Definitely concerned.

RHD is slammed. Hanna is working a dozen major cases. A Hollywood stalker slaying. A violent container hijacking out of the Port of LA. The shooting death of a Russian gangster's daughter. The look in Drucker's eyes says he should not be adding this case to his load.

"ID?"

"None," Drucker says. "Rausch and Sansara have detectives canvassing nearby gas stations, banks, convenience stores, for video in case a camera caught the killer's vehicle." He is practically thrumming with a low sense of wariness. "You want to add this to your caseload?"

"Ask me in a minute." Hanna's attention moves across the desert floor.

Two years ago, maybe even last year, Drucker wouldn't have asked that. But Hanna can't concretely explain why he's here. He can't explain why the scanner call propelled him to send Drucker out when two veteran detectives from RHD were already rolling.

He walks away from the long edge of the grave. Where the glare of the spotlights fades to shadow, he points at the ground.

"Her other shoe." He glances around. "She lost it running."

"She broke free?" Drucker says.

Hanna shakes his head. "Footprints here. Men's shoes. Men, plural. Then hers, running, unevenly. With one man following." He whistles at the photographer and crime scene unit. "They brought her out here, let her go, then chased her down. They caught her and put a shotgun barrel flush against her back and pulled the trigger. Dug the grave where she fell and dragged her in." He feels cold now.

The photographer and techs tramp this way.

Hanna points. "Get measurements and impressions."

He returns to the grave. His scalp is tight. Under the lights, the young woman's skin is green and waxy. He dabs at his upper lip. His gaze stutters from the entry wound down to her ankles.

"Ligature marks." It's crawling under his skin, a strange feeling, about the marks. "They bind her, they take her out here—this is somebody confident they could turn this hillside into a rabbit hunt, with a young woman who would never be missed."

It's not the guy, though. Or not just him. It's her. Jane Doe.

She looks simple and small. Horrific, a nightmare inflicted. He kneels beside her, searching for signs.

"And in Los Angeles, who is unlikely to be missed?" he says.

Drucker looks calm, deeply concerned, and dogged, like he senses something meaty, and dangerous, and wants to tear into it. "No tire tracks aside from the dirt bike," he says. "Just boot prints, animal tracks, her footprints."

"So, they walked her out here from the car."

"Kept the perp's vehicle clean."

"And for the fun of it," Hanna says.

"Nothing improvised." Drucker scrutinizes the scene thoughtfully, the way a mountain lion is thoughtful. Homing in. "Quick, efficient. Carried out by a guy who has a routine. And partners. And having a routine and partners means he's sure as shit done it before and ready to do it again."

Hanna trusts Drucker's experience and instincts. He circles the body, checks the dark ground around it.

The RHD detectives return. Sansara has a keen and leery look in his eye.

"Captain." Respectful, if perfunctory.

"I'm taking this," Hanna says.

Sansara's shoulders lower. "We're already up and running."

"Yes, you are. Nevertheless."

Rausch, no-nonsense, a weightlifter, steps up beside her partner. "Sir. This goes beyond murder. Rape Special has the contacts—I have the contacts—on the Fig track, Alameda, the Van Nuys track, to investigate whether a pimp or a john did this."

"Great." Hanna turns from their affronted faces. "Those contacts? Start working them. Rausch, you're with me and Drucker." He heads for his car.

66

Downtown at Parker Center, Hanna sweeps into RHD. The fluorescent lights give off a magnetic hum. The concrete-and-glass offices of the Major Crimes Unit spread across the floor, open plan, industrial minimalism. Clean lines of sight for an elite unit within an elite division. Maps on whiteboards. Assignments, open cases. Men and women are on the phone, on the computer, their faces sharply lit under desk lamps. They glance up as he slides past. A few nod to him. The graveyard shift isn't his assigned watch, but he rolls through at all times of the day and night.

The stack of files on his desk is two feet high. Half of it is bullshit administrative crap. The glass on the door says CAPT. VINCENT HANNA, COMMANDER, MCU.

He has one minute, he knows, before Rausch storms in, then Sansara, to bitch about him getting yanked from the case. Hanna stands behind his desk, adrift but feeling a rip current cutting across his horizon, pulling. He wants to swim toward it.

Drucker appears, filling the doorway. "ME's at the scene."

"You saw how torn up the sole of her foot was?" Hanna says.

"She kept running after she lost the shoe."

"Sliced to shit, but she endured it, for a chance to get away."

"That why you're taking this?" Drucker raises his hands. "I mean, I'm down. Hundred percent, Vincent."

"I expect you to be, because we are full-bore from here on."

"Of course."

Hanna's gaze falls on his desk. The 150 reports from subordinates he needs to review and approve. Staffing requests. Interagency memos. Purchase orders for tactical supplies and equipment.

"Uniforms and detectives are looking for video up and down the 210," Drucker says. "Autopsy will give us more."

Hanna drums his knuckles on the desk. After a second, he nods.

Drucker turns to leave. He turns back, then glances over his shoulder at the office floor outside. He lowers his voice. "Got a call from the DA's office."

Hanna drops heavily into his office chair, biting his thumbnail. "Oh, yeah . . . What do they say? Or I don't wanna know?"

"The evidence in the port hijacking case, the recording of the interview with the CI?"

Hanna stares at Drucker's chest.

Drucker leans on the desk. "Vince, the prosecutor doesn't have it. Says you never submitted it. She needs it for trial."

The recording. *Shit.* "What did you tell her?"

"I told her I've been reviewing it, I didn't know she needed it for trial prep already. My mistake, so sorry, our wires got crossed. I told her the recording will be on her desk at eight a.m. tomorrow with an affidavit and a chain-of-custody log."

"Good."

Drucker looms in front of the desk.

"Right," Hanna says. "I'll make sure everything gets to her."

Slowly, Drucker nods. Hanna feels a coiling tightness in his chest. Drucker's nod says, *How long am I covering for you?*

"Anything else?" Hanna says.

"You tell me."

Hanna says nothing. Drucker turns and leaves.

The route from downtown to Los Feliz is busy, the night a glimmering grid. Hanna's wired now, but exhaustion is still dragging at him, humming through his veins. This slaying. Why was the young woman killed? Kidnapping, rape, trafficking, drugs? He rolls down the car window. The Santa Anas seem to rasp over his skin at a molecular level. Drucker's gaze lingers on the backs of his retinas. He doesn't want to think that Drucker is right.

But Drucker usually is. That's why he's in MCU. He's insightful, tough, honest, and canny. They all are, on his team. Drucker, Casals, and the detective he has co-opted into this new case, Kath Rausch.

He rolls past dark corners and brightly lit homes and swings up to his place. The recording that the assistant DA needs has been sitting there for weeks. He forgot about it. Forgot that he should have returned it to Evidence.

His condo is a refurbished loft with polished concrete floors and halogen track lighting. It smells of cigarette butts, Armani cologne, and the sour laundry that the Armani cologne is meant to cover. The recording is under a pile of newspapers on the dining room table.

He should never have brought it home, never have removed it from the sealed evidence bag. But concentrating—getting any real work done—when he's in his report-fucked office is impossible. He slips the recording back into the evidence bag. He presses the heels of his palms against his eyes.

In the kitchen, he pops the lid off a prescription bottle of Adderall. The scrip is real, if not his. One twenty-milligram pill once a day. He downs three dry. Waits for the hit, the energy, the focus. Wanting to feel on top of it, confident of everything and aware. That euphoria evoked when he's on the scent of something big.

He'll get a racing heartbeat and agitation, knows all this shit. But he's gotta tie up the hijacking case with a bow. He grabs the evidence bag and hurries out the door.

Back in the car, rolling down Sunset, he thinks about the Jane Doe. Barely out of puberty, chased down, shot, and dragged into a hole in the dirt off a droning freeway. Destroying hope had gratified her killers. He sees her hair fanned out under the camera flash. Feels a dank chill.

He gets his cell phone and hits speed dial.

The phone rattles as it's picked up. "Vincent, hey."

"Hi, sweetie."

"You're in a cruiser," Lauren says.

"Crown Victoria, the queen of prowl cars."

"You're not coming by, are you?"

An ache, a premonition, settles into him. "Can't, cruiser's like a shark, it has to keep moving. Just checking in."

The city swells up around him, the billboards, the lights, the buzz. The downtown skyline gleams with a Vaseline shine.

"Everything's status quo," Lauren says. Her voice is still breathy, almost rushed, like she's running behind, or after something just out of reach. But it's genuinely bright now. Strong.

"You ready for the exhibition?" he says.

"Just about." Plates and silverware clatter. "Redoing the frame on the watercolor. It needs black, something glossy."

High school art exhibition. New school. Small, all girls, room to breathe, room to thrive. Lauren has been there eight months. It seems to be sticking. That lets the fist around Vincent's heart ease up a millimeter or two.

"Nervous?" he says.

"Yes."

He rolls around a bend, pulse high. "Lean into that. It means you'll be excited, fully open to it. It means your art is vital. Alive."

"I'll try." She exhales. "Promise."

"You're going to stun them," he says. "Love you."

She pauses and seems to turn a corner into a quiet room. "You, too."

It's a natural place to end the conversation, but he doesn't hang up. The pause stretches.

He wants to hear another voice. One that's slow, and smoky, and mellow. He can picture her, dancer's legs crossed on the sofa, head cocked, cigarette lifted to her lips.

Lauren's voice quiets. "She won't talk to you."

Justine. Married six years, divorced four. The heat had drained, and the anger, and for a while, it seemed that a softer connection was being sustained.

He squeezes the steering wheel. His skin feels electric. He wishes the jolt was from the Adderall, not from the emotional slap, but he's still waiting for the amphetamine bang. He thinks, *Hurry up.*

Lauren's off this stuff now—that's one of the last things Justine told him.

The very last thing she told him was: *Speed won't give you the power to track your prey in the dark. That glow you feel? It isn't x-ray vision. It's self-incineration. Understand?* And the door shut in his face.

He holds the phone. The night prickles by.

He lives alone. Sleeps on his own. Anybody new he hooks up with, it's physical. Touch and go. Justine and Lauren have been the two women in his life, removed, kept at a distance. Held by a thin tether, fraying.

He doesn't want to put Lauren under any strain. "Later, kiddo."

He heads back to work.

67

Drucker stands in a corner of the autopsy suite. Detective Kath Rausch stands beside him, arms determinedly crossed. The medical examiner and autopsy technician approach the stainless steel table. The black body bag lies atop it, zipper shining under the hanging surgical light.

Hanna paces in the background.

It's been three days since the victim was found. Still no ID, but

Rausch has turned up surveillance tape from a gas station up I-210 from the burial site.

At 1:42 a.m., headlights cruise past, heading into the hills. An American sedan, older, heavy flanks, big engine. At 3:03 a.m., the car returns and pulls into the gas station. The driver stays at the wheel. White man. Two men get out, one white, one Black. The pump islands partially conceal them. One man squeegees the windshield. The other takes a plastic garbage bag around the side of the station to a dumpster and comes back without it. They drive away.

That was it. Hanna had said, *Play it again. Slow motion.*

Rausch rewound and replayed. When the men exited the car, Hanna said, *Stop.*

The image was blurred, patches of light and dark. The men's features were too indistinct for identification. They seemed ghostly, smeared.

Can you zoom?

Rausch shook her head. *The techs can. And maybe can improve the gain and contrast.*

Three men. Organized, Drucker said.

What it tells us—the body dump was done by the blur people. Hanna set his hands on his hips. *Rausch, check that dumpster. If we're lucky, it hasn't been emptied.*

Already did, she said curtly. *Got the bag. Going through it.*

Now, the ME snaps on latex gloves and reaches for the overhead mic. "Beginning exterior examination." He unzips the body bag.

With her body faceup, the shotgun exit wound in the victim's upper chest is horrific. Drucker and Rausch stand silently. Hanna continues to pace.

The ME speaks into the mic. "The face is partially skeletonized. There's evidence of predation. Birds and larger mammals as well as insects."

He gently turns the victim's head. "The left eye is missing. The orbital socket is scoured clean." He tilts the surgical light to shine directly into the empty socket. "There are . . . marks on the medial orbital wall."

Hanna continues pacing heavily in the shadows.

"Scorch marks," the ME says.

Drucker feels a sharp prickle up his spine. Hanna stops.

"Burn mark, circular, roughly eight millimeters in diameter." The ME straightens. "Somebody put out a cigarette in her eye."

Hanna hears the ME's words, hears the click of the assistant's camera, peripherally sees Drucker straighten, feels electricity pour off Rausch.

"Premortem?" she says. "Post?"

Drucker's intake of breath is audible. "Man, this is some dark shit."

Hanna seems to freeze-frame. He looks hard at the ME. "Burned with a cigarette."

The pathologist is carefully examining the rest of the woman's skull. "Earlobe, nose, and, yes, the eye."

Hanna's chest all at once feels hollow. "The marks on her ankles."

The ME frowns. "I'll get to them."

"Now," Hanna says. "Let's go."

Grudgingly, the pathologist moves down the table. He adjusts his glasses. "Yellowish-brown furrow in the tissue, hard to the touch, parchment-like from the drying of abraded skin. Ligature." He turns her foot. "The angle . . . this—the inverted V where the knot of the ligature pressed into her ankle—it's consistent with gravitational suspension."

"She was hung by her feet?" Hanna says.

The ME nods. "And there's a detectable pattern on her skin. The ligature material must have been hard." He scrutinizes the marks. "It's indistinct, but these impressions resemble the links of a chain."

Hanna feels a few seconds from a dark implosion. "Otis Lloyd Wardell."

Drucker turns. "Who?"

Hanna walks on autopilot to the autopsy table. "Otis Wardell is in Los Angeles."

"You know the killer's name?" Drucker says.

Hanna closes his eyes and dips his head as though an anvil has been hung around his neck. "It's him. He is alive. Twelve years and he is alive and on repeat."

Standing as still as a totem, he gives Drucker and Rausch a summary. The Chicago home invasions. Rapes, bludgeoning deaths. The auto repair shop torture killing. Wardell's disappearance.

Then he shakes his head, clearing it. "This is a new MO for him, the shallow grave."

He takes out his phone and punches a number.

Casals picks up. "Robbery-Homicide."

"Guess what? We have a ghost," Hanna says.

Validation. The edges of his intuition sharpening into view. *Trust yourself,* he thinks. He feels like he's peering over the edge of a crevasse. The long-suppressed hunger rises. That excoriating case. The hunger to hunt down a man who destroyed lives recklessly and ravenously.

Otis Lloyd Wardell. Hanna's blood rushes. *You motherfucker. You're in my city. And you don't know that I know you're here.*

68

Thursday night, 11:30, the street is busy. South Figueroa, four lanes, below the Coliseum, the used-car lots closed, the churches quiet. Gas stations wildly bright, active. And strip malls, convenience stores, the massage parlors with the neon-pink signs. The motels. The motels. The women on the corners, strutting. The cars lining up for them, men shadowed inside, rolling their windows down, saying, *Come here, girl.*

He cruises. He's making his rounds.

The locals, the neighborhood residents, they drive down this boulevard, they lock their doors and pull down the shades. People passing through, off the 110, driving to USC up the way, they keep their hands at two and ten on the wheel, and they see only the traffic lights and fast-food joints. They see nothing else.

But when you have eyes, it's all you see. And he has eyes. Because these are his motels, his massage parlors. The girls on the corners grind in his rooms. Those rooms rent at fifty dollars for fifteen minutes, which is all the time they need for motel dates. He takes a cut of the cash they get from every trick. Their pimps pay him a tax: twenty dollars for every hundred.

Five motels, two massage parlors. He makes the rounds every night, checking his payout, how many girls are in; making sure everyone's kicking back.

He pulls into the Outskirts Motel. COLOR TVS. NO PETS. All rooms face a central courtyard, one way in, one way out. The desk clerk sits in a cubicle behind scratched ballistic glass with an amplified speak-thru and slide-across cash tray, like a movie theater ticket booth.

He parks and is buzzed through a side door. "Whatcha got?"

The clerk, Kultar, is listening to a transistor radio. His clothes are clean but faded. "Smooth rotation. No problems."

He opens the cash drawer. He scans the motor court and the rooms, dingy curtains drawn, busy, *ka-ching*.

"Better be no fuckin' problems," he says.

"No, boss. Everybody is acting like gentlemens."

He grunts. The Outskirts is what hood denizens call "busted." A pimpin', hoein', dope-buyin', dope-slangin' paradise. A body ain't stepping up in here unless they're about some dirt. And that is *exactly* how he likes to keep the place.

He loves owning motels. They're his kingdom. He can shoot through, collect the night's money, maybe smash a girl if the mood strikes. They're all available to him. The pimps all send girls at the same time. Nobody causes strife, either. He allows no gangster crap, no pimp beefs, no ruckus at his motels. And under no circumstance does anyone bleed or die on the property. If it's an overdose, carry 'em out. Let 'em die in an alley. And this motel is so far south, right down on the city limits, that the LAPD don't bother hitting it. They don't even realize it's in LA.

Kultar has the balance sheet. He scans it. The Outskirts is a turn 'n' burn joint. He's got five pimps coming in, each with four to five girls. That's reliably twenty girls grinding simultaneously.

He goes by Smoky. John Francis Smolenski. It's on his driver's license. Nobody here calls him Otis. His crew wouldn't dare say the name Wardell. He has gained a few pounds—muscle, yeah—and wears his hair moussed tall. The scar through his eyebrow isn't distinctive to anybody except women he meets in bars, who think it makes him tough but vulnerable, a hot lay who needs mothering. Back in Chicago it's listed as a distinguishing mark on his criminal jacket. Here, nobody cares.

"The cleaner been in?" he says.

"Yesterday, like you asked."

Girls who are fresh off the boat usually clean the place before getting turned out, sent to the real job that's been lined up for them in massage parlors or on the corners. But this week he paid a homeless woman to wipe down the rooms. Let her watch color TV while she ran a rag around bathroom sinks. Catch some Jerry Springer. This week, he sprang for bleach.

All because of the bitch. The Asian girl was supposed to get on her knees between his legs. But she gagged at the sight of his cock. Rage pulses behind his eyes.

First, she shrank from him into the corner of the room. Started *crying,* loud, the TV didn't cover it. Then a music video came on. Tupac Shakur rapping "Dear Mama" over the Spinners' classic "Sadie."

What the fuck? he muttered. *Stop crying.*

Tupac, big doe eyes, moaning over his mom. The girl cringed back against the wall.

He sing about his mama. I sorry. Song mean much for me. I love my mother, too.

Fuck Tupac. His mother was a crackhead. Wasn't even a real Black Panther. She wasn't shit! She was a no-good whore. Stop crying and come here.

That's when he unzipped his jeans and grabbed her head, and she gagged. Then she bolted for the door, and he pulled the claw hammer from under the newspapers on the nightstand and hit her in the back of the head. After that, almost to the end, she was semiconscious. She only fully woke up when he pushed her into the scrub and whispered, *Run.*

Fuck her.

He tells Kultar, "The cleaner never comes back. See her 'round here, run her off."

He checks the condom supply. Each girl gets one per customer. Not that he gives a damn about the spread of disease, but so that he knows the churn. Count the condoms and he knows how much each girl owes.

The desk clerk turns. "One thing, boss."

He cools. "One thing you shoulda told me when I came in."

"I am trying to be organized. I apologize."

"What one fucking thing?"

"Eazy-D."

Outside, a white Honda with chrome rims skids to a stop on the street, music pounding. A spidery man in sagging jeans and a tank top jumps out. A girl is walking toward the corner. The pimp runs up, grabs her by the hair, and punches her in the stomach.

Wardell turns away. Not his business. "What about Eazy-D?"

"His balance sheet. It don't add up," Kultar says.

His chest heats. "That so?"

Outside, the pimp reaches into the girl's panties and pulls out cash she has stashed there. He shoves her toward his car.

"He is shorting you on the motel's cut," Kultar says.

"When's the last time you saw him? He come around when, six a.m. or so?"

"It has been several days."

Shorting him on his cut? Ain't happening. Wardell heads out. Eazy-D needs finding.

69

Chris strides toward the Santa Anita Club House, looking fresh in a cobalt suit and silver tie. Hair razor cut, shorter than he ever wore it here. Horn-rimmed glasses with clear lenses. Dark scruff. A toned frame—still rangy, but leaner, more angular. Smooth.

Walking straight across ground where he's still a wanted man. For the un-homecoming.

Ana forges ahead with an eager lope, boldly unrefined. Eyes front, taking in everything and everybody. Her brown leather duster sweeps behind her. She's dressed up, for her. Taupe sweater, black jeans over Dr. Martens. Her hair is pulled into a high bun and secured with a butterfly clip. Sunglasses propped on top of her head.

"You're supposed to wear those on your face," Chris says.

"It's LA. It's fashion." She says it with her usual dry self-confidence. She has never been to California.

Ana has lived in London and knows the scrappy, crazy streets of Ciudad del Este, but the hustle and flash of Los Angeles are fresh to her. Alluring. Filled with white teeth and false smiles. Dreams, the cynicism that feeds on dreams. American attitudes seem foreign and strange. Chris is her cultural translator, her anthropologist.

It's been four and a half years since he left. He hopes he's ready.

Much has changed—and nothing. Ana's been working full-time for the family business since she earned her MBA from the London School of Economics. She's still battling her father's dismissive attitude toward her. David Liu is grooming her brother to take over. Felix still mixes partying with business. He has a baby now, with Reynalda Chen, Claudio Chen's sister. With the baby they generate a Chinese greeting card image of a nuclear family. It both sidelines Ana even more and papers over the enmity between the families. Babies soften bitterness, and Felix and Reynalda's relationship, while capricious, promises the hoped-for merger. In that light, Felix has begun proposing joint ventures with the Chens.

That galls Ana. Her relationship with Felix is wary and resentful. They circle each other like a cobra and a mongoose. Chris isn't sure sometimes which is which.

And Chris is working with Ana's semiautonomous business unit, Mercury Partners International. The Lab, he calls it, where tech projects get cooked up. Blue sky or quick and dirty—they brew it all.

The morning sunshine seems to bleach away shadows. He's rolling the dice. They have tickets to Singapore in ninety-six hours. From there they'll hop by ferry to Batam, Indonesia, forty minutes away.

Chris Bergman is traveling with bulletproof ID: a Canadian passport obtained via Paraguayan sources in the Canadian embassy in

Asunción. Ana travels on her legit Paraguayan passport—she doesn't need a cover ID.

Chris has warned her that there's a fugitive warrant outstanding for Chris Shiherlis—he's a wanted felon and potentially still on the LAPD's radar—but has omitted details. They'll be careful. They're always careful; their relationship is hidden from the family.

It's risky. But Ana said, *Come with me,* so he did. That's how it works.

In and out. All business. *Big* business. They're in Southern California pursuing avionics systems for the Lius' clients.

Through Walter Huang, Ana's uncle in Alhambra, they're meeting with engineers who work in aerospace. The Liu organization already has systems for anti-jam GPS and full global access via satellite-based command and control, with intelligence, surveillance, and reconnaissance capabilities. Systems that can outwit the DEA, Coast Guard, and FBI, or, for kleptocracies, insurgencies, or client states, that can outlast whomever their enemies are. The Lius' biggest customers are obtaining airframes—drones to surveil disputed borderlands and trafficking routes. Now they want missiles to take down their opposition. Weaponry that will repel surveillance aircraft and airborne attacks by rivals. If Ana can sell those clients missile guidance packages with cutting-edge IP, they'll drool.

He's here. He hopes it's not a fatal error.

The racetrack feels both familiar and alien. An earlier version of him would have felt an itch, a yen, to lay down money on the Daily Double; would have gotten here for breakfast at six a.m., chatted up the trainers and wannabe jockeys exercising the Thoroughbreds, and bet the month's rent on a long shot, then stood at the rail while the horses thundered by.

Today, he sweeps into a VIP elevator, up to a private suite above the finish line. It's laid out with hors d'oeuvres like this is a state dinner, though Chris knows this is meant as an out-of-the way mission to impress. Waiters bring in pitchers of ice water and trays of dim sum. A wide-screen TV fills one wall, playing a travel show on low, scenes of leis and surf.

Ana greets a young man in his thirties, a cousin from Alhambra.

He has a solid SoCal accent, looks casual in his Hugo Boss suit with no tie, hair slicked back. He's familiar with her but deferential. Ana's not tall, wears no jewelry and only a Timex on her wrist. And she dominates the whole fucking room. Chris loves it.

The cousin shakes his hand. "Darrin Huang."

Oldest son, Chris knows, of the man who set up the LA portion of the trip.

"Chris Bergman."

Their first guest soon arrives. Raymond Zhang is a Southern Cal native, an engineer who works for an aerospace defense contractor. He's here to be . . .

Bought.

It's considered commerce in Ciudad del Este, Hong Kong, Nairobi, Shanghai. In Ana's view, this deal isn't transgressive. It's business liberated from artificial regulatory constraints imposed by state legal systems. She has an incentive program for this man to provide valuable IP to the Lius, to Mercury, her Skunk Works.

This is the USA. Here, they like judgmental labels, like "bribery."

The next guests soon appear. The American Chinese guest is tall and athletic. The two mainland Chinese guests are quiet and stiff, even though they're safely beyond their own borders. And Chris knows they have not been followed by anyone from the Chinese consulate. They have come into the country on tourist visas, separately, to visit grannies and uncles and to go to Disneyland with their little American nieces and nephews. And to have a day out at the races, a good Chinese tradition.

Ana welcomes them and lets them admire the fabulous view of the track and the mountains. She discusses the handover of Hong Kong sovereignty to China. She encourages them to enjoy the food. Chris is adept with chopsticks now. He watches the men, noting how they behave, how nervous they are, whether they're eager or slippery.

The television switches from the travel show to local news. It's a weird flashback, seeing anchors he hasn't thought about in almost five years but recognizes immediately. Their handsome faces, their mannerisms, their fame-whore gaze at the camera. Their voices, the ones that talked about his bank score turning downtown into Beirut back in '95.

Ana knows some of his past. He has been open that he's come up a rough road, that what he did in the USA was heavy duty. Not even forgivable in Ciudad del Este. He will be careful here. This under-the-radar visit will be pure business, a glide through an itinerary before they fly to Asia. She trusts that.

The rest she doesn't need to know.

She is confident that he is 100 percent aligned and dedicated to her ambitions. *Their* ambitions.

Darrin Huang takes the athletic Chinese American and the stiff Chinese men onto the balcony. The local news runs through familiar tropes. A movie-star divorce. A car chase on the 91 Freeway. A reporter on a rugged hillside along the 210 talking about a murder. Sources in the medical examiner's office say the girl was the victim of a particularly brutal shotgun slaying and previously had been tortured. The LAPD's Robbery-Homicide Division is leading the investigation. That one arrests Chris's attention. To him, the room goes quiet.

Ana is staring at him.

Zhang, the garrulous engineer, leans over a heaped plate of food. He's eating ravenously. Ana's stare gets through to Chris.

Chris returns a look that most people, he has learned, read as opaque. Ana will correctly read it as mirroring her opinion. The engineer is hungry, needy, full of want. Eager to grab everything they will offer him.

Let him eat. Then they'll tell him what he needs to do if they are to fill his bank account.

Ana turns back to the man. "You understand, the purchase of the guidance packages is only one element of our arrangement."

"And you have that locked in, right? No way this is going to come back to bite me?"

"None at all."

She has tied up the transaction with a bow. End-user certificates have been purchased that show the guidance packages going to Ethiopia. They're fake. After hopscotching the globe, the systems will end up with the Lius' buyers, coca growers in Bolivia and Colombia.

She leans in. "You will also provide the software. The source code."

That way, Ana will be able to build more systems of her own.

"Yes, yes." Zhang is near to sweating. "Nobody will know."

"How will you assure that?"

"I head the systems engineering division. Nobody checks my work. Anything anybody would find, I tell them it's a bug, I'll get right on it." He looks up. "I'm good. That's how."

Chris speaks casually. "We want to see your manufacturing facility. The assembled guidance systems."

Ana slides Chris a new look, understanding that he wants to assess quality control, the reliability of the deal and of this guy.

Zhang pauses, then nods. "Off-hours. I'll have to finesse it so there's no record of you coming on-site."

"Excellent," Ana says. "Let's discuss the source code delivery. How many files? How big?"

He reaches for another helping. "Big," he tells her. "Terabytes. I can post them to a dark server. Limited life span. Give you the key, you grab them, then they disappear."

She shakes her head. "I'll provide you with external hard drives. That way there's no footprint."

Chris leans back. They are scoring like champs. So how come he feels like he's on a knife's edge and could fall either way?

70

Stepping out of the elevator on the fifty-third floor of the Library Tower an hour later, stoked from the Santa Anita meeting, Ana admires the skyscraper. "A statement building. Mega. And seismically secure."

"It blew up like a winner in *Independence Day*," Chris says.

She eyes him questioningly. "That, too."

An overstuffed attorney leads them to a conference room where two older Chinese men in suits wait to meet them. Ana greets them with proper deference in Mandarin, then switches to English.

Chris sits beside her at a gleaming conference table while the lawyer's PA brings coffee on a silver tray. Now he feels strangely ill at ease, like the building is swaying, though there's no earthquake. He's here as Jeffrey Christian Bergman, director of operations for Mercury Partners International—a shell surrounded by half a dozen other shell corporations owned by the Lius. But he's suspicious, contentious—what is he feeling? Fuck it. This meeting is about financing the guidance system deal by running money through Southern California real estate.

Ana has negotiated the purchase of small strip malls in LA satellite cities like Monterey Park. Places with a strong Chinese American population, where her family has connections. Those properties will be a funnel for washing funds. Funds that will buy them the hardware, software, and engineers they're after.

The suits across the table acknowledge him politely. Who do they think he is? Somebody from the hard side of international military-adjacent commerce, who knows his way around hard men and hard places? Probably.

A paralegal has just brought in multiple sets of documents when another man arrives. Ana stands. Again, in Mandarin, she speaks deferentially. Bows. Chris gets some of it.

Uncle Walter.

It's her cousin Darrin's father. Sixties, blousy suit, hatchet face. He's the surety, the guarantor for the financial side of the transaction. Local. Family. Organization man. Using Walter Huang means Ana's Skunk Works is firmly anchored to the family business.

Walter nods perfunctorily at him. Chris returns it. "Sir." It chafes.

Two men follow Walter into the room. One is white and in his thirties. European. He nods brusquely. "Jakob Gögel."

He's here on behalf of Felix.

That chafes. Felix wants some clown to babysit Ana's deal? The guy's German. Curt. Juiced, with a thick neck and tattoos leaking out below his starched cuffs. Remote eyes. Ex-military, Chris thinks.

The second man wears a Brooks Brothers suit without a tie. Horn-rims. Ethnic Chinese. Chris has seen him before. He has the solemn stolidity of an accountant. He takes a seat without introducing himself. He was standing beside an SUV with Claudio at the Itaipu Dam. What the hell's he doing here?

Walter signs documents and then pushes them to Yuan, the new man. He signs on behalf of the ostensible financiers—another shell corporation fronting for the Liu organization. They finish in ten minutes. The lawyers push their chairs back.

Gögel sets new documents on the table. "We are not finished."

Walter slides the papers toward Ana. "An addendum."

Abruptly wary, she reads and freezes. "'Right to examine bank accounts and audit financial records at any time'? No."

The third man, the accountant, speaks emotionlessly. "Yes. I'm afraid the answer has to be yes."

"'Spyder Ventures LLC shall have full access and, if deemed necessary, implement supervision . . .' What is Spyder? What is this? I don't . . ." She trails off. Understanding dawns in her eyes. Spyder is a joint venture.

Chris's pulse begins to thud. Ana presses her hands into the table.

Walter looks at her. "Before the money transfers, I, Mr. Gögel, and Mr. Yuan are to see all of Mercury's records, with a forty-eight-hour right to cancel the deal."

Chris is staring at Mr. Yuan.

Ana rises. "This is not our agreement. I must speak to my father."

"I have already spoken to him, niece," Walter says.

Her cheeks flush. She can't hide it. She looks like she's been slapped across the face.

Gögel sits like a hunk of wood. "Felix has reservations. We are here on his behalf."

Chris looks at Mr. Yuan. "And whose behalf is he here on?"

"Claudio Chen," Mr. Yuan responds. "Felix's partners have reservations, too."

Partners, Chris thinks. *Since when?* Ana, covering the raw anger and outrage, is boiling inside her head.

"Your new deals here are too independent," Walter says. "Your father has let you have a length of rope to form this business unit. I think he's indulged you. But on this really big deal . . . ?" He eyes her. "You are swimming in water too deep."

Looking stung, she presses her lips tight, formulating a reply.

Chris eyes the men. "Who's making bank here?"

Yuan gives him a dismissive glance and turns to Ana. "The Spyder partners think this should be vetted and managed more thoroughly."

"Really? How about we hire McKinsey or Arthur Andersen?"

Ana shoots Chris a look. He reins it in.

"Apologies," Chris responds.

Walter Huang has not taken his cold stare from Ana. "We will audit, and if supervision is required, Spyder will appoint a managing director."

She looks right through him, her face expressionless. A look Chris reads as: *If you think I'm doing that, you're insane.* These men want Ana to give Felix unlimited access to her work, as if they're entitled automatically to strip her of it.

Chris eyes Gögel. *And who the fuck are you working for?*

Ana's look sweeps across all the men and lands on Walter.

"Thank you, Uncle," she says, and grabs the pen, scrawls her signature, and walks out.

Chris can't believe it.

He catches up with her outside in the breezy afternoon. He pulls her aside. "What the fuck was that?"

She looks down at his hand gripping her arm. "Not here," she hisses, and starts for their car.

Chris catches Ana again and they step sideways, out of sight, while Walter, Yuan, and Gögel get in a silver Mercedes. He wants to see who's riding with whom. An acid taste rides the back of his throat.

"Who the hell is Yuan?" Ana says.

"They're trying to kneecap you. Yuan works for the Chens. An accountant. What did you sign that for?"

She inhales, turns away.

"Hey, you're tough, a genius innovator," he says. "Don't let them—"

"Uncle Huang is my elder. That's what's expected. Felix is . . . a pig." Her eyes flare. "Spyder. Joint venture. I know that means Claudio is trying to steal this deal. What I signed buys time. I don't give a shit what I signed. We have more work to do."

She heads for their car.

And the irony, Chris knows, is that David Liu will mistakenly respect Felix for showing initiative at last. Chris stands in the plaza. A buzz seems to vibrate in the air, static electricity humming around him. The street, downtown. Slipstream, time loop. He can't shake it. And he's fed up watching Ana be dismissed.

71

At the Beverly Hilton, everything gleams. The white facade. The Lamborghini and the Bugatti parked outside the entrance, placed like ornaments. The pool, electric turquoise. Ana strides across the sun-drenched marble lobby, wanting to get up to their suite, log on, contact her father.

Chris stops. "I'll catch up with you."

She pauses, holding the elevator door, and raises an eyebrow.

"I need to work through this," he says.

"So?" And she gestures toward the lobby, as in *What's wrong with upstairs?*

"I want air and sunlight."

"And nostalgia?"

Her tone is pointed. She's like a goddamned electron microscope, reading him.

"I'll be back."

She punches the elevator door button, lips pursed.

At the concierge desk, he says, "I need a car."

Fifteen minutes later, he's in a black Alfa Romeo, slipping through traffic on Wilshire beneath towering palm trees. He fires up a virgin cell phone and calls Paolo.

"*Oi. Como vai?*" Paolo says.

"*Tudo jóia.*" It's all cool. Portuguese—it's manageable these days, and so is his relationship with Paolo. "Sunny and clear. One cloud, maybe two."

"Yeah?"

"This guy Felix sent. Gögel. Who is Gögel?"

"Ex-military, NATO spec ops, team leader. Now a business consultant. Geographic focus on the Americas. Big into anabolic steroids. What you need to know?"

"Is he Felix's asshole, or does he have other loyalties? He's traveling with Yuan, the accountant who works with Claudio Chen."

"Did Gögel insult Ana?" Paolo says.

"Dude isn't subtle." Chris shifts gears. "And two and two is two and two. Are they both fronting for Claudio?"

Paolo mutters a curse. "I find out."

Chris thinks: Muscle, a hard case, dark background . . . Why does Felix want him here? Why would Claudio want him here?

"*'Brigado, irmão. Tchau.*" He ends the call.

He is not going to let anyone cut into Mercury's deals. Her deals. Maybe somewhat *their* deals. *They will not get in our way.* He drops down a gear and aims downtown.

He never expected to come back like this. He never expected to become Ana Liu's minor business partner or imagined that they might steal game-changing technology. Tech that can be used the way a buyer wants to use it. Gear even the DEA doesn't have the budget for.

He didn't want to return to the United States, and especially not to California. He's a much smarter pro than when he left and a hell of a lot more cautious. But Ana wants him along on this deal. So does her father. And Paolo. They want an American sentinel on the ground with her. And a man. A smart and lethal man.

Meanwhile he can't contact anyone. He feels the impulse. He has to remind himself there's too much risk. They may still have an eye on Charlene. LAPD has to still be on the lookout. It's too dangerous.

Business. Get in, get out. Everything else waits.

But Felix and these two clowns are throwing up roadblocks, trying to piggyback onto and take over what was supposed to be her deal. And his deal. No fuckin' way. Not now.

He accelerates. Years in Paraguay. Earning. For himself and for them.

Now he's in a place to get his family out.

He thinks of how much money he's stashed in offshore accounts in the Caymans and in shell companies with accounts at Citi and HSBC. A real estate investment trust in the Seychelles that owns part of a shopping mall in Köln. He's diversified. He learned that from Ana: hedge against catastrophe. Spread the wealth. Lose one stash, you have another cache. Backup. Security.

The money is safe. Accessible. So, what's he going to do?

He has lived a parallel life in Ciudad del Este, telling himself that Ana is completely separate from Charlene. Ana, too, has been realistic about the limited life span of their romance. And that's what it is. Way more than a hookup. More than sex. A partnership, still as intense and powerful as when they began.

Clear your head, vato. Drive. Slough off the old shit that's holding you back, so you can think your way all the way up to next.

Windows down, it hits him full force. The velvet brush of an ocean breeze in late afternoon. It's action—fractal, arterial, the feeling everything is possible. Sexy, rich, dangerous Los Angeles. He drives straight to Flower Street.

Perverse impulse.

The Far East bank is exactly as it was. But he's a different man living in a different world now.

He can see that day, feel the sun on his face. Walking out, duffel so full of cash he could *smell* it, the Lincoln right there at the curb. Floating. Scoring. Breedan at the wheel, chill in his dark gray shirt and sunglasses. Neil beside him, staring straight ahead. Michael in the back seat, grinning, pumped. Winning. Nothing but winning! Chris feels it now. His face pulls into a smile on its own. The car's right there.

Busy sidewalks. A bus lumbers by.

Two men in funereal suits across the street. Long guns. The Black

LAPD detective's shotgun swinging up. The other guy, Chicano or Native American, with an ArmaLite. In a millisecond, Chris opens up with the CAR-15. Zero hesitation. Three-shot bursts.

Fuck them.

Shooting their way out of the ambush.

Slammed.

Neil pulling him to his feet.

Get up!

A horn honks. Chris brakes for a red light. His heart is slamming against his ribs.

Come on, come on.

He turns the corner. His skin is cold. He leaves the memories and powers onto the 110 Freeway to the 10 West to PCH and Malibu, his mind slurring, the sun and the ocean glittering, the day sinking.

On PCH he does *not* roll by Neil's house. He's sure it's still there. The surf pounds beyond. The breakers roll. He swallows. Why the hell is he doing this?

Hard right onto Malibu Canyon Road. He winds through the Santa Monica Mountains and drops down into the Valley and jumps eastbound onto the 101, the Alfa smooth and powerful, a roiling well of dark energy inside him, impelling him.

And he finds himself on his old street in Sherman Oaks, doing this dangerous, thrill-a-minute dark shit that's too good to resist in a car that's not his and years later, the suburban facade too bright.

Somebody else lives there now. A woman. There is what was.

He keeps driving. Not his house. Someone else's house. Not his wife. Someone else's beautiful wife to come home to. Magazine-perfect front, where somebody else is on the rise, or maybe faking it and pretending they have it made when they don't.

Why's he doing this? Dancing with disaster. If he's recognized by a neighbor. 'Cause Ana guessed right and her eyes told him not to.

Stop it, he thinks. *I'm fucking myself up on purpose.*

He puts the pedal down.

..

The sun is dropping, the golden hour especially golden in California, and it feels retro to be standing in a phone booth. Chris smells old paper, ink, and hot metal pawed by greasy fingers. Traffic rushes past. The number rings.

"Blue Room." The voice is rough, hoarse, familiar.

"Hey, Nate," Chris says.

There's silence on the line.

"Good to hear your voice," Chris says. "Been a while."

He hears a jukebox in the background, conversation, glasses clinking.

Nate finally speaks. "Things all right there?"

"Outstanding. But I'm not there. I'm here."

Nate's voice flattens. "Here."

"Yeah. Let's meet up."

Another pause. Nate's probably running through every possibility. Bad news. Good news. Danger. The need for self-protection. Whether to trust the phones. Chris doesn't.

"What's it about?" Nate says.

"Business," Chris says. "Opportunities. Strictly a positive."

"When?"

"I'm free. Remember that restaurant in the Valley, great greasy breakfasts . . ."

"Our book club spot. Still has the early bird special, if you're close enough to hit that."

They're talking about a parking garage on Burbank Boulevard. Close enough? Chris turns. The Blue Room is across the street, its neon sign glowing. Burbank Boulevard is a quarter mile away.

"Doable."

"Enjoy. I'll catch you later." Nate ends the call.

The garage is nearly empty. Amber evening light is hitting Chris in the eyes as he leans against the hood of the Alfa when Nate rolls up in a new burgundy Cadillac deVille.

He gets out, looks around warily, and sets a cold gaze on Chris.

He's wearing a bolo tie, hammered silver, to go with the leather coat. New twinge in his stride, maybe arthritis in his knee.

Chris smiles and ambles toward him, hand out. "Good to see you."

Nate grips his hand, seeming simultaneously curious and guarded. "Wouldn't have laid odds on you being on the other end of that call, much less in LA."

"Strictly business. Then I'm gone. Man, I owe you," he says. "For getting me outta LA and hooking me up with the Liu family."

"You look like you're doing all right."

"Better than all right. I met your Liu guy today." Letting that hang there.

"No. You met Walter Huang. Marvin Huang, that guy was okay. He was in McNeil for tax fraud. Died last year, and now his asshole brother runs it."

"How'd the rest work out?" Chris asks.

"Everybody got paid. Breedan's widow, Cerrito's family, and Kelso got his end."

"What about that girl Neil had?"

Nate shakes his head. "Civilian. World of trouble. I wouldn't go near her. She was in his car on his way to LAX. That led RHD and that cop, Hanna, to my doorstep."

"They lay a glove on you?"

"No. They were all up inside my stuff like colonoscopy police. I doubled up on secure comms. Still do."

"I never met her. He never talked about her. The only woman he hooked up with like that, that I knew, was Elisa."

"I remember," Nate says.

"When we got there, Neil had taken out four of them. Didn't bother burying the bodies, and the fifth got away."

Chris pictures a night in El Centro a million lifetimes ago: Elisa braiding her daughter's hair while making some smart-ass remark to Neil with a smile, and something smelling like roast pork and garlic simmering in the oven, and Neil laughing. Neil never laughed.

The other image in his memory is of her dead on that road along the Mexican border, wounded like that to pin Neil down, trying to stop the bleeding, while the fifth asshole fled. He thought Neil was hit, but it was Elisa's blood he was drenched with, holding her to his chest.

She must have put herself on the spot, Neil figured later and told Chris. Walked into it. To save her kid? Alert them? He didn't know. After that Neil was never the same. Then he cut himself off from the little girl, fearing that contact with him put her at risk. Like if someone wanted to get him, they would go for her. He was toxic. Attachments to him got you killed. Look what he brought down on the kid's mother.

Neil hunted for the fifth man for a time. All that came back were pieces about a home invasion crew in Chicago. Aaron Grimes had been tortured. That's probably how he tripped to the Mexicali score.

Chris looks at Nate, shifts. "I want a meetup with Kelso."

"Tell me about you," Nate asks.

Nate is like a coyote, quick and careful, adept at sliding into spaces, making things happen, then getting out. Separate, never part of a pack, free. Chris knows he got his bachelor's in finance while in Folsom, knows he's smart and stays up to date.

Chris runs him through life in the tri-border free-trade zone in Paraguay. His work for the Liu organization. His migration from working security to transnational business dealings.

"Kelso. Is that doable?" he asks.

Nate's already narrow eyes narrow another millimeter. "It's doable."

Chris nods. Neil was the one who met with Kelso. Chris merely followed the game plan.

Nate eyes him uncertainly. "He don't sell scores no more."

"I don't buy scores no more. He still out there, grabbing data bouncing around off the ionosphere?"

Nate nods. "He's still Mr. Wizard with a keyboard."

"There's a piece in it for you if anything comes of it."

"Okay."

"LAPD?"

"You're still high on their hit parade." Nate stares, his squint like x-ray vision. "You're different. You changed."

"A lot's happened," Chris says. "One day I may even mature into young adulthood. There is one exception."

"Do I wanna know what that is?"

"Probably not," Chris says. "Robbery-Homicide Division. Vincent Hanna?"

"He runs the Major Crimes Unit within RHD now. He is no one you want to go near."

Chris gazes at the orange sky.

"Thought you'd be demanding to see Charlene," Nate says.

"I may."

"Easy. She moved back to Vegas with your kid. She's in the phone book. Charlene Delano." Nate eyes him carefully. "And forget Vincent Hanna. I won't lift a finger."

"Neil was my brother from a different mother. You do for me, I do for you. From all the way back in Folsom," Chris says.

"Yeah? I could say the same. And what do you think crosses my mind when that asshole cop strolls into the Blue Room every once in a while? I wish I had that motherfucker on the yard. But I do not. And I will not go there. My loyalty is with the living." He doesn't say anything more. Then he adds, "On Kelso, gimme a day."

Chris nods, jaw tight.

He gets back in the Alfa. When he shuts the door, the plush quiet feels alienating. He drives away, gripping the gearshift.

Nate watches Chris's taillights disappear down the ramp of the parking garage. The growling engine fades, then roars away on the street.

Nate thinks Chris hasn't just stitched himself back together after his bloodstained escape from Los Angeles. And it's not only that he's operating on a different plane. It's more than that.

Asking about Hanna . . . he can understand that. Charlene . . . ? Nate was expecting a volatile demand. Insistence. This man is tightly put together now. Linear. Tuned in to a lot more than he lets on.

Nate takes out his cell and calls Kelso. "Got something. Could be interesting."

72

Eazy-D lives with his mother west of Alameda, near Thirty-Eighth Street. He's a Low Bottom Blood but bunks with Mommy, and in the morning Wardell stomps away from her tiny bungalow, frustrated. Her boy has disappeared. Ain't been home for three days.

Three days since word went out that cheating Smoky was a life-shortening error.

Eazy-D is burrowed into some rathole, missing his mama's cooking, and Wardell isn't going to wait for him to poke his skinny ass into the daylight. He knows someone else who can help locate the pimp. But she won't open the door to Wardell any more than the White House butler would. Doesn't matter. He knows a way in.

Three hours later, he's on a road lined with towering palms and emerald lawns, the grass so green it might have been watered with Lucky Charms. The sun is brilliant. The white van has NONSTOP PARTY SHOP painted on its flanks.

The four men inside wear Dockers and identical royal-blue polo shirts. They follow the winding street past ten-foot hedges and homes with wrought-iron gates.

"Slow down," Wardell says from the shotgun seat.

He hasn't done this for twelve years. Not since he drove off in Neil McCauley's work car, stuffed with millions in cash. He gunned away from that bloody back road and kept driving, all the way to the Pacific Ocean. In LA, he got himself a new name and a new line of work on McCauley's money. On Figueroa, motels sell for around ninety grand each. With the five he's bought, all moneymakers, he is now an entrepreneur. A backstreet mogul.

But the skills come back. He points and snaps his fingers. "That's our bull's-eye."

Tick-Tock turns in at a Tudor-style mansion with laurels lining the drive.

The people who own it are loaded. Helena Benedek plays tennis in diamond bracelets. Belongs to the Junior League. Her obese Anglo husband, Jerrold, is heir to a retail jewelry empire. Midrange shit, but franchised out the ass in malls nationwide. Jerrold works downtown, marketing engagement rings to blue-collar chumps. Helena supplies girls to pimps like Eazy-D and banks her own dough.

Tick-Tock—Isaac Wells—parks on the circular driveway. The van is full of helium balloons. They unload, guns under their shirts, balloons obscuring their faces.

Wardell pulls down his ski mask. "Party's here. Pop the cork!"

A rage-filled smile spreads across his face. He rings the bell.

The maid goes down first, easy. One punch, *boom*. Wardell kicks the door shut. He finds Helena on a love seat in the conservatory, her middle-aged face empty with surprise, as round as the balloons that are now floating to the top of the two-story foyer. Pink lipstick, eyes like onyx.

"What's this crap?" she says.

He holds a Smith & Wesson semiautomatic at his side. "You tell me where Eazy-D is, that's what's this crap. And I want that girl's papers." He mimics her Vietnamese accent. "Unnerstan, mamasan?"

She cools a few more degrees. "I don't know where he is. Take off mask. You fool nobody."

"Masks for your neighbors."

"You will regret coming into my house."

"Me?" Wardell says. "I don't have to worry about Immigration."

"I 'Merican citizen," Helena says. "I donate symphony. United Way. Save whale. You are a sewer toad."

"And when the cops find your stash of passports and IDs you grabbed from the slope girls you import? Fifteen-year-olds you promised good American jobs, who end up six weeks later butt-fucked with no papers, working off their transport down on Figueroa for a couple years?"

He spits on the floor.

Helena stands up, showing teeth. "And Mr. Smoky, he tries them out, yes? Get high on his own supply. And when a girl won't work off her ticket? Fights back? Huh? You like that too much, don't you?"

She pauses. The rest hangs in the air.

"I not only person police might get call about," she says.

He says nothing, knowing that Helena has the dead girl's documents somewhere, maybe in this house. She could be a link back to him. A liability.

He speaks over his shoulder as he takes a Bic lighter from his pocket. "Tick-Tock. Gimme a cigarette."

73

The aerial house looks exactly the way Neil described it. A shabby hilltop fortress in East LA gangbanger territory, surrounded by microwave and cell towers. There's a camera in the steel gate. Chris bets the barbed wire on top of the cyclone fencing is electrified. Hacker NORAD.

He buzzes and the gate powers open. At the top of the driveway, the faded yellow house overlooks the city in one direction and twelve lanes of the 10 Freeway in the other. Cars like bits in a stream, or electrons racing down the rails to the gate of a transistor to become a zero or a one.

Kelso calmly waits at a patio table in the shade, a mantis folded into a wheelchair, beard brushing his chest. He wears a T-shirt that says THERE ARE 10 KINDS OF PEOPLE IN THE WORLD. THOSE WHO UNDERSTAND BINARY, AND THOSE WHO DON'T. He extends a meaty hand. "Shiherlis."

Chris shakes. Kelso gestures at the seat across the table.

Chris sits. "How you doin'?"

"Good. You taking a census?"

"Nate says you shifted focus, doin'—"

"This and that."

"He says you perform dark magic, tunneling through the web."

Kelso smiles. Beatific. Cryptic. "That and this. And you're not a carder in the market for zero-day exploits."

"Not today." He leans on his knees. "I need a guide who can . . . help me discover if there are some advanced ways we can do our business.

Buy services and sources. We do transnational deals that move digital and material objects securely. We move money, have security, and can get heavy duty, if needed. And all of that is executed outside US territory and jurisdiction. And we're not in the drug trade."

"You've retooled."

"Movin' with the moves." He shrugs. "We work out of a free-trade zone in South America. And I have an exceptional partner."

"What's the commodity?" Kelso asks.

"Electronics, hardware, software, engineering, manufacturing. Lots of cross-border reach. Like that."

"Why me?"

"Nate says you got the keys to the kingdom. You can access the ultimate dark Yellow Pages underneath the smiley-face graphic user interface in the underside of the web nobody sees."

Very fancy description. "What kind of tech?"

"Avionics."

Kelso eyes him. "Specifically?"

Chris pauses, considers, then says, "Comms. Signals intercept. Navigation."

Kelso raises an eyebrow. "Sounds like a DoD purchase order." He taps his fingers on the table. "Navigation. You talking guidance systems?"

Okay. "If I was," Chris says, "who wants those? Where would I unload them?"

"There's market segmentation," Kelso says. "Entry level, that's shoulder-launched missiles. Cheap. Can take out a helicopter or a piñata at your kid's birthday party. Midlevel? Surface-to-air and air-to-air missiles. You're talking about state actors, countries with air forces. The top? Inertial navigation systems. Those ride in ballistic missiles. Rockets. Theater, intercontinental." He leans back. "Who wants this stuff? Who doesn't? Religious freaks in the mountains. Third world right-wing paramilitaries the US government won't fund anymore. Shining Path. Rogue states. Everybody wants to defend themselves from enemies real and perceived. And to project power."

Inside the house, a woman walks into the living room. She's Black, with braids wrapped atop her head, typing on the laptop she carries.

Kelso crosses his arms. "What do you call what you do?"

"Globalized enterprise in a free-trade environment," Chris says.

"Euphemism. UN calls it 'transnational organized crime.'"

Kelso's abstract smile remains. Inside, the woman gets an apple from a bowl on the kitchen counter and saunters down a hall. She is younger than Kelso, and hot, and fully engaged with her laptop screen.

"If there are tools to innovate better ways to do what we do, I want to learn about that and put them to work," Chris says.

A closed IBM laptop sits on the table. Kelso sets a heavy hand on top of it. "You can get all kinds of shit online. Heroin. Identities. Goat fetish porn. Access to the British House of Lords. Coders. Guns. Plastic explosives." The computer stays closed. "There are markets. But you're not gonna stumble on them."

Chris stares at the laptop. "How do I discover them?"

"Nate's wrong. I'm not an explorer. I'm a navigator." Kelso settles into stillness. "You need introductions. A chain of trusted connections. And state-of-the-art encryption."

"Start with the encryption." That way, he can at least keep information from Felix.

"Okay. I'll price out a package." Kelso tilts his head. "The rest I can also provide to you." He leans forward. "But we ain't going window-shopping at the mall. I can do it—when you know exactly what you want. Not before."

He glances at the antennas and dishes bristling in the yard.

Chris feels electric. There is a way out. Salvage. Victory. He reaches across the table and shakes Kelso's hand.

74

When the girl steps off the bus in her Wilshire Center neighborhood and gets home near four in the afternoon, her roommate's on the apartment sofa, finishing a term paper, eating Doritos. Tina is also her cousin. She looks up. "Hey, girl."

She smiles. "Gotta rush. My shift starts in an hour."

In her bedroom, she takes off her medallion of Our Lady of Guadalupe and hangs it on her vanity mirror, beside a photo of her late mother. She turns on the radio and slips into her waitress uniform, singing along to Lenny Kravitz's "Always on the Run."

She's twenty. She's working and going to community college. She's doing okay. She progresses. She survives.

The diner is retro, with a '50s sheen. It sits on a busy stretch of Century Boulevard near Jesse Owens Park. The booths are turquoise, the lights red with Sputnik-style sparkles. The burgers are fat, juicy, and bad for you.

On weeknights, the Backstretch is loud with the dinner rush. The grill men flip and shout with the rhythm of a drum line. The crowd's a mix of construction workers, basketball fans heading to games at the Forum, and guys who run nearby pawnshops. Those guys arrive with the Racing Form and sweat ringing their armpits. They order BLTs with a side of slaw. They keep track of the clientele and the waitresses.

The girl is slim and strong, hoisting a serving tray onto her shoulder and weaving through the tables to a booth. Her voice is bright. "Here you go."

She serves, the dishes clattering. Clubs, meat loaf. The men, in their forties and fifties, are laughing and giving each other shit over the Lakers.

"Anything else?" she says.

One guy with a combover like a dead hamster drinks her in. "We'll let you know, hon."

She moves to the next table, takes an order, swings by the counter, hands it over.

She's worked here for a year and knows the regulars, knows who's a tourist, who's sketchy, who's liable to grab her ass. She keeps an eye on Dead Hamster Hair and his hands.

It's a steady job. It's above the table. She's above the table, pretty much.

No trouble. She smiles at customers, and they tell her they like the way she grins. Her eyes are dark, her hair mahogany, pinned up for work.

She bustles over and sets down waters and menus at a window booth. "Here you go."

"Thanks, sweetheart," one man says.

"I'll be back to get your drink orders." She turns.

A hand snags her forearm. "Get me a Michelob."

She takes out her order pad and a pen. "Coming right up."

She heads across the diner. Her vision seems swimmy.

She hurries past the kitchen, knees softening. In the women's room she slams open a stall door, presses her hands against the sides. Her stomach heaves. Sweat coats her forehead.

The man in the booth who wants the Michelob.

In his forties. Handsome, pale, in a tight polo shirt and jeans. Confident. A scar through his eyebrow.

A scrim of memory bleeds red across her vision. Tío Tomás dead on the floor of the abandoned ranch house. Her mother running in. A man, a man, a man, *that man in the booth,* his voice like poisoned oil.

Honey, you're home.

It's him. The man who murdered her mother.

Gabriela barely sees her own feet as she stumbles to the manager's cramped office at the back of the diner. He's at his desk, pasty, sucking on a giant soda.

"I'm sick," she manages.

75

The evening is sun-shocked and Wardell's in a sweet mood. He hasn't found that fucker Eazy-D yet, but he has just won big on the Daily Double at Hollywood Park. Watching his maiden come home off the backstretch—that was magical.

They're in the fence's regular booth by the window. Fabbiano's an old railbird who hangs out here, up the road from the racetrack. His combover is dyed gopher brown.

"The Sox won last night."

Fucking White Sox, Tick-Tock thinks. *This here is Dodgertown.*

But Fabbiano, Tick-Tock thinks, grew up in Chicago. Wardell likes to surround himself with guys from the Chi to talk hometown old times, even though Wardell has fugitive warrants from Illinois.

In this noisy diner, nobody can hear. If they could, Wardell wouldn't be arranging to lay off the merch from their score.

"Mounted stones," Wardell says.

She leaves via the rear door. Shivering, she shoots a look back at the Backstretch and dodges across Century Boulevard toward the bus stop. The windows reflect the evening sun, but inside, the men sitting in the booth form a sickening display. She feels like scorpions are crawling up her back.

Tick-Tock squints against the glare coming through the window, watching her hustle away, fast, like she just stuck a fork in a light socket.

He taps Wardell on the arm. "You scared the shit out of that girl. You know her or something?"

Wardell frowns. "What girl?"

"Waitress. Mexican chick. She bugged out, dude."

Wardell turns toward the window. Traffic. It clears briefly.

76

Wardell sees the girl reach the bus stop and stare back at the diner with a stricken expression.

Tick-Tock points. "Her. With the birthmark on her neck. Chick's sure as hell acting like she knows you."

Wardell glares for a heated second. The girl is looking straight at him. Cars pass on Century, interrupting his view. When they clear, she is not there.

The locket he tore off Elisa Vasquez's neck. *Te amo—Gabriela.* The girl at the bus stop even looks like her mother. He sees it now.

He's been made.

He explodes out of the booth, shoves a waiter aside, and storms out to the sidewalk. The bus is pulling away. The girl is gone.

Gabriela slides into a seat and leans her head against the window as the bus rumbles away.

Wardell. The name pounds through her mind like a falling hammer. She can see him, leaner, meaner, hot, angry, the scar standing out white against his rage-reddened face.

Backhanding her mother, throwing her on the dining room table, tearing her shirt.

She presses the back of her hand to her mouth.

Twelve years, no news, no understanding; just emptiness, struggle, and the blank, terrorizing, stomach- and soul-churning feeling of falling, of everything that held her being ripped away, suddenly, without explanation.

Until Explanation walked in and sat down in a blue vinyl booth and asked for a beer.

Neil is gone. Marcos, her cousin, is in Mexico. Neil's friends—she has no idea. She was a little girl. She remembers their names. Trejo, joking in Spanish, his eyes glittering. Michael did dumb magic tricks for her, clearly a dad. The tall boy with the blond hair who taught her to play cards. Blackjack. Always moving, always looking like he was about to break into a run. Chris.

All gone. No one to reach out to.

She can't simply hide. She can't return to her apartment and bolt the door and scream and scream, though that's what she feels like doing, screaming, here, on this bus, screaming so loud the windows and roof and tires explode. Her breath catches. Her chin trembles.

Wardell. Well fed. Well dressed. Swaggering in.

The bus lets her off a couple of blocks from her apartment. Quick look. Busy road, nobody paying attention as she climbs down. When it pulls away, she stands alone on the street.

Working up her courage, Gabriela walks to the LAPD's Hollywood Station. She has never been in a police station. Cops are people to be avoided, always. She lives a legit life, works above the table, has her taxes withheld. She's a US citizen. In the world she was born into, cops are hyenas. They are fed, if at all, in the form of *mordita*. Bribes. They have their world, their goals, their cliques and turf.

They have power. They have resources. Here, they troll the streets.

She walks through the doors. The lobby is coldly bright, the walls a dull beige. Wanted posters are tacked up. There's a thick glass partition at the desk.

She approaches the officer who's writing on a clipboard on the other side.

"I want to make a report," she says.

She's taken to speak to the detective on duty, Anglo, who sits forward at her desk like a bulldozer. She listens to Gabriela's clear description of the man called Wardell and her halting explanation that she knows he's "a robber and a murderer." The detective writes it down.

Gabriela says, "I want to stay anonymous. When you look for him, I don't want him to find out my name."

"You're here. I see you. I have it," the detective says, then seems to see fear blight Gabriela's expression. "Your name won't be made public," she finishes.

Gabriela nods, uncertain. "I saw him at the diner where I work. The Backstretch."

The detective writes that down, too.

Back out on the street, Gabriela feels a sense of inchoate rage and terror. The sunny evening feels different now. Ominous. Like it took forever, but the world has turned, as it was always going to do. Always. She walks toward her apartment building.

Survive.

Gabriela Vasquez tells herself that every single day. It's her prayer. She touches a photo she has at home. It's her remembrance and promise to her mother, Elisa. *Survive.*

In the station, the detective turns to her computer. She enters the information Gabriela gave her.

"Huh."

Otis Lloyd Wardell. Chicago. Wanted for murder, rape, felony murder, armed robbery. Wanted for questioning by the Major Crimes Unit within RHD in the slaying of the young woman found buried off the 210. Washed-out face with a scar through his eyebrow.

She writes up a contact report, prints a copy, sends a digital version of the file into the LAPD system, flagged. She calls RHD.

"Report on a person of interest in the Jane Doe murder off the 210, coming your way."

Wardell has doubled back to the diner. Tick-Tock stands outside the door.

"I know who she is." Wardell is breathing hard. "Her mother. She was in a crew I knew."

"What's that mean?"

"Her family, they're smugglers. Outlaws. That's how she recognized me." He glares. "We gotta get to her before she can drop a fucking dime on me."

Tick-Tock shakes his head. "Outlaws? Man, she ain't calling no police."

"You're gonna roll the dice on my life?" He pokes Tick-Tock in the chest. "I don't want BOLOs all over SoCal issued on my ass. Go fucking find her."

Storming back into the diner, he heads down the hall and raps his knuckles on an open office door. The manager looks up, harried. Wardell instantly throttles back down.

"Question for you, my friend. I just stopped in from outta town to see my niece, and one of the girls, very nice girl, told me she went home sick . . ."

77

Music rolls through the Beverly Hilton. There's a party in the ball-room with a big band, women in lamé so shiny it could power a space station. When Chris enters the hotel suite, the sheers on the balcony door are swirling in the warm breeze.

Ana's outside, braced against the balcony railing, back to him, hair streaming in the air, soaking in the lights of Century City.

He slips his hands around her waist from behind. She continues staring at the skyscrapers. After what feels like an endless minute, she rests her head back against his chest.

He lets the dusk cover them. "Met a man this afternoon."

She doesn't turn.

"Dude's way ahead of the curve, has been for twenty years."

"What curve?"

"Cyber tech."

She turns.

"He worked on DARPA, building the net in the first place. He knows every way in and out and all the plumbing underneath."

"And?"

"You want to get out from under Felix's thumb, right? Get past these clowns talking down to you? So, you're thinking build a facility halfway around the world in Batam?"

"That's not the only reason. Batam's like an Asian Ciudad del Este, wide open. But Singapore's only four and a half miles across the Malacca Strait."

"That's great," Chris says. "But I'm starting to think there's some-thing else."

"What do you mean?"

"I don't know. I'm thinking there's some other ways to be doing this. It's like an idea . . ." He gestures into the air. "Right there."

"I don't understand."

"I don't, either. Pretend you're in a room, ten feet by ten feet. That's your world. Then in your peripheral vision you start to see a door. You start vibing that maybe this small room isn't all of it. Maybe it's inside a much larger room holding a whole inventory of new possibilities."

"Where are you going with this?"

She steps out of his arms and turns. Her expression is reserved, but there's curiosity in her eyes.

"What if some of your family's holdings and facilities in Paraguay can be sourced in parallel, from outside the Liu organization? Independently. What if you were able to cut the cord of dependency? What if you were able to shop for independence?"

"How?" she asks.

"His name's Kelso. He operates from a hilltop in City Terrace. Lots of hardware, and encryption as sophisticated as NSA."

Ana is listening.

"What gave you this idea?"

"The world is going global. National borders and jurisdictions are fading. You want out from under these clowns who can't shine your shoes? Let's go exploring."

Her eyes narrow, gleaming. "When can I meet Kelso? On my way back from Asia?"

He hasn't seen Ana thrilled like this in a while.

"Sure."

Ana brightens, kissing him. "This could be something."

"I know."

There's a pause, and then a melancholy cast comes over her.

"What?" he says.

"My mother. She wanted to be a doctor. For a Chinese diaspora woman of her generation, that was not happening. Inherited culture can drown hope and ambition . . ."

Ana turns to the starship Century City buildings.

"What about you?" she says.

"Me what?"

"Your family. You never talk about your family. All you ever told me is you grew up here."

"East of here." Chris resets. "Paramount, California. Meatpacking, cracked earth, a couple of dusty palms. The main industrial product is alienation. That's also a successful adaptation to the environment."

"What did your mother do?"

"What did she do? She got knocked up with me at seventeen on the night my father shipped out to Germany. He got drafted into the army when he was eighteen. Three weeks after he deployed, he and two other idiots got killed doing a thrill ride on the no-speed-limit autobahn outside Stuttgart.

"She blew through the death benefits and then became a go-go dancer at the Mello Yellow in Gardena. Cindy the Surfing Queen. Hung out with a biker set, part of the Mongols, for a while. Paramount— getting high in the mid-'70s—was like hippie drug culture from Topanga and Laurel Canyon trickling down to the working-class.

"Last time I saw her was in 1979. Too many acid trips landed her in Camarillo. That's a state mental hospital. I had just gotten out of juvie. I went to see her. She still looked like a teenager. She had red hair and this wash of freckles across her nose. She didn't recognize me. I tried to talk to her for a long time. It was like I was the adult."

He remembers the pale cream-and-green high-gloss institutional walls. That stuck in his mind. Maybe the high gloss made it easier to hose it down.

"She was doing psychedelic hand jive and told me, 'I know where my head's at, someone find my body.'

"She died while I was in San Quentin."

"How?"

"They said a car crash."

Ana says nothing. She'd never heard any of this before. He would simply evade the question.

"Why?" she asks.

"Why what? Why was I in Q?"

She nods.

"'Cause I got caught." Simple. "I was doing robberies and shooting pharmaceutical-grade morphine I scored off a nurse at Kaiser Permanente in Harbor City. At one point I couldn't tell if I was doing crime to support the drugs or if the drugs were the excuse to do the robberies because that was as big a high."

He looks at her with an attitude that says, *You wanted to know me? Okay. Know me. And if you're gonna tell me to fuck off, do that right now.*

"Basically I had an incomplete command of my facility to navigate from any one moment in time to the next thing I wanted."

He looks at her.

"Did you spend time in therapy?"

"No." He goes on: "I had a guy, was like my older brother, who helped me straighten my ass out when I got transferred to Folsom. It's with him that I got real. He read me like an x-ray. Told me things about *myself* that he had picked up from *himself.* He read. He got me reading. I got serious about doing crime. He was there for me and I was there for him. He saved my life."

"In prison?"

"And on the street."

"What happened to him?"

"He made a mistake. He was with this girl. He lost his navigation, which had been, like, perfect. Like Vasco da Gama. So, he walked into this trap set by a guy who knew what he might go for. And that guy killed my brother out near LAX."

"Who was he?"

"He was a cop in LA."

"Where's he now?" she asks.

"He's right here."

His eyes, filled with the forest of lights from the high-rises, linger there. Then they turn onto her.

"What now? Have I told you more than you wanted to know?"

He feels tainted. *Is it over?*

Ana takes his hand and kisses it.

"What's that for?" he asks.

She changes the mood. "Let's order food."

She goes inside and orders room service while she boots her PC and logs in to the hotel's network, front-ending her VPN at the same time. She is a wonder. Chris never stops being magnetized by her. He hasn't lost her. He hasn't lost . . .

"Surf and turf," she calls out to him. "I'm going to shower."

She turns on the stereo and heads for the bathroom. Chris leans on the balcony railing, soaring.

LA at night. Bright lights. Everything there spread out in front of him. *Maaaaan* . . . A flat constellation that goes on forever . . . *City of light,* Jim Morrison sang. *Or just another lost angel, city of night . . .*

But the traffic, the music, the party rocking downstairs; the cars, the money—the vibe. Like the night he met Charlene. That singular, brilliant, lightning-struck Las Vegas evening. He pauses, inhaling. Being here. Feeling it. Chris lets the city he left, and longed for, and fears, and dreads, and dreams of, sing up to him. It rides circuits in his bloodstream like five milligrams of morphine. This is natural, ambition making the difference. This is mojo risin'.

Charlene. His pulse hammers. *Where are you tonight?*

Chris thinks she's met somebody. Thinks, doesn't know. The photos stopped coming. The last arrived nine months back. Beautiful, sunny. Nothing since.

It bugs him, but he allows himself only a moment of jealousy. He can't blame her. It's survival. He's glad she possesses that skill. Keeps her and Dominick safe. Someone touching her flesh, though, that thought drives him nuts.

Stop it.

He misses her. He aches for Dominick. God, does he.

From the shower, Ana sings with the stereo, her voice sweet and raw in the reverb.

He has a phone number that Charlene mailed him for emergencies. He's never called it. He doubts it will work anymore. But he brings the phone out onto the balcony. Heart pounding, he dials.

There's a lag in the connection, a delay—call forwarding? The phone rings.

Heat spreads through his chest. The sounds of the city ride to him. Hope and fear build with every ring.

> Hills are filled with fire.
> If they say I never loved you,
> You know they are a liar . . .

Does he still love her? Yeah. What the hell does that mean for him, here, now? A parallel reality?

"Hello."

That voice. Clear and calm and confident, even answering a call.

The night lights up, brilliant, hot, filling him with electricity.

"Hello?"

He hears music in the background on her end, hears her breathing.

His lips part, but he can't bring himself to speak. He hangs up.

Charlene stands in the kitchen with the phone in her hand. A dry wind gusts outside, bending the ponderosa pines. Her voice drops to a whisper. "Chris?"

Nobody's there.

She slowly, carefully hangs up. Her fingers linger on the phone, heart racketing in her chest. The call sounded long distance. It was sent via call forwarding.

Was that Chris calling on a random weeknight from somewhere so distant?

78

Hanna ends his call and drops the phone into its cradle. He is crackling. The stack of folders in his office is straightened up. He has requested a civilian clerk to assist with the files.

When he walks out onto the unit floor, Drucker hands him photos from the mansion where Helena Benedek was beaten unconscious.

The marble atrium is covered with blood and detritus from the first responders' attempts to resuscitate her: used gloves, syringe caps, and torn paper packaging. The ceiling is crowded with silver Mylar helium balloons.

"Their ruse. Party planners," Drucker says. "Having some sick fun. They tore jewelry off the victim, a diamond tennis bracelet, the maid says. Everything else was a variety pack of gratuitous psycho shit."

"Return to Forever," Hanna says sharply. "Wardell cannot abandon his own MO even if it identifies his ass."

Casals pushes through the door, loose limbed, sharply dressed. A question in his eyes.

Hanna nods at his office phone. "Just got off with Rick Rossi. He's still with Chicago CID."

"Anything?" Casals says.

"Wardell has been off their radar since the torture-murder at the auto repair shop."

"Twelve years."

"Warrant remains active for the home invasion and murder of James Matzukas. Felony murder for the deaths of Wardell's crew at the Colson house firefight. Work cars guy, Aaron Grimes. Federal fugitive warrant, flight to avoid prosecution, all that. But yeah. Wardell turned into Casper the Ghost and disappeared in a puff of smoke."

Drucker walks to his desk. "What's CPD sending us?"

"Photos, Wardell's jacket, known associates, original reports the responding officers and detectives wrote up on the Aaron Grimes murder.

"Work up an age-progressed drawing."

Casals sets his sidearm in a desk drawer. "If he was dormant, twelve years is a long time, Vincent. Means he had money from somewhere. Now, maybe he ran out."

"Or he got a yearning for his old-time religion of rape, torture, and murder," Hanna says. "Whatever, he is here now."

"How'd Rossi sound?" Casals asks.

"Settled in." Hanna half smiles. "Like Shakespeare Station's his home away from home and he plans to stay there the rest of his life

in a BarcaLounger, TV and remote control. Easton's retired." He gives
Casals a look. "Novak's running the unit."

What goes around comes around, Hanna thinks. *When you fall, you land
where you were aiming for all along. So you better find a way to hang on,
brother. Get back up. Drive forward.*

For a moment he sees Wardell staring at him from behind a ski
mask, black eyes flat and vacant. Two seconds before Wardell drove
at him with a carjacked Mercedes.

He turns to his detectives. "Wardell is about dominance. He always worked slick and tight. But professionally, he's a bottom-feeder.
Came in when a family was at home, terrorized them—that was his
MO. But sticking around to carry out a rape instead of *boom*, in, *bang*,
out . . . that is his indulgence. That's where the River Styx kicks in. He
acts from deviant psychology, not operational necessity. That is his
weakness. Knowing that about him is our way in."

He pours a cup of coffee. One Adderall this morning, no more.

"Wardell always cased homes ahead of scores. Drucker, show his
photo to Helena Benedek's neighbors. Their gardeners and maids.
Their dog walkers. Mail carriers, newspaper boys, and school bus
drivers." He drinks half the cup. "Wardell used tipsters to get inside
info on his targets. In Chicago, he had a car valet who provided intel
and duplicated victims' house keys for him."

When Hanna turns, Casals is looking at him silently.

"Get a list of every establishment Benedek frequents or has visited
in the last two months," Hanna says. "Anyplace she handed over her
house keys. Anyplace she revealed her home address and financial
status. Gyms, pools, places where the staff has access to lockers or
where Wardell could bribe someone to hand over customer info. Let's
see if any business she frequents prints out appointment schedules
with names and addresses. What do they do with the printouts? Who
collects their trash?"

He turns to Drucker. "Run Wardell's MO to the FBI. ViCAP. Maybe
he's been active someplace else over the last twelve years and the
database will kick it out. No guarantee another jurisdiction uploaded
the information to the Bureau, if it even exists. Try it anyway." He

turns away and back. "When you talk to the FBI? Do not tell them you have a multistate series of torture-murders. Do not let them think they can assert federal jurisdiction. I don't want anybody else movin' in on us."

Drucker picks up his phone. Casals waits.

"That girl who survived," Hanna says, "Jessica Matzukas." Heat drills through his head. His breathing feels tight. "We take Wardell off the board, we can finally tell her it's over."

Drucker nods. "Amen to that." He looks at the whiteboard where their open cases are listed. "Let justice roll down like waters. And righteousness as a fucking steamroller."

Hanna breathes through the shaft of heat piercing his head. That's new. Rage restrained? Revulsion uncoiling? "Wardell starts fires. He can't stop. We find his trail and track him by the smoke and burn marks."

A near-forgotten memory surfaces.

"Casals. Long time back—after I left CPD—you told me word came that Wardell's second-in-command got killed in a gunfight."

"Hank Svoboda, yeah." Casals says. "He and three other men were found shot to death down by the Mexican border. A back road outside Yuma."

"1988?"

Casals nods. "Four bodies, bunch of shot-up vehicles." He takes off his glasses. "I talked to a Yuma County deputy back then. He said there was a lot of blood on the road. Somebody else had been removed. Too much blood, couldn't have survived. I thought maybe that was Wardell."

Hanna considers it, wondering.

The door swings open and Detective Rausch strides in. "Pham Thanh Thuy."

Hanna spins. "That's the girl in the shallow grave?"

Rausch nods. "The garbage bag we recovered from that gas station dumpster contained her clothing—with contact powder marks on the back of her blouse. And cigarette burn holes. She was stripped after death." She puts her hands on her hips. "We also found her purse. No ID, but it contained a letter to her. We went to the address and found her sister. Shitty apartment, crowded with girls who are on the stroll." She opens a notebook. "Sister's Pham Huong Lanh. She works the Fig track. She's seventeen."

"Trafficked?" Drucker says.

"The sister knows maybe five words of English. Four of them are *hey, baby,* and *cash money.* She's skittish. Terrified. Thanh, I gather, was her younger sister." She shakes her head. "I showed her Wardell's photo. She couldn't hide her reaction. Horror show. She knows him."

"He her pimp?" Hanna says.

"No. The fifth English word she knows? *Motels.*"

Hanna is on his way to the door. "Let's go."

79

The Outskirts Motel, on Figueroa below 120th Street, is bubblegum pink with peeling orange trim. It's dim and pulsing with secret energy. Hanna and Drucker swing into the courtyard in an unmarked car around midnight.

It's the fourth dump they've hit tonight, from the list Pham's sister provided to Rausch. At every place, when they flashed Wardell's photo, the desk clerks shook their heads. *No, never seen this man. Don't know him,* they said in a bored Cantonese, Honduran, or Boston accent.

The Outskirts's porch lights are piss yellow, giving the clerk behind the speak-thru window a jaundiced cast. A bony guy, hunched, in a Manchester United T-shirt.

Hanna leans on the counter. "What's your name?"

Drucker pounds on the locked door to the clerk's cubicle. The clerk says nothing. Out on the corner, late-model cars are lined up. Young women in baby dolls and string bikini bottoms walk among them. Two cars pull into the motel courtyard.

"This place is like a drive-through at three in the morning." Hanna cups his hand to his mouth and booms, "I'll have a Double-Double, fries, a Coke, and a blow job on the side."

Making them for cops immediately, one girl throws a pink high heel at him.

Drucker's battering fist echoes across the courtyard.

The door opens on a chain.

"Your name," Hanna says.

"Kultar," the clerk says.

"Kultar. Where's your boss?"

"I don't have a boss. It's some corporation, I don't know."

"Unlock the door before Sergeant Drucker starts shouting, 'Police,' and your customers all bug the fuck out. 'Cause the boss you don't have is gonna hate that."

Kultar unlocks the door.

The cubicle smells like sweat and stale takeout. Like his own place, Hanna thinks, laughs.

Drucker fills the space. "Your boss's name?"

Hanna scans the desk, stacked with notebooks and ledgers. "You handle the books, the night's tally. Somebody comes by? Who's the guy that collects the money?"

Drucker towers over him. "I see enough health and fire code violations here to drag your ass downtown and back a dozen times."

The clerk raises his hands. "Smolenski. Mr. Smolenski. I don't know where he is, how to contact him. He not come by in days."

Hanna glances at Drucker, then back at the clerk. "Why not? Because of the girl we found dead in a shallow grave? What do you know about that?"

Kultar recoils. "Nothing!"

"But Mr. Smolenski does? What's his first name?"

"John."

"Who knows where to find him?"

Kultar gazes out the filmy ballistic glass window.

"The girls?" Hanna says. "A pimp?"

Kultar hesitates. "Perhaps Eazy-D."

..

Back in the car, Hanna and Drucker radio Rausch; she's in another unmarked, up Figueroa near USC.

"Eazy-D, I know him," Rausch says. "Squirrelly kid, real name's Calvin Page. Tennis shoe pimp with big doe eyes. He Romeos the girls, but he's mean."

"The clerk at the Outskirts says Wardell is after this pimp for shorting him his cut of the cash the girls earn grinding at his motels."

"Lately I've seen him rolling in a black Suburban with chrome rims and a big blue-and-silver star on the back window."

Hanna and Drucker find him two hours later, cruising a darkened street two blocks from Figueroa, headlights off, staying in the shadows while he keeps track of his prostitutes. Drucker cuts him off and forces the Suburban to stop.

The window comes down and a bass beat that must weigh four tons rolls out, along with the smell of weed. Eazy-D has both hands on the wheel.

"Easy, son," he says.

Drucker gestures him out. Eazy-D jumps down from the SUV. He's five-foot-six, in saggy Bugle Boy jeans and raggedy sneakers. He looks like he's late for tenth grade math class.

Hanna gazes at him like he's an apparition. "How you gonna chase down your girls with your pants below your ass crack, Calvin?"

"Don't have to chase nobody." He gestures at himself. "They want this."

"One of your girls over there, she's wearing eight-inch pink plastic heels, and even she could outrun you."

"What you hassling me for?" Eazy-D says. "You ain't Vice. I ain't seen you around here." He gives Hanna a dismissive up-and-down. "And, man, you do look like you been a-round."

"Hasslin' you?" Hanna points at the blue-and-silver star on the Suburban's back window. "Cal-vin! If I were hassling you, I'd impound this piece-of-shit SUV for riding around LA sporting the mother-fucking Cowboys."

"I don't—"

"What's wrong with you, Cal-vin?"

"Ain't doin' nothin', man. Sticker came wit' this! I'm not a fan."

"No?" Hanna queries. "Then I've got to arrest you for mopery."

"What's that?"

"Mopery in the third degree," adds Drucker. "You mopin' here, you've been seen mopin' there."

"So, where," says Hanna, "the fuck did the dude go?"

"What dude?" Eazy-D says.

"You trying to be stupid or were you born that way?" Drucker says. "White dude, greaseball motherfucker with a scar through his eyebrow who owns the Outskirts."

Eazy-D shrugs. "I don't—"

"Don't say 'don't,'" Hanna warns him.

"'Cause then we *don't* find him," Drucker says. "He finds you."

"'Cause we know he's lookin', 'cause we know you're holding back his end from your girls rolling in and out of his motels. And he's looking for your ass. And you are starting to waste my motherfucking time."

"Hold on, hold up." Eazy-D glances around. No other traffic. Small homes barricaded against the night are dark. "Man, I ain't holding out. I lost a girl. He got to do reconstitution."

"'Reconstitution'?" Drucker says. "You mean restitution?"

"Yeah. That."

Hanna turns dead-on to face him. "Lost her. She get confused and take the wrong bus? You look for her in the lost and found?"

"No, man. This girl, the one you found out by the 210."

"Oh, that one," Hanna says quietly, dropping his voice, as if now the puzzle is solved. "Where is he?" The change of tone is spooky.

"He lives in this weird-ass house south of here." He shakes his head. "That girl, she was part of my stable—supposed to be. She didn't get with the program. He told me he was gonna regulate her. Then she disappear. Which is why I didn't kick back. Unnerstand? See, 'cause Smoky got to pay for the girl, and that's why Smoky and his people are looking for me."

Hanna feels a cold drip down his spine. "Smoky, he 'regulates' girls who don't get with the program? That it? Other girls disappear?"

Eazy-D harrumphs. "What you think?"

"Where's this weird-ass house?" Drucker says.

They arrive with SWAT, four a.m., ballistic vests, Hanna wide-awake with no chemical stimulation, heart turning over, *bam,* against his ribs. The house is in a development of identikit ranch homes. It's the goblin in the bunch, a stone bunkhouse from the 1920s, huddled back amid a stand of overgrown oaks and sycamores. It's dark. It's silent.

They go in with a no-knock warrant, the short battering ram smashing apart the doorjamb. Flashlights on the rifles of the tactical team. Hanna, Drucker, and Rausch behind them. They swarm room to room, like wasps, eyes adapted to the night, blood pounding in their ears.

"Clear," the SWAT leader shouts.

Hanna reaches a bedroom. Messy. Empty. He swings back to the kitchen. Dirty dishes crusted with days-old food. Mail all over the floor beneath the slot in the front door. He kicks it.

Wardell knows they're after him. He's in the wind.

80

He paces. Inside the man-cave garage at Tick-Tock's house in Gardena, Wardell paces, relentlessly. A one-eared pit bull watches him warily from a dog bed.

When Tick-Tock comes in, Wardell spins on him. "You better have good news."

"Police raided your house. SWAT."

"Goddamn it."

Tick-Tock has tried calming him. Tried hiding the Maker's Mark from him. Tried feeding him. Wardell threw the plate of spaghetti his wife cooked at the wall. Tick-Tock has sent his wife and kid away now, early morning, before Wardell woke up. Tick-Tock grew up in Lynwood, a tough brother, but Wardell going ballistic scares even him.

"Fucking LAPD," Wardell says. "They're onto the motels."

"Name behind all them motels comes back to Smolenski, though, right?" Tick-Tock says.

"It don't matter! They're onto me."

He kicks the dog. It squeals and scurries away. Tick-Tock's blood pressure bumps way up. He holds out his hand, and the dog cringes to his side.

"Twelve years in LA. I ain't starting over *again*. Miami, or Toronto, or fucking Belize."

"Beaches in Belize supposed to be nice."

Wardell spins. "Fuck you."

Tick-Tock raises his hands. "So maybe it all blows over."

That won't happen, Wardell thinks. The motels—if the cops have them, he might have to burn those connections. It'll fuckin' kill him, but he'll do it. He has cash. A fat pile right now, because he laid off $300k in mounted stones he got from Helena Benedek. He can ride it out.

What he's thinking about is who dimed him.

His motel kingdom was built with money he scored off Neil Mc-Cauley on a back road outside Yuma. Cash he drove away with, leaving the rest on the pavement, nothing but blood bags and car carcasses. Leaving McCauley holding the dying woman.

Leaving a loose end behind, who made him at the diner.

"That fucking waitress." He turns on Tick-Tock. "I told you we had to look for her before she could go to the police to say, 'I saw Otis Wardell sitting here in this booth.' That bitch."

Tick-Tock nods placatingly. "I know. Other shit intervened. Not your fault, boss."

Wardell kicks a stool over. "No, asshole. It's *her* fault." He begins pacing again, ready to blow. He speaks to the air. "We are coming for you, Gabriela. Your whore mother couldn't get away, and you won't, either."

Dime him? He's going to get this bitch.

81

That afternoon, Chris hooks up with Nate at the back door of the Blue Room. The last time Chris stood here he was half dead from a gunshot wound, taking a car for the near-catastrophic meet with Charlene. How the wheel spins. Nate hands him a manila envelope.

"Kelso's woman delivered this." He sees that Chris is wondering about her. "They're what he calls a bonded pair. Trustworthy."

Chris glances inside. A zip drive.

"Encryption program," Nate says.

"Good." Chris holds out his hand. Nate shakes. Chris holds on. "One other thing. Vincent Hanna."

"What about him?"

"What can you tell me? Residence? Habits?"

"You stay away from him, is what I'm telling you. Thought you grew up."

"When it comes to Neil? That's the exception."

"What the fuck do you think runs through my mind when that jagoff strolls into the Blue Room every coupla months?"

Chris sees the fire behind Nate's ice-blue eyes.

He continues: "I don't do shit and I ain't telling you shit. Don't make me regret I answered the fucking phone when you called. The past is buried. They think you're dead or gone. You gonna blow that? Dig that up? You crazy? They will bury you. And me."

Nate's forefinger jabs Chris's sternum. Not gently. The Nate on the yard at McNeil is in the room. "You live with it."

Chris breathes. "Forget I asked."

"Forgotten." Nate nods.

Chris drives to the top of Mulholland, a serrated ridge above the city. The sunshine hits windows all around him, gold and crimson. He parks the Alfa and gets out into the warm wind.

He phones the Nevada number. She answers. This time he doesn't hesitate.

"Charlene, it's me."

Even under the rush of the wind, he hears an intake of breath. He shuts his eyes, willing her not to hang up.

"You called the other night, didn't you?" she says.

It's a relief. "I didn't know what to say. But I'm talking now."

"I'm listening."

He feels immensely distant, yet on the verge of being burned. "I got the photos you sent." It sounds lame. His voice seems to have a loose bolt in it. "I heard you're in Vegas."

"Since last year." She pauses. "I wasn't staying in LA. What for? Everything else was gone." Her voice turns raspy. "I'm taking care of Dominick. And myself."

"I wish . . ."

"God. Me, too. So much, do I wish."

Chris lets the wind scour him. He feels an intense longing for the past.

"I've been working in real estate," she says.

"Good."

"And I need to let you know," Charlene says. "I'm with somebody."

Chris says nothing.

"I've been with him for over a year. He works in the casino business." Another pause.

Chris waits. Her voice strengthens, like she knows this is no time for evasions.

"He's taking a managerial job at the Venetian in Macau."

"Macau." It sinks in. "You're going with him?"

"Yes. Dominick will be in a good school. Yes, I'm going with him."

He takes a beat. "It sounds solid."

"It is. Steady and quiet."

"Very adult," says Chris.

"Something wrong with that?"

On edge all of a sudden. Old Charlene.

"What's funny?" she says.

"Nothin'. Reminds me, is all. Good memories."

He walks to the lip of the road overlooking the city, trying to see clearly and speak calmly.

"Sounds like . . ." He searches for the guts to be real. "You've hung tough and built a good life for you and Dominick."

"Yeah. And it's nice to hear you say that."

Her voice is as beautiful as ever. He feels a passionate gravitational pull to her. His sun and stars. "I promised you . . ." He clears his throat. "Look, I'm going to call again. A day, two. It'll be twenty-four to forty-eight hours. I'll call and we'll set a meet."

"Set a meet."

That chill. She just went so cold, so fast, that Chris feels freezer burn.

"I'll call you. We'll figure it out."

"You set a meet with your crew, not with your wife."

"Charlene—"

"Think harder, Chris."

That's the end of the call.

Later, Chris sits in the Alfa, stereo cranked, long shadows stretching ahead of him. The beat thuds through his chest—Ice Cube, "Check Yo Self." He's been sitting for a while. Thinking. Churning. Wired.

Scanning.

Across the street, the white facade of Parker Center bakes the view, a towering white cuboid. Beside it, in a multistory parking garage ringed with gray metal fencing, car windshields shine.

The garage gate opens, and a Crown Victoria pulls out into the sun. At the wheel, sunglasses on, a carrion bird in a sepulchral suit: Vincent Hanna.

Chris starts the engine and follows.

Hanna pops a red light. Chris waits patiently. *King of the city, fuck him.* Hanna gets caught by another red a few blocks up. Chris continues.

Look at this guy, he thinks. *Cruisin' around, drawing breath on planet*

Earth. "*Maybe I'll catch a movie, go get a pizza.*" And Neil, as close to a brother and soul mate as Chris ever had, is in the ground, rotting somewhere.

After a few miles through traffic, Hanna turns into a parking lot cut into a hillside and bounded by curved steel picket security fencing. Gym bag in hand, loosening his tie, he walks into Title Boxing Gym.

Chris cruises past.

82

The buildings at the aerospace company are single story, bare bones, industrial, even the engineering wings. Security is strict, but the engineer has access. Raymond Zhang runs the department. He lets Chris and Ana in. Ocean fog is damp on the ground at the El Segundo facility. It's three a.m.

They move past the locked doors to the manufacturing center, the clean rooms where techs wear coveralls and booties and masks to prevent contamination of the electronic components.

"You see," Zhang says. "All in-house. US made. Surface-to-air aerodynamic missile guidance systems. Homing guidance systems, with accelerometers and the latest software. Electromagnetic sensors as well as heat-seeking systems. Lockheed Martin and General Dynamics buy these components. Northrop Grumman."

He swipes a card and leads them across a parking lot to another locked facility.

"Surveillance cameras?" Chris says.

"No."

"I see them on the ceilings and the electrical poles."

"Not tonight. I turned them off. Set up an executable program that tripped a short circuit facility-wide. I have noted this fault in the log. I am currently running a diagnostic. The cameras will be offline until that process completes. I'm frequently here at this time of night. It'll appear normal."

Chris wanted to verify that this guy is all that he says he is and that he'll carry through. The man sweats and is twitchy. But so far, so good. Chris cuts a glance at Ana.

"I have the hard drives for you," she says. "When will you deliver the software?"

"Tomorrow."

Zhang opens the door of the warehouse and turns on the lights. It's cavernous and cold. The racks of components go on and on. They're compact. Stacked, packed, wrapped in plastic.

"Product comes from production and assembly and is stored here for shipment," he says.

"These are the guidance systems themselves?" Chris says. "Not barcoded?"

"We have other means to keep track. This isn't Walmart."

"Where are these going?" Chris says.

"US and foreign militaries," Zhang says vaguely.

Across the aisle, behind yellow tape, are racks labeled QC.

"Quality control?" Chris says.

"Those are defective units."

"Lotta units there."

Ana frowns. "Problems in the clean room? On the assembly line? Or with the software?"

Zhang shakes his head. "This is merely one manufacturing facility among a dozen in the United States. Defective units are shipped here, disassembled, then sent to a recycling and disposal plant in Kentucky."

"What happens when a guidance system has a defect? It targets Sea World?" Chris says.

"Possibly. Which is why the software includes a mission abort override."

"Self-destruct command?" Chris eyes the packages. "No barcodes on those, either. Just stickers. Like poison control. Mr. Yuk is warning the air force this gear's bad."

"Essentially." Zhang looks antsy. "Have you satisfied your curiosity?"

Ana nods at the door. "Your office, please."

They head out. Chris takes one final look at the racks of guidance packages. Zhang turns off the lights.

The fog surrounds them as they walk to the car.

"He badly wants money," Ana says. "He'll play."

Yeah, Chris thinks. *Raymond Zhang will play.* The subtle threat that the Department of Defense, and his wife, might learn of his secret second family in Phoenix has sharpened his motivation to provide the software Ana desires. After that, the carrot. His payment. Her smile. Chris's presence, which helped her win the engineer with charm, promises, and just enough fear.

"You finessed him," Chris says. "A-plus."

"Gracias."

He scans the empty streets, head swiveling, threat assessment ingrained.

"Looking for something?" Ana shoves her hands in her jeans pockets. "Wishing?"

He hears the menace behind her bland tone. "Habit."

The fog dampens sounds on the street. The warning signs flash red in his head.

Her voice is glass smooth. "You're thinking about your wife, though."

He holds his fire, setting himself mentally. When they approach the car, he turns to her. "Of course I am."

Ana's eyes are burning. "This is where you lived with her? Los Angeles."

"That's right."

He breathes evenly. Tries to. Wants to keep the black box closed. To her. To himself. Even a once-upon-a-time outlaw knows that talking about his wife to the woman he's sleeping with is deadly. Dangerous all around.

Los Angeles. He's here, and if he works it—hard, fast, putting his heart into it—he can set up Charlene and Dominick's out. Nate can arrange documents for them. It's possible.

The lock on the black box rattles. He tries to slam it shut. They're not why he's here tonight.

He wonders when he stopped making their out the first, last, constant drive in his day.

"The place stirs up memories. More than I expected. I'm working it out," he says.

"Are you going to see her?" Ana says.

"It's not just her." He pictures the cop, Hanna, who killed his *brother*. "And she moved to Las Vegas."

"That's not an answer." The detonation behind her eyes is seismic. "You are pursuing her. On this trip. My trip. You found this out when?"

"The other day."

"You are talking to people I don't know."

"We're in America, Ana. C'mon, Los Angeles was my home."

"Will it be again? If you can bring Charlene back?"

It's the first time he has heard her say *Charlene*. She has always been oblique. *Your family. Your wife. Them.*

"I don't know," Chris says.

"Are we over?"

The words are simple, direct, and piercing. And behind them, he hears pain.

"Chris. Tell me. Are we done?"

"No. I'm here with you and flying to Singapore on Friday."

"Bullshit, bullshit, deflection. Denial. 'Oh, look, there's a squirrel,'" she says. "Four years with you, Chris. Bloody hell, you think I know only your name. I know you inside and out. I want more than smoke and mirrors. Are you going to reunite with your family now or not?"

"I told you from the beginning."

She freezes. For a second, she looks like she might explode.

"No—Ana, I don't know."

"You have never been indecisive before. I think you need to reexamine your feelings and your commitment to being truthful with me."

"You said no strings," he says.

"And I started it. And here we are. Secret romance."

"You never wanted your family to know. I honored that."

Her voice rises. "And I honored *your* family. I've never pressured you to give them up."

"I never lied to you."

"Don't start now. Do you love me?"

"I do."

Holy fuck. It comes straight out. Raw exposure of something he has never admitted to either of them. Ana's lips press tight.

"I love you, too," she says. "How fucked up is that? How inartful. So un-Taiwanese of me. What a betrayal to the course I set," and she turns away from him.

"Life happens as we make it happen. We're making this happen. But it's not so predictable."

"You can't have both. Not me and your wife and son. It's impossible."

"I would never—"

"You're right, you would never. I would never let you." She reins her emotions back. "The freedom we felt was never free. I should have known."

"We can't do this right now."

"And we can't pretend it's not happening." She laughs abruptly. "I don't want this to end."

"I don't, either."

Her gamma-ray gaze could strip him down to atoms. "I'm not the one who's taking time from business to pursue the other woman."

Anger flashes. "The 'other woman'?"

"I don't care. I knew what I was getting into. I don't see myself as a woman who'd be okay breaking up a family with a young child."

Her entire being vibrates with an unexpressed . . .

"But now? I don't care." She gets in the passenger seat and slams the door. Looks out the window.

Near four the next afternoon, Ana and Chris pick up the hard drives from Zhang at a mall parking lot off the 405, then drive back to the hotel in deathly silence. Well-traveled streets. Stores that were here forever, some mom-and-pop groceries—all gone. Used to be LA was fresh, nothing had rotted and decayed during the Depression and World War II building pause, like cities in the Midwest and East Coast. Here, everything was new and clean. Full of hope for the future. Now, it's all cheap construction that won't last twenty years.

Chris swings the Alfa to a stop inside the hotel's porte cochere entrance and reaches for the ignition. Ana puts a hand on his arm.

"No," she says.

His hand rests on the key. "What do you mean?"

"Leave it running."

She's right there, so present, focused, aware. In tune with him but right now looking into herself for a decision. And he sees that she intuitively knows everything.

"Ana. Tell me."

"Take care of everything you need to take care of," she says. "And whatever the other thing is that I can't put a name to that is snaking around inside of you. Take care of that, too. I'm going to Singapore.

"Go meet with Charlene. We were so smart. We were supposed to be only business. And the romance was . . . transitory, extra. It is so buggered. Our future is rolled together, and I want you. I'm not trying to convince you of anything. But I expect to know what our life together will be. Or won't. I need to know what you're going to do." She's cold, honest, and won't be manipulative.

The engine gutters. He watches her in the sunlight, momentarily blank.

She's his if he wants. She's not going to interfere in his decision about Charlene and Dominick.

"I gotta sort myself out," he says.

Her shoulders shrug, as if to say, Yes.

"Take care, love." She climbs out and strides into the hotel.

Five p.m., going off duty, Hanna swings his car into the boxing gym lot. He wants to warm up skipping rope, then hit the speed bag. Sweat out impurities and distractions in the gym's old body smells and stained walls. Focus.

A block away, there's a hillside. On top is a derelict two-story house built nearly a century ago when this hilltop was a rural idyll from the small city along the Los Angeles River. Windows and doors gone now. It's an empty skull. Its cracking stucco is covered edge to edge with Maravilla and Big Hazard tagging. In the shadow on the downhill side among tall pampas grass stands Chris Shiherlis.

He watches Hanna go into the gym. He has a perfect line of sight down into the gym's parking lot cut into the hillside. There's no windage to worry about. The hillside blocks that. With a flash suppressor/silencer, the shot will be invisible, nearly inaudible. A giant's fist will punch from nowhere. The round, traveling four times faster than sound, will take down Vincent Hanna before he hears it. Then Chris will hop on the 101 to the 110 South to the 105 West to the Bradley International Terminal at LAX and fly the hell out of Dodge.

Hanna's regular pattern. That's what he was looking for. Wednesdays and Fridays after work, he hits the boxing gym. Chris will be there.

Right now he crosses and gets into the Alfa.

83

The Alfa drives like a black shark. The interstate is empty once he clears Los Angeles and heads across the desert toward the Nevada border.

After an hour, the sharp focus of his intent softens enough to ask himself, Is this conviction? An imperative about the man who killed his brother from a different mother? Is this impulsiveness in an excellent and perverse masquerade?

At night, the glow of Las Vegas is visible from twenty miles out, a neutron blast from an empty bowl of desert. Sizzling, writhing, calling. Tonight, Chris rolls past the turnoff for the Strip. Feels distant from it. He's aiming for somewhere else.

The address Nate gave him is in a new neighborhood northwest of town. It's midevening when he exits I-15 and dives into a development with neat streets and playgrounds. When he turns off his headlights, he can see the stars overhead. The mountains, toothy and black, are a blockade along the horizon. Above them, salting the heartless sky, constellations dazzle.

He slows and turns onto a winding street. His hands are tight on the wheel, tighter now that he's going fifteen miles an hour than when he was razoring up the fast lane on the freeway.

It's a two-story house with palm trees, ponderosa pines, and white oleander outside. Spanish tile roof. Packed in among similar houses— the American dream, desert edition. The lights are on. The blinds are up. This is a calm suburban neighborhood. Nobody here has hidden themselves from prying eyes.

And he sees. It's a different world they live in. Families all along the street. Baseball field around the corner. Kids on bikes.

He parks across the street and turns off the engine. The big front windows give a clear view into the living room. He sits a moment. He did not alert them. Didn't call. Just came.

He rolls his neck and breathes, rehearsing what he's going to say when he rings the bell.

He is still gripping the wheel when he sees Charlene.

She walks into the living room from the kitchen, talking at someone over her shoulder. His breath snags.

In old jeans and a sleeveless white blouse, casual and perfect, her walk is the same. Like a lioness, relaxed, ruling. Her sandy curls are loose and long. Even from across the street, from the darkened interior of the car, he can see how her face glows. She is at home. It surrounds her, serves her, suits her.

Right there.

She drops onto the couch and tucks one foot under, the same athletic ease, her face animated. Something makes her laugh. She stretches an arm across the back of the sofa.

Dominick runs in, agile, balanced. A boy. A little boy. Strong, active, perfect, beautiful. His son. The human being he and the woman across the street created from themselves.

His heart is hammering in his ears.

Dominick jumps up and down in front of Charlene, fingers spread like starfish, leaning forward, talking to her. Excited, his face alight. She tilts her head, that quirky mannerism that reveals a youthful side Chris knows she never got to enjoy. She laughs.

He exhales.

He puts his hand on the door handle.

A man walks into the living room. Tall, with a construction worker's build, fit but not overmuscled, and a corporate haircut, late thirties. He wears a polo shirt and jeans, horn-rimmed glasses. He's a legit citizen.

Charlene says something to him, casually, ease on her face, and picks up the television remote. She flicks the TV on as the boyfriend sits beside her on the couch. He pats the cushion, and Dominick climbs up beside him with a book in his hand.

Rage flares, blue hot. *The guy is holding something of* mine, Chris thinks. *I can walk across that street in eleven seconds and . . .*

The boy leans close to the man and holds the book out.

It's a totally ordinary slice-of-life moment. Chris knows it, knows how rare that is, how rare in his own life it has ever been. How sparkling and precious it felt when *he* was the one with Dominick on his lap and Charlene beside him.

Across the street, the rapport among the three in the living room is apparent. A wave sweeps through Chris, tidal, overwhelming. To get out of the car. To pull Dominick into his arms, smell that sweet little-kid smell. To touch Charlene.

And it's obvious their world is complete. *Their* world. Charlene and Dominick's. And theirs, perhaps, is not his world anymore.

The wave, an undertow, drags his hand to open the car door. *Right there.* Across the street. Across a chasm. He has come so far. For them. Hasn't he?

He takes his hand off the door handle. Before he can think twice, he starts the engine and pulls away. The darkness feels like a tunnel. An abyss. It runs up through the gears. Accelerates. It feels like his heart rips from his chest. He drives away.

84

Batam, Indonesia, crowds the top of a small island in the Malacca Strait. It's a city of a million people, and it's a grungy counterpoint to gleaming Singapore, visible ten miles across the water, but the wild east side is where anything goes. Ana rides in the back of the Mercedes, heading for the meetings she set up overnight, hoping Chris is not going to restart his family. That he's rolling the dice with her.

The trip necessitates meeting with ethnic Chinese Indonesians and Singaporeans, but not in strict Singaporean territory. The car jounces on the rough road. The equatorial air is thick, the greenery grasping. There are probably three thousand ships anchored in this four-and-a-half-mile-wide piece of oceanic real estate at any one time. Piracy is a rite of passage for teenage males in Batam, when testosterone levels start to rocket. Staring at the bright lights of wealthy Singapore across the strait—*let's go get some*. Usually they prey on coastal freighters or palm oil tankers, as opposed to thirty-five-knot Maersk container vessels or LNG tankers. Ana watches families eating late meals in the stilt houses near the water's edge linked with fragile walkways. On the other side of the road are the family shops, crowded with kids and painted turquoise, pink, and blue.

The point is, if you're moving anything by sea from anywhere in the Asian Pacific across to the Indian Ocean and the whole of Arabia, you go through the Malacca Strait, and its tightest point is Singapore. The Arabs, Indians, Malays, and Chinese did it a thousand years ago, following the trade winds. Trade winds blow east six months of the year and west the other six, filling sails, pushing the trade each way. This is where they got their name. After the Suez Canal, destinations included Europe.

Opposite Singapore is Batam. If it goes well, Batam will be where Ana sets up the next outpost of Mercury Partners International.

Live here? No. Live in Singapore, a forty-minute ferry ride away.

Along with all manner of technicians, programmers, banking, communications—everything they need.

She powers up the phone. Call Chris? *No.* Not yet. Instead, she calls her father.

Felix answers. "Sister."

"Brother." She's used to saying it robotically, compartmentalizing her emotions. Shutting away everything that Felix is. "How is your son?"

"Fat. He looks like Reynalda. I want one that looks like me."

Revulsion tightens Ana's throat. The insinuation makes her queasy. The things Felix does and wants that she has rejected, which she has never told her parents, never ever told Chris.

"And business?" She half expects him to mention the Mercury deal, but he doesn't.

He lets out a sigh. "Paolo is twisted about something. But what's new?"

"What is he twisted about?"

"Who knows? Kittens in the security office, something."

"Put Fù Qīn on."

"He's busy." Felix turns away, covers the receiver, talks to somebody else. Laughs. Dismisses her, even though she's calling on an encrypted phone from half a world away.

She expects this treatment by now, but acid anger and hopelessness still churn in her gut. And something else. A sense of disquiet. Some ripple on the surface of a lake.

"Is Father busy with this thing that has Paolo twisted?"

"No, Madre de Dios, he's in meetings." His voice turns sly. "Though I like the way you keep saying *twisted*."

"Bloody hell. Grow up." She hears him laughing as she hangs up.

The Mercedes bounces along. *Fuck you, Felix.* The ripple on the lake seems snakelike.

Chris has intuitions, flashes of insight. She's the methodical one. She gets her regular cell phone from her handbag. She calls Singapore Airlines.

"I need to change my reservation. Yes. Singapore–Los Angeles."

85

Hanna is pumped on espresso when he rolls into MCU at nine a.m. He's just come from the assistant district attorney's office. The prosecutor has the evidence he nearly lost, from the container hijacking case. They're squared. Off his back. He's buzzing.

"Drucker, Rausch," he says. "Where are we on Otis Wardell? Whaddaya got?"

Standing at his desk, Drucker ends a phone call. "John Smolenski is a false identity. Fake Social Security number, fake birth date. No arrests, no record of him obtaining employment in California. Doesn't own property in his name in LA County. No business licenses, leases, court filings."

"He's playing shell corporation three-card monte with the motels," Hanna says.

"Twelve-year fugitive flight? He sure as shit got good at doing something else."

"The robbery victim?" Hanna says. "Connections, common denominators?"

Rausch spins on her desk chair. "Yeah. Helena Nguyen Benedek. The common denominator between her and Wardell is trafficked girls. I talked to Vice. She may have season tickets to the opera, but she human traffics Vietnamese girls and turns them out to massage parlors and a regular old-school brothel in Montebello."

"Then he and his crew were not there only to rob her," Hanna says.

Casals approaches with a cup of coffee. "Expect them to lay off the jewelry, all the same."

Hanna tosses his keys on his desk and picks up his messages. A uniform passes through, delivering mail and files. She hands Hanna the daily brief, a summary of tips, developments in active cases, wants, warrants, and urgent matters from around the LAPD.

He leafs through it, glances at Casals. "Fences?"

"On it."

Hanna runs his finger down the page, speed-reading. He skims past something. Stops. Goes back. His blood starts racing.

A short paragraph about a citizen reporting the sighting of a wanted murderer. Then the name, circled and highlighted, makes the room go ice cold and muted: Otis Wardell. *Ms. Vasquez states that Wardell killed her mother and uncle twelve years ago in Yuma, Arizona.*

Hanna shouts for Drucker and Casals. The report is from a detective at Hollywood Station. Hanna sees her name on one of his message slips. He grabs the phone.

"Yeah, Detective Macy," he says. "Captain Vincent Hanna, RHD. This report. The citizen who says she saw a man named Wardell. Name and address."

Drucker's and Casals's heads turn. Hanna scrawls on a sheet of notepaper.

"Thanks." He tears the note off. Drucker grabs the car keys.

The apartment building is gray with red and white trim. Bottlebrush trees line the front steps. Approaching the third-floor apartment, Hanna and Drucker hear pop music. The door opens promptly when Drucker knocks.

"Gabriela Vasquez?" he says.

She's petite, with an athletic build and quick dark eyes. At the sight of their badges, she turns to wood, instinctively raising her defensive shields at the sight of two cops, Hanna thinks.

"We're here about the report you filed," he says. "We're here about Otis Wardell."

She steps back. "Come in."

In the kitchen, Gabriela offers Hanna and Drucker seats at the thrift-shop table. Posters hang on the walls: TRAVEL FIJI. Textbooks cover the coffee table. Calculus worksheets. A paperback of *Jurassic Park.*

"I didn't think anybody would come so fast," she says.

Drucker hands her Wardell's 1988 mug shot. "Is this the man you saw at the Backstretch?"

The photo seems to strike her like a snakebite. Her breathing quickens. Her eyes dilate. Then she cools, like a sheet of glass, a one-way mirror.

"That's him."

Drucker leans forward. He's broad-shouldered and can look dangerous—is dangerous, to the wrong people. But he softens his voice and speaks warmly. "Tell me everything you can. Take your time. This man, who was he with?"

Gabriela spends a moment gathering herself. Then she talks.

Hanna listens. *Guarded.* That's the word that comes to him as her story unwinds.

Drucker's tone is gentle. "You told Detective Macy that Wardell killed your uncle and—"

"He killed my mother."

Agonized. Determined, Hanna thinks. "At the diner, did Wardell talk about where he was staying? Where he works? Where he was going after he ate?"

"He took hold of my arm. To order a beer." Her lips draw back.

"Do you think you're in danger? Did he recognize you?"

"I don't know. He didn't act like it. He barely paid attention to me."

Hanna nods. "This ranch, the house where you saw him when you were little."

"Where I hid." Her voice diminishes.

"Yuma. Whose house was it?"

"I don't know. My mom had a temp job, cleaning."

She picks at a thumbnail. Hanna reads pain. Nerves. Strength. And elision.

"Did you meet the owners?" he asks. Gabriela shakes her head. "Did the house seem like it belonged to wealthy people?"

"It was old and plain."

She goes on. How Wardell and his men drove up. Tío Tomás, killed. Her mother arriving. Wardell beating her, burning her with a cigarette. "Then he dragged my mom out to a car and took her away. I never saw . . ." Her voice catches. "Never saw her alive again."

Hanna feels a goad, scents something just out of reach. "Did she know Wardell?"

"No." She blinks and draws herself up. "No. You think she *knew* him? She was terrified." She shakes her head, indignation rising, then raises a hand. *Stop.* "I know she didn't. Wardell kept asking questions, like . . . who was she, what was she doing at the house."

"What else?"

She flushes. "I don't know. I was eight. I remember her talking to *me* in code, telling me to run without tipping him off."

"What do you think he wanted?" Hanna says.

"He was after some people. He wanted money. Like he was hunting them. He was looking for both. He took my mom to barter her, then killed her. That's what I think."

Hanna's already checked: Gabriela's clean. No record. Legit. A City College student. Her uncle wasn't. Tomás Vasquez came from six generations of border rats. Low-level smugglers. In his twenties and thirties he smuggled refrigerators and TVs into Mexico, small loads of pot on the way back. And there's no record of Elisa Vasquez's death in Arizona. If she died there, it was never officially recorded.

Gabriela's eyes are hot. Hanna slows down.

"Four men were killed in a gunfight on the border outside Yuma in 1988. We think they were Wardell's crew."

A new emotion sweeps through Gabriela's eyes. Surprise? Confusion? She looks like she wants to shout, *Good.*

"He came with about four men," she says.

"He was after some*body.* He tortured your mom for information. Who did he want?"

Her face turns stony. She shakes her head.

"Where was your dad?" Hanna asks softly.

"He died when I was little, a car wreck." Emotion stripes her face. "My mom and I . . ."

Abruptly, she stands. She goes to her room and returns holding a snapshot that's been folded in half.

"That's my mama."

In the photo, Elisa Vasquez is young, fit, and vivacious, her gaze tough but wry. She and Gabriela look alike. Hanna reaches for the photo. After a brief hesitation, she hands it to him.

Then he unfolds it.

And Vincent Hanna about falls through the floor. Opposite Gabriela's mother is Neil McCauley.

Gabriela's eyes brim. "That was her man."

Hanna reveals nothing. The photo moves through the air as it's handed to Drucker. Drucker reads Hanna and regards it with a prepared flattened affect.

Hanna's pulse is tripping. "Tell me about this guy. Who was he?"

"That was Neil."

"How'd he and your mom get together?"

"I don't know."

"What was he like?"

"Why do you want to know?"

The moment expands, tenuous, depthless. Hanna's heart feels hollow and hungry, and full of whirling sparks.

"Our paths crossed," he says. "I knew him a little."

Gabriela holds his eye, as if this is a test, as if she has taken a chance, and Hanna has earned something from her by his answer.

"Do you remember much about him? You said you were eight?"

"That's right."

"What was he like?"

"What I remember most is he treated me like we were the same kind of age. He listened. He paid attention, you know. He didn't talk down to me," she says. "He drove me to school sometimes. Once he brought me a present, a little statue of the Water Tower, from Chicago."

"He was from Chicago?" Hanna keeps his tone level.

"No, I think it was a business trip."

In the photo, Neil McCauley is younger, lean, and rough and looks vividly present. His arm circles Elisa Vasquez's waist. He seems utterly at ease, bright with affection but alert. Always alert. And at home.

"He was a quiet guy. He didn't talk to talk. But he talked to me," Gabriela says. "I always knew he was there. He could be very serious. Whenever we walked someplace, he always took my hand."

"Like you were a family."

She nods.

Drucker glances at Hanna and speaks softly. "Was Neil at the house that day?"

Gabriela's gaze goes distant. "No. I only saw him later. After. He was broken up. He's the one who told me about my mom . . ." She lowers her head, then looks up, eyes glistening. "They were happy." Her voice breaks. "*We* were happy. Things were good for a while. Then it was over."

Drucker stands. "Thank you," he tells Gabriela. "This is hard, we know that, and the other thing you should know is that this is a major piece of help."

"Anything you remember, and anything you need, you call this number," Hanna tells her.

He and Drucker give her their cards.

"This is my personal cell, okay?"

She nods.

"You get scared, you can't sleep, you just wanna talk, I don't care about the time, you call me. You understand?"

She nods.

"No. Tell me you will do that."

His insistence is a little unusual, she thinks. "I'll call."

Hanna nods. "Now you and your roommate, you have to leave. Pack up. You recognized him, maybe he recognizes you. I can try to get you into a women's shelter, but that's not like instant coffee. Is there someplace you can go?"

"I'm not going to any shelter. Some dormitory with strangers? Indefinitely?" She steps back.

"You're not safe here. Especially from this guy."

"My family here can take care of me better than anyone. My cousin Manny, he's Tina's brother, we'll head to his house."

Manny's a mechanic, a take-no-shit guy, who lives on a hill in Boyle Heights with five dogs and a hazy view of downtown.

"A patrol car's outside. It will wait here until you go. They'll escort you to Manny's. Then I'm going to have rotating units outside his house keeping an eye on you."

She hears concern behind Hanna's words.

"All right. And what are you going to do?"

"What are we going to do?" Hanna scans her face. "We are going to find him. And we are going to take him down."

They shake her hand and walk down the hall, filling it, black suits, like ravens, swooping away. She shuts the door and leans her forehead against the wood.

Four men shot dead on a border back road. It churns her heart in a way she can't decipher. Neil must have done that, trying to save her mother. But Otis Wardell got away.

Take him down.

Do it, Captain.

You knew Neil, whatever that means because he was in the Life with my mom. But you connected, somehow. Bring Wardell down. Do it for Tío. For my mother. For me.

Do it.

As they drive back to Robbery-Homicide, Hanna radios Casals. "Wardell came into the Backstretch on Century Boulevard with two men. One sleazoid white guy Gabriela's seen there before. One young Black guy with a 'Time's Up' tattoo."

"Bring her in to look at mug shots?" Casals says.

"No. Bring them to her," he says. "But that's not the headline."

He and Drucker are buzzing, stunned.

"The girl's mother, who Wardell killed? She was living with Neil McCauley," Hanna tells Casals.

Silence on the other end. Hanna gives him a moment to take it in.

Wardell's crew was shot into Swiss steak down near Mexicali, shortly after he fled Chicago. Wardell tortured and killed Tomás Vasquez and abducted Elisa Vasquez, trying to find out what?

"From what Gabriela told us, Wardell may have been looking to rip off another crew's score. Maybe on the Mexican side." He looks at Drucker. "Big money on the border is cartel money. Wardell wouldn't have the balls, but Neil would."

Did Wardell try to rip off McCauley?

"If he did, he barked up the wrong tree," Casals says to Hanna.

Hanna's jacked with a rush that things are turning his way. He's closing. Investigation: 90 percent data sorting. A grind. 10 percent rush.

"The shootout . . ." he says to Casals.

"I'll contact the Yuma County Sheriff and Arizona state troopers."

"And I want an x-ray of the Vasquez family. Their background, connections, any ties to McCauley's crew, going back to cave paintings." He ends the call.

We were happy. Hanna feels like he was hit by a two-by-four. McCauley, Elisa, and Gabriela. Neil was Gabriela's father for a while, the exact opposite of what McCauley told him. *No attachments.* So maybe this was before that. Maybe this was why that.

Elisa killed. He didn't stay connected to his stepdaughter. *"When it rains, you get wet." When you get next to Neil, you get dead.*

Drucker looks over from the wheel. "Are you going to tell Gabriela we killed Neil McCauley?"

We? Me. This girl is anchored, striving, surviving in life despite everything. Tell her?

"No fucking way."

Hanna imagines eight-year-old Gabriela. Remembers Jessica Matzukas. Sees the ruined body of Pham Thanh Thuy in a shallow grave.

Women, children. Innocents. Sisters. Lovers. People. How many has he encountered? How many are looking for him to end Wardell? They all sit at his table. They look at him . . .

Third Street rolls out toward downtown. He punches the number into his cell. Lauren picks up on the fourth ring.

"How'd it go?" Hanna says. "The art show."

"Killed it." She sounds surprised, like joy snuck up when she thought it couldn't. "Somebody called my style 'abstract emo,' which, no, but it got people nodding their heads."

Hanna savors the buoyancy in her voice. It won't last, but every time she feels a moment like this, it keeps her here. Then a version of being "here" with positivity builds in memory that maybe pulls her away from the downhill ride.

"I'm not surprised. I knew it," he says. "I'm gonna commission you to paint one for me. I'll hang it in the RHD lobby and make all these jerks who work for me"—he winks at Drucker—"salute when they walk by."

"Hi, Lauren," Drucker shouts out. "Congratulations."

Hanna ends the call. Sunlight pierces the windshield. He feels a fog scatter and focus clear, adrenalized. His nerve endings ring.

86

Chris Shiherlis pulls the dusty Alfa into the Beverly Hilton porte co- chere, tired, gritty-eyed. At sea. He flips the keys to the parking valet and palms him a twenty. It's late. He has been driving for more than a day through the desert. In the lobby he passes the bar, ignoring the music and laughter, the flower arrangement, and the cut-glass vibe. He stops at the front desk, waiting to talk to the concierge.

Upstairs in the suite, Ana is on her burner flip phone on the bedroom balcony.

In his office in his walled estate overlooking the Paraná River, Da- vid Liu is on his hardline talking to his daughter while sipping yerba maté from a silver straw in a traditional leather gourd. He puts it down to deal with her irritation about Walter Huang and Felix. Felix is only taking his place, he reassures her in Taiwanese. That's all.

"It's natural he'll make mistakes. You're there to show him the way."

Ana's about to react to the condescension when—

David Liu's office door slams open. "Who the hell are you?" she hears in angry Spanish. And David Liu throws himself sideways, rip- ping open a desk drawer for a handgun he won't reach in time, as

two men in balaclavas open up with nine-millimeters at the moving
target . . .

Ana hears gunshots muffled by the phone and she's shouting, "*Bà!*"

The doors of the elevator open with a whisper. Chris exits and walks
by banana-leaf wallpaper from the elevator lobby. He rounds the
corner, approaching the door to their suite. He cards it and walks
through, nearly tripping over Ana's suitcase. He's surprised. She's
back early.

Then he hears screaming from the bedroom: "*Paolo! Talk to me!*"

Chris flies through the suite. City lights obscure the view outside
the bedroom balcony windows. He finds Ana next to the bed, frozen,
phone in hand. A cold blade moves through Chris's back.

"What happened?!"

She points at her open laptop on the bed while shouting into the
phone, "*Paolo!*"

Chris lifts it.

"I was on with Paolo! The call cut out." She tries again, pacing frantically, furious, crying.

A video is paused. Chris hits Play, scrolls the video in reverse. It's
footage from the Lius' home security video system. The high, wide-
angle lens shows David at his desk on the phone, speaking in Taiwanese.

"We were talking. He was talking to *me*," Ana says.

In the video David Liu's office door flies open. David shouts, moves
to the right. Chris's stomach tightens.

Gunfire. Pounding. Two gunmen. Two nine-millimeters, an H&K
and a Beretta. David's blown back against the wall, falls behind his
desk; blood blooms on his white shirt.

Chris pauses the video. The two shooters are frozen in the doorway. Balaclavas. He hits Play. They back out. He switches to the grid
displaying the twelve security cameras. There they are, exiting the
main house. He hits that camera. They're taking off their masks. Paraguayans or Arabs. Sudden shots echo. Gunman One's slammed to

the ground. The other spins, firing. He's gunned down. Shouts erupt, chaos. Someone moves in and shoots the first gunman in the head.

He pauses. Their eyes rivet together. "Where's your dad?"

"Paolo got him to the ER. He's critical. Unconscious. That's all I know." Ana claws at her hair. "When the gunfire came . . . I heard everything. Then nothing. So, I accessed the security cams."

He pulls out his phone. "Felix?"

"He's okay, Paolo was telling me, then Paolo's call dropped." She shakes her head, wild. "Paolo was hit, too, but he had on a vest."

Chris rewinds the video and watches again. Her shock fills the room. At the same time, he feels himself move inward, dropping into that automatic groove: the even heartbeat, his senses amped, attention pinpointing on the most important parts of the immediate present.

And now he picks up the anomaly. It's from an exterior camera, the drip of something else. It's the gunmen's attitude. Leaving the property, they seem unafraid. Their body language says it. They're moving across the grass to the gate to the road, as if to hail a taxi. Suddenly, they're cut down. The new shooters' faces are unseen. But they approach. When Chris hits Pause, it's because he sees a sinewy arm. It's partially exposed in a rear shot, carrying a twelve-gauge. What he sees is part of a tattoo: a two-headed snake. Motorbike Man.

"Chen security."

She spears him with her look. "Felix came back from the casino with Claudio Chen. Invited him in to party."

"Just Claudio?" Chris says.

"And his entourage. They were at the pool house together. When my father and I . . ."

Chris feels a sudden emptiness. Fucking Felix. If he thought Claudio Chen had anointed him part of his posse, he would have welcomed his whole asshole squad. The Chens gained access to the family compound.

"Chen's security killed both shooters," Chris says.

She thinks of her father. The error inevitably involving Felix. A broken sob. "Oh, Bà."

Chris takes her in his arms.

"I have to get home," she says.

"No." Chris thinks. "Where's the sat phone?"

He grabs it and heads to the balcony. This time, Paolo answers. His voice is thready.

"*Irmão*," Chris says. Brother.

"I should have seen it. Knew something was brewing. I parked Mr. Liu's Montero and was walking back. But I . . ."

Chris speaks low and straight. "The shooters."

"Never seen them. They say Lebanese or Syrian. The Barakats? That makes no sense."

"No, it doesn't."

Paolo coughs. "And now they are dead. That is convenient."

"Too convenient. And you're not sloppy. I know that. Felix?"

Paolo doesn't answer. The silence stretches.

"Okay," Chris says. "*Tchau, cara*."

He looks at the skyscrapers across the street. Inside, Ana makes another call. Speaks Mandarin. When Chris goes back in, she hangs up.

"I just called Uncle Walter in Alhambra. Let him know. The conversation. Something was . . . not right." She freezes, and her eyes widen.

She rushes to her laptop on the coffee table. There's a spasm of anguish as she sees her father on the screen. Then she minimizes the window, pushes through, and opens a private browser window. Types. Stops. Frozen.

"I'm locked out." She's hitting the keys again. "I can't access anything. The Mercury network. Nothing. Shit." Tries another route. "My passwords are disabled." Looks up with shocked surprise. Holding her breath, she pulls up online banking. Access Denied. She settles back on her knees. "I'm cut off. Totally."

The Lius have been hijacked by the Chens, unwittingly aided by the number one son. Now they're moving rapidly to sideline Ana.

Her phone rings. She gives Chris a look. "Felix."

She takes a second to set herself and answers. "*Hermano*."

She listens to her brother. She begins to pace. As they talk her anger seems to cool, then to distill and harden. When she hangs up, she stands silently.

She throws the phone against the wall.

Her tone is scathing. "He says we are fortunate that Claudio's security was on-site when the attack came. The Barakats have taken out Fù Qīn. Now Felix must protect the rest of our family, and there is only one way to defend the Liu organization." She looks ready to rip someone's skin off. "Ally with the Chens. Taiwanese with Taiwanese."

"Bullshit," Chris says.

Her face is dark. "My father may die. Felix just sold us out."

She picks up the phone, dusts it off, and pitches it straight back at the wall.

Chris goes to the sideboard and pours her a vodka. She hesitates, then tosses it back. Drops onto the couch. Small. Stripped to the bone.

She looks at him.

"Do nothing. Call nobody," he says. "Don't move. Wait for their move."

"Why?"

"Because you don't know enough yet."

She looks up, her gaze briefly flaring, before subsiding back into shock.

Her computer chimes. Her webcam has turned on. She checks the screen, and her eyes go stony.

Chris reenters from the bathroom. She gestures Chris to stand back, out of frame. She puts on headphones and answers a video call in Spanish.

Across the room, Chris paces.

If she was angry before, Ana is now a barely contained typhoon. After a minute, she says, "*Comprendo.*" Then she looks up. "Chris just arrived. He will understand, too."

She gestures him to the screen, pulls off the headphones, and puts the call on speaker. Chris rounds the table and sees Claudio Chen, bright-eyed, crackling, and looking both satiated and hungry. He's wearing a Stetson tipped back on his head, a western snap-button shirt, and a two-carat diamond drop earring. He barely seems to register Chris.

"He was saying he's praying for my father. With the threat to the Liu family and to preserve it, the deal for the guidance system software should go forward. It is imperative to retain posture and continue cash flow so competitors don't perceive vulnerability and try to move in. The deal will go forward through Uncle Walter," she explains to Chris, looking unlike herself. "And the Chens will help by administering it."

"Really?" Chris says.

"Felix has agreed." Her tone is near absolute zero.

Claudio's gaze glides over Ana like a knife. "Yes, he has. And you do understand? In our temporary merger, as in all mergers and as of now, to properly administrate we cut back duplicate functions. Two become one. So, for now, corporately I will lead. Ana will work for me. Yes?" He answers his own question. "Good. We must have clear, top-down authority. Competitors will look to see if there is weakness in Taiwanese enterprises, Liu and Chen. They must see there is not. The wagons are circled. Everybody understands. Correct?"

After a cold moment, she nods.

Claudio ends the call.

She turns to look at Chris. Outrage, pain, incredulity.

"Let him have it," Chris says.

"Have what?"

"The deal. Forget the deal."

She looks at him. She's taken aback by his assertiveness. What is he talking about?

"Leap right to this place. In this moment," he says. "We do our own deal. 'Cause that's where this is at and what it's about right now. All of it."

"I have to get home." She sneers at the webcam. "Claudio, 'Stay and complete the transaction.' Fuck him. My father . . ."

"Ana, it's a setup."

"It's family."

"I don't know from family. I do know from rip-offs and setups. You go home now, you are over and out. Do not go. You'll do what? Become your father's caretaker, if he survives. They will push you into the background. They want you docile. So they can rip off your ideas and move you to the bleachers. And you? You won't tolerate it. And then anything can happen to you. Who's there to protect you? Felix? And the worst is you'll have lost the timing to make the moves because that timing is right now."

She shuts her eyes. He stands close.

"I can't clear my head."

"This is what is." He absolutely knows this is true. "The Barakat hit team is bullshit. The Chens probably hired two freelance Arab shooters, then whacked them on the way out. A double takeout so they can't talk. Claudio put it at the door of the Barakats." He holds her eye. "Assume Claudio told Felix to put Gögel on the Liu family payroll. He's Chen's dog. And assume he's working with your uncle and cousins here, too. And I'm sure there's a team watching us. This is not improvised. It's planned."

She turns aside.

"Ana?"

"Felix. What part of my fucking gene pool becomes a Felix? Explain that to me. How is he my brother? Right in my face and I still can't process it. I told you once, he thought I should make a match with Claudio. He actually wanted to pimp me to Claudio. And now this with my father?"

"Pimp you?"

"He jokes, but it's no joke. I'm sure he fantasizes some bent threesome. Or whatever's in his febrile mind." She brushes that away with ridicule.

But it's a silver needle drilling into Chris's head.

"Fuck *me* for thinking this would go any other way." She laughs at herself.

Blood running buzzes in his ears. *Shut that down.*

"Chris . . . ?"

"Money," he says. "Felix *locked* you out of everything, including the Mercury bank accounts, right? You're hosed. And we're getting another room but keeping this."

"Chris!" She flares.

"What?" he says, ratcheting down.

"I'm not rolling over for them, Claudio, any of them." She breathes. "What's the deal?"

That's more like it.

"Call Raymond Zhang. Get us into the aerospace warehouse."

"Why?"

"'Cause, that's where the heart of the deal lives. In those crates."

"I'm locked out. I have no control over those units."

"We will manufacture our own, but we need to get in there for a template."

"Great. How?"

"I have money. You have money stashed. Hedged. Baby, we will set up our own outfit."

She doesn't move, looks frozen.

He looks her in the eye. "You're ambushed? We assault the ambush. Where's the manufacturing facility? Technicians, programmers, transportation, banking, security, all of that? I will show you." He raises the envelope he got from Kelso. "This is a door. We are goin' to try to go through it. If we do, on the other side, we will intercept these motherfuckers."

She picks up her phone. So does he.

"Kelso," he says.

The nighttime view from the aerial house is sparkling. On the streets below, a gunshot echoes. City Terrace gangbangers. Normal night sounds. The woman, Dalilah, lets Chris and Ana in and leads them to a windowless secure room. Gray egg-carton acoustic tile covers the walls. An electric hum runs in the background. Kelso sits before a bank of monitors.

He speaks over his shoulder. "You know what you want?"

"You vet me with your contacts?"

He spins. "Yeah."

He raises an eyebrow at Ana. Chris introduces them and they nod, acknowledging and silently assessing each other.

Chris indicates Kelso's screens. "Let's go to the store."

"My consulting fee is ten K per hour."

"Done."

Kelso turns to one of the computers arrayed before him. He loads a browser Chris has never seen.

"What's that?"

"Freenet. It got released a couple months ago. It accesses sites that aren't indexed on the open web. Aren't findable via commercial search engines—Yahoo!, Google."

"How?" Chris asks.

"It's a peer-to-peer platform. Decentralized network. It's a distributed system for storing and retrieving stuff. Strong anonymity protection. It's dark net versus open net, call it the 'dark web,' whatever. And our search is bouncing through onion routers in seventeen different countries and my core message is in my own Agency-level encryption. We are anonymous ghosts."

Ana watches. Kelso accesses a site and slides the cursor across an image of the Taj Mahal. He stops on a specific pixel and clicks. The image dissolves, and they plunge into a deeper level of the internet.

"Steganography?" Chris says.

"Like knocking on the door of a digital speakeasy. You have to know what part of the picture to go to, exactly where to go, and how to gain entry."

A portal comes up. An image, like the Grim Reaper in an empty shroud, appears.

"The hardware store," Chris says.

"More than that. What do you need?"

"I need to replicate guidance systems."

"Big ask."

"I'm not asking you to be Raytheon, man. We need electrical engineers, programmers, skilled fabricators, and a source for chips. Can I get that?"

"Of course."

"Show me."

"*Let your fingers do the walking.* Like the old Yellow Pages, but underground Yellow Pages. You can get anything. Your next question is how do you know they're reliable, since there's not a Better Business Bureau operating in the dark web? Here's the answer: I know how."

"So, I can move money electronically from somewhere to somewhere, untraceable. Right?"

"Right."

"And a manufacturing facility. And they don't know who we are. After we're gone, we were never there. Comms? Transpo? Security?"

Kelso says, "Where you going with this?"

Chris knows where. He sees it in a flash. It's as if he's suddenly elevated ten feet in the air, looking down on a structural blueprint with all its interconnecting components and the workflow among them.

Can he score only the components of Ana's brick-and-mortar Liu family business he needs without their physical infrastructure?

Done right, he and Ana can duplicate all she's been locked out of. And they can run it with NSA-grade Kelso encryption.

"I want to build an entire transnational organized operation out of component parts and services we buy off the dark web."

"Evanescent infrastructure," Kelso says.

"If that's what I mean, that's what I want."

Ana's watching Chris carefully.

"I'm going to need a medium-sized plane to move goods from A to B from people I don't want to know and they never know me, so long as it doesn't fall out of the sky. Agency-grade comms. If I hire PMCs, they gotta be ex-SAS, Israeli paratroopers, Spetsnaz, like that. Not retirement home rent-a-cops. You vetted me—you vet them, too."

"Of course. These nav guidance systems," Kelso asks. "What do you need? Hardware? Software?"

Ana opens her laptop. "Hardware. We have the software. Here. Specs and codes."

Kelso scrolls. Looks up at her sharply. "This antenna reads both GPS and GLONASS?"

"That's right. And without degradation. Seamless switching between the two systems."

The look they exchange deepens. Kelso's expression turns respectful and excited.

"Wow." He turns to Chris. "A guidance system that can access both US and Russian navigation satellites. That's ninja-level shit, man. You can put a missile through a window anywhere in the world. You can escape jamming attempts, circumvent urban canyon effects . . ."

"Minimize disruption from solar flares, improve accuracy at high latitudes," Ana adds.

"Like I told you, I have an exceptional partner," Chris says. He steps up to Kelso, holds his gaze, seeing the thing in its entirety. He nods. "Okay, man. Let's go."

Kelso runs his fingers through his beard. "Where do you want to build this?"

"Electronic Neverland," he says.

"Banking location." Kelso turns to his keyboard. "Caymans, Liechtenstein, or Manila?"

Chris scans the new world in front of him. He sees Ana, roused out of where she was, watching everything Kelso does. She nods. She's with it all the way.

"I'll be right back," he says.

He walks out the sliding glass door and crosses the grass of Kelso's hilltop to the farthest point at the edge of the hillside. Below and beyond him is downtown LA seen from the east. Thousands of head- and taillights flow through the aorta of the 5 Freeway, the 101 and the 10 splitting off north of downtown. It holds him for a moment in ennui.

He stands there, singular under the palm and night sky. Behind him, adjacent to Kelso's modernist house, is the thick aluminum post supporting a forest of microwave transmitters and cellular repeaters. They tower like a monument to signal traffic. The city seems to murmur to him. Its lights agitate, constantly in motion. But it can't see him, can't hear him.

He has the number memorized. He enters it. His heart thunders.

"Hello."

One word, that voice, that pull, that beauty, that creator, the one who made him a son. *My sun and stars.*

"Baby," he says.

Charlene takes a breath. "Chris?"

He closes his eyes. He takes the money he's accumulated and kicks back to Barbados or somewhere with Charlene and Dominick. That's the rest of his life for a while.

Or his life is what he's living right now, sinister Paraguayan streets mixed with death and hot love—and is hot love too good to last? He's here on the cutting edge of whatever this is becoming. Who will he become? The roulette wheel turns. Place your bet or walk away. It's right now.

"Charlene," he says, and just saying her name twists him around. One more breath. "Go to Macau. Go with your guy. Go make a life. I will always love you and Dominick. I'll always be there, as long as I'm alive." His voice has a hairline crack. "Don't tell Dominick you talked to me. Go get what you're building now. That's what you want."

There's nothing else on her end for a long beat. "I don't need your permission."

Chris laughs.

"What's funny?"

"You never did, and you're tough as hell, as usual."

"Here's tough. What about Dominick? He has a right to his father."

"What I'm trying to say is, here's the big picture. You stood by me. But you know the life you want. I know what that is. You should have that. I have to trust my son to you. This is fucked up. This is a knife stuck in my heart.

"But it's the life I been dealt," he goes on. "And I'm living that life. You don't want any part of that. You shouldn't have to have the questions: 'Is he going to show up someday? Walk in the door? Become a problem?' And Dominick should not get screwed up by the same shit as I was. No father. Or some guy on the run who doesn't come home, and then he thinks there's something wrong with him because of that when there isn't. I don't want to pass that on, generation to generation. So go make your life with your guy that you want for you and him. You'll do a great job. That's what I mean. I'm trusting him to you. I know you will do right. That's why I called."

He hears her soft exhale. "I'll hate you for a while."

"I know."

He ends the call. He stands in the shadows, empty, hollow. Taking in the night. Traffic. Palms. The wash of city lights.

When Ana wants, she can blend into a wall. Little sister, barely seen, a smudge that interrupts men's views—she has a lifetime's practice. She walks through the aerospace warehouse, wearing an ID borrowed by Raymond Zhang from the locker of an off-duty night shift worker. The young woman looks vaguely like her. But she has a clipboard and a reflective vest. Chris has told her that nobody questions a person with a clipboard and a reflective vest with a label on it. Ever. She blends like she's a transparency.

Still, her heart is pinging. She has never done this.

Zhang clears her path, disabling the warehouse security cameras. "Ten minutes."

A muscle jumps in his cheek. She doesn't care if he has a stroke, as long as he waits until she is gone. She has paid him a hundred grand.

"Out," she says.

He goes.

She needs to switch only three guidance packages. One to serve as the template for their own batch. Two backups. Redundancy. A hedge.

Ducking under the yellow tape into the QC aisle, she boxes the swapped units, slaps on a shipping label, and carries them to shipping and receiving. Her legs are trembling.

The shipping clerk barely gives her a look. Still, she wants to run.

Then the UPS truck pulls up. Chris gets out wearing a brown driver's uniform. Her nerves calm.

She disappears out the front gate of the facility and sheds the ID and the vest, breathing, gulping air. Telling herself not to express anything, no emotion, to anyone.

At shipping, Chris runs a scanner over the delivery label and walks out with a salute. He drives away in the truck, which he stole from the street in front of an El Segundo apartment complex. Dumps it two miles away in a vacant lot.

At a FedEx store in Long Beach, he arranges to ship the guidance units.

The man at the counter types in the address. "Long way."

Chris gives him a face of wood. He takes the receipt and strolls out.

Batam, Indonesia. He hopes a long way is far enough.

87

The garbage truck is what keeps Gabriela from hearing the sound at first. She's just dashing into her apartment to grab her calc textbook.

At her cousin Manny's house, an LAPD patrol unit has been parked outside most of the time or cruising the block. This morning she walked out to get the newspaper, and some blond-haired cop sitting in the car said, *Hey, get back inside.* Her cheeks heated. Like he was her boss? In her mind, she saw her mom shaking her head. Back in the house, pissed off, she realized she was missing her calc textbook. She wasn't going to screw up her GPA. She got in her car and pulled out through the alley.

Gabriela grabs the book, then hurries to her bedroom to get some fresh clothes. She drops her backpack at the foot of her bed, changes into lug-soled black boots, and pulls on a jean jacket. Below, in the parking lot behind the building, the garbage truck's brakes hiss.

There's percussive clanging as trash cascades into the hopper, the chime of glass breaking.

Then the engine grinds, the truck pulls away, and she hears noise in the hall: clicking, scraping sounds. She steps from her bedroom and peers at the front door.

The knob is rattling.

She hears a metallic clack. Her breath catches. A pick is being inserted.

The lock flips and the knob turns. She pulls back into the bedroom and silently shuts the door. Putting her ear to the thin wood, she hears footsteps.

Papers rustle on the kitchen counter. A heavy step crosses the creaking linoleum.

The apartment phone is in the kitchen. She doesn't have a cell. They're on the third floor. She can't call the police, can't jump. She locks the bedroom door. Her heart thunders.

The footsteps move into the living room, then stalk to the bathroom. The shower curtain screeches on its rail as the intruder pulls it aside.

Wardell. It has to be Wardell.

Breathing. A cough. The door to Tina's room squeaks open. Footsteps circle and return to the hall. Pause. One door left. Hers.

It doesn't matter how he got her address, how he knows. It's him. He's here.

She backs away from the door.

Wardell shakes the knob. Puts his hand to the bedroom door. It's flimsy particleboard. He raises his knee and kicks. The wood splinters around the lock and the door flies open.

He enters. He sees nobody. The furniture is poor-girl shit. The bed is neatly made. He ducks and raises the bedspread to peer underneath. He turns to the closet. Flicks open his switchblade. Striding across the room, he throws the closet door open.

Clothes, shoes, a backpack. He rifles it, dumping crap out.

Fuck her. No girl.

Outside the window, a decorative wooden railing runs horizontally along the exterior of the building, painted dark red against the gray stucco. It's two inches wide.

Gabriela stands on it, toes clinging to the wood, pressed tight to the wall of the apartment building three stories up. The wind blows her hair around her shoulders.

She heard her bedroom door smash open. Now, inside, she hears reckless noise. Her legs are shaking. She flattens her face against the wall and tries to claw her fingertips into the stucco.

The noise in her bedroom intensifies, then stops. The door crashes against the wall, like somebody's kicked it again. Distantly, she hears the front door slam open.

Then silence.

She waits, clinging precariously to the side of the building, fearful that the pounding of her heart might launch her backward into empty air. She listens and counts to sixty, knowing that Wardell is tricky. Slick. Sneaky. He could be lurking inside.

Finally, delicately, she pushes the bedroom window open and clambers back in.

Clothes have been pitched out of the closet. Dresser drawers are tossed. She shudders, queasy.

Did he follow her from the Backstretch? Did another server give up her address? *Mierda.*

She balls her fists, shaking. Then, outside, she hears voices crossing the parking lot. Two men. She steals to the window.

Wardell strides away. With him is the Time's Up tattoo guy who was at the diner. Wardell's neck is red. He gestures as he talks, slashing motions.

"Bitch thinks she can hide." He shakes his head. "I'm the all-seeing eye. I left her a sign."

Gabriela stares at her bedroom wall. A pair of her panties has been pinned above her headboard, stabbed through the crotch with a butcher knife. Beside it, words are scrawled in her scarlet lipstick.

BYE WHORE.

88

In their new hotel room, Ana paces on an encrypted sat phone call. "The exchange must be at the same time. I board the ship. I inspect the cargo. Only then."

Beyond the window, a glazed blue afternoon sky soars above the mountains. The television plays in the background to cover her conversation. She shuts her eyes as the translator on the other end speaks to a military functionary in an office seven thousand miles away. She can hear a desk fan rattling and desultory traffic outside an open window.

The functionary says, "'*Uwafiq*."

Her Arabic is basic, but she recognizes the word *agree*.

"The chartered plane carrying the guidance systems will already be airborne," she continues. "When I am satisfied with the crude, I will signal the flight to land at al-Watiya."

The functionary listens to the translation and again accepts her terms. She clenches a fist.

"You must guarantee that the flight will have advance landing clearance. Approval from Tripoli. We do not want it shot down."

She is negotiating the first segment of a three-way deal. Libya is cash poor because of embargoes but oil rich, so Libya will pay for the guidance systems with crude. Two hundred of their units for five hundred thousand barrels of Es Sider–grade oil and an aging tanker to carry it. Ana will then sell that oil and ship to somebody for money. At today's Brent Crude spot price, that could be an $11 million deal. If the spot price swings, up or down, who knows.

She listens to the translator and nods. "Excellent."

She ends the call, exhales a slow, thrilled breath, and turns to Chris. "It's on."

His glance is coolly satisfied.

They're set. Packed. Both anxiety and possibility are in front of them.

Their first transaction is the sale of the stolen guidance packages. Those packages will be in secure storage in a guarded warehouse in Jakarta. The buyers: found through an encrypted link via the underground web. The transpo: a Marshall Islands–registered container ship, from Indonesia to Dar es Salaam to South African mercenaries fighting for Denis Sassou-Nguesso's Cobra militia seizing power in the Congo with backing from France and Angola. The other container transshipped in the sea-lanes near Sri Lanka and heading to Basra. End user certificates, bought and paid for by Kelso. Their online bank accounts, newly created.

Their second transaction is the big test. It's the sale of systems they're manufacturing themselves—the sale she has just finalized with the Libyans. The software is being installed by a programmer and a team of technicians from Singapore in an idle factory outside Batam city. Singapore, with its plentiful supply of everything, a short ferry ride away.

LA is finished. Tonight Ana will fly out of Burbank to San Francisco, then to Jakarta. Chris will fly from LAX through Singapore and meet her. He is pumped.

He's making it happen. They've stayed here, going through the routine motions, to avoid raising suspicion. To all appearances, their deal taken over by the Chens is proceeding. Claudio is pleased. So too then is his acolyte, Felix.

And that blows Ana's mind. She and Chris know goddamn well that the Chens were behind the hit on her father. Felix buys Claudio's version of events because he wants to. His self-deception is blinding, narcissistic, almost lovesick—and profitable. Which is despairing and bitter to Ana. It infuriates Chris.

Ana turns to her laptop. "I need five minutes. We're almost done."

Chris steps to the window. The sheers are closed. This room is one floor below and two spots over from their suite. As he scans the street, a television news anchor says, "The LAPD has identified the young woman buried in a shallow grave near I-210 as sixteen-year-old Pham Thanh Thuy.

"According to Captain Vincent Hanna of the Robbery-Homicide Division, Pham, who was shot to death, had recently arrived from Vietnam."

Chris stills.

His vision zooms out. *Done? Am I done? No.*

"No suspect has been arrested. Detectives continue the investigation . . ."

Ana would think he's crazy.

He stands watching the street, his back to her. He hears her typing.

She's breathless. "It happened." She turns toward him, astonished.

He looks. She's talking about a video—security footage captured outside a warehouse in Ciudad del Este.

"Our kill code in the guidance packages the Chens took over. Their client must have powered up a surface-to-air missile for initial startup and testing."

The warehouse explodes. Overpressure, shock wave, flame. Walls turn to toothpicks.

"Beautiful." Chris nods. "Let's go."

She scans the screen. Hesitates.

"What's wrong?" he asks.

"Nothing."

"What are you worried about? I know that look."

"Felix?" she says.

"What about him?"

She catches Chris's arm. "Whatever we do—whatever *you* do—look out for him. Okay? He's my brother."

"He's a piece of shit."

"I know he's a piece of shit. And at the same time he's my brother. Blood is blood. Promise you'll look out for him."

"Okay." Chris nods.

"I mean it. Promise."

"I promise." He looks at her meaningfully. "Okay?"

She slams her laptop shut. Her phone rings. "Zhang."

As she answers and puts the call on speaker, Chris again checks the window.

Zhang sounds fevered. "What has happened? What have you done?" He speaks over the sound of a racing car engine.

Noise erupts from the phone. The metallic *bam* of a collision. Zhang shouts, "No—"

There's yelling. Then the flat pop of semiautomatic gunfire.

Chris looks out at Santa Monica Boulevard for a sign. Nothing yet.

The call goes dead.

"*Fuck.*" Ana's eyes pin Chris's. "They know."

"They'll be here in a heartbeat. Take the back stairs," he says. "Radio silence. Hit the road, I'll back you up."

She straightens, but looks off-balance. "We're going to have to deal with them."

"That's right." He grabs her hand. "I'll make sure you aren't followed. Ana. We go. We build. Then we deal with them."

Standing in the old world, she's uncertain. She inhales.

Then she squeezes his hand. "Okay. I'm with you."

She runs out. When he gets downstairs, he sees Ana pull away onto Wilshire in a bland Ford compact, sunglasses on, her hair swept under a cap. On Santa Monica, a Mercedes pulls to the curb—Gögel. Ana U-turns at the light and heads west. Chris takes the Alfa and follows at a distance, checking his mirrors. He watches Ana swing onto the 405, clear of tails.

He heads south.

The storage unit is behind an abandoned supermarket in Torrance. He doesn't have a key, but he has bolt cutters. The lock snaps with a clang and he rolls the metal door up.

An armory is inside.

He and Neil paid for this locker five years in advance. Chris turns on the light and pulls the door down.

Handguns, two Benelli semiauto twelve-gauges and a cut-down Remington 870. CAR-15s, an H&K G36 assault rifle with a collapsible stock, a TAC-338 sniper rifle. Suppressors. Blades. Cleaning kits. Stacks of ammunition.

89

When Hanna pulls out of the hospital parking lot, the sky is streaked red with sunset. He drives toward the boxing gym, impatient, running mental calculations. Helena Benedek, the procurer of immigrant girls, including Pham Thanh Thuy, is on life support. They'll get nothing on Wardell from her. But the jewelry Wardell stole from her will fund an out for him. The motels generate his debased wealth but will take too long to unload. The stones, though, will net him ready cash. Fast. Figure twenty-four hours before he's gone, tops.

The motels, Wardell's latter-day money . . . Hanna still doesn't know what went down on the border, but McCauley was involved, his lover died, and a little girl was orphaned. He pictures young Gabriela Vasquez, her child's hand secure in Neil's. Then plunged into the void.

Yet Gabriela has her feet on the ground, working, going to school, living life. She's haunted, though. Scarred. Hanna saw that. And if Wardell recognized her, when she recognized him, he won't want her dropping a dime on him. She'll be hunted.

He radios dispatch to connect him to his unit.

Rausch answers. "I'm walking Wardell's photo to businesses up and down Century. So far nobody's recognized him, or at least admitted to it. Casals is at the Backstretch."

"Keep going." Palm trees flash past, sun-etched. He keys the radio again. "Casals?"

He slows and turns in at the gym. Sam answers. "I got a lead, Vincent. On Wardell's fence."

On the hillside above the gym, waiting in the Toyota Supra he boosted outside a multiplex movie theater, Chris watches the Crown Vic pull in and stop, but not in a slot. Chris kills the engine and picks up the TAC-338 sniper rifle, with a flash suppressor attached, off the floor in the back. He climbs out of the Supra and takes up his concealed firing position. A focus comes over him, frosty. He's waiting for Hanna to pull into a slot, get out of the Crown Vic, grab his gear bag, and walk across the parking lot.

Hanna to Casals, "Give it to me."

"The regular at the diner who fits Gabriela's description. He's Wayne Fabbiano. They know him. He runs a TV and computer store in Pico-Union. Fabbiano's Electronics. A laundry list of priors, receiving stolen goods."

Hanna spins the wheel and guns the car back onto the street.

Hanna screeches away.

"Shit." Chris races back to the car and pulls out to follow him.

The display window at Fabbiano's Electronics is crammed with cheap televisions and Nintendo sets. A buzzer rings when Hanna steps through the door into a smoky yellow light.

The place is cramped: narrow aisles, shelves towering overhead. At the back, the proprietor sits behind a messy counter. His yellow guayabera blouses over a bowling ball stomach. Beside him, a circular fan nudges the nicotine-tinged air around the store.

Drucker stays by the door. Hanna ambles toward the proprietor, eyeing the aisles from behind his shades. No other customers. Beyond the counter, a closed door leads to the back of the store. No noise, no music or TV, no indication anybody is back there, though that's a preliminary assessment.

He walks up to the desk, badge out. "Wayne Fabbiano. I'm Detective Vincent Hanna. That's my partner, Jamal Drucker. We are looking for a guy you know. His name is Otis Lloyd Wardell."

Behind Hanna the sun blares through the windows, backlighting him. Fabbiano squints up. His combover is dyed pancake-syrup brown. Just for Fences brand, maybe.

Fabbiano purses his lips, shakes his head. "Haven't made his acquaintance."

"'Acquaintance'? Like in a dating service?" Hanna moves closer, as if he has x-ray vision and can see his thoughts. "What the fuck is that on your head? Your spirit animal?"

Fabbiano folds his hands across his belly. "Joker, huh? Look, Detective, I don't know no Wardell. So, unless you got a warrant or some such or want to buy yourself a Walkman? Great. Otherwise . . ." and he indicates the door.

At the door, hearing this, Drucker flips the OPEN sign to CLOSED and moves a display to block the view.

Hanna listens closely to the ambient sounds of the store. The whir of the fan. The silence otherwise. Nobody moving around in the storeroom behind Fabbiano. No customers.

He grabs Fabbiano by the front of his shirt, jerks him across the counter onto the floor, and puts his foot on his neck.

Fabbiano throws his hands up, clawing. "Son of a bitch."

"Otis Lloyd Wardell," Hanna says, soft and flat.

Fabbiano squirms, slapping, trying to remove Hanna's foot.

"Fuck you, jagoff," he hacks.

"Fuck me?" Hanna's hand grabs Fabbiano's face like a vise, forcing the eye contact Fabbiano wants to avoid. His weight bears down on his foot, choking the man.

"Mounted stones! You just fenced them. Otis Wardell. Look in my eyes, you prick. I will crush your larynx. That's in your throat. You'll be speaking out of a Walkman with a mic to your neck."

Fabbiano goes limp and raises his hands in surrender. "Don't know where he lives. Have a phone number, it's a service he uses."

"His car. His crew. C'mon!"

"A Firebird," Fabbiano says. "Black. New."

"License plate."

"Dunno."

"No good. Wrong answer." Hanna steps down on his throat.

Fabbiano is close to choking. "Wait, wait! The car, I installed a Lo-Jack. It has LoJack!"

"Name it's registered under?"

"Bhalla," Fabbiano gasps. "Kultar Bhalla."

Hanna yanks him up. "You warn Wardell or Bhalla or any of Wardell's other motel clerks, you're going down. You clear? And I don't mean to the LA County lockup."

Fabbiano nods.

Hanna marches him down a hall and locks him in a storeroom. Fabbiano pounds his fist on the door.

Hanna leads Drucker out of the store. "He'll keep overnight."

In the reddening sunshine, they stride toward their cars. Hanna says, "Activate the LoJack tracking signal on the Firebird."

Drucker nods, pensive. "The company's gonna need either a warrant or a foolproof stolen vehicle report that'll stand up with the state computer system."

They look at each other.

And he adds, "Vincent, did you just see that guy steal a black Firebird?"

"I sure did. You better go write up a report."

A block away, Chris idles in a no-parking zone, hand on the gearshift. Hanna fires up the Crown Vic and squeals a U-turn. Chris follows.

Driving toward Parker Center, heart high in his chest, Hanna radios Casals. Gets no response.

"Casals, copy?"

With a burst of static, Casals replies. "Copy. The man Gabriela described who was with Wardell at the Backstretch, young Black guy with ink, just turned the corner. He's walking toward the diner."

Hanna's pulse jumps. "Keep him in sight." Heading for the diner, he puts the pedal down.

..

Drucker is sitting in his unmarked car, typing on the ruggedized laptop docked in front of the dash, when Hanna phones.

"Vincent."

Revving engine on Hanna's end. "Guy from Wardell's crew just walked into the Backstretch."

"On my way."

"Got the LoJack running?"

"Need another fifteen, twenty minutes." He hits keys, rapid-fire, then starts the car.

At the wheel of the Supra, Chris hangs back in thick traffic on Century Boulevard near the Forum. The palms have a ruddy tinge in the dying light. Pedestrians stream by in the crosswalk. Buses pass in front of him. He eyes the streets. Hanna is a block ahead.

Chris taps his fingers on the wheel. Focused. Like he's holding his breath while a ball spins around the roulette wheel, waiting for it to drop.

Then Hanna swings around a corner and parks. It's an inconspicuous location. He jumps out and hurries along Century.

What's he doing? Surveillance? A takedown?

If it's an arrest, when it goes down Hanna will be 100 percent focused on that.

Which will present an opportunity.

Chris pulls past the street where Hanna parked, swings around the block, and pulls to the curb. He keeps eyes on Hanna's car and waits.

At the apartment, Gabriela shoves clothes in her gym bag and calls Tina, warning her not to come home, go straight to Manny's after work. Her keys are shaking in her hand as she hustles for the door. In the ransacked kitchen, the phone rings.

The number on the display is the Backstretch. She picks up.

"Miss Vasquez? Detective Wells, calling for Sergeant Drucker."

His voice is curt. She brings herself up short. "Yes?"

"We need you to identify an accomplice of Otis Wardell. Can you get down here?"

"The Backstretch?"

"We received a tip. The accomplice is meeting someone here. Park on the street in the next block, opposite McDonald's. An officer will come outside to meet you. We will keep you out of sight."

She checks her gut. Nods to herself. "I'm on my way."

The door slams as she runs out.

In a hallway at the Backstretch, Tick-Tock replaces the pay phone receiver. He pockets the card Wardell found on Gabriela's kitchen counter. SGT. JAMAL DRUCKER, ROBBERY-HOMICIDE DIVISION. He gets his cell phone and hits speed dial.

"She's coming."

90

Hanna hears the answering machine pick up as he parks the unmarked out of sight of the diner. His stomach tightens. He jogs along Century. When the tone arrives, he speaks urgently.

"Gabriela. It's Captain Hanna. We are closing on Wardell. If you hear this, wherever you are, stay there. Lock yourself in." He crosses an intersection. "I'll contact you again when it's safe for you to leave."

He ends the call. His heart is hammering again.

Gabriela grips the wheel as she drives to the Backstretch. There's a burnt-orange sky. Her chest is tight. Wardell's voice seeps through her head. She cannot rid herself of it. *Honey, you're home.*

Beneath it is another voice, tenuous yet ever steady. *Mariposa. Run.*

Not this time.

In her bedroom, she found a locket hanging on her headboard on a string. It was the locket she gave to her mother the Christmas before Elisa died. The photos inside, of her and Neil, were faded and wet with spit. She cleaned it up and is wearing it. *Not this time.*

On her way to the diner, she swung by Manny's place. She used his phone to call Robbery-Homicide. Hanna was out.

When she walked back to her car, Manny followed, frowning, uneasy.

You sure? he said.

Never more sure.

On the phone, she'd left Hanna a message. *Important,* she told the detective. *Get it to him. Wardell found my apartment. He knows it's me.* She'd kept her voice steady. *I'm on my way to meet Detective Wells and Sergeant Drucker at the Backstretch. I want to make sure you know.*

Manny watched as she squealed away from the curb. The gun she got from him is under her jacket, in the waistband of her jeans. A silver revolver, growing warm against her skin.

She wants protection. She wants an equalizer. Manny taught her to shoot at a range in Sylmar.

She wants to see Wardell taken down.

Sunset in her eyes, she drives toward the diner.

91

The alley up the block across from the Backstretch has fetid water trickling down its center. The dumpsters smell ripe. Wardell is parked in the shadows, slumped low in the Firebird, drumming his hands on the wheel.

Inside the diner, Tick-Tock is watching. He'll phone if the girl turns up via the back door. 'Cause she's slippery. Wardell checks the restaurant windows. The bus stop. The McDonald's.

And then he sees her in his rearview mirror.

Gabriela drives cautiously along Century, hyperalert. She doesn't have the skills her mom did but knows about spotting surveillance.

Nearing the Backstretch, she turns off and cuts parallels back and forth through the neighborhood. She glances down an alley. She swings back around to Century. Two blocks from the diner, on a side street, a Crown Vic is parked, whip antenna on the back.

Cop car. She pulls over near the McDonald's and hauls change from the cupholder to feed the meter. The sun is falling behind the buildings, shadows cooling. Her heart is banging like a snare drum.

Hanna is in a clothing store a block from the diner, shady side of the street, at the window, when RHD phones him.

"Vincent, you got a message from a Gabriela Vasquez. She said she's heading over to meet some RHD 'Detective Wells' at the Backstretch. There's no—"

"Goddamn it!"

Outside, an old Subaru eases down the street. Hanna catches sight of the driver in the sunset. It's her.

"Goddamn it." He hangs up.

Drucker is in a building across the street with a different angle on the diner, two uniforms with him. His laptop is open. SWAT has been alerted, but it will take time for them to gear up and deploy.

"Drucker," Hanna radios. "Gabriela just drove by me. Green Subaru, heading west."

"Copy," Drucker replies, his tone doubling for *shit*. "See her."

An alert arrives on his screen.

"Got the LoJack."

"Where is he?"

His blood goes cold. "A narrow cross street off Century. Looks like an alley. He's sitting still." He looks out the windows. "He's here, Vince. He's across the street from the diner."

He runs for the door. Across the street, Hanna does the same.

••

That Subaru—it's her. Comin' behind his back, treacherous chick. Wardell gets out of his car.

At the parking meter, Gabriela pours quarters into the machine, her gaze locked on the diner.

The hand comes around her neck from behind swiftly. Lips press to her ear.

"Shh. Hold still, or you'll die right fuckin' here."

The voice is hoarse. The man has a meaty presence. Tic Tac breath. The tip of a knife presses into her side. Traffic slides by mindlessly.

The gun Manny gave her is jammed in the back of her jeans. Her breathing quickens.

"Don't even think about it," Wardell says. "I'll slit you down to your pussy."

He digs the knife against her side, her kidney, the stiletto switch-blade aimed slightly up, the tip honed so sharp that she thinks it would slide halfway through her body before she knew she was dead. Without turning her head, she looks up the street. Does anyone see?

But this looks like a lover is holding her close. Nobody is going to intervene.

Wardell slides his free hand down her ribs and beneath her blouse and takes the revolver.

"Think you're sly, huh?"

She smells his cologne. His sweat. She is trying to keep from peeing herself. To think.

He nudges her up the sidewalk, his arm tight against her side, the knife.

She scans the sidewalk ahead. People walk. Cars pass. He's pinning her arms too tight to claw him in the eyes. Stomp on his foot, maybe. The knife presses harder. The tip pokes through her shirt, then her skin. Scream, jerk, kick him, he'll stab her.

Wardell moves her along. "That's it," he says. "Evening stroll. Just like that."

Then, a block away, she sees an intense dark-haired man in a black suit and a blue shirt, wearing shades, striding down the sidewalk toward her.

Hanna.

She keeps breathing. Wardell walks her straight ahead.

Across the street, paralleling Hanna, comes Drucker. Tall, his face iron, moving smoothly, like a large torpedo. Two uniformed cops behind him.

They're a hundred yards away, across a busy intersection. But they're coming. She lifts her chin, hoping Hanna will see her.

He stops at the corner, a red light with heavy traffic, waiting for a dump truck to pass. His head turns, searching. She stares as if she can connect to him telepathically.

He zeroes in on her and stills. Their eyes lock.

A bus stops in front of him, blocking the intersection.

Wardell yanks her sideways and pulls her down an alleyway.

He throws her against a black Firebird and pins her. "Sneakin' in like an alley cat." He whips electrical tape around her wrists, then wrestles her into the car and binds her hands to the door handle. He fires up the engine and pulls onto the street in front of the diner.

He glares at her. "Stop it with that *poor little me* look." There's something unnerving, inhuman, in his gaze. Hunger. "Enjoy your last-chance power drive."

She looks at her bound hands.

"Nope. Get that door open, I'll drag you along the asphalt at sixty miles an hour."

He cruises past the diner. Inside, a guy stands, throws cash down, and rushes for the door. Gabriela recognizes him. Wardell's flunky, Time's Up.

"You smile to my face, then dime me. Yeah? Who's laughing now?"

She sees part of a shotgun on the floor in the back seat. He's planning to take her somewhere isolated and kill her, just like her mother. He's eager. She has never seen a smile look so enraged.

••

Drucker gets across the intersection first. He's eighty yards from the diner when he realizes that Gabriela is no longer on the sidewalk.

Into his radio he says, "Vincent, lost sight of her."

Back at the intersection, Hanna dodges around the bus, sticks his hand out, and zigzags through cross traffic. Brakes squeal. Horns honk. His vision burns. Fifteen seconds earlier, he locked eyes with Gabriela. Wardell was on her like a pelt, forcing her to walk. Now they're gone.

He hears a throaty engine.

Across the street, Drucker turns to watch a car emerge from an alley and drive east on Century. It's moving faster with every fraction of a second.

"Black Firebird," Drucker shouts. "Gabriela is in the passenger seat."

The car tears past Hanna, up the boulevard. The sun flashes in the driver's eyes. Flat, black, so dark they don't seem to reflect any light. As Hanna spins and runs after it, the Firebird passes vehicles on the wrong side, skates through a yellow light, and veers back into traffic.

On the run, Drucker shouts instructions into the radio, all units, the description of the Firebird. Hanna's car is parked in the next block. He whistles.

"With me."

Drucker dashes across Century. They sprint for the unmarked as the Firebird screams east in traffic.

The Supra idles on the side street, rumbling. On Century, traffic rolls and pedestrians pass in the crosswalk. Hand on the gearshift, Chris eyes the road, analyzing ingress, egress. Where to set up, when to ambush Hanna. How to get out. *Improvise*, he tells himself.

He checks the flash suppressor on the CAR-15. It will be even more critical to be stealthy. Then his watch. He has an hour before check-in closes for his flight out.

A screech of tires snaps his head around. On Century, a black Fire-bird squeals out of an alley and races east.

Behind it, Hanna runs along the sidewalk. He jumps in the Crown Vic. A Black detective joins him.

Chris spins the wheel and pauses. It looks like a pursuit is about to go down. That'll bring more cops. He can't hang on Hanna's tail.

He pulls a tight turn and roars around a corner to parallel Hanna and the Firebird a block from Century. At the corner, he sees the Fire-bird race through an intersection, then flashing lights—the Crown Vic.

Wherever the guy's going, Hanna's following. Chris can vector in.

Wardell blasts along Century Boulevard, his whole being buzzing. *Wasps in his heart. Worms in his brain,* Gabriela thinks. She presses away from him as he busts the speed limit, skating through red lights. She tries to maneuver her wrists in the bindings, but the tape is painfully tight. The sun has fallen low, flashing red along the horizon as they sweep past car washes and gyms and drive-throughs, towering blue sky beyond them, the ceiling of the world, blind to her.

She tries to reach the passenger window switch.

Wardell cuts her a confident glance. She can squirm and struggle all she wants.

He swerves across a lane and back, narrowly avoiding a pickup. She closes her eyes, pulls it together, then turns and looks over her shoulder.

"Nobody's coming, bitch." He exhales a grunt. "You, smiling in the diner, then running to the fucking LAPD. Yeah? Go on, piss yourself. See how you like it. You got the grit to put up with that kinda shit? Fucking assholes in the South State projects, laughin' their ass off. Till I wasn't that guy anymore. Humiliation's *good* for you. Think you could stand up? Uh-uh." He mutters out his window, "Fuck them."

They turn south onto Crenshaw, and Gabriela's heart drops. Traf-fic is thin. Pine trees picket past. The 105 Freeway is a couple miles ahead. If he gets on a freeway, she's done. He can break free from the city, from people, their eyes, lose them in the mountains, the desert. He is in full flow, confident that he is unstoppable.

She has to do something. Anything.

Wardell swings wide to the left and slews past slower traffic.

Two blocks away, Chris speeds south, paralleling the Crown Vic with its flashing lights bouncing off buildings, chasing the Firebird. They're accelerating. Maybe heading for the 105 Freeway.

"C'mon, c'mon." He needs to get ahead. He floors the Supra.

Hanna, with Drucker in the passenger seat loading shells in a shotgun, bombs down Crenshaw, dash light spinning. He flips the headlights to flash left-right-left in sequence. On the radio, Drucker booms commands, calls in the air unit, more ground units. Armed and dangerous. Female hostage, age twenty. Gabriela Vasquez.

Hearing her name, Hanna's vision seems to scope. He hits the siren, veers into opposing traffic, and jams his foot to the floor.

Wardell slaloms through traffic, smooth, wired. Signs are lit up, dusk descending. They pass soul food restaurants and taquerias. He swings into the bus lane, along the curb, and guns it across an intersection against the light.

Accelerating again, he checks Gabriela out as if she's a flank steak. His face sours. He flicks at her mother's locket, which Gabriela has added to the chain beside her religious medallion.

"Wearing that next to the Virgin Mary? Your mama was a devious bitch. Thought she could con me? That bitch got learned. I got the whore mother; now I got the daughter, too."

Horns. He slurs past swerving vehicles. Shoots a glance at her, her large eyes.

"Think they're gonna rescue you? 'Cause they're the badass police?

They think they're gonna fuck me up? I'll show you *bad,* what I'm gonna do to you and then them. And then *real* bad. 'Cause I don't give a fuck what happens to me."

Windshields gleam under the streetlights. Everything is bright and fractured. The sky overhead, deep blue.

He looks in the rearview mirror. "Fuck is he?"

Who's he looking for?

Gabriela realizes he's looking for the guy she saw as they drove past the Backstretch, who stood up and ran out. Backup. Wardell had backup when he killed Tío. He's bringing it to watch him kill her.

Then, in Wardell's eyes, looking for Tick-Tock, she sees instead a flickering reflection. Blue and red. Flashing lights.

Gabriela's heart leaps. A police car is coming, fast, against traffic, far back but gaining. Tears sting her eyes. Wardell exhales through his teeth.

Foot heavy on the gas, he swings wide left, lining up for a right-hand turn at speed. But as he cuts the wheel, a delivery truck pulls into the lane next to him, cutting him off. He jerks the wheel back, misses the turn, and keeps going, the engine now racing.

The police lights in the mirror pulse, holding Gabriela's eyes. The 105 is ahead. But at the intersection with the on-ramp, the light is red, and traffic is heavily backed up. She thinks, *Come on.*

But Wardell doesn't slow. He throws the wheel left, bounces over the median island, and accelerates.

Gabriela sees the signs. WRONG WAY.

He powers onto the freeway off-ramp, skidding onto the dirt shoulder, heading east—onto the westbound 105. Gabriela's skin shrinks. She presses herself back in her seat.

Wardell slams into a wooden road sign, shattering it. Dust flies. Cars on the off-ramp swerve wildly out of his way. Finding room on the hard shoulder, he checks the mirrors. Then he pulls out a cell phone and speed-dials.

"Cops are on me. I need to switch cars. Meet me at Broadway and Manchester."

Gabriela tries to keep breathing. They rocket along the shoulder, freeway traffic racing in the opposite direction mere inches from her. Ahead is the massive four-level interchange with the 110.

Wardell plans to lose the cops on this wrong-way run, then swing off at the next exit and dump this car. He might get through the interchange and make it to a surface street. That'll be far enough. Tick-Tock will be waiting.

And he said, *I need to switch cars.* Not *we.* She sees the shotgun in the back seat.

Horns blare. Oncoming traffic swerves. They curve up onto an elevated transition ramp, careering through a long left-hand turn.

Booming south on a broad surface street, Chris spots the Crown Vic flashing by. Hanna is in pursuit.

Chris scans the street ahead. Then his eye is taken by the soaring transition ramp and the guy driving against traffic through the huge interchange. What the fuck is going on? He has to be aiming to get off the freeway ASAP. There's an exit ramp four blocks east. He heads for that.

Chris knows he'll beat both cars there. When Hanna drives down that ramp, Chris will be waiting.

As the concrete ribbons of the interchange curve past, in the side mirror Gabriela sees fiery embers of sunset. Ahead, the gleaming spires of downtown. Headlights. Wardell pours on more speed. Maybe sixty-five, maybe seventy miles an hour. Bad crazy.

"You are worse than your whore mother. Dime me to the PD. PD ain't getting me." He presses his thumb against her temple and shoves her head toward the window. "*Pow.*"

The flashing lights of the police car have fallen back, receding to pinpoints.

An oncoming station wagon swerves as they pass it, sideswipes another car, and smashes the concrete guardrail. Wardell glares at the road ahead, coming down the transition ramp to the 110 the wrong way. Now, with the full width of the 110 to her right, Gabriela sees an on-ramp ahead. If Wardell makes that into an exit, in the next few hundred yards he'll be into the maze of surface streets. Tick-Tock will be waiting. That will be it.

No surrender.

Swift as she can, Gabriela draws up both knees, twists, and kicks Wardell in the head.

His skull cracks against the driver's-side window. She kicks him again and his head fractures the glass. He reaches—flails—a hand from the wheel, swiping at her leg, and she nails him a third time, in the jaw. His head hits the metal doorframe.

He loses control. She feels it, the wheels sliding as he reels, the tires squealing, the acceleration sending them into an out-of-balance, uncontrolled turn.

The Firebird veers across two lanes of traffic. She sees a pickup and an SUV, headlights. A tanker truck behind them. She balls herself into a fetal position.

The crash is loud and brutal. The Firebird takes a hit, spins, smashes into the oncoming pickup. The hood crumples. Steam blows, the horn blows, the windshield shatters and falls in.

They smash to a stop. Wardell slumps over the wheel, blood streaming down his face.

Gabriela's field of vision shrieks white. Adrenaline pounds through her. The windshield presses on her, a crackling sheet of pebbled glass. Horns blare. Screams. She shoulders out from under the fallen glass. Traffic is snarled, cars smashed, some turned on their sides. Ten? Twenty?

Wardell slumps, motionless. She tears at the electrical tape with her teeth and jerks her hands back and forth. Then Wardell inhales raggedly, rousing. His arm moves. She wriggles one wrist loose, then the other. He blinks. A slow eye turns to her. She shoves the door open. He raises his head. He grabs for her and snags her locket, jerking her head back.

She snaps the thin chain and scrambles out. Bruised. *Jesus*, her leg. Wardell rises and lunges after her, an anaconda. She runs.

92

Foot down, Chris aims toward the Firebird. His headlights eat the asphalt. The on-ramp to the southbound 110 is dead ahead. He's less than a block away when the Firebird's headlights round a bend on the freeway, coming straight at him on an intercept course.

To his right, on the freeway, he sees the black car scream around the turn against traffic. Flashing lights follow behind it. Chris punches it. Then yards before reaching the ramp, the Firebird veers out of control.

Chris downshifts. "Fucking hell."

The crash is concussive, a chain reaction high-velocity pileup. Louder than shit.

Chris pulls over, jumps out, and runs toward the freeway, SIG jammed behind his back and H&K rifle held along his leg with the stock collapsed, camouflaged against his black jeans in the rapidly falling dark. Ready to take down Hanna from a distance.

When he runs up the on-ramp, he sees chaos. Headlights, taillights, steam blowing from shattered radiators. Glass everywhere. The Firebird is in the middle of the roadway, wedged amid four cars it T-boned. It's crumpled like old aluminum foil.

In the distance, the spinning lights of Hanna's Crown Vic flash from the 105 transition ramp. Chris's pulse drums. Hanna's coming. The scene is chaos. Chaos provides cover. Chris pans the mayhem. He has to hurry if he's going to do this. Set up. Scope this out.

Two hundred yards ahead, a man crawls from the wrecked Firebird. Covered in blood. Staggering this way.

Shotgun in his hand. He raises it, points, and fires. A fleeing young woman, injured, puts a pickup between them. Sheet metal takes the blast.

She's a girl, maybe twenty, limping forward toward Chris, dodging between cars. Strands of black electrical tape hang from her wrists.

She has escaped from the guy with the shotgun, is all Chris knows.

Now she's caught in the glare of headlights as she flings a look behind her. Chris sees her eyes, her resolve. And the butterfly birth-mark on her neck.

For a second, he nearly stops. She resembles Elisa.

He starts moving toward her. He knows her. Now he runs.

It's Gabriela Vasquez.

She dodges between the gaps of stopped cars.

The man behind her, closer, fires the twelve-gauge. He misses. Now he moves to his left for an open angle on her.

She stumbles this way through the pileup. The driver's gun barks again. She flinches but keeps coming. Chris, in a full sprint toward her, raises the H&K. His agitated front sight slides across the driver. He fires a three-shot burst anyway, to give her cover.

Gabriela sees him, stutters to a stop. Is he shooting at her, too?

He yells to her, "C'mon! Gabi!" And he gestures toward himself.

She digs in and runs, eyes brilliant. Stopped now, he aims past her and opens up with three-round bursts. The driver's disappeared in the melee.

Hanna's scraping the Crown Vic along the cement wall on the shoulder of the 105, the wrong way, pursuing Wardell. Halfway to the crashed Firebird, wrecked cars block his way. The drivers are out. He screeches to a halt. The 110 is littered with smashed vehicles. Smoke is rising.

"Goddamn it," Drucker says.

Hanna and Drucker leap out, Remington shotgun in Drucker's hands, and run. Massive pileups. Cars, trucks. Drucker hears screams, smells gasoline.

He hears gunshots.

He sees the smashed Firebird—empty. He advances through the cracked light. Smoke swirls. Distantly, Drucker catches sight of a bloody man with a shotgun in his hand. Running recklessly at a tangent, Wardell swings up and fires.

Return fire booms from farther up the freeway, sharp, echoing—a high-powered rifle. Who the hell is that?

People in wrecked cars duck, crying, or fling themselves from their vehicles to the ground. Wardell pumps the action and fires again. A UPS driver caught in the crossfire is knocked flat.

The rifle cracks a three-shot burst.

Running, skin prickling with adrenaline, Drucker peers through the chaos. A hundred fifty yards away, barely visible in half-shattered headlights, a man stands by Gabriela, laying down covering fire, as they move away.

Wild. People scatter, yelling. Two are hit by shotgun pellets.

Drucker shouts to get down. He runs through the swirling smoke of a white Ford pickup with flames boiling from under the hood, slammed into the back of an eighteen-wheeler. The driver is unconscious. The doors are crushed. Raising an arm to block the fire's stinging heat, Drucker puts a foot against the frame of the truck and yanks the driver's door partway open.

He sees Hanna racing forward toward Wardell on the other side of the freeway.

Drucker yells, hauls one more time on the crumpled door. It opens wide enough to pull the driver out. The man thuds to the pavement.

Drucker leaves him and runs on, raising his weapon. Between smashed cars, Wardell is glimpsed veering in and out of sight. Drucker aims. His background's clear. When Wardell flashes into view again, he fires.

The shot hits an empty vehicle. Wardell turns and sees him.

And off to his left he sees Hanna running along the retaining wall with his Benelli shotgun.

93

Hanna runs. Wardell's eyes locked on him. Then he turned and ran— toward Gabriela. Hanna loses him behind black smoke from a Toyota pickup, its gardening tools sprayed across the freeway, and a Volvo wagon, both on fire now.

The River Styx is kicking in.

Traffic is jammed to a stop. Headlights glare. Wardell dodges between cars. Hanna pounds after him, breathing hard.

..

The interchange is clotting to a stop: pileup blocking the southbound, rubberneckers slowing on the northbound. Hanna and Wardell are now out of sight. In the wrecked and backed-up traffic, the dark, the headlights turn everyone to silhouette. Drucker can no longer see Gabriela.

He works his way toward the center barrier, looking for a path through the wreckage and smoke. To his right, from behind him, a car on the northbound side scrapes along the center median. It's a black Dodge Viper, pouring it on, heedless of traffic.

The man at the wheel, a young Black guy, sees Drucker and slows, headlights blazing. A window comes down.

Drucker spins behind an empty truck, putting the engine block between himself and the car. Gunshots hit the pickup.

Wardell's crew. His backup. Armed and mobile.

Drucker spins out from behind the truck, shotgun to his shoulder, and fires at the car. Two shots, three. Double-aught buckshot. The Viper goes loose, hits the median barrier, and stops.

Drucker approaches, Remington centered on the motionless driver. Gone, hit in the head.

He turns and races after Hanna.

Gabriela's lost her sense of direction in the chaos. Cars are at crazy angles. More gunshots. Drivers' doors suddenly open, blocking her. Looking over her shoulder, fearing Wardell is right behind her . . .

Suddenly she's grabbed from the front. She screams. Tears away.

"Gabriela?"

She hears the voice. Turns. His eyes are familiar. It's Neil's friend from many years ago. A rifle's slung from his shoulder, aimed down the freeway.

"Come on. Come on."

Chris runs with his arm around Gabriela's waist. She is dazed but determined, running, though blood seeps through her jeans. The freeway is chaos.

"Who's chasing you? Is there more than one?" Chris rasps.

"The man who killed my mother."

On the move, he shoots her a look. Behind them, more gunfire, rounds banging into sheet metal, shattering glass. Chris spins. Pushing Gabriela behind him, he raises the H&K.

In the crush of stopped traffic, through smoke and headlights, figures are silhouetted against the red glare of flames. Wardell slides sideways into view for a fraction of a second. Chris doesn't have a shot.

Hanna runs in, searching. Through the wreckage behind him he spots the crashed Viper and shotgunned windshield. He races forward, squinting against headlights. He spots Wardell, a lurching shadow a hundred yards ahead.

Wardell slides toward the concrete center median and sees the Viper. Tick-Tock dead. He turns and runs in the direction Gabriela went. He peers through the windows of snarled vehicles.

Hanna catches a glimpse. He races, closing the distance to get in range. Wardell grabs a door handle on a Volvo. Locked. He backs up a step and aims the shotgun through the Volvo's window. The people inside scream. He squeezes the trigger.

Empty. He drops the shotgun and pulls a pistol from his waistband.

Hanna lines up, fires. Wardell abandons the Volvo and disappears beyond an eighteen-wheeler.

Hanna sprints after him, coat flaring, breathing heavy. He gets fifty yards. Wardell slips out from behind the big rig.

Headlights. Shadows. The night spins across him. Wardell's gun arm is extended, his semiautomatic up.

What Hanna sees is the muzzle flash. Then he hears the shot. The round hits him in the thigh, a sledgehammer knocking his leg out from under him.

The night tilts, a wild swing. Stars and freeway lights sweep across his view, as if the bindings that hold him to the world are cut. Numbing, deep pain. Dazed. How'd he get here, on the ground?

People in cars scream, trying to hide under vehicles or drive out of the wreckage-turned-shootout, backing up suddenly, crashing into each other, trying to U-turn. Some bail out and flee. Headlights are above Hanna's eyes, a white flare, sharp. Feet run in all directions. He's numb. He has his weapon in his hand. Who's a civilian? Who's Wardell? Where's Gabriela?

The Benelli's bolt is locked open. Out. Empty. He tosses it aside. With a guttural cry, he levers himself up. He leans against an empty car. Blood pools under him. Lights whirl. He draws his Colt Combat Commander, fighting against the shaking in his arm.

Rifle fire cracks the air.

Rounds hit the back window of an SUV. Wardell breaks cover, jerking into view from behind a truck, spinning, searching for the gunman. He shoots into the distance. Hanna tracks his line of fire. Hears return fire, sees a flick of exhaust from a muzzle, sees a man with a rifle. *The fuck?*

Then Hanna centers on Wardell. He zeroes his aim. He fires.

Wardell drops, hit, out of sight.

Hanna pulls himself up and takes a step, but his leg buckles. He slides down the empty car to the pavement.

Get up. Come on. He rolls to his knees, trying not to scream, keeping hold of his Colt. His radio is crackling.

Wardell. He has to be sure.

Panicked people flee past him. Hanna lowers himself to the asphalt and peers under cars.

Twenty feet away, Wardell presses himself up and staggers to his feet.

Hanna's pulse pounds, agonizing. Gritting his teeth, he claws himself up and lurches behind a pickup truck tipped on its side. He thuds down, his back against the hood, into a black crease of shadow. He holds his gun on his lap, his heart thundering, a weird, unwinding sensation spiraling up through him.

Wardell wants Gabriela. Even now, he wants to kill her. Hanna needs to make him want something else more.

He takes a breath. "*Wardell.*"

His right side is not entirely in shadow. He's striped with head-lights, his gun arm, his shoulder. He inhales to straighten, to get a view, to remember how to talk into the radio.

He stops. Just stops.

He lets the light fall across him and he stills. Waiting.

Among the running footsteps, the jagged zigzag of fear, one set of feet staggers near. Hanna can't see all of him yet. He catches flashes. Hears it—a metallic click, the magazine of a semiautomatic handgun being dropped, hitting the road. Another being inserted. Slammed home. The slide being racked, chambering a round.

Hanna watches a shadow rise above him, a manifestation, taut, dark face in grayscale. The man's chest heaves. A strobing flash of headlights in his eyes. Rising above, taking over the view, looming, Wardell pitches into view.

Bleeding. Staring down. Gun held close by his leg, finger on the trigger.

Wardell's eyes tag Hanna's. He raises the Beretta. "April Fool's, mo—"

Hanna shoots him in the chest. The .45 round slams through Wardell's sternum like the punch from a giant, destroying his heart. Two more rounds crash into him.

Wardell falls back to the pavement. His gun clatters away. He raises his head and gapes at Hanna incredulously.

Hanna steadies his Colt. Wardell's eyes spark and he bares his teeth, hissing. Hanna holds his gaze. Lines his sights on Wardell's forehead. Takes his time. Pulls the trigger and blows him away.

Chris and Gabriela cut down a side street, into gloom.

Beyond a warehouse he stops and looks back. Nobody is coming. He lowers the H&K.

He turns to face her. She takes a second. It's dark. It's been forever. It's a different world. Shadows and ghosts.

She inhales. Goes still. "You're Chris?" she says.

"Yeah."

She puts a hand against his chest. Her eyes are bright.

"Let's get out of here."

He wraps an arm around her shoulders, rifle in his other hand, and leads her away, unbound, surprised, feeling a wild wave of relief. Gabriela Vasquez. Elisa's kid.

Nobody's going to touch her. Not now.

The red Chevy pickup swings away from the curb on Broadway, heading into a nondescript spread of businesses and apartment buildings off the interchange. Despite the cacophony of sirens and flashing lights back on the freeway, this block is shuttered and empty. Chris stands on the sidewalk and watches the truck go. In the passenger seat, Gabriela looks out the rear window of the cab. Her cousin Manny is at the wheel. Her expression is somehow both fiery and wistful.

She puts her palm against the glass and holds it there, a farewell.

He stands in the cooling night as the pickup drives away, his hand raised.

Gabriela.

Live your life, girl. Live and remember.

The taillights vanish around a corner.

He drops his hand.

He turns and walks back toward the freeway, rifle tucked along his leg, dark, invisible. The massive concentration of lights and sirens ahead tells him the confrontation is over. Whatever happened, it's done.

His car's nearby. He could get behind the wheel, drive away, avoid the chance of being seen. His adrenaline, this feeling it's a pivot point, won't let him do that.

He scales a chain-link fence, hikes down the concrete embankment beneath the interchange, and slides through the shadows beneath the freeway ramps to the other side. When he returns to the street, the view, the gleaming night, reveals the cars crashed on the 110. Matchbox toys, upended. Fire trucks have arrived, and LAPD black-and-whites, parked at forty-five-degree angles at the foot of on-ramps, lights spinning. Uniforms are directing traffic. The scene is no longer chaos. The cops own it.

Pedestrians mill, shocked, some bloody. He joins them, gets a clear view of the carnage.

Amid the popcorn flash of emergency lights, a clot of EMTs and cops gathers over a body on the roadway. Man flat on his back, arms thrown wide.

Jeans, boots, T-shirt. The shooter. Someone named Wardell. A corpse.

A few feet away, paramedics attend to another man. A detective. Behind them, pacing, are two Robbery-Homicide cops Chris recognizes.

Drucker. Casals. His shoulder feels a weird ache. The EMTs are working on a gunshot wound.

Vincent Hanna. Down, maybe on his way out.

From the angle between Hanna and Wardell's body, Chris figures Vincent got the drop on the guy. Point-blank.

Okay.

Chris stands in the stark light. *It isn't your time, Hanna. Not tonight.*

He walks away.

94

On the freeway shoulder, Hanna sits on the bumper of the ambulance. The paramedics have put a pressure dressing on the gunshot wound and are prepping him for an IV line. Drucker and Casals circle like hawks. The adrenaline wearing off, he's light-headed and cold.

Drucker sees. "Hey, you over there," he says to a medic. "Get a blanket over here."

"I'll be fine," Hanna says.

Casals, rarely talkative but always there, says, "Damn right. Now, let 'em do their goddamn job, Vincent."

Wardell's body lies ten feet away. The medical examiner kneels beside it. Crime scene techs are setting out evidence markers, counting the cartridge casings on the road and the bullet holes in wrecked cars, and in the dead man.

Hanna looks at Drucker. "Gabriela." His voice sounds raspy.

"She got clear."

"How?"

Something on Drucker's face. Hanna sees.

"What?"

"You got this guy," Drucker says. "Wardell, he's gone. Stop asking about everything else. We got that."

Something in Drucker's eyes, more than just taking Wardell off the map.

Gone, *bang*. Done.

The paramedic flicks his finger against the back of Hanna's hand to raise a vein for the IV. The night feels untouchably distant. A high hum swoops in, carrying him someplace.

Wardell. Twelve years. Too many victims, too much pain. People killed. Gabriela's mother.

Something here he isn't connecting. Tight. Weirdly unbreakable.

Hanna puts a hand on the paramedic's arm. "Later for the IV."

"Sir, we—"

"Casals." Hanna groans to his feet. "We check Wardell's car yet?"

He throws an arm over Sam's shoulder. With Drucker, they work their way to the demolished Firebird.

Hanna slumps against the car as Casals aims a Maglite at the interior. Trash and pebbled safety glass cover the seats. Drucker combs through it. The flashlight's beam catches a glint of gold.

"What's that?" Hanna says.

Drucker hands him a locket on a broken chain. "*Te amo—Gabriela*."

Hanna pops the clasp. The photos inside are faded. He runs his thumb across them. His head clears. He turns to Drucker. "You see him?"

Drucker gives him a burning look. "The man who pulled Gabriela out? I'm not sure."

Hanna gazes up the road, at lights, darkness. Death, flight. His heart drums in his chest. He nods to Drucker slowly.

He looks back at the locket. On one side, Gabriela. On the other, Neil McCauley.

He closes it and holds it tight in his hand.

95

It's two a.m. when Drucker gets the surveillance tape from an office building on Broadway. He and Casals are beat but wired, the post-adrenaline crash hitting, not enough coffee on the planet to sharpen him up to where he wants to be.

It's a construction firm, and they'd rousted the facilities manager at home, got him in to get them the tape. He and Casals crowd around the monitor. The video rolls.

The camera captures everything from the moment Otis Wardell races toward the building on the stack interchange. The car is a black streak. Wardell briefly visible, a smear; Gabriela in the passenger seat. As the Firebird flies down there's a disturbance in the car. Wardell swerves. Spins. Hits traffic, spins another time, gets hit again.

Drucker shakes his head. "Brutal."

Gabriela punches the passenger door open and fumbles her way out and flees into the still-burgeoning multivehicle wreck. Wardell soon follows, wobbling, bloody, gun in hand.

"Damn," Drucker says.

"She forced him to crash," Casals says.

"Must have. Jesus."

And then, up an on-ramp on foot, comes the man, running smoothly, jacked, his head on a swivel. H&K rifle with collapsible stock slung from his shoulder in his hands, low, half hidden.

The tape is low quality. The light is poor. The distance is bad, the focus.

But now Drucker is 100 percent certain.

Casals looks over Drucker's shoulder, takes a breath. Exhales.

The man on-screen looks different from how he did the last time

Casals saw him. But when he aims his rifle at Wardell, standing solidly in front of Gabriela on the roadway, totally committed, looking for a shot, his face is to the camera. Drucker freezes the tape.

It's Chris Shiherlis.

"What the hell is he doing here?" Casals says.

Drucker hits Play again. Shiherlis puts a hand on Gabriela's back and sends her running down the ramp as he backpedals, weapon up.

Drucker stops the tape.

He walks outside. Casals follows. The air is cool. The roads are empty. The city rises around them, glimmering. A faint wind brushes the back of his neck. He stands in the middle of the street and stares into the shadows.

Shiherlis, you are good.

And I'm going to find you.

The night closes in.

96

Andaman Sea, 6°01' 27.0" N, 96°57' 12.1" E

March 16

In the sea-lane in international waters between Indonesia and Thailand, Ana stands at the high bow of the oceangoing tug. The sky is pearly with humidity. The ocean breeze whips at her face as they pitch over the chop of the bow wave. The tug's diesels throttle down to match the eight knots of a veteran long-range oil tanker. They ease alongside through four-foot swells that roll past the tanker's hull. Laden with crude, it rides low, unaffected by the waves that rock the tug.

A rope-and-wood-slat ladder unfurls down the side of the ship.

She signals to the men with her. Timing the swell, they all climb. Halfway up the side of the hull, Ana looks across the towering plane of corroding steel plate toward the bow, 210 meters long and 70,000 deadweight tons; she feels like an ant. If she were agoraphobic, this would be a bad place. She climbs up.

On the ship's deck, a few of the Libyan and Filipino crew members are assembled.

The heavyset captain sidles toward her. A nickel-plated semiautomatic shines in his waistband.

Ana braces herself on the rolling deck. "Permission to come aboard."

He eyes her and the men she has brought: a petroleum chemist with a silver lab case and heavily armed, wide-bodied private military contractors—a mix of Israelis and English and Welsh ex-SAS, mostly bearded. The tanker's crew eyes them warily. The PMCs' expressions are indifferent.

"Granted." He gestures broadly. "She is ready for inspection."

Ana is on the bridge above the sea, shining gold white in the late-afternoon sun, when the chemist reappears with his glass pipettes of thick dark oil.

"All tanks are full. The crude has an API gravity of thirty-seven degrees and sulfur content of point-three-eight." He shows her one pipette. "Top-quality Es Sider crude. Per spec."

She takes the sat phone and steps outside. Her call connects her to a small twin-engine Antonov An-26, a medium-sized cargo plane, carrying the bartered guidance systems and circling lazily off the coast of Libya.

"You are go to land," she says.

Singapore

March 17

The tropical night is hot, and Chris is halfway through his chili crab at a Boat Quay noodle house. Behind him is the gleaming skyline. Skyscrapers with Olympic-sized rooftop pools. The Fountain of Wealth—the world's largest fountain—illuminated by a laser light show. Construction cranes everywhere. To Chris it makes Los

Angeles look like the 1.5 world. He's about to crack a claw when his sat phone blinks awake. It's Claudio, initiating contact.

Chris answers. "Yeah."

"We know what you did." Claudio's tone is calm.

Chris says nothing. He lets the silence float.

After a beat Claudio continues: "We fucked you up, you fucked us up. So, I'm thinking maybe that is a kind of equilibrium. Which means the only thing happening right now is we are ruining each other's commerce. That hurts both families."

Chris takes a shallow sip from a cold bottle of Tiger Beer. "I'm listening."

"We can keep at this, but then both families make less money. If your guidance systems do what you claim, with our sales, distribution, finances, and transportation, we all get rich. We should end this. So, I will take the initiative. I propose we find a way to work together." His voice is confident. "We must negotiate a truce."

Chris sets down his beer. "Maybe not a bad idea. I'll talk to Ana."

"Okay. Mr. Yuan will—"

"We don't want to meet Mr. Yuan. What do I want to meet Mr. Yuan for?"

A casual pause. "Then I'll send Felix."

"Fuck Felix. You want us to consider working together? We talk to you, face-to-face."

From the longer pause on the line, Chris can practically see Claudio carving a skull in a tabletop with a steak knife.

"You're manufacturing the units yourself, yes? Or outsourcing?" Claudio asks.

"Ourselves."

"So fast. You have a reliable supply chain?"

"Of course."

"I should lay eyes on this operation to see that it's real."

"You want to see it? You can see it. Then we see if there's a deal."

"Next week. I'll be in touch with details."

Claudio ends the call. Chris finishes his beer in one long pull. *Good.*

••

On the patio at the Casino Paraná, Claudio tosses the phone on the table. Across from him in the morning light, Felix looks eager, if uncertain.

"You're going to make a deal for us to partner with them on the systems they're fabricating?" he says.

Claudio stares at him like he's an idiot. "I'm going to seize their hardware. I'm going to burn the balls off Ana's technicians until they give me the guidance system code that reads both Russian and US GPS coordinates. And then I'm going to kill that blond motherfucker."

Herons swoop past above the deep river gorge where the Paraná runs toward the huge Iguazú Falls. Felix blinks, repeatedly. "Bergman, okay. Fuck him. But Ana comes home." He straightens his shoulders. "And I'm going with you."

"Big brother going to protect little sister?" Claudio smiles and stares at Felix for a moment. "Okay. You come. Leave Paolo here to look after your father."

Claudio loses interest in Felix and shifts his attention to the row of TVs monitoring the play of punto banco, blackjack, and craps.

A minute later, Felix jogs down the steps past the gigantic roulette wheel in front of the casino and into a waiting Range Rover. Paolo is at the wheel, pale and bandaged, just out of the hospital.

"Where we going?" he says.

Felix wipes his brow. "You're not. You stay and watch over my father."

Paolo cuts a glance at him in the mirror. "Right now, I mean."

"Home." Felix clenches his jaw. "Home sweet fucking home."

Paolo pulls out. His gaze slides from Felix to the roulette wheel's blinking neon.

Malacca Strait, 4°15' 59" N, 99°36' 21" E

March 24, 0145 Hours

The sea is flat, moonglow a thin shimmer on its surface. The lights of distant container ships wink in the night near the Sumatran coast.

On the walkway outside the bridge of the tanker, Ana hears twin engines snarling on the near-black void of the water. A go-fast boat is inbound, running dark.

The tanker captain has the go-fast on marine radar. He points. "One minute."

Ana spots its milky luminescent wake. She nods crisply. The buyers are arriving.

She bartered the guidance systems to Libya for oil. Now she's selling the oil for cash.

The deal has been done in the dark depths of the hidden web via Kelso's register of verifiably reliable players. Both the tanker and its cargo are being purchased by an oil-starved, sanction-hit refinery in Myanmar, a country of unimaginable natural resources and human capital being starved by its pariah regime. Cities dark at night. Factories rotting. People starving. The rich slavering to gain and hoard the nation's wealth.

The go-fast swings alongside with a growl.

Ana beckons her men and heads for the bridge.

Batam

0150 Hours

The factory huddles on the outskirts of the city, bare bones, which is all Chris and Ana need for a pop-up operation. Ceiling fans rotate beneath a corrugated metal roof. Indo-pop plays on a boom box. Chris walks the catwalk above the assembly line.

The third shift is cranking. Even in the middle of the night, workers bust their humps assembling guidance packages. They're mostly locals, some from Cambodia and Sri Lanka. They live in a dormitory on a red-dirt road behind the factory. They're diligent. They grind and send the cash home to their families.

Chris peers out the cantilevered windows at the top of the building into the heavy night air. Insects buzz in the trees. He checks his watch. The buyers should be boarding the tanker. He gets his phone to text Ana and stops. Up the road, he thinks he hears tires whine on tarmac.

Headlights flicker through the distant tree cover. Chris's pulse pings. Then they're gone.

The convoy of SUVs rolls through the heavy darkness. Riding shotgun in a Toyota 4Runner, Claudio hears a man's voice over his walkie-talkie.

"Staging."

"Inbound," he replies. "Thirty seconds."

He gives the driver a throat-slashing motion. The man kills the headlights. The other SUVs follow suit.

Ahead, Claudio's men are creeping through the trees outside the factory, sliding silently through the shadows.

He has brought a heavy crew: four of his best men, plus private contractors recruited via a Chinese Indonesian in Palembang who belongs to the Taiwanese Bamboo Union triad. The contractors are Bamboo Union enforcers and Indonesian ex-Kopassus.

In the back seat, Felix breathes steadily, his eyes gleaming. "They're set?"

Claudio's mercs reconned the site last night and earlier today. They clocked shift changes and counted the number of workers on the assembly line. The factory is rectangular, flimsy, will be easy to isolate and control. Their stealthy approach has put them in close proximity for the assault. At this hour, the people at the site will be fatigued. Slow. When Claudio shows his face, he'll draw Chris and his security's focus. He'll set them off-balance, distract them, lowering their readiness for his crew's violent, dynamic entry. And he wants them to see his face. To know it's him.

Felix says, "We're good?"

Claudio ignores Felix. Into the walkie-talkie he says, "Status?"

In reply, he hears two clicks. *In position.*

One fire team will secure the dormitory. They'll enter, overwhelm, zip-tie, and gag everyone inside; silently slit the throats of anyone found outside so they can raise no alarm. The rest—his core security people, backed up by the Indonesians—will take up breach points outside the factory and await a signal to enter. The Indonesian gunmen are large, rugged, and ready to rock.

When Claudio gives the order, they will hit the factory.

The convoy swings up in front. Six of Claudio's contractors are already stacked along the wall beside the front door, ready for the assault. At the back, he knows, two more flank the rear door, in position to stop any target who tries to escape him.

Claudio racks the slide on his SIG pistol. "Let's go."

He climbs out and moves quickly toward the door.

The meeting with Bergman has been carefully scheduled. For tomorrow. Claudio's here a day early.

He's here to take back what's his.

Chris hurries down the catwalk stairs. He's halfway along the assembly line when the door opens.

Motorbike Man walks in. Cocksure, tattoo writhing on his forearm. Hands empty, but he's undoubtedly strapped. Behind him come three more Chen security and two large-boned Indonesians with long hair, looking ruthless but cool after their air-conditioned drive from the airport. Chris counts bodies.

In walks Jakob Gögel. Beneath an aloha shirt and loose jacket, the veins in his neck pop. The whites of his eyes are a briny yellow.

"You here to audit my books?" Chris says.

Gögel sends him a look as flat as a blade, but agitation writhes beneath the surface. "Americans. Can you ever simply shut up?"

Through the door steps Claudio Chen. Chris takes him in for a full two seconds.

He's dressed like a vampire at the court of Versailles: frilled shirt, high-collared black velvet jacket. Blue-white contacts make his eyes nearly colorless. It's a fucking look.

Behind him comes Felix, in a yellow-and-black *Game of Death* tracksuit.

"Hey, guys." Chris lifts his chin in greeting. Keeps his voice level.

Claudio's security spread out in front of him. Felix sniffs.

Chris notes the men's positions. His pulse is regular but pounding. "How's your father?"

"We flew him to São Paulo, he needs specialists. And for security"— Felix blinks; he is coked to his fingertips—"we sent Paolo with him for protection."

"Smart." Sidelining the head of Liu security. "Reprisals against the Barakats?"

"When the time is right."

Claudio peers around. "And Ana is . . ."

"Elsewhere."

"Busy girl." He scans the assembly tables, the components. "That she could invent this . . ." He waves vaguely at the building. "Barbie Dreamhouse."

Gögel smiles.

"And fortunate she has you to work with." Claudio steps up to Chris, close, too close, his unsettling habit. "Why don't you call her. Get her over here."

Gögel scans the factory floor and climbs the metal stairs to the catwalk. Chris is chill, but thinks, *Fucker.* Taking the high ground, the German patrols, checking out the windows, then stations himself so he has an unobstructed view of the entire factory floor.

Chris fights his longtime instinct to smash Claudio's face. He holds as still as ice. He doesn't turn his head. To the workers, he says, "Take a break."

On the line, the workers exchange glances and set down their tools as they turn to leave.

Felix wipes his nose. "This isn't a problem. We need to work out details. It's fine. Everything is fine. We need to sort this out, and then Ana will come home."

Chris cuts him with a look. "Stop talking."

Felix raises his hands. Claudio stands with his arms loose at his sides. Chris knows he plans to murder him and Ana. No question. But Felix, Chris thinks, has convinced himself Ana is going home, forgiven. His brain's fried.

"How about a drink?" Chris says to Claudio.

Chris gestures toward an office and walks ahead of Claudio and Felix to the doorway, deliberately offering his back to them. He hears Claudio not move and then start to retreat. The hair on Chris's neck stands up.

In his earpiece, a quiet voice speaks. "Six outside. There's two stationed to cover the exterior approach to the door with overlapping sectors of fire."

Chris keeps walking.

The voice says, "In ten. Nine. Eight."

He walks, counting down in his head.

He reaches *one,* drops, and from outside, gunfire cracks open the night.

Aboard the oil tanker, Ana stands at the chart table, surrounded by navigational maps and racks of communications gear. Despite the heat, she is cool. She is about to take delivery of millions of dollars. US cash money. Footsteps clatter on the exterior metal staircase. The buyers step through the hatch.

"*Mingalarbar,*" she says. *Hello.*

The four men are skeevy, sweating through their silk suits. One carries a computer and satellite phone. One smokes a Marlboro. Two, dead-eyed, look like Burmese military. They start to open their coats wider. She sees SMGs suspended under their loose suit jackets. Then they stop.

Entering from both open hatchways is Ana's tactical team: the ex-SAS with British SA80s, the former IDF commandos carrying Galils aimed at the deck but set for three-round bursts.

Ana types on her laptop. "I am now fulfilling delivery of the shipment—five hundred thousand barrels of light sweet Libyan crude—and the vessel. On time, per contract. At today's Brent spot price plus the agreed ten percent premium for the crude, and the discounted price for the tanker, the total due is $15,349,000. I'm ready to complete the transaction."

She writes account and routing numbers on a page torn from her Moleskine and pushes it across the table. "Bank details."

The smoker looks Ana up and down: a small woman in a hoodie and track pants.

"I speak to the boss." He takes a slow drag and scans her men.

"I'm the boss," she says. "You talk to me."

He exhales a cloud of smoke.

The ship rolls with the swell. Ana nods lightly. "A cyclone is developing in the Bay of Bengal," she says. "You'll want to get your nifty go-fast boats back to shore and offload this crude at the refinery before the storm makes landfall."

She offers a pleasant expression, as if this had been the expected social nicety.

The smoker laughs sourly. He tilts his head. Lets silence stretch. He eyes her tac team. Weighing something in his head.

Ana shakes her head. "Whatever you are thinking about, like changing this deal? Don't."

She looks at one of the Israeli mercs. He drills a glare through the smoker's forehead. The light in the smoker's eyes—whatever he'd planned or thought he might still pull off—fades to nothing.

Ana links a secure sat phone to her laptop and connects.

"The funds," she says. "Send them. Now."

The buyer picks up the paper with the bank numbers, opens his screen, and types.

Workers scatter. Outside, gunshots multiply.

Gögel sees out the windows from the catwalk, draws his Glock, turns toward Chris.

Chris is through the office door as Gögel fires. Rounds clang against the steel office wall. Chris has his CAR-15 that was propped inside the door.

Claudio clocks the sudden appearance of Israelis and Brits in stack formation, hard-eyed and bearded, in body armor, already firing.

Instantly, a Chen Paraguayan gunman goes down, hit by three

rounds from a Galil. They're smooth and fast. A wide-bodied Welsh ex-SAS, firing his SA80, takes out two Chen mercs.

Behind the building, rifle fire rakes the night. Outside the front door, where the Chen team is stacked up, Chris's men ambush them from an L-shaped formation inside the tree line. The short side of the L hits them from the front in enfilade. Three drop, and as the rest start to counterattack, the long side of the L pounds them with flanking fire.

Beyond the assembly line, Motorbike Man returns fire at the PMCs and scrambles for cover. He turns toward Chris, who's exposed.

In the open back door is Paolo, hazel eyes brilliant, cast on his shot-up arm. With an H&K MP5 on a sling, he rips Motorbike Man to ribbons.

Gögel runs along the catwalk, firing. Chris dives beneath it, rolls onto his back, and shoots straight up. The CAR-15 shreds the metal flooring.

Gögel cries out gutturally and topples to the factory floor. Chris rolls and aims the CAR-15 at Gögel's head. He holds Gögel's gaze. Pulls the trigger.

Outside, Claudio's second fire team abandons the dormitory and rushes toward the factory. From a camouflaged hiding place they've occupied since the morning, two ex-SAS snipers with scope-mounted rifles start to pick them off. They drop one after the other.

In a corner of the factory floor, the last of Chen's security tip over a metal file cabinet and fire erratically at Chris's mercs and at Paolo. Claudio is behind heavy machinery with them, his SIG pistol in his hand. Freaky contacts glaring, he rocks in place, trying to decide what to do. He straightens—to see Chris? To fire at Chris? The second that part of his head clears cover, Chris rolls out, prone, from the side of a workstation, and unleashes a three-round burst. Claudio's head jerks back. He crashes to the floor.

Felix runs.

Outside, one of Claudio's remaining gunmen, firing wildly, retreating, hits Felix in the ribs. Paolo puts the gunman down. Felix plunges on, his bright yellow tracksuit spattered red. He staggers into the darkness and falls.

Chris follows.

Chris finds Felix on his back in the dirt, the insects singing, heat lightning flashing in the distance over the Strait of Malacca. As Chris approaches, Felix crabs backward. His face is striped with revelation, seeing Chris for real.

"Can . . . we can work out a deal . . . ?"

"You thought I wouldn't know you were coming early?" Chris says.

Felix is trying to figure it out, Chris can tell. Felix sees Paolo's here. What's there to figure out? Paolo tipped Chris and Ana. And Chris got to work, arranging for an Indonesian broker of pirate crews and security contractors to provide intel and mercs with heavy-duty experience and local expertise. He was tracking Claudio's group from the moment their flight departed Guaraní in Ciudad del Este. He had transponders placed on all the vehicles waiting for the Chen party at Batam's Hang Nadim Airport. Chris knew how many security Claudio brought and identified the Indonesians as well-trained and violent former military. Chris has been ready for this attack for days.

"We weren't going to . . ."

"To what?"

"Believe me," Felix says. "She would have been fine. She's my sister!"

Chris settles a look on him.

Calm voice. The SIG in his hand. "She told me all about that."

Felix looks at Chris.

Chris's eyes are cold.

He fires.

From inside the factory, Paolo sees a muzzle flash.

Batam

0645 Hours

When Chris meets Ana at the airstrip, the morning sky is still black. Stars sizzle overhead. A vein of indigo lies along the eastern horizon, as do the lights of three thousand vessels anchored outside Singapore. She jogs down the stairs of the charter jet, practically vibrating with purpose.

When she approaches him, he says, "Done."

She feels a profound harmonic within.

She nods, gratified, and glances across the tarmac. Paolo is standing by the car.

"Felix?" she says.

Chris holds her gaze.

Ana is like fireworks. Thrilling and brilliant. A lover, a miracle. She is better off without Felix. Chris has improved both their lives. But tell her? She could never be with him again. Never touch him. Never work with him. Blood is blood.

He puts his hands on her shoulders. "He's gone. He was caught in a crossfire."

She looks at him. A fissure cracks her composure. Innocent, welling grief. She takes a ragged breath, squeezes her eyes shut. He embraces her. Her body shudders. Flashing into her mind is Felix as a nine-year-old, and she's seven with her big brother, who takes her hand. She was little sister. Blood is blood. Chris holds her tightly. She presses herself to his chest.

And his pulse feels electric, dark, powerful.

97

Hanna slides onto the barstool. The place is enchanting, with dark booths and a cobalt-blue glow. Bottles of amber spirits gleam, underlit, behind the bar. "Gimme Shelter" on the jukebox. The drink comes without asking.

Nate sets a double bourbon in front of him, then sets his hands on the bar and stands there. The music plays. They look at each other.

Hanna smiles. "What are you *not* gonna tell me about Chris Shiherlis?"

ACKNOWLEDGMENTS

Michael Mann

Charlie Adamson could recite whole scenes from films from memory. He and Dennis Farina, his partner, would role-play during all-night stakeouts as detectives in Chicago's elite, and sometimes lethal, Criminal Intelligence Unit. They both had roles in my 1980 film *Thief*.

It was in 1963 that Adamson was focused on the actual Neil Mc-Cauley, whom he killed in a chase and gunfight.

By the late '80s, I had encouraged Charlie's writing and produced a TV series he created, *Crime Story*, in which I cast Dennis as the lead. He had become a serious actor, with roles in *Miami Vice* and *Manhunter*. We worked together in various combinations on *Thief*, *Crime Story*, *Manhunter*, *Heat*, and *Luck*.

Charlie's insights and humor illuminated aspects of Hanna. His understanding of McCauley helped me imagine his character. While I was in Chicago in 2009, in the thick of preparing *Public Enemies*, Charlie knew he was on the edge and called to say goodbye, with typical clarity in his frankly emotional way. He died the next day.

Farina, across the years, became one of my closest friends and a highly accomplished actor. He, too, left prematurely, in 2013.

I'm grateful to former LAPD Captain Tom Elfmont, with whom I spent the majority of weekend nights for six months, chasing radio calls from one crime scene to another in advance of *Heat*.

Don Ferrarone and Lou Milione, with their intellectual rigor and insights, brought clarity to operating outside the social contract in the wild and dangerous places on the planet. Those thanks extend to others on the international-operations side of the DEA, and at the top to Jack Lawn and Michele Leonhart.

I received invaluable help exploring human narratives occurring day to day on the streets of LA from the unique Robert Deamer and the multi-talented Dana Harris.

For bringing me into their lives, I'm grateful to professional thieves John Santucci, for his immense help on my film *Thief,* and the irrepressible and supremely literate Jerry Scalise.

The ultimate reward I receive as a writer and director, a beneficiary of extraordinary treasures, is from the all-in commitment and art of Al Pacino, Bob DeNiro, Val Kilmer, Jon Voight, Tom Sizemore, Diane Venora, Amy Brenneman, Ashley Judd, Danny Trejo, Tom Noonan, Dennis Haysbert, and the entire *Heat* cast. Simply, they made everybody alive.

Meg Gardiner has been a great collaborator, and I'm deeply appreciative of the way she accompanied me into the worlds of *Heat* and the other venues we explored. She's a great and gracious coworker and a bold talent.

I want to thank Brian Murray and Liate Stehlik at William Morrow/HarperCollins for believing in this project and Michael Mann Books. You have been great partners throughout this entire process.

Meg Gardiner and I were very fortunate to have Jennifer Brehl as our editor. Her incredible insights throughout the editing process made an important difference, and her passionate support of this book was invaluable.

At William Morrow, I want to thank the following individuals who made important contributions to this book: Jennifer Hart, Danielle Bartlett, Kaitlin Harri, Julianna Wojcik, Ryan Shepherd, Nate Lanman, Chantal Restivo Alessi, Mark Meneses, Sam Glatt, Jeanie Lee, Bonni Leon-Berman, Julia Wisdom, Phoebe Morgan, and especially Andy LeCount, who helped champion this project from its earliest days.

My attorney, Harold Brown, is unique. A poet, a friend, and a young man of the old school of committed, principled people representing motion picture artists, who always is about "making something from nothing rather than nothing from something."

My relationship with Shane Salerno has evolved over twenty-five years. From an eleven-year-old who loved, and had his imagination permanently damaged by, *Miami Vice* to a collaborator and brother and, ultimately, my literary agent, who first presented to me the idea of an imprint, sincere thanks for believing in and sticking with this. It continues to be a great ride.

At my own company, I want to thank Darice Wirth and Bryce Forester for their tireless work assisting me on the book. And my amazing daughter, Becca Mann, whose caring for this and other pieces of my work has kept them faithfully organized.

Among the many, those I want to thank who were so pivotally important to the making of the film *Heat* include producer Art Linson, who told me I was crazy to consider not directing it; Peter Jan Brugge, the masterful logistician; the magisterial cinematographer Dante Spinotti; my dear friend and brilliant editor Dov Hoenig; editor Billy Goldenberg for all his great work; Kathy Shea; Elliot Goldenthal; Moby; and my pal since 1979, Gusmano Cesaretti, for his visual imagination and our many explorations.

I am especially grateful to Arnon Milchan for believing in this film from the very beginning, for writing the checks in collaboration with Warner Brothers, and for his unique respect for the artist.

I want to thank Peter Giles for reading the audiobook. When I hear his voice, I see what I wrote as cinema.

Nothing is possible without the spirit and heart and solidarity of my wife, Summer, and the very components of my life, Ami, Aran, Jessie, and Becca.

Meg Gardiner

Novels spring from authors' imaginations but reach readers' hands thanks to the dedication, support, generosity, and expertise of many others. Boundless thanks go to Jennifer Brehl, who immersed herself in the world of *Heat* and did a fantastic job editing this book. This book is better because of her dedication and hard work. I want to thank everyone at HarperCollins, including Liate Stehlik, Jennifer Hart, Danielle Bartlett, Kaitlin Harri, Julianna Wojcik, Ryan Shepherd, Nate Lanman, Chantal Restivo Alessi, Mark Meneses, Sam Glatt, Julia Wisdom, Phoebe Morgan, Andy LeCount, and the entire team at William Morrow/HarperCollins; my agent, Shane Salerno, for first suggesting me to Michael Mann, for bringing me into this project, and for protecting this book during a long development process; Ryan Coleman, Deborah Randall, and the entire team at the Story Factory; Bryce Forester for his tireless work; and Darice Wirth, Becca Mann, Reed Farrel Coleman, and those whose unique insights and willingness to share them inform the novel: Jerry Scalise, Stephen Donehoo, Dana Harris, Bob Deamer, Matthew Betley, Ann Aubrey Hanson, and Paul Shreve.

Above all, my gratitude goes to Michael Mann. He invited me to join him in expanding the iconic world of *Heat*. I appreciate his trust that I could help bring this story to life. Working with him on this project has been a privilege and an honor.